These powerful tyc...
play e...

After ...
BRIDEGROOM
BOSSES

Available next month:

After Hours
BOARDROOM
BARGAINS

Ruthless bosses by day, seriously
sexy lovers by night!

After Hours

BRIDEGROOM BOSSES

CATHY WILLIAMS

JESSICA HART

SUSAN STEPHENS

M&B™ and M&B™ with the Rose Device
are trademarks of the publisher.
Harlequin Mills & Boon Limited, Eton House,
18-24 Paradise Road, Richmond, Surrey TW9 1SR

AFTER HOURS: BRIDEGROOM BOSSES
© by Harlequin Books SA 2010

Sleeping With the Boss © Cathy Williams 1998
Business Arrangement Bride © Jessica Hart 2006
Dirty Weekend © Susan Stephens 2007

ISBN: 978 0 263 87394 8

009-0510

Harlequin Mills & Boon policy is to use papers that are
natural, renewable and recyclable products and made from
wood grown in sustainable forests. The logging and
manufacturing processes conform to the legal environmental
regulations of the country of origin.

Printed and bound in Spain
by Litografia Rosés S.A., Barcelona

Sleeping With the Boss

CATHY WILLIAMS

Cathy Williams is originally from Trinidad, but has lived in England for a number of years. She currently has a house in Warwickshire, which she shares with her husband Richard, her three daughters, Charlotte, Olivia and Emma, and their pet cat, Salem. She adores writing romantic fiction and would love one of her girls to become a writer – although at the moment she is happy enough if they do their homework and agree not to bicker with one another!

CHAPTER ONE

ALICE pushed open the glass double doors to the office block, and at once had that comfortable feeling of coming home. She had just returned from a fortnight's holiday in Portugal—two weeks of hot weather, blue skies, blue sea, cocktails round the pool every evening with the girl she shared a flat with. And at the end of it she had boarded the plane back to a grey, cold England that was emerging reluctantly from bitter winter to sulky spring, with a feeling of muted relief.

Most people dreaded the thought of their holiday ending.

'I could stay here for ever,' Vanessa had told her four days into the holiday, luxuriating at the side of the pool with a drink in one hand and a cigarette in the other.

'You'd be bored stiff after a month,' Alice had said, rubbing suntan cream evenly over her body in the hope that a golden tan might endow her with at least a glowing, healthy look. She had long abandoned any ambitions of glamour. She was simply too thin and too unremarkable for that.

'Okay,' Vanessa had conceded. '*For ever* might be a bit much, but I wouldn't spit in the face of an extra two weeks.'

Alice had obligingly agreed, but by the end of two weeks she had had enough, was itching to get back behind her desk.

Now, she pushed through the double doors, headed towards the lift, and wondered whether it wasn't rather sad that she had actually missed her work. What kind of

statement was that about her personal life? She was
thirty-one now, and it didn't take a leap of imagination
to see herself in ten years' time, a quiet little spinster
who pottered at home on weekends and looked forward
to Mondays. Not a pretty scenario.

As usual when she started thinking along those lines,
she pushed the thought to the back of her mind. There
had been a time when she had been brimming over with
enthusiasm, when she had made her plans and dreamed
her dreams and had been young enough and naïve
enough to assume that most of them would fall in line.
That was years ago, though, and she could hardly remember the girl she had been then.

She opened the door of her office to hear the sound
of a telephone being slammed down from her boss's
office.

Was this what she had missed? She was hanging up
her coat when he yanked open the connecting door and
confronted her with his arms folded and a thunderous
frown on his face.

Alice looked back at him, unflustered. Over the past
year and a half she had become accustomed to Victor
Temple's aggression. He could be intimidating, but he
had never intimidated her. Or at least he had initially,
but she had refused to crack under the ferocious impact
of his personality, and after three weeks' temping she
had been offered the job permanently.

'Well, I needn't ask whether you had a good time or
not.' He confronted her, arms still folded, as she made
her way to her desk and switched on her computer.

'It was very pleasant. Thank you.' She looked at him
and was struck, as she always was, by the sheer force
of his physical presence. Everything about him commanded immediate attention, but it went far beyond the
mundane good looks of dark hair, grey eyes and a mus-

CATHY WILLIAMS 7

cular physique. Victor Temple's uniqueness came from a restless energy, a self-assurance and an unspoken assumption of power that defied description. When he spoke, people automatically stopped in their tracks and listened. When he walked into a room, heads swivelled around, eyes followed him.

In the beginning, Alice had been amazed at the reactions of perfect strangers towards him. He had taken her out for lunch a couple of times, with clients, and she had seen the way men frowned, as though trying to place him, simply because he seemed to be the sort of person who should be recognised, the way women stared surreptitiously from under their lashes.

'Spent all day swanning around a pool, turning into leather?'

Alice looked at him and wondered, not for the first time, how she could possibly enjoy working for a man for whom common politeness was a concept to be blithely ignored, unless it suited him.

'And very relaxing it was, too,' she said, refusing to be provoked into a suitable retort. He had positioned himself directly in front of her desk and Alice sat down and pointedly began sifting through the mail she had brought from Reception, efficiently extracting the bits she knew she would be expected to deal with.

However infuriating and demanding Victor Temple could be, they somehow worked well together, and gradually, over time, he had delegated a sizeable workload to her. He trusted her. Advertising was a demanding business to be in; some of their clients could be sensitive and temperamental. Alice knew that he found her useful in dealing with them. She never allowed her attention to waver and was clever at soothing frayed tempers whenever he wasn't around to deal with them personally.

In return, she was paid well. Far better, she knew, than

she would be in any other job on the open market. It was a blessing and a trap at the same time, because leaving would have meant a huge cut in pay and she had become accustomed to a certain level of comfort over time. She could afford her holidays abroad, the occasional meal out at an expensive restaurant. Could even run to the odd designer outfit, if she chose to; but she never did. Designer clothes, she acknowledged, called for designer-style bodies—on her they would hang sadly around her thin frame, tacitly admitting defeat.

'Well, at least one of us had a relaxing fortnight.' He managed to make this sound as though she had deliberately connived to ensure that his fortnight had been a stressful nightmare.

'Has it been very busy here?' she asked, abandoning her inspection of the computer screen in front of her and looking up at him. He had perched on the edge of her desk and showed little inclination to move. 'How did the Finner campaign go? Have they signed up?'

'Just.' His mouth twisted and he gave a short, mirthless laugh. 'No thanks to that airhead temp you employed to cover you.'

'Rebecca came very highly recommended by the agency,' Alice protested. 'I wouldn't have taken her on otherwise!' She paused and frowned at him, shrewdly working out in her mind what had happened. She had seen it before. Perfectly level-headed girls who somehow became flustered adolescents by the time Victor was through with them. He had the unnerving habit of issuing orders like bullets from a gun, and any signs of inefficiency were treated with scathing contempt. His patience was something he kept on a very short leash.

'What agency? The agency specialising in idiots?'

'Don't be ridiculous. I'd hardly take on someone I thought was incompetent, would I? That would just mean that I'd return from holiday with a two-week back-log of work to be done.' She glanced at the stack of files on the desk out of the corner of her eye, and thought that they closely resembled a two-week backlog of work.

Victor followed her gaze and said triumphantly, 'Point proved. The girl barely knew how to type.'

'Her speeds were well above average.'

'She went to pieces every time I attempted to dictate something to her.'

Alice looked at him with clear-eyed comprehension, mentally picturing the scene. Victor's definition, she suspected, of *going to pieces* no doubt meant that the poor girl had asked questions along the way instead of following what he was saying, which would have been punctuated by frequent telephone interruptions and emerged as the basis of a letter which she would have been expected to translate into lucid, crystal-clear coherence with full background knowledge of the client. Poor girl. Next time, Alice thought, she would make sure that she employed someone older, with enough presence of mind to bounce back after a day of Victor Temple's demands.

'There's no need to give me that look,' Victor said irritably.

'What look?'

'The look that implies that somehow it's my fault if I end up with a temporary secretary who apparently hasn't completed her course. I'm a perfectly reasonable man.'

Alice nearly laughed out loud at that one. 'Oh, absolutely,' she murmured, restraining herself. 'Could I get you a cup of coffee?'

'Bring it into my office. I want to go through some files with you. We've just got a new client on board. Some titled fool who wants us to do a discreet advertising campaign for his stately home. Refuses to let anyone deal with it but me.'

'Stately home?'

'I'll discuss it with you in my office.' He stood up and raked his fingers through his hair. Alice looked at him and it flew through her mind—a thought so brief that it barely left an indentation—that she had yet to come across a man as compellingly attractive as Victor Temple. The angles of his face were hard, bordering on arrogant, but for all that there was a certain underlying sensuality about him. It was there in his mouth, in his dark-fringed eyes, in the supple grace of his body. He never worked out and probably wouldn't recognise the inside of a gym if he saw it, but his body was sleek and well-toned. A lean, athletic body which was apparent beneath the cut of his suit.

Was that one of the reasons why they worked so well together? She could acknowledge, in a detached, clinical way, that he was almost frighteningly good-looking, but he did not appeal to her. Tall, dark-haired and handsome all added up to the sort of man she knew, instinctively, was best avoided. She had already made one mistake in that direction and it was a mistake she would never repeat.

In turn, she was quite simply not his type. He did not sport a line of ever-changing women. She had met them both, and they both slotted into the same category—sexy, blonde and, at least from the outside, highly undemanding on the intellectual front. They had both struck her as the sort of women who accessorised what they wore to match their lipstick and nail varnish, and in high winds would somehow still manage to hold onto an immaculate hairdo and impeccable make-up.

His last secretary, who had left six months before she had arrived, had been, according to some of the girls in the office, a fifty-something harridan with a penchant for tweed skirts, even in summer, and sensible shoes. Then had come a dizzying and unsatisfactory array of young girls, none of whom had stayed the pace.

Alice knew that what he appreciated in her were her mind and her lack of obvious sex appeal. It was either a flattering or alternatively depressing comment on her, depending from which side of the fence it was viewed. As for her, she welcomed it with relief.

When she went into his office, he was on the phone; he leaned back in his chair and motioned to her to sit down, watching her as she did so.

Alice was suddenly acutely conscious of her appearance. There had been nothing in the slightest way sexual about his look, but there had been a certain unexpected appreciation there—must a flicker, but enough to register in her subconscious. The applications of sun cream had done the trick, eventually. She had not developed a deep tan, but there was a pale bronze glow about her which was quite becoming.

She sat down now, smoothing her skirt with her fingers, and gazed straight ahead of her, out through the window to the oppressive blue-grey sky outside. Glow or not glow, she didn't need a mirror to tell her what she lacked. Her straight dark hair, falling to her shoulders, was shiny enough and easy to look after, but, coupled with her fine-boned face, somehow managed to give her a background, girl-next-door look, and she lacked curves. She knew that and it didn't bother her except, occasionally, when she happened to be in the company of someone blatantly sexy, at which times she would feel the smallest twinge of envy that there was an entire world of clinging, low-cut dresses that would for ever be out of her range.

'Hello?' She heard the deep timbre of his voice and refocused her attention back to the present.

'Sorry. I was miles away.'

'And not a particularly pleasant place, judging from the expression.'

Alice blushed and looked down at the notepad on her lap. Sometimes it was easy to forget just how shrewd Victor Temple could be when it came to reading other people's minds. His own, he kept suitably under lock and key.

'Just thinking what needs doing when I get back home,' she improvised, and he raised his eyebrows with a certain amount of sarcastic amusement.

'Well, so sorry to drag you back to mundane office matters.' He sat back with his arms folded and subjected her to a leisurely stare. 'I can't imagine your flat being anything other than scrupulously tidy,' he drawled, which brought more colour to her cheeks and she returned his look with a flash of sudden anger.

'It's a mess,' she said flatly, defying him to contradict her. 'Books everywhere, clothes everywhere, dishes not washed.' She stared down to conceal the rebellious glint in her eyes. Did he think that she was prim and proper and precise? Did he think that, because she was efficient at work and well organised, she was exactly the same out of work? For all he knows, she thought, I could lead a scorching and raunchy life the minute I leave this office block.

'I'm impressed,' he told her, amused at her tone of voice. 'Vanessa not pulling her weight?'

'Post-holiday clutter,' Alice said, stifling an inclination to scowl. 'We've hardly had time to unpack our cases.'

'Why don't you get a cleaner?'

'Because it's an unnecessary luxury.'

'Don't I pay you enough?'

'More than enough,' she said, restlessly wondering where this conversation was leading. She glanced at him from under her lashes, trying to determine his mood. 'I happen to rather enjoy cleaning,' she murmured finally. 'I find it relaxing.'

'You're the first woman I've ever heard say that.'

Perhaps you mix with the wrong sort, she felt like telling him. Not that he would have appreciated women who wanted to tidy his house for him. She thought that he would probably run a mile if he were ever to be confronted with a domestic type. Domesticity was not a characteristic he would find especially appealing in a member of the opposite sex. He didn't want cosy nights in watching television, he didn't want home-cooked meals, he didn't want the little lady ever to wear an apron and attempt to tidy him up into a candidate for marriage.

'You were telling me that you have a new client on board?'

'I have a file here somewhere.' He pulled open the drawer of his desk and rummaged briefly inside, frowning. 'Now where did I put the damned thing? I was sure I stuck it in my drawer.'

'Perhaps Rebecca filed it away,' Alice said helpfully.

'Why would she do that?' Victor asked irritably.

'Because she might consider it one of her duties? Filing tends to come into the job specification for a secretary. Even for those who don't complete their secretarial courses.'

He slammed shut the drawer of his desk and favoured her with a narrowed look. 'Sarcasm, Alice?' He raised his eyebrows expressively. 'Since when?'

Alice didn't say anything. Normally, she bit back any retorts she might have fermenting in her head. Normally, she maintained an even, placid demeanour. She did her job and very rarely allowed herself the luxury of personal input. But two weeks in the sun had stirred something inside her. There had been a lot of young couples there, blissfully wrapped up in one another, oblivious to the outside world. The hotel specialised in honeymoon holidays, and from that point of view had not been chosen with a great deal of foresight, because for the first time Alice had been conscious of her own relentlessly single state. True, Vanessa was single as well, but her life was brimming over with men. She emanated a certain vivacious attractiveness that drew them in droves.

Her own situation was, she acknowledged realistically, slightly different. No men beating a path to her door, although she had a few male friends who occasionally asked her out to dinner, or the theatre, and it was only now, strangely, that she felt the lack of them. Perhaps, she thought, because she had crossed the thirty threshold. Time suddenly seemed to be moving faster. The gentle breeze that had flicked over the pages of the calendar was gathering momentum, flicking those pages faster and faster.

She smiled at Victor, meeting his speculative look with studied incomprehension, and decided that any restlessness was best left at home, or at least locked away in a compartment in her head that was inaccessible to anyone apart from herself.

'What did you and that flatmate of yours get up to on holiday?' he asked curiously, and Alice could have kicked herself. Victor Temple enjoyed getting his teeth into a challenge. For the past year and a half, she had shown him one face, and although at the beginning he had asked polite questions about her outside life he had quickly realised that answers would not be forthcoming, and he had soon lost interest.

Now, stupidly, she had afforded him a glimpse of someone else behind the efficient smile.

'Oh, the usual things,' Alice said vaguely.

'Really? Like what?'

'You said it yourself: we swanned around the pool and turned to leather.' Most of the couples, she thought, had looked young enough to be her children. Or perhaps she just felt old enough to be their mother. A sudden, sour taste of dissatisfaction rose to her throat and subsided again. Whatever was the matter with her? she wondered irritably. She had never been prone to self-pity, and she hoped that she wasn't about to become a victim of it now.

'You couldn't have spent a fortnight doing just that.'

'We went to the beach a few times as well.' She would have liked to somehow draw the subject back to the stately home, and the portfolio of other clients awaiting attention, but she knew that to have done that would only have succeeded in sharpening his curiosity still further. In a minute, he would become bored trying to extract information from her and he would give up.

'Good bathing?'

'Cold.'

'And what about in the evenings? What do young single girls get up to when they go abroad on holiday?' He grinned, amused at her discomfort, which annoyed her even more.

'I would have thought that you knew the answer to that one,' Alice said evenly. 'After all, we do enough advertisements on the subject.'

'Ah, yes.' He sat back and gazed at her thoughtfully. 'Nightclubs, bars.' He paused. 'Sex.' He allowed the word to drop between them, like forbidden fruit, and she went bright red.

'I'm not that young,' was all she could think of saying by way of reply.

'You mean that you're too old for nightclubs? Bars? Or sex? Or all three?'

She snapped shut her notepad and glared at him openly. 'What I do on holiday is none of your concern, Mr Temple. If you're really that interested in finding out what the young single female gets up to on holiday, then I suggest you go along yourself and find out firsthand. I'm sure that you'd find no end of women willing to show you.' She heard herself with dismay and confusion, alarmed that he had managed to provoke her into a response that was extraordinarily out of keeping with her normally unobtrusive work persona.

'Well, well, well.' He linked his fingers together and inspected her. A long, deliberate and leisurely inspection that was as unwelcome as it was disconcerting. She could feel her nails biting into the notepad and for the life of her she couldn't think of a way of wriggling out of her embarrassment.

'Quite a show of temper,' he said, in the voice of a scientist who suddenly discovered that his experimental mouse had unexpected talents.

'I'm sorry,' Alice said in as brisk a voice as she could manage. Now she felt like bursting into tears, which was ridiculous. She had obviously been doing too much thinking and Victor's insinuations that she was a dull bore didn't help matters. 'Perhaps we could get on with...'

'Oh, no, not so fast. I'm intrigued.' He linked his fingers behind his head and continued to stare at her. 'I was beginning to wonder whether there was anything behind that efficient veneer.'

'Oh, thank you very much,' Alice muttered.

'Now I've offended you.' He didn't sound contrite. In

fact, he sounded as though he was enjoying the situation enormously. The devil, she thought, works on idle hands. He had spent two weeks like a bear with a sore head and now he was catching up. He was relieved that she was back and relief had awakened some dormant desire to have a bit of a laugh at her expense.

'Not at all,' she said, gathering herself together.

'You never told me what you did on that holiday of yours. Something obviously happened. You're not your usual self. What was it? Did you meet a man?' He smiled as though amused at the thought of that. 'What was he like? Do you realise that I know very little about your private life? Considering the length of time you've been working for me?'

'Yes.' And that's just the way I'd like it to stay, her voice implied.

'I hope you're not thinking of deserting me to get married and have babies.'

Alice winced. The prospect of that couldn't have been further from reality. Marriage? Children? She had buried any such thoughts a long time ago. It seemed like decades ago.

'You've never struck me as the sort of girl who wants to rush into all that,' he continued musingly, not bothering to wait for her reply. His grey eyes held a question, one she refused to answer. None of this had anything to do with him.

She held her breath, not knowing whether to reply or maintain her silence in the hope that he would eventually shut up, and was saved a decision by the telephone.

It was a protracted conversation, and by the time he got off the phone he had obviously forgotten all about her and her private life. He opened one of the files on his desk, and Alice breathed a sigh of relief.

As he dictated letters to her, and her hand flew over

the notepad, turning pages, she realised that she was writing, listening, following orders, but with her mind halfway to somewhere else.

She didn't want Victor Temple showing any sort of interest in her, even interest of the most casual nature. She had become accustomed to their well-tuned, impersonal relationship. Now she could feel her eyes drifting to him, surreptitiously taking him in, just like all those women whose eyes travelled over him whenever he was in their company.

She woke from her semi-reverie to hear him talking to her about his latest project.

'It's a rather grand house.' There were a series of photos which he began to extract from a folder, flicking through them, turning the pictures this way and that with a frown. 'Handed down through the generations. The gardens have been landscaped by someone rather famous. The inside of the house itself is quite special, and apparently there are all manner of royal connections, albeit in the past.'

'Why have the owners come to you?'

'Owner. Just the one chap and I gather the cost of running the place is proving to be a strain on his bank balance. Reading between the lines, I'd say that the chap in question has eaten his way through quite a bit of the family money and now finds himself with a title and not much else to go with it.'

He looked up and tapped his fountain pen on his desk. 'Usual story. Large family inheritance which has gradually been whittled down through the ages. Now there's just the house and the upkeep is fabulously high. Our client figures that if the house is opened to the public he might be able to recover some of the costs of running it. Our job is to sell it, discreetly.'

'Oh, right.' She was almost back to normal now, thank

heavens. Mind firmly anchored on the task at hand, and
Victor back to his usual self. That brief moment had
been unsettling to say the very least.

'Have a look at the photos. Tell me what you think.'

He handed the large, glossy prints to her, and Alice
felt a cold chill of horror spread through her. It started
in the pit of her stomach and gradually spread through
her body until she felt as though her limbs had frozen
completely. She couldn't move. She could hardly think
straight. She sifted through the photographs with shaking
hands and then placed them on the desk in front of her.

'Well? What do you think?' He looked up from the
file, which he had been scanning.

'What sort of advertising campaign does he have in
mind?' Alice asked faintly. Her brain, which had been
temporarily numbed, now began working in overdrive.
There was no reason, she told herself, that this project
should intrude on her life. There was no need for her to
involve herself in it in any way whatsoever. She would
remain calm, cool, collected.

Victor's eyes narrowed. 'A series of spreads in one of
the more prestigious country magazines. He wants to
open the house and grounds to visitors. In due course,
he has plans to turn the place into a country hotel.'

'I see.'

'Where the hell are you this morning, Alice?'

'What do you mean?' She attempted a smile but the
muscles in her face felt stiff.

'I mean,' Victor said very slowly, with exaggerated
patience, 'you look as though you've seen a ghost.
You're as white as a sheet. Don't tell me that you've
picked up some bug on holiday. I don't think I can stand
another fortnight with a temp.'

'No. I'm fine.' She swallowed, and rummaged around
in her head for something intelligent to say about the

campaign. 'Yes! It doesn't sound as though it should be a terribly difficult job. I mean, the house more or less speaks for itself.'

'Right. That's what I thought.' He began explaining what he had in mind, while she half-listened and nodded—she hoped in all the right places. 'I've made an appointment for us to visit in a week's time.' He snapped shut the file. 'We should get more of a feel for the place when we see it.'

'We!'

'Naturally. I'll want you there to observe and take notes.' He scrutinised her face. 'Why? Is there a problem with that?'

'No!' There wasn't *a* problem with that, she thought wildly. There were several thousand problems with it. 'It's just that I'm not sure whether I shall be able to find the time...I mean, it looks as though Rebecca has left quite a backlog of work to be brought up to date. And then, some of the accounts are a bit behind. I shall have to devote some time to chasing them...' Her voice drifted off into silence and he looked at her as though she had taken leave of her senses.

'You can clear the backlog in a matter of a day or two,' Victor said slowly, as though talking to someone mentally deficient. 'And Sam's handled some of the overdue accounts. I made sure that she brought them up to date. Any more excuses?'

'I really would rather not be on this particular job,' Alice confessed flatly, when she couldn't think of another excuse to give him. It made no difference anyway. She recognised that glint in his eye. She could throw a million excuses at him and short of her taking to her bed with a broken leg he would simply demolish them one by one until he had got what he wanted. Namely, her presence there.

'Why not?'

'I'd rather not go into it, if you don't mind. I'm only asking you to respect my request.'

'And I'd rather you *did* go into it, if *you* don't mind. When I hear what you've got to say, then I'll tell you whether I shall respect your request or not.'

Typical, she thought with helpless, frustrated despair. Typical, typical, typical. Anyone else would have simply nodded and let the matter rest. Anyone else with even an ounce of sympathy would have trusted that her reasons were valid, and would have acquiesced to her request. But not Victor Temple, oh, no. If he saw a Keep Out sign, then his immediate response was to try and get in. And he wouldn't be content to try and find the easiest entrance. He would simply take the quickest route and would use whatever methods he had at his disposal. The man was a shark.

How could this have happened? How could the one man in the world she wanted to have nothing to do with, with the one stately house in the world she would rather never have re-entered, have chosen the one advertising company in the country she worked at to promote his wretched place?

She knew how, of course. Victor Temple ran the tightest ship. His advertising firm was highly respected because it was highly successful.

But, she reasoned, she need not divulge any of her private affairs to him. She nodded, defeated. 'All right. I'll come with you. Perhaps you could give me the precise date so that I can enter it into the diary?'

'*Dates.* We'll be there for a total of three days.'

Could it get worse?

'And do you mind telling me why,' Victor said casually, before they moved on to other things, 'you've changed your mind?'

'Yes. Actually, I do.'

The shrewd grey eyes looked at her carefully, as though he was seeing her for the first time.

'What a day of revelations this is turning out to be,' he said dryly. 'First your little display of temper, and now some deep, dark secret. I'm beginning to wonder what other surprises you have in store for me.'

'It's no *deep, dark secret*,' Alice told him, and she punctuated the lie with a light laugh. 'And I don't have any surprises in store for you, or anyone else for that matter.'

'Well. I suppose we shall just have to wait and see.' He returned her laugh with one of his own, but she could tell from the expression in his eyes that his curiosity had been aroused, and she contemplated the prospect of three days at Highfield House with sick trepidation.

They said that you could never really leave your past behind. Sooner or later it caught up with you.

Now her past was catching up. All she could do was ensure that it didn't sink its claws into her.

CHAPTER TWO

THE following week was a nightmare. The pace at work was frantic. It seemed as though hundreds of clients had all decided to descend upon them at precisely the same time. The phone hardly stopped ringing, and the meetings were endless. Victor could exist indefinitely on a diet of no sleep—his stamina was amazing—but Alice could feel her nerves shredding as she trudged to meeting after meeting, taking notes, writing up minutes and in between catching up on everything else.

Portugal and sunshine seemed like months ago. And it didn't help matters that Highfield House hung over her head like a dark cloud, full of the promise of thunder.

Her capacity to remember amazed her. All those years ago, and still she could recall entire conversations with James Claydon, as though they had taken place the day before. And it seemed as though each passing hour added another little snippet of recollection, another small, bitter memory of the past she had spent four years trying to forget.

On the morning they were due to travel up, her nerves had reached such a point that she felt physically ill when she went to answer the door to Victor.

He had decided against having his chauffeur drive them and as she pulled open the door she saw, immediately, that he had not dressed for work. No suit. In its place, dark green trousers, a striped shirt and a thick cream woollen jumper over it. Alice looked at him, taken aback by his casual appearance, and after a few seconds

23

of complete silence he said sarcastically, 'I do possess the odd change of clothes.'

'Sorry.' She bent to pick up her holdall, which he insisted on taking from her, and then followed him out to his car—a black convertible Jaguar which breathed opulence.

'There really was no need for you to wear a suit,' he said as she settled into the passenger seat. 'This is supposed to be a relaxing three-day break. We'll stroll round the grounds—' he started the engine and slowly manoeuvred the car out '—have an informal, guided tour of the house so that we know which rooms will lend themselves to the most flattering photographs, discuss the history of the place.' He shot her a quick, sidelong look. 'No power meetings. I'll expect you to make some notes along the way, naturally, but that's about it.'

'I didn't think,' Alice said, glancing down at her navy blue outfit, the straight-cut skirt and waist-length jacket, and the crisp white shirt underneath. The sort of clothing that was guaranteed to make the most glamorous woman totally asexual. She had chosen the ensemble deliberately. She supposed that she would meet James at some point during their stay, very likely as soon as they pulled up, and she needed the sort of working gear that would put her in a frame of mind that would enable her to cope with the encounter.

With any luck, he might well not recognise her at all, though it was highly unlikely. She had changed during the past four years, had cut her hair, lost a fair amount of weight, but most of the changes had been inside her. Disillusionment had altered her personality for ever, but physically she had remained more or less the same.

She tried to picture him, after all this time and with so much muddy water stretching between them, and her mind shut down completely.

'I hope you've brought something slightly less formal than what you're wearing,' Victor told her. 'We don't want to intimidate the client. Which reminds me. There's a file on the back seat. Read it. It contains all the background information you need on him. Might find it useful.'

Alice hesitated. She had debated whether she should tell Victor that she knew James, or at least had known him at one point in time. After all, how would she explain it if he greeted her with recognition, as he almost inevitably would? On the other hand, she had no desire to open that particular door because Victor would edge in before she could shut it, and then subject her to a barrage of questions, none of which she would be inclined to answer.

In the end, she'd decided that she would go along with the premise that she didn't know their client from Adam, and if James greeted her like some long-lost friend, then she would simply pretend that she had forgotten all about him; after all, it had been years.

Years, she thought on a sigh, staring out of the window and making no move to reach behind her for the file. Four years to rebuild the life he had unwittingly taken to pieces and left lying there. Four years to forget the man who had taken her virginity and all the innocence that went with it and for three years had allowed her the stupid luxury of thinking that what they had was going to be permanent.

She could remember the first time she had ever laid eyes on him. It had been a wet winter's night and she had been working for his father for almost a month. Despite that, she had still not seen most of Highfield House. There had been just so much of it. Rooms stretching into rooms, interspersed with hallways and corridors and yet more rooms. And of course Henry

Claydon, wheelchair-bound, had not been able to show her around himself.

She could explore, he had told her, to her heart's content, and had then proceeded to pile so much work onto her that she had barely had time to think, never mind explore the outer reaches of the house.

She had loved it, though. Sitting in that warm, cosy library, surrounded by books, taking notes as the old man sifted through files and documents, watching the bleak winter outside settling like a cold fist over the vast estate and beyond. So different from the tiny terraced house in which she had spent most of her life before her mother died. It had been wonderful to look outside and see nothing but gardens stretching out towards fields, rolling countryside that seemed to go on and on for ever.

She had grown up with a view of other terraced houses and the claustrophobic feeling of clutter that accompanied crowded streets. Highfield House was like paradise in its sheer enormity. And she'd loved the work. She'd loved the snatches of facts, interspersed with memories, which she had to collate and transcribe into a lucid format, all part of a book of memoirs. She'd enjoyed hearing about Henry Claydon's past. It had seemed so much more colourful than her own.

She had been working on, alone, in the study, when James Claydon had walked through the door, and against the darkness of the room, illuminated only by the spotlight on the desk, he had appeared like a figure of the night. Long, dark coat, dark clothes. And she had fallen in love. Hopelessly, madly in love with handsome, debonair, swarthy James Claydon.

'Do I get an answer to my question?' Victor asked. 'Or do you intend to spend the entire journey with your head in the clouds?'

'What? What question?'

'Oh, good heavens,' he muttered under his breath, 'you're as good as useless like this. I hope you intend to snap out of it sufficiently to be of some help to me on the trip. I don't want you drifting down memory lane when you should be taking notes.'

'Well, I *did* ask whether I might be excused from this particular job.'

'So you did. And you never gave me your reason. Is it the house? You lived around here, didn't you?'

Alice looked at him, surprised that he would remember a passing detail on an application form from eighteen months back.

'Well? Didn't you?'

'Not very far away,' she admitted reluctantly. It had been her first job after her mother died, and London the bolt-hole to which she had fled in the wake of her miserable affair. Still, the first she had seen of Highfield House had been when she had applied for the job of working alongside Henry Claydon, even though the name was well enough known amongst the townspeople. It was a landmark.

'How close? Everyone knows everyone else in these little country villages, don't they?'

'No,' Alice said bluntly. 'The town I grew up in was small but it wasn't *that* small. People who live in the city always imagine that anywhere fifty miles outside of London is some charming little hamlet where everyone is on first-name terms with everyone else.'

'And it isn't?' Victor exclaimed with overdone incredulity. 'You shock me.'

'Ha, ha.'

'Oh, dear. Don't tell me that your sense of humour has gone into hibernation.'

Alice shifted uncomfortably in her seat. She couldn't quite put her finger on it, but something had changed between them, almost unnoticeably. It was as though his sudden curiosity about her background had moved them away from the strictly working relationship level onto some other level, though *what* she couldn't make out. Whatever it was, it made her uneasy.

'So, what's the town like?' He glanced at her and continued smoothly, 'Might be interesting if we're to find out how saleable Highfield House is for visiting tourists.'

Alice relaxed. This kind of question she could cope with. 'Picturesque,' she said with a small frown as she cast her mind back. 'The high street is very pretty. Lots of black and white buildings which haven't been mown down in favour of department stores. There's still a butcher, a baker...'

'A candlestick maker...'

She smiled, almost without thinking. 'Very nearly. Or at least, there was when I was last there.'

'Which was...?'

'A few years ago,' she said vaguely.

'Any historic sights nearby?'

'Remains of a castle. I'm sure there must be quite a bit of history around it, but if there is, then I'm the last person to ask because I don't know. Stratford-upon-Avon's not a million miles away.'

'Sounds good. Any stately home that's open to the public can only benefit from having interesting surroundings.'

'Yes, that's true,' she said, wondering for the first time whether the town would have changed much, whether her mother's old house was still standing, whether Gladys and Evelyn who had lived on either side were still finding things to argue about. She had not given any of this much thought for years, but as the Jaguar ate up the miles she couldn't help casting her mind back.

'So Highfield House is close to the town centre…?'

Alice glanced at him and his face was bland. Interested, but purely from a professional point of view. Or at least that was what his expression told her.

'Not terribly. At least twenty minutes' drive away and not readily accessible by public transport.'

'Set on a hill, though, from what I remember from the photos. Quite a commmanding view.'

'Yes.'

'And correct me if I'm wrong, but there was an old man there, wasn't there? James Claydon's father, I believe.'

'That's right.' He had never known about her infatuation with his son. James had only appeared occasionally. She could remember anxiously looking forward to his arrivals with the eagerness of a teenager waiting for her first date. And he inevitably would arrive with flowers, or chocolates, or little trinkets which he would bring from London, or wherever else he had been. And there would be a few days of stolen heady passion, followed by weeks of agonising absence.

'Died… Can't quite remember when…'

'After my time, I'm afraid,' Alice said shortly. 'I'd already left for London by then.'

'Ah, so you *did* know at least something of what was going on at Highfield House. Wasn't the old man a widower?'

'Yes, he was.'

They had cleared London completely now, and she looked out of her window, marvelling at how quickly the crowded streets gave way to open space. It was still very developed, with houses and estates straddling the motorway, yet there was a feeling of bigness that she didn't get in the heart of London.

Victor began chatting to her about one of their clients,

a problem account, and they moved on to art, music, the theatre. She could feel some of the tension draining out of her body. He was good at conversing and could talk about practically anything. His knowledge stretched from politics to the opera and he spoke with the confidence of someone who knew what they were talking about. It was a valuable asset when it came to dealing with other people, because he was informed enough on most subjects to pick up on the slightest hint of an interest and expand on it. He could put people at ease as smoothly as he could intimidate them when the occasion demanded.

She rested her head back and half-closed her eyes, not thinking of Highfield House or James Claydon, or any of those nightmarish thoughts that had dogged her for the past few days.

'What made you decide to come down to London to work?' he asked, digressing with such aplomb that it took her a few seconds to absorb the change of subject.

'I thought that I might get a more invigorating job in the capital,' she said carefully.

'So you swapped the open fields for the city life.' It wasn't a question. It was more said in the voice of someone thinking aloud. Musing, but with only the mildest curiosity expressed.

'It's not that unusual.'

'Quite the opposite.' He paused. 'What exactly were you doing before you came to work with me?'

'Oh, just a series of temp jobs,' Alice said, dismissing them easily.

'And before that?'

She gave him a guarded look. 'I wasn't working for a company,' she said evasively. On her application form, she had not extended her work experience beyond her temporary jobs, all of which had earned her glowing references; and because she had joined the firm as a temp herself there had been no in-depth questioning about her work background. Her experience within the company and the fact that she had worked smoothly with Victor had been all that was necessary.

'Still at secretarial school?'

'No.' The nakedness of this reply forced her to continue. 'I worked freelance. Actually I was transcribing a book.' Well, it was the truth, shorn of all elaboration, and Victor nodded thoughtfully.

'Anything interesting?'

'Not particularly.'

'Was it ever published?'

'I have no idea.' She doubted it. At the time, Henry Claydon had shown no real rush to finish his memoirs. It was a labour of love, something of a hobby. He'd certainly had no need of any money it might have generated. No, she was sure that it had remained incomplete.

'Bit odd for you to take off for London in the middle of a job like that...'

She didn't care for this line of questioning. She knew where it was leading, but she was wary of the circuitous route. This was how Victor was so clever at manoeuvring people into revealing more than they had bargained for.

'The money wasn't very good,' Alice told him, truthfully enough, 'and it looked as though it was a book that could have taken decades to write. I simply couldn't afford to stay in the end.' It was a sort of truth.

'He must have been disappointed.'

'*He?*'

'He or she. Whoever was writing this mysterious book. You must have built up some kind of rapport, working in such intimate conditions.'

Alice shrugged. 'I suppose so, although, to be fair, I *did* give him six months' notice.'

'Ah. So it was a *him*.'

'That's right.' She could feel him testing her, trying to persuade confidences out of her. She had given him the irresistible—a shady past lying underneath the crisply ironed shirts and the sober working suits. When she thought about it, she realised that it had been a mistake to react to those photos. She should have agreed instantly to the trip up and then promptly cancelled at the very last minute, when it would have been too late to rearrange the whole thing. True, she would not have been thanked by any of the secretaries who might have found themselves replacing her, but then she would have been spared the ordeal that lay ahead. And, almost as important, she would have been spared Victor's curiosity, which, once aroused, might prove unstoppable.

'What kind of book was he writing?' he asked casually, and Alice suddenly realised where all his questions were leading.

Victor Temple thought that she had been having some kind of affair with Henry Claydon. Except he had no idea that Henry Claydon had been her employer at the time. She could almost hear his brain ticking over.

'Documentary of sorts,' she said, thinking that this could be her way out, as far as revealing too much of her past was concerned.

'Lots of research?' He gestured to her to check the map, glancing across as she laid it flat on her lap and followed the road sequences with her finger. They had left London behind and she felt an odd stirring of nostalgia as the open spaces became more visible. Over the past two days the weather had cleared, and as the Jaguar silently covered the miles everywhere was bathed in sunshine. The sky was a hard, defined blue and everything seemed to be Technicolor-bright.

'A fair amount.'

'You're not very forthcoming on this chap of yours,' he said idly. 'Can't have been a very interesting job. How long were you there?'

'Three years.'

'Three years! My God, he must have been a methodical man. Three years on a book! And one that wasn't even completed by the time you left.'

'Oh, yes, he was terribly methodical.' That was the truth. Henry had indeed been very methodical, despite a charming inclination to side-track down little paths, little reminiscences that brought his recollections to life. 'And, of course, he wasn't writing *all* the time.' If Victor thought that she had been having an affair with this mysterious stranger, then let him. He should never have assumed that she was fair game as far as his curiosity was concerned anyway.

'No, I guess he had to work occasionally? To pay the bills?'

'He did work in between, yes.' She paused, leaving his unspoken assumptions hanging in the air. 'Do you mind if I have a quick look at the file on Highfield House?'

Victor glanced at her with a quick smile. 'Sure. Good idea. You can tell me what you think. We never got around to that, if I recall.'

'So we didn't,' Alice agreed. She stretched back, just managing to grab hold of the file, and began to leaf through it, grateful that Victor was driving and couldn't read the expression on her face as she scanned the photographs of Highfield House.

It hadn't changed. The grounds looked as immaculate as she remembered them. There was a picture of James, standing with his back to the house, leaning elegantly against the side of his Land Rover, and her heart gave a little leap of unpleasant recognition. It was difficult to define any sort of expression on his face, but he appeared to have changed very little. Some weight had settled around his middle, but it did very little to detract from the overall impression of good looks. Was he married now? Victor had said nothing to intimate that he was. No Mrs Claydon had been mentioned. On that thought, she snapped shut the folder and returned it to the back seat.

'Well? What are your thoughts?'

'It's a large place. What does the owner expect to do if it's opened to the public?'

'Restrict his living quarters to one section of the house. Shouldn't be too difficult in a house of that size.'

'I can see why he might need the money,' Alice said, injecting as much disinterested speculation into her voice as she could. 'Must cost an arm and a leg running a place that big. The grounds themselves look like a head-ache. Heaven only knows how many gardeners he would need to employ.'

'Not as many as in the past. I gather, from the cov-ering letter that was sent, that quite a bit of the land has already been sold off. Still, there are still two formal gardens, including a rose garden, a miniature maze and a small forested area.'

Alice remembered the forested area well. She used to enjoy walking through it in the early evening, after they had stopped working. In spring it was quite beautiful, with the trees coming into bloom, and in autumn the leaves lay like a rich russet carpet on the ground. The three years she had spent there seemed as elusive as a dream, yet as clear as if she had been there yesterday.

She worriedly bit her lip and hoped that James would

not overreact when he saw her. If she played her cards right, she might even manoeuvre to confront him on her own, when Victor was safely tucked away somewhere. That way, she could tell him to keep quiet about their relationship, that she had moved on from the past and she did not need reminding of it. He had always, she thought reluctantly, been a very decent sort of person. Things had ended on a sour note but in retrospect that had been mainly her fault. Reading too much into a situation. Not understanding that wealth preferred to stick to its own.

She felt faint with humiliation, even now, as she remembered the surprise and dismay on his face when she had mentioned marriage, commitment, a long-term solution, the apology in his voice as he'd stammered through his explanation. That he wasn't ready to settle down. Oh, he liked her well enough, and he was basically too decent to say outright what had been written all over his face: that as a long-term proposition she simply was not suitable.

Alice rested her head back against the seat and could feel her heart hammering madly in her chest. She hadn't thought of that traumatic conversation in years. At first, she had been able to think of nothing else. Every word had burnt itself into her brain until she had thought that she was going mad, but gradually, over time, she had made herself think of other things whenever the temptation to dwell on it had risen inside her.

She had learnt to reduce the entire episode to a philosophical debate. It was the only way that she could put it behind her. It had altered her whole approach to the opposite sex, she had sealed off her emotions behind locked doors, and that was how it would have stayed if fate had not intervened. If Victor Temple had been more sympathetic. She heard him dimly saying something to her and she murmured something in response.

'What the hell does *that* mean?' he asked harshly, breaking into her reverie, and she pulled herself up with a start.

'For God's sake, Alice! What turn-off are we supposed to take? That map's in front of you for a reason!'

'Sorry.' She studied the map, not having a clue where they were, and eventually, when she asked him, he pointed out their location with an ultra-polite precision that only thinly veiled his irritation with her.

She was never like this at work. Usually, he had only to ask something once and she caught on, competently carrying out his instructions. But then, her head had never felt as woolly as it did now.

'Look,' he said, after she had stumbled out their route, frowning hard in concentration because her brain just didn't seem to want to co-operate. 'I don't know what the hell happened up here, but it was years ago. Haven't you managed to put it behind you by now?'

'Of course I have,' she said quickly. 'I'm just a little rattled at coming back here after all this time.'

'Must have been quite a miserable business if it's managed to keep you away from your home for so long.'

Alice could feel her defences going into place. She had been a private person for such a long time that the ability to confide was alien to her. And anyway, Victor Temple, she thought, was the last person on earth she would wish to confide in.

She glanced across at him and wondered whether she would have been susceptible to that animal charm of his which other women appeared to find so irresistible, if experience hadn't taught her a valuable lesson.

Hard on the heels of that came another, disturbing image. The image of him in bed, making love to her.

She looked away hurriedly. Thank heavens she was immune to his charm, she thought. If James had been a catastrophic mistake, then the likes of Victor Temple would have been ten times worse. He was just in a different league, the sort of man destined to be a danger as far as women were concerned.

She licked her lips and put such silly conjecture to the back of her mind.

'He probably doesn't even live in the area any longer,' she heard him say.

'Who?'

'The man you had your affair with. The one you were working for.'

She knew that he was taking a shot in the dark, and she opened her mouth to contradict him, then closed it. Let him go right ahead and think that. It suited her.

'I can't imagine you having a wild, passionate fling,' he said with slow, amused speculation. He looked across at her and their eyes met for a brief moment, before he turned away with a little smile on his lips.

'What sort of time scale do we have for this project?'

'Not a very adroit change of subject, Alice.'

She could discern the laughter in his voice and was unreasonably nettled by it. Just as she had been earlier on. He had categorised her, stuck her on a dusty shelf somewhere. Another spinster-to-be, past her sell-by date. Age had nothing to do with it but, reading between the lines, she was, to him, so unappealing sexually that she disqualified herself from the marriage stakes.

'I don't have to explain my private life to you.'

'Do you to anyone? Is there another man in your life now?'

'No, and I'm quite happy with the situation, as it happens.'

'Really?' He was enjoying this conversation. She

could hear it in his voice. 'I thought all women wanted to get married, settle down, have children. Keep the home fires burning, as they say.'

Alice winced inwardly at that.

'Not all, no. This is the twentieth century, in case you hadn't noticed. There are lots of women around who prefer to cultivate their working lives.' She had never spoken to him like this before, but then their conversations had never touched on the personal before. Or at least not *this* personal. On a Friday he might ask her, in passing, what plans she had for the weekend, but he had never shown the least interest in delving any further.

'I think that's something of a myth,' he said comfortably. 'I personally think that most women would give an arm and a leg for the security of a committed relationship.'

Alice didn't say anything, not trusting herself to remain polite.

'Wouldn't you agree?' he persisted, still smiling, as if pleasantly energised by the fact that her common sense was struggling to hold back a desire to argue with him.

She shouldn't say anything. She knew that. She should bite back the urge to retort and, if she had to speak, should take refuge in something utterly bland and innocuous.

'You seem to find ones who don't want committed relationships,' she was horrified to hear herself say.

'What on earth do you mean?'

Alice wished that she could vanish very quickly down a hole. She had gone too far. There was nothing in his voice to imply that he was annoyed, but he would be. Cordial though he could be, he kept a certain amount of space around himself and barging in with observations on his private life was the most tactless thing she could have done. He *was* her employer after all, and she would do well to remember that. She could have kicked herself.

'Nothing!' She almost shouted it at him in an attempt to retrieve her remark. 'I didn't mean anything.'

'Oh, yes, you did. Go on. Explain yourself. I won't fly into a fit and break both your arms, you know.'

Alice looked warily at him, the way she might have looked at a tiger that appeared friendly enough for the moment, but could well pounce at any minute.

'I—I was being sarcastic,' she stammered eventually. 'It was uncalled for.'

'Right on at least one of those counts, but, before you retreat behind that cool façade of yours, tell me what you were thinking when you said that. I'm interested.'

Interested, she thought suddenly, and unlikely to be offended because she was just his secretary, and when you got right down to it her opinions would not matter to him one way or the other. She felt stupidly hurt by that.

'Okay,' she said with energy. 'You said that most women want commitment. In which case, how do you feel about breaking hearts when you go out with them and refuse to commit yourself?' This was not boss/secretary conversation. This was not what they should be talking about. They should be discussing the route they were taking, the weather, holidays, the cinema, *anything* but this.

'I give them a great deal of enjoyment.'

Alice could well imagine what nature of enjoyment he had in mind, and more graphic, curiously disturbing images floated into her head.

'Well, then, that's fine.'

'But would be more fine if I slotted a ring on a finger?'

'Not for you, I gather.'

'Or necessarily for them. What makes you think that they don't tire of me before I have a chance to tire of them?' He looked across at her and grinned at the expression on her face. 'Well, now, I expect I should take that as a compliment.' Which made the colour crawl into her face, because she knew that he could see perfectly well what she was thinking. That he was the sort of man a woman could not possibly tire of. When, she wondered in confusion, had she started thinking like that?

'I recognise where we are now,' she said. She closed the map on her lap. 'We should be coming into the town in about fifteen minutes. Highfield House is on the other side. I can show you which signs to follow.' She stared straight ahead of her, and before he could return to their conversation she began talking about the town in great detail, pointing out places she remembered as they drove slowly through, covering up the lapse in their mutual detachment with a monologue on the charms of the town she had left behind.

As they headed away from the town and back out towards the countryside, she began mentally bracing herself for what lay ahead of her.

The sight of Highfield House, rising up in the distance like a matriarch overlooking her possessions, made her feel faint with apprehension. Her voice dried up.

'Impressive, isn't it?' he murmured, misreading her sudden silence.

'Yes, it is.'

'And you can breathe a sigh of relief. We're out of the town now and I take it there were no sightings of your past…?'

'No. No sightings.' Breathe a sigh of relief? If only!

CHAPTER THREE

THE car pulled smoothly up into the huge courtyard outside Highfield House and Alice fought the urge to slide
very low down into her seat, so that she would not be
visible to whoever happened to approach them.

Which, as she saw with a great wave of relief, wasn't
James, but a girl of about nineteen, dressed in a pair of
jeans and a jumper and holding a duster in one hand.
She pulled open the door, stood there with one hand on
her hip, and waited for them to emerge. Alice wondered
what had happened to the staff who had been in atten-
dance when Henry had been alive. There had been a
middle-aged couple who had lived in permanently, and
three cleaners who came in twice a week, in addition to
the gardeners and a cook.

Victor was the first to open his car door and as he
walked up to the house Alice hurriedly sprang into action and flew behind him, sticking on her jacket in the
process.

Up close, the girl looked even younger. Her yellowish
hair was pulled back into a ponytail, and she was chew-
ing gum.

'We're here to see James Claydon,' Victor said, and
was met with frank, adolescent appraisal.

'Not here.'

'And where is he?' he asked stonily.

'Gone to the vet's with the dog.'

'The blasted man could have called and asked us to
drive up another day,' he muttered darkly to Alice, not
much caring whether the girl at the door heard or not.

41

'A bit of an emergency, it was,' the girl explained helpfully, straightening up. 'Anna, that's the dog, got into some bother with one of the fences out towards the paddocks and the vet said to bring her down immediately. He should be back, he said, in about forty minutes and in the meantime I'm to show you where you'll be staying.'

She had now turned her frank appraisal to Alice, but after a few seconds she resumed her fascinated inspection of Victor, who had stuck his hands in his pockets and was scowling.

'Brought any bags?' the girl said brightly, and Alice smiled at her. It wasn't her fault that she had to deliver a perfectly acceptable message to someone whose tolerance level of other people was close to zero. It had also cheered her up, momentarily, not to be confronted with James.

'In the car,' she said. 'Shall we fetch them?'

'And I'll show you up. By the way,' the girl said, focusing a little more on Alice and steering clear of the gloweringly silent Victor, 'I'm Jen. I come up here to clean twice a week.'

'Must take you for ever,' Alice said as Victor strode towards the car to get their bags. 'I'm surprised there aren't any...staff...' What on earth happened to all of them?

'Used to be. God, I hate chewing-gum after a while.' She removed a piece of tissue from her jeans pocket, folded the chewing-gum inside it, and returned it to her pocket. 'But now there's just me, and of course the gardeners. Actually, it's not too bad. I only have to clean part of the house; the rest is closed off. And James, that's Mr Claydon, isn't fussy. In fact, he's hardly up here. Comes and goes. You know.'

She led the way up the stairs, relishing the break in

whatever it was she had been doing, chatting interminably the whole way up and finally depositing them in
their bedrooms.

'I'll be seeing you later,' she said cheerfully to Alice,
who looked around her room, grateful that it had not
been her old one.

'What?' She looked vaguely at Jen.

'I'm here for a couple of days. Cooking, you know.'
She propped herself against the door-frame and grinned.
'Home economics was the only thing I did well at
school. My cooking's a darn sight better than my cleaning.' She flicked the duster unenergetically at the door-
frame as though swatting a fly. 'More fun, too.'

As soon as she had disappeared, Alice positioned herself by the bedroom window and sat on the window-
seat, staring out. The house, she thought, hadn't changed
internally at all. It didn't seem as though even an orna-
ment had been rearranged. But thoughts of the house
were not on her mind. She wanted to wait for James. As
soon as his car pulled up, she intended to run down to
meet him so that she could steer him clear of mentioning
anything to Victor that might indicate that they once
knew each other. That, she decided, had the saving grace
of both safeguarding a part of her life which she had no
intention of exposing, and doing away with the awk-
wardness of a meeting neither of them would have
wanted.

She had rehearsed the conversation in her head a million times by the time the Range Rover pulled up outside. It seemed like for ever, but when she looked at her
watch she realised that it had been under forty minutes.

For a few seconds she watched as he got out of the
car, released the dog from the boot; then she headed
down the stairs quickly, taking them two at a time and

looking around to make sure that she wasn't being observed by Victor.

Why, she wondered, did it matter so much whether
Victor found out about her past or not? Everyone had a
past and nearly everyone's past had a skeleton of sorts
in it.

But, for some reason, it did. For some reason she
found the idea of him knowing too much about her unsettling. It was as if some part of her suspected that if
the distance between them was eroded, then something
would be unleashed, although she wasn't sure what.

She almost ran into James as he was tossing his jacket
over the huge mahogany table in the hall. He spun
around at the sound of her footsteps, no doubt expecting
it to be Jen, and whatever it was he had been about to
say became a strangled gasp of shock. They stared at
one another, speechless, and finally he said. 'My God!
Alice Carter! What on earth are *you* doing here?'

Confronting your fears was always easier than fearing
the confrontation. Alice looked at him and thought, He's
just a man, a jigsaw piece in a puzzle that has its place
amongst all the other pieces. And her memories of him
had somehow given him a status that reality, now, was
quickly dissipating. He was neither as tall nor as good-
looking as she had remembered. He looked weaker than
she remembered, less of a force to be reckoned with.
She hardly even felt bitter now, although time might well
have succeeded in accomplishing that.

'I have to have a word with you, James,' she said
urgently, glancing over her shoulder.

'But what...*what* are you doing *here*?' He looked
dazed.

'In the kitchen,' Alice said, grabbing his arm and half-
pulling him in the general direction of the kitchen.

She half-expected to find Jen there, relaxing with a

cup of coffee and probably smoking a cigarette, but when they got there it was empty. She looked around her, struck by the familiarity and the strangeness of it all. The same weathered bottle-green Aga, the same solid wooden units, the same huge pine table, even. Nothing was out of place. It looked as though it was seldom used, as no doubt was the case if what his cleaner had said was true.

'I can't believe it's you, Ali,' he said, regaining his power of coherent speech. 'My God, you've changed. You've had your hair cut!' He made it sound as though, in four years, having one's hair cut was a reckless adventure.

'Sit down, James.'

He sat down and continued to stare at her in the manner of someone who was looking at a ghost. The fact that he had been caught off guard also helped to boost her confidence. She had spent days agonising over what her reaction would be when she finally saw him for the first time in years, dreading the memories that would surface. A sense of purpose had melted all that into the background.

'You look great,' he said, observing her with the same boyish enthusiasm that had won her over in the first place; except now it did nothing for her at all. Oh, he had been enthusiastic all right, until it had come to the crunch. Was it any wonder that her impressions of men tended to be a little jaded? If and when she ever found a man, she would make sure that he was a solid, dependable type. Charm was something that she would steer well clear of.

'I'm here with Victor Temple,' Alice said, cutting short any temptation he might have had to go over old times. 'I work for him.'

'Ah, so you're here to see the house.' His face clouded

over. 'Bit of a shame, Ali, having to do all this. Dad would have hated it, but I ran into a bit of trouble over one or two investments. Couldn't really see much of a way out. Not to mention the fact that this monstrosity's eating away my inheritance.' He scowled, and Alice was startled by the sudden rush of irritation that she felt towards him.

'Please don't call me *Ali*,' she said. 'Victor knows nothing about us and I'd like to keep it that way.'

'How could he know nothing about us? Surely you must have told him that we had an affair the minute you knew that I was the client in question?'

'No, I didn't.'

'Why not?'

'Because, James, I'd rather forget about you.'

'That's not very nice.'

'Nor, if I recall, were you,' she said coldly, and he had the grace to flush.

'I explained at the time…'

'Look, James, it's not important. It's in the past and that's where I want it to rest.'

'Why?' He looked at her shrewdly. 'Why does it matter whether your boss knows about us or not? Are you two having an affair? Is that it? And the less he knows about your past the better? You haven't pretended that you were a virgin when you met him, have you?'

'No! And no, we most certainly are *not* having an affair!'

'You really *have* changed,' he said slowly. 'You used to be much more…'

'Pliable? Gullible? Those the words you were searching for, James? Or maybe just plain stupid.'

'Less hard.'

'Experience tends to do that to a person.' She stifled the attack of bitter resentment that had flooded her throat like bile. There was no point in bitterness, no point in resenting the past. You couldn't change it, after all; the most you could do was learn from it.

'If it's what you want, I'll keep quiet about us, but I think it's ridiculous. And he's bound to guess sooner or later.'

'How do you work that one out?'

'The way you react to the house, for a start. You'll trip up by recognising something.'

'I'll make sure that I'm careful, then, won't I?' She paused. 'When did your father...?'

'A few months after you left.'

'I'm sorry.'

'He missed you, you know.'

Alice felt a lump in her throat. 'I missed him, too.' She had written to him a couple of times and when, after a few months, he had stopped replying, she had assumed that he had forgotten about her. It had hurt that she couldn't explain to him her real reason for leaving, and she certainly had not been able to stick around, not given the circumstances.

She stood up and was about to leave, when she heard footsteps outside and the door was pushed open. Jen stood back to allow Victor to brush past her and he looked at the two of them narrowly; then he moved forward and held out his hand to James.

'Victor Temple. And I see you've already met my assistant.'

'Yes, Alice—may I call you Alice?—and I bumped into one another in the hall. Pleased to meet you. Jen, why don't you make us all a pot of tea and bring it into the conservatory?'

Jen muttered something inaudible and looked as though the last thing she wanted interrupting her leisurely cleaning duties was the further task of boiling the kettle, making some tea and playing waitress.

The three of them moved off, with Alice following James in the manner of someone who was on unfamiliar ground, and as they walked towards the sitting room, making polite conversation on the way, she looked at the two men. Years ago, she had thought James to be the perfect combination of charm, brains, sophistication and good looks. Next to Victor, he seemed hollow and insubstantial. He was shorter, to start with, but the differences lay not so much in the way he compared physically to the other man, but in his character. Victor was clearly far more dominant a personality. He was discussing the house now, asking questions, his eyes assessing his surroundings, absorbing it all so that he could work out the best way of selling the place to the general public.

The sitting room, which had been the most used room in the house and clearly still was, had undergone a superficial face-lift. The walls had been repainted, with peachy colours replacing the original bland magnolia, and the flowery sofa had gone. In its place was another, deeper in colour and co-ordinating with the curtains which, also a new addition, hung to the ground, draped in an artistic swirl on the floor.

'Most of the place is unchanged since...' James laughed and sat down, elegantly crossing his legs and glancing at Alice, who avoided his gaze completely '...well, since time immemorial. There's a small gallery in the west wing, housing a couple of rather decent impressionist paintings and a few more modern affairs. I shall take you both on a tour a bit later. What do you think of what you've seen?' He directed the question at Victor, but his eyes were on Alice.

Victor sat back and gave him a succinct and profes-

sional appraisal of the rooms they had passed, then rattled off a series of questions on the precise size of the
place, what exactly the intention was in opening the
house to the public, and where James's residence would
be located.

Alice listened in silence, her head tilted to one side
as though riveted by the conversation, but her mind was
a million miles away. Down along memory lane:
James's hand on her, excitedly exploring, that glorious
feeling of being in love, of living in a dream world,
making plans and thinking thoughts and weaving dreams
that would never materialise.

She closed her mind there, locking away the painful
memory. If she let it out of its closet, she knew that she
wouldn't be able to restrain the tide of bitterness that
would flood through her and her face would give everything away. And in the very deepest part of her had been
the wound that hurt the most, the sickening knowledge
that her short-sightedness had been her own downfall. It
would have been so much easier if James had been an
outright cad, but he hadn't been, however long she had
spent afterwards dwelling on every hateful aspect of his
personality that she could muster. No, the truth was that,
for whatever reasons, he had simply not wanted her in
the end.

Jen appeared pushing an ancient trolley, on which several valuable pieces of a bone-china tea-service were
interspersed with mismatching mugs. She had arranged
several biscuits on a plate, and she took her time transferring everything from trolley to table.

'That'll be all,' James said, when she showed little
inclination to leave. 'I'll be mother and pour the tea,
shall I?'

To Alice's dismay, he poured hers, adding two tea-
spoons of sugar, inadvertently remembering the way she

drank it, and she snatched the cup from him, hoping that
Victor had overlooked this piece of familiarity.

'You might like to explore the town,' he was saying
now. 'Perhaps tomorrow. Get a feel for the place.'

'Good idea,' Victor agreed. 'Although Alice is already
familiar with the place.'

Alice could feel her face going pink, and she forced
herself to smile brightly at James. 'I used to live around
here,' she contributed, trying not to sound strangled.

'Did you, now?' James grinned openly and raised his
eyebrows in an interested question. 'Amazing that our
paths never crossed!'

Victor was looking at them both, sensing something
in the atmosphere but unable to put his finger on exactly
what.

'Hardly,' Alice said coolly. 'We would have mixed in
very different circles.' If James thought that he could
play cat and mouse with her, then he was very much
mistaken. He was right. She had toughened up a great
deal since he last knew her. She was no longer the impressionable, dithering idiot she used to be.

'Quite so,' James agreed in an overdone way. 'And
of course I was away most of the time. Boarding-school,
then university.'

'As Victor says, I know the town, although I haven't
been back here for a few years—'

'How odd!' James said, interrupting her.

Alice ignored him as efficiently as she could without
appearing rude. 'And I can happily show him around.'

'I shall make sure that there's a car at your disposal.'

'I brought mine up; we can use that,' Victor murmured. Normal conversation resumed, with Victor asking questions about the history of the place, which eventually led to the indefinite plan of turning the house into
an exclusive country hotel.

'Do this place good to be opened up completely,' James informed them. 'Damn building is gathering cobwebs.'

'You mean you want to turn Highfield House into a resort?' Alice asked, aghast at the idea, and Victor frowned at her.

'That's the general idea,' James replied cheerfully, giving her his full, undivided attention. 'Of course, it'll be tastefully done, absolutely in keeping with the history of the place. Might have to work a swimming-pool into the scheme of things...'

'Swimming-pools tie in with the history of the place?' Alice asked caustically, ignoring Victor, whose lips had thinned in black disapproval of her remarks. 'You'd never get planning permission.'

'Possibly not,' James said ruefully. 'Shame.'

Next, she thought acidly, he'll start considering introducing a disco or two, to appeal to the younger crowd. Henry would be turning in his grave. He had always told her that the house was far too big, but the privacy and peace it afforded him was worth it. Now here was his son, ruminating over swimming-pools, discos and pinball machines.

'I never realised that you had such strong opinions on country houses,' Victor said coldly to her, reminding her of her position without overtly reprimanding her, and Alice flushed.

'N-no, of course I haven't,' she stammered, aware that James was looking at her and wondering whether his remark about swimming-pools hadn't been a deliberate ploy to try and catch her out.

'Then perhaps you could see your way to sticking to the brief in question?'

'Of course,' she said faintly, retreating into silence as the conversation resumed.

If she could get out of the wretched tour of the house, then she would, because she was certain that there would be more of the same, more sly, provocative remarks from James, designed to appeal to his amusement at finding her trapped in a situation of her own making.

And it was as awkward as she had anticipated. He forced her into observations on everything, from the rugs on the floor to the wallpaper on the walls. He asked her pointed questions about where she had lived, and remarked so often on what a small world it was that at the end of two hours she would gladly have walked out of the house even if her job was on the line.

As they wearily reassembled in the sitting room later that evening, Alice turned to James and, unable to resist the desire to strike back, asked sweetly, 'And is there a Mrs Claydon anywhere? I don't recall any mention of whether you were married or not...'

James flushed darkly. 'I *was* married,' he said ruefully, and Alice continued to smile politely as her mind feverishly replayed their final conversation four years ago.

What sort of woman had he married? she wondered now. A debutante with an impeccable accent and a winning way with horses? She suddenly wished that she hadn't attempted to get her own back by goading him.

Victor glanced at his watch, and made some noncommittal remark to defuse what they could both see might prove to be an uncomfortable situation. But James continued with an awkward show of *bonhomie*. 'Didn't last very long, as it turned out.' He gave a short, bitter laugh.

Alice looked uneasily in the direction of Victor, whose face was unrevealing.

'On paper, the perfect match.' He looked directly at Alice. 'We all learn lessons from experience, don't we?'

'Some of us deserve them more than others.'

'Could I have a word with you, Alice?' Victor's voice was icy and furious.

'She was as eager to be shot of me as I was of her, in the end. A messy divorce. The ideal match wasn't quite so ideal after all. And now, if you'll both excuse me... Dinner will be served in the main dining room at eight.' He gave them both a half-bow, and left the room. As soon as the door was shut behind him, Victor turned to her, his hands thrust aggressively in his pockets.

'Do you mind telling me what all that was about?'

'I don't know what you're talking about,' Alice said, knowing full well what he was talking about but refusing to lower her eyes and accept the well-earned rebuke timidly.

'In case,' he said in a low, silky voice which was far more forbidding than if he had shouted, 'it's slipped your mind, James Claydon is a client. Your behaviour has been utterly unprofessional.'

'I apologise.' She stuck her chin up and met his stare evenly.

He walked towards her slowly and she could not have felt more intimidated if she had been unarmed in a jungle and faced with an approaching tiger on the lookout for its next meal.

'I should dismiss you on the spot.'

'Well, why don't you?' she asked, her cheeks red. She had gone so far that it was impossible to back down now, but she didn't much care. Wounds had been re-opened and she felt as though, appalling though her behaviour had been—especially to Victor, who had no idea of the past that was being played out under his eyes—she had been operating on instinct.

It had given her no satisfaction to learn that she had been replaced by a woman whose pedigree had been insufficient to secure the marriage. And if James had learnt his lessons, then hadn't they been learnt at *her* expense? Her naïvety and her innocence were now just a memory, and she ached for the girl she had left behind.

Now, she blinked back the unshed tears and continued to stare at Victor, daring him to sack her.

'I'm prepared to give you the benefit of the doubt,' he said grimly. 'But don't try my patience beyond its limits. I expect you to be civil tonight. If you have to speak, I expect your remarks to be utterly impersonal. We're here to do a job.'

'Yes.' She struggled to get the word out, and lowered her eyes miserably.

'You're not going to go sentimental on me, are you?' Victor asked gruffly, and he tilted her chin up so that she was looking at him.

The very personal gesture, the feel of his fingers on her face, made her breath catch in her throat. He had never touched her before. At least, not deliberately. Not like this. She stared up at him, unable to breathe.

'I wouldn't dream of it,' she managed to whisper, and he smiled at her.

'Good.' He lowered his hand and she resisted the temptation to rub her face where his fingers had touched. Her body seemed to be suddenly on fire. 'I shall see you at dinner, in that case.'

It was all too much, she thought later as she dressed for dinner. James, her past, Victor. She felt as though she was spinning out of control, as though the iron railing that sectioned her life had dissolved into a bundle of useless shards, leaving her at the mercy of every passing emotion.

She remained silent throughout the meal, only speaking when appropriate, making sure that her remarks were as innocuous as possible.

Jen, surprisingly, had produced a wonderful meal, but it seemed to go on and on and on. One course, then another, then another, and it was well past eleven by the time Alice was finally back in her bedroom.

She made sure that the door was locked. She didn't trust James. She had looked up a couple of times at dinner to find him watching her. What had he been thinking? Clearly the dissolution of their relationship had been a minor blip on his emotional horizon. A regrettable incident over which he had not spent an undue amount of time agonising. Doubtless he would have been surprised had he known just how completely he had managed to alter the course of her own life.

No. For him, she was back and with his marriage washed up she wondered whether he saw her as fair game. Worse, in debt to him for keeping silent about their past.

Maybe he had changed. Who could say? But at least then, when she had known him, he had displayed the blinkered insouciance of someone whose aim in life was to have an enjoyable time, without assuming too many cumbersome responsibilities. Although Victor was no creature of domesticity, she instinctively felt that his approach to the opposite sex was of an altogether different nature.

Which brought the whole subject of Victor to her mind. She had felt him watching her over dinner as well, carefully vetting her remarks, and strangely enough, although there had been nothing personal in his hooded glances, she had been more acutely aware of him than she had been of James. That brief touch, when he had slipped his fingers under her chin, seemed to have taken over all rational thought processes. Crazy.

She hoped that she would have put the whole ridiculous episode into perspective by the following morning, because they would be spending the day together. Getting a feel for the town. She had tried to sound enthusiastic about that, but in truth she felt exhausted at the prospect. Under normal circumstances, this was the sort of job that she would have adored. A couple of days in a country mansion, exploring a picturesque town, discussing the brief with Victor, parrying ideas, something she now saw that she enjoyed far more than she had ever admitted to herself.

Unfortunately, these were not normal circumstances. She couldn't wait for their short stay to come to a close, at the end of which she would make sure that it no longer intruded on her life, come hell or high water.

She appeared the following morning in a suit very similar to the one she had travelled up in, to find that James had already departed to do some business in Warwick. Victor was in the kitchen, being administered to by Jen, whose voice could be heard from the hall.

He looked at her as she walked in, and said immediately, 'Isn't that a bit workmanlike for a trip into the town centre?'

'I'm afraid it's all I've brought with me,' Alice said, sitting at the kitchen table and pouring herself a cup of coffee.

He had clearly come well prepared for a casual yet potentially important proposal. What was it about his informal clothes that made him seem much more dangerous than his normal attire of suits? Was it because it implied a sort of relaxed attitude that she found difficult to cope with? She had succeeded all those months in seeing him only as her boss, in ignoring every other aspect of him. Now, unexpectedly, she found herself seeing him more and more as a man, and a devastatingly attractive one at that. Was it because he was in different surroundings? Because she was finding it difficult to slot him into the category which he had formerly occupied in her head?

She took refuge in her coffee, declining Jen's offer of a full cooked breakfast.

'And those shoes hardly seem sensible for traipsing around a town.'

Alice fidgeted uncomfortably. She hadn't thought. She had just packed an assortment of clothes that would bolster her self-confidence. It hadn't really occurred to her that they might be doing any exploration of their surroundings.

'I'm afraid they're...'

'All you have...' he finished for her. 'Perhaps,' he said, reclining back in his chair and subjecting her to a long, cool appraisal, 'you ought to get a change of outfit.'

'Oh, no!' Alice said hastily. 'These shoes are perfectly comfortable.'

'For an office.'

'There's a good clothes shop on the high street,' Jen chipped in, as though she had been part of the conversation from the start. 'A department store. Sells shoes, too. You could get a whole new wardrobe there, as a matter of fact.' She eyed Alice. 'The boss is right. No good tottering through the town in that get-up.'

Alice thought that she might well strangle the girl given half a chance. In a minute, she thought, Jen would pull up a chair and fully join in with the conversation, never mind the little technicality of cleaning, which was what she was paid to do. There were dishes stacked in an ungainly heap on the counter. She had obviously become bored with the washing-up the night before and had decided to leave it for a better moment.

'I really don't think that it's necessary to buy an entire

new wardrobe to cover one day's worth of walking through a very small town centre,' she said coldly.

'I agree entirely.' Victor stood up. 'The one outfit will do nicely, and something to wear tonight, if the only option on the menu is another suit.'

Alice didn't say anything, but she felt cornered and harassed. In a minute she felt sure that Jen, whose area of specialisation appeared to include everything bar cleaning, would take it into her head to start on the subject of make-up. She drained her cup before that could happen and followed Victor out to the hall, feeling a complete fool now in her work clothes. She couldn't think how he had managed to make her feel positively girlish the evening before.

'Can you direct me to the town centre?' he asked a few minutes later as he started the engine of the car, and Alice nodded.

'Congratulations, by the way,' he said as they left the house behind and headed towards the town.

'On what?' She tried very hard not to sound utterly resentful and evil-tempered. She forced herself to remember that personal assistants, despite the title, had no personal feelings—or at least none that were brought into the work environment, however deceptively casual that work environment might be.

'On being the perfect assistant.'

'Thank you very much.' She stared out of the window and began pointing him in the direction of the town centre.

This little trip was becoming more bizarre and nightmarish by the minute.

Shopping with Victor Temple for clothes? What next? she wondered.

CHAPTER FOUR

THE town centre was as Alice remembered. In fact, as they drove into the car park and began walking through, she got such a feeling of familiarity that it was almost as though she had stepped back in time. Back to when she was much younger and would cycle in to pick up shopping for her mother. A loaf of bread, some meat from the butcher's, bits and pieces which she would balance precariously in the basket at the front.

In her high heels, she had to walk very quickly to keep pace with Victor, who strode along with his hands shoved in his pockets, glancing around him with a practised eye. He stopped abruptly, looked at her, and said, 'Shall we do this properly? You haven't eaten anything yet. Is there a coffee shop around here? While you eat a full cooked breakfast, you can fill me in on the place.'

Alice pulled her jacket around her. It was, she had to admit, inappropriate gear for a stroll through a town on a day when the sun was fighting a losing battle with a biting cold wind. Her shoes were not designed for anything other than a few paces in an office and the backs of her feet were beginning to show promise of developing irksome blisters. She should have brought her older pair with her, but then she had had no idea that marathon walks were going to be part of the working agenda.

'There's somewhere to have a cup of coffee in the department store. Just around the corner.'

The walked quickly along the street. It had been pedestrianised, which was a vast improvement on when she was last there, because the pavements were narrow and had had the tendency to become sickeningly over-crowded with people avoiding the possibility of being mown down by passing cars. Here and there, in the cen-tre of the road, there were eye-catching arrangements of flowers. In summer, she imagined, it would look quite delightful.

They reached the department store with some relief, and once inside she saw that that, too, had undergone drastic surgery. It had been modernised. They travelled up the escalator and she looked around her, taking in the hygienically sanitised cosmetic counters, where the sales assistants all seemed to wear white or pale blue outfits and vaguely resembled nurses.

'Just coffee, thanks,' she told Victor, once they had reached the coffee shop, which was much bigger than it had previously been, though, as far as she was con-cerned, less appealing.

She found them a table, and when he joined her she saw that he had bought her an enormous jam-filled doughnut, which he proceeded to shove towards her with a command for her to eat it.

Alice smiled politely and tentatively took a bite. She rarely indulged in sweet things, generally because she simply forgot to buy them when she did her weekly shop.

'You look as though you're testing it to see whether it's been filled with poison. Don't tell me that you're one of those women who are permanently on a diet.'

Alice took an enormous bite, so that the jam spurted out around her sugar-coated mouth. She wished that he would stop staring at her. Jam doughnuts and an air of dignity didn't go hand in hand. She wiped her mouth, fighting a smile.

'No, I don't diet.'

'You just don't eat very much.'

She shrugged. 'Food isn't a very big part of a single woman's life, or, at least, not mine.'

'Which is one thing to be said for a non-single state.'

She didn't answer that. Instead, she began telling him about the history of the town, what little she knew about it, and the surrounding places of interest that might attract the public to Highfield House as a result. For a while, they discussed various formats the campaign could take.

'Of course,' he said, sipping his coffee, 'James Claydon has a point when he says that turning the place eventually into a country hotel of sorts is a good idea. I'm quite sure that a conservation trust could be induced to maintain at least some of the running costs of the land. Why were you so vociferously against the idea?'

'I just think that it's a beautiful house, but a lot of its beauty lies with its potential for complete solitude.'

'Which doesn't appear to be what the master of the house craves. It seems that he's hardly ever around. Checks up on the place now and again but he prefers to spend most of his time in London.'

Hadn't that always been the case? In the three years that they had known each other she realised, thinking back, how little she had seen him. The open countryside offered nothing along the lines of fast living, which was what James had always liked. His father might well have found inner peace in the sprawling, stupendously beautiful estate, but the same could not be said for the son.

'What do you think of him?' Victor asked unexpectedly.

'Why do you ask?' Had he suspected anything? There was very little that he missed, and if *she* had noticed James's eyes on her on more than one occasion, then it was more than likely that Victor had noticed as well.

'Curious.'

'He seems very nice,' Alice told him cautiously.

'*Nice* is such a strange adjective. It says everything and nothing at the same time, don't you think?'

'He doesn't strike me as the sort who would get a great deal of pleasure from playing lord of the manor and showing tourists around his house.'

'I should think he'll employ someone to cover that. He'll have to, in fact,'

'What do *you* think of him?' She finished eating the doughnut as unobtrusively as possible and waited for his reply.

'I think,' Victor said seriously, 'that he's a perfectly pleasant human being, but one inclined to use the world to his own advantage.'

'Doesn't everyone?'

'In varying degrees.' He paused. 'I should think that James Claydon's primary objective in life is the pursuit of pleasure. *His* pleasure, with everyone else's taking second place.'

Years ago, she would have risen up in arms at that description. She had been so totally taken in by his superficial charm that she had failed to see that behind the boxes of expensive chocolates there was very little. He was like one of those boxes under a Christmas tree in an expensive store. Beautifully gift-wrapped, but empty inside.

'I wouldn't know about that.' She toyed aimlessly with her coffee spoon.

'I should think that his father despaired of him.'

'I wouldn't like to speculate on that,' Alice said crisply.

'Why not?'

'Because…because…' She couldn't think of a good reason. Except that Victor had been right in his assessment of James, and to agree with him would only serve to remind her of her own stupidity and lack of insight in the past.

'Because you don't agree?' he asked smoothly. The grey eyes on her were curiously watchful.

'I can't say that I know him well enough to make any generalisations on his character,' she lied. 'Anyway, he *is* a client of ours,' she finished lamely.

'All the more reason to try and ascertain precisely what sort of person he is. That way we know how to target the campaign.'

He had an argument for everything, she thought. If he chose to, he could argue that grass was blue and would probably end up persuading you that you were colour-blind for thinking otherwise.

'From what he said to me, he leads something of a playboy existence in London. I should think that even when he was married...' Victor's mouth curled at the mention of that, and Alice could read disapproval on his face at James's cavalier interpretation of the failure of his marriage. 'Even when he was married, he still continued to live by his own rules. I feel very sorry for any woman who happens to come into close contact with him.'

'Why?' Was there something being said here that she wasn't quite grasping?

'Because,' Victor said slowly, 'she would find it hard competing with his ego.'

'You seem to have reached an awful lot of conclusions, considering you've only known him a very short time.' He might have played havoc with her life, she thought grudgingly, but Victor's opinions were a bit on the dramatic side, weren't they? He had managed to take a few strands of James's personality and weave them together in such a way as to turn him into the amoral, utterly unscrupulous cad she had almost wished he had been, if only to ease her self-recriminations in the aftermath of their affair.

'First impressions and all the rest.' He finished his cup of coffee and stood up, waiting for her. There was something terse in his manner that she couldn't quite put her finger on and she told herself that she was imagining things. Being paranoid. It was easy, given the odd combination of circumstances that had brought her back to this spot.

'I suggest,' Victor said as they headed one floor down, 'that you buy something for walking in, unless you have a pair of trousers secreted away in your bedroom, and something a little less austere for tonight. I've asked MacKenzie and Bird to come up so that we can hash through some details with Claydon, find out precisely what he has in mind and what size spread he intends us to do.'

He had his back to her, and she looked at him and automatically at the interest he was generating in various members of the opposite sex who were travelling up in the parallel escalator.

If a woman would be mad to get involved with James Claydon, she wondered how Victor would categorise himself. Surely he couldn't think that he was perfect husband material? Perfect husband material didn't attract stares the way he did.

Since it appeared that she had no choice in the matter of clothes, she said, as soon as they were on the appropriate floor, 'If you like, we can arrange a time to meet up. Perhaps outside the store in an hour's time? Eleven-thirty?'

'I don't like,' he said, looking down at her, which stopped her in her tracks. 'I'll help you choose what to buy.'

'There's really no need.'

'I suppose not.' He took her by her elbow as though holding onto her before she decided to take flight, and began walking around the floor. He clearly felt no need to inspect anything. He dismissed entire sections at a glance, while Alice struggled to find some composure in between the various waves of confusion lapping over her. She didn't want this. She hadn't wanted to buy any wretched clothes in the first place, and she certainly had not expected him to chaperon her every move.

'Right.' He ran his eyes over her assessingly. 'A pair of jeans, I think. There.' He pointed to some and she stood where she was, not moving. 'Off you go. What size are you?'

'This is ridiculous.'

'I'm rather enjoying myself, actually.'

I'll bet, she thought acidly. Next you'll be asking me to do a few twirls so that you can inspect the fit.

'And let me have a look at you in them. I don't trust you. I have a feeling you might just grab hold of the first pair that feels remotely comfortable, simply so that you can cut short this little exercise.' He grinned a wicked, knowing grin that did something peculiar to her insides, even as she found it irritating.

In the end, she tried on six pairs of jeans, six different makes, and after the embarrassing ordeal of parading in the first pair she adamantly refused to repeat the procedure.

'You'll just have to trust me to choose some that fit,' she told him, red-faced and mortified as his grey eyes swept over her, reminding her of her considerable limitations figure-wise.

Then came the mortification at the desk, when he insisted that he pay for the clothes.

'I'd rather you didn't,' Alice said through gritted

teeth, trying to remain composed for the benefit of the cashier, who was looking at her as though she was made to reject an offer from someone else to foot the very overpriced bill.

'Nonsense. It's on the company.' And before she could protest further he had whipped out his credit card and was signing the slip of paper.

Then the outfit for that evening. She found herself being steered towards the most inappropriate outfits, things that she would never have dreamt of wearing in a million years.

'What's wrong with *this* one?' Victor asked impatiently, after she had politely refused even to consider the previous five he had pointed out to her.

'It's too red,' she said, not looking at him. And in case you're interested, she wanted to tell him, its *redness* isn't its only drawback. It's also too short, too tight and too daring for me.

'How can something be *too red*?' he asked bluntly. 'And why isn't that suit you're wearing *too blue*?'

'I should have done this on my own,' Alice muttered resentfully.

'You still haven't answered my question.'

'I don't like red clothes,' she said defensively. 'Red doesn't look good on me.' The truth was that she had never owned anything red in her entire life, or at least not so far as she could remember. There might have been a red coat in her distant childhood, but certainly not once she had crossed the puberty threshold. She had never been inclined to draw attention to herself and she wasn't about to start now, at her ripe old age.

'How do you know until you try it on?'

He was doing this on purpose. She knew it. Trying to get under her skin and provoke her into a suitably untypical reaction, at which he would be deeply amused.

'I could never wear anything like that.' She stared at the little dress hanging on the rack next to her and almost shuddered at the thought of herself in it.

'Why not?'

'Because it's just not *me*. Is that a good enough reason for you?'

'Nope.' He took it down and virtually frog-marched her to the changing room.

Alice shut the door behind her and ill-humouredly removed her clothes, avoiding inspecting herself in the mirror. Mirrors in changing rooms, she knew from experience, reduced all but the best figures to ungainly proportions. Her legs always appeared too skinny, her body too straight, her bust non-existent.

She stuck on the red dress and looked at her reflection with jaundiced eyes, prepared for the unspeakable.

She looked good. Or do I? she thought uncertainly, turning around as far as she could go so that she could inspect the back. She decided that it must be the remnants of her tan which accounted for it, because the dress was the most flattering she had ever worn. It was in soft, jersey cotton, fitted from the waist up, but then flaring down to mid-thigh. The neckline was rather low-cut, but then the long sleeves compensated for that, so that she didn't feel at all exposed in it.

She slipped it over her head, stuck back on her suit, which now seemed even more unnaturally drab in comparison, and reluctantly told Victor that it would do. She made sure that she didn't look him in the face when she said that, because she knew that she would scream if there was any hint of a smug smile there.

'And now,' he said, 'we can have a little drive around. Spare those feet of yours any further walking.'

They drove through Warwick, past the castle, then along to Stratford, which, from the inside of a car, safely

protected against the chill wind, looked almost too perfect. She remembered coming to Stratford when she was
a child, going to plays with her mother, who, for some
reason, had been intent on making sure that Shakespeare
was thoroughly drummed into her head.

Unexpectedly, she found herself telling Victor all
about those trips into Stratford.

'I always enjoyed the outing,' she mused with a sigh,
'but the plays were a little more difficult to get to grips
with.'

'You mean that as a ten-year-old child you couldn't
see the virtues of *King Lear* and *Hamlet*?'

'Oh, no, we never ventured near those!' Alice exclaimed with a laugh. 'Mum wasn't a sadist. I think even
she knew that that would be pushing her luck.' Then,
afterwards, there would be a treat of some sort or other.
Usually an ice-cream cone. Considering how little
money there had been, she had led a charmed life. Or,
at least, had never felt lacking in anything. Shakespeare
plays and ice-cream cones seemed a long time away
now, she thought sadly. Her mother would have liked to
see her settled down, perhaps with a child or two.

'Hungry?' Victor asked, and she nodded.

'Starved.'

'We passed a pub on the way here. How does that
sound to you?'

'Fabulous.' She looked at him and their eyes met and
tangled, and she was the first to look away, confused.
An hour and a half ago, she'd been infuriated with him
for putting her through the ordeal of buying clothes she
neither wanted nor needed, and yet here she was now,
as relaxed as she had ever been, actually enjoying his
company. Almost as if they were two absolutely com-
patible friends instead of an employer and his employee.

Had she somehow climbed onto a rollercoaster without knowing?

She reminded herself that Victor was adept at being charming. He had an inherently persuasive personality. This little outing was nothing at all special to him. He would have been exactly the same if he had found himself in the very same situation with his previous secretary, the fifty-year-old harridan in the tweed skirt and support tights.

It was important not to let it go to her head.

They ate lunch at a picturesque pub which served food that didn't quite live up to its surroundings, but was perfectly passable; then, as they were getting into the car, he turned to her and asked her where she had lived.

'Oh, nowhere special,' Alice said, gesticulating vaguely in an easterly direction.

'Why don't we drive out, visit your old house?'

'What?'

'There's no need to rush back to Highfield House. It's too late to think about starting a comprehensive tour of the grounds. Seems a little idiotic to come all this way to your part of the world and not visit the place you used to live.'

'I...I'm not...' The suggestion was unexpected enough to throw her completely off balance. 'Well, why not?' she said doubtfully into the silence. There was a reason why not. She knew that. It hovered at the back of her subconscious, just out of reach.

It took them much longer than it should have to get there, because the streets all looked the same, especially after several years' absence, but eventually there they were, parked outside what used to be her old house. Lived in, and proudly so if the front garden was anything to go by. It was very small, but bursting with colour, and the small patch of grass was mown so perfectly that it looked almost manicured.

'The front door has been repainted,' was all she could think of to say, and it seemed pitifully inadequate considering the sentimental pull she felt inside her.

'How long did you live here?' he asked, with a gentleness she barely paid attention to.

'All my life. There was never the need to move on, you see. Dad died, and there were just the two of us, and besides, Mum liked being reminded of…being surrounded by her memories. When I got older, I used to tell her that she should move on, start afresh, but she always said that she could never do that.'

'You must have been a great source of strength for her.'

'She used to tell me that I was the bane of her life, but yes, you're right.'

They sat in silence for a while. There was no activity in the house, or at least none that she could see, which was a shame because she would have liked to see who was living there. She wondered what her mother would have made of her now, and felt a lump gather in her throat, which she had to dispel by swallowing and blinking very rapidly. The last thing Victor Temple needed was a puffy-eyed, sobbing personal assistant.

'Would you like to go in?' he asked. 'I'm sure the owners wouldn't mind, once you'd explained that you used to live there.'

'Oh, no.' Alice laughed a little shakily. 'I don't need reminding of the place. I have all the memories I need inside me.' She fished inside her bag, extracted a handkerchief, and dabbed a runaway tear from the corner of her eye. 'Right, then,' she said briskly, 'shall we head back?'

'No more places of interest you want to visit?'

She knew what he was thinking about. The fictitious ex-lover he imagined she had tucked away somewhere close by, possibly still hammering away at his fictitious book. She shook her head, and he started the engine of the car. On the way back, he made sure that the conversation was work-oriented, which she appreciated, and she was even more heartened to find that James was nowhere around by the time they arrived back at Highfield House.

And even more heartening was the fact that dinner was not going to be the painful process that it had been the evening before. It would be strictly work, more or less. David MacKenzie and Derek Bird were co-directors in the agency, one in the creative field, the other in accounts. There would be some polite chit-chat—that was inevitable—but from what she'd gathered the wheels would begin churning into action. The practicalities of the campaign would be discussed, fees would be agreed on, professional meetings would be arranged.

With any luck, she thought later as she relaxed in the bath, she would be able to fade nicely into the background with her stenographer's notepad in hand and her working hat firmly in place.

The past few days had been a muddle of emotions. It would be a relief to get back into the routine of work.

She felt the very smallest of qualms when she began dressing.

She had washed her hair and blow-dried it very carefully so that it gleamed and swung around her face, just touching her shoulders. Then some make-up. Then the red dress. She could hardly believe the finished version of herself that stared back at her from the mirror.

The men were all assembled in the drawing room by the time she finally made it downstairs. Alice took a deep breath, imagined that she was in her normal suit, and walked in. Dave was the first to break the stunned silence that greeted her entry.

'Good God!' he exclaimed, standing up and walking towards her. 'I don't believe it! Tell me that you're not little Alice Carter.'

'I'm not little Alice Carter,' Alice said obligingly. 'Hi, Dave.' She could see Victor in the background, standing with his back to the French doors, a glass of something in his hand, and was tempted to scour his face for his reaction, but resisted the impulse.

'You bloom at night,' Derek said warmly, moving forward, and Alice smiled at both of them. They were both family men, in their forties, and she liked them both. They treated her as their equal, taking their cue from Victor, and frequently used her as their testing board for some of their layouts.

'Like some rare and mysterious flower?' she joked.

'You took the words out of my mouth,' Dave said. 'Have you ever thought about a career in advertising? Perhaps working for a difficult and temperamental man?'

'I'm sure Alice would be the first to agree that I'm the least temperamental and difficult man she's ever met,' Victor drawled, from the background.

'But if those are the qualities that she wants,' James said smoothly, strolling across to her and handing her a fluted glass of champagne, 'then I would be only too happy to oblige.'

A split second's silence greeted this, then it was back to business. She sat down with her glass in one hand and her notepad balanced on her lap and made a mental note not to glance in James's direction. She hadn't liked the look in his eyes over dinner the night before, and she cared even less for the sentiment expressed behind his remark. To the disinterested onlooker, it could well be interpreted as a bit of polite flirting, but to her it sounded very much like an invitation. He had eliminated her from his life without his conscience getting in the way, and he must be completely mad, she thought, as the conversation picked up around her, if he thought that he could re-enter her life as though they had parted company the best of friends.

Over dinner, a splendid spread which was served by Jen and two of her pals, from the looks of it, she kept her eyes purposefully averted from James, who was opposite her. When he spoke, she tilted her head to one side and listened, but her eyes remained fixed on the wall behind him, even though she could feel him willing her to look at him.

The nuances of atmosphere were lost on David and Derek, but several times she saw Victor looking narrowly at her, tuning in to James's reactions, and she made sure that she gave him no reason to suspect that there were any undercurrents between them.

'Well, then,' James said, once the cheese and biscuits had been cleared away, 'I suppose you boys want to get down to business.' His face was slightly flushed from drinking too much wine and Alice thought that if they didn't get down to business pretty soon, then they might just as well forget it because James's contribution would be less than zero. No one else had had very much to drink and when Victor caught her eye she could tell from the expression on his face that his thoughts were moving in precisely the same direction as hers.

'We'll need somewhere with a table,' Victor said, standing up and pre-empting any further inroads into the bottle of port strategically placed in front of James.

'Pick a room!' James said expansively. 'The drawing room's the best bet. Square table there; we'll just sweep the chess set off and get down to whatever needs to be gotten down to!' He beamed at them, bellowed to Jen to show them the way, which was unnecessary since she was at the table clearing the dishes, and as the other three men were going ahead he brushed past Alice and tugged her back towards him.

'You look delicious, Ali,' he said, with a vague slurring of his words.

Alice disengaged her hand from his arm and stared back at him coldly. 'You've had too much to drink, James. Now, why don't we just head to the drawing room so that you can get down to work?'

'You never used to wear dresses—' he ogled her appreciatively and Alice's teeth snapped together '—as revealing as that.' He fingered the sleeve of the dress and she pulled her arm away.

'I didn't want to be here, James,' she said, stiff-faced, 'but now that I am I would appreciate it if you could keep your distance.'

'Now, now, that's not a very the-customer-is-always-right kind of remark, is it?'

She didn't answer. Instead, she headed towards the dining-room door, with James trailing behind her with a disgruntled expression on his face.

'We always used to get along rather well,' he said, catching up with her but fortunately keeping his hands to himself.

Alice stopped and folded her arms. 'Not well enough, if I remember.'

'Marriage wasn't the be-all and end-all, *isn't* the be-all and end-all.'

'Certainly not marriage to me, anyway,' she said with remembered bitterness. Funny, but seeing him again had put her past into perspective. She had spent years telling herself that she had had a lucky escape, that James Claydon, however infatuated with him she had been, had been all wrong for her. As wrong for her as she had been for him. Now she actually believed it.

'You don't still hold the past against me, do you?' he asked, as though mystified by her blank refusal to pick up where they had left off.

'No. I don't hold anything against you. To be perfectly honest, I feel very sorry for that poor wife of yours.'

'Poor wife indeed. You never met her! She made my life hell.'

'I'm sure you deserved it,' she said vigorously, finding it hard to relocate the rancour that had dogged her for so long.

'Don't you feel *anything* being here again?'

'It was pleasant strolling around the town and seeing what's changed.'

'I mean *here*. This house. We had good times, didn't we?'

'Oh, yes. We had very good times, skulking around and having a clandestine affair behind your father's back.'

'You never complained.'

Alice didn't have an answer for that. He was right. She had never complained. She had meekly accepted his pathetic explanation that his father had impossibly high moral standards and would never in a million years have condoned their sleeping together under his roof, however vast the roof was. It would, James had told her repeatedly, kill him.

'More fool me, then,' she muttered to herself.

'Look, Ali, seems stupid for us to be working together...'

'We are *not* working together. I happen to be up here in the capacity of Victor Temple's secretary. You're working with *him*.' She couldn't believe that she had got herself into a state over meeting James again after four years; she couldn't believe that she had overblown his importance in her life to such an absurd extent.

'Well, whatever. The point is, we're going to cross paths quite a bit from now on...'

'Not if I can help it.'

'And I always did regret the way our relationship ended. I mean, I really missed you, Ali.'

Oh, *please*, Alice thought, and she eyed him sceptically, bring on the violins.

'I spend most of my time in London, as it happens,' he said, when she made no comment. 'What's the objection to meeting up now and again? Just friends?'

'And the cheque is in the post,' Alice said.

'What?'

'Never mind. We really should be getting a move on. They'll be wondering where we are.'

'They'll be drinking port and brandy and not giving us a moment's thought.'

Alice began heading off towards the drawing room, and James reluctantly followed.

'What do you say to the odd meal out?' he asked, stopping her by putting his hand on her arm, and Alice turned to him.

'Thanks but no, thanks.'

'What harm can there be in that?'

'Look, James, you don't *need* to pursue me. I'm sure there are hordes of available young women out there who wouldn't say no to your offers of dinner and whatever else you have in mind.'

'I'm getting older and the young women are getting younger. Besides, they bore me. I need a *real* woman.'

He looked so pathetically sincere that she sighed.

'Okay. Maybe a meal if we happen to cross paths at some point in the future. But that's all, James. Nothing else.' It was worth the lie simply to terminate the conversation.

'A meal would be fine.' He grinned happily at her and was about to say something else when Victor appeared, seemingly out of thin air because she certainly hadn't heard him coming.

He looked at them and then said in a hard voice, which carried only the slightest nuance of courtesy, 'I hope I'm not interrupting anything, but we're waiting for you two. Would you mind?'

CHAPTER FIVE

VICTOR was in a foul mood. Alice had sensed it the evening before, when they had retreated to the drawing room and spent three hours working. Oh, he'd been as professional as he always was, rattling off ideas like bullets from a gun, bringing James sharply back down to earth when some of his offerings were too far-fetched; but when he had addressed her it had been in clipped tones and she had had to bite back the retort on the tip of her tongue on several occasions.

Now, as they trudged through the gardens, she stole sidelong glances at him, perplexed.

Derek and Dave had already left for London, and James, after forty-five minutes of tramping along with them, clearly bored by the outdoors, had vanished as well to take the dog back to the vet for a check on its foot.

'Stupendous gardens, aren't they?' Alice asked, generating some small talk if only to break the silence. They didn't look splendid. The weather had broken, and everywhere was sogging wet and bedraggled. The wind had picked up overnight as well, so that they were both walking quickly, with Alice huddled inside a waxed jacket which he had borrowed from James, and her feet slipping about uncomfortably in a pair of green wellingtons, also borrowed and several sizes too big. It was raining, a thin, persistent rain that made her feel as though she was walking in a cloud.

'If you care for this sort of thing,' Victor replied in a dismissive voice.

Alice didn't say anything. She knew from experience that the best way to handle one of his moods was simply to ignore it. Or else to be ultra-polite and friendly.

'He's going to have to get his act together and do something with these gardens,' Victor said, stopping and staring around him with his hands in the pockets of his waterproof coat. 'If he imagines that tourists are going to pay to wander around on estate that's seen better days, then he's in for an unpleasant surprise.'

'It doesn't look that bad,' Alice said mildly. 'The weather isn't helping things at the moment.'

'Gardens that don't look *that bad* aren't going to do, though, are they?' Victor glanced at her witheringly, as though challenging her to defend the indefensible, which of course she didn't.

He moved on, heading towards the copse, and Alice trailed behind him, half acknowledging his point that everywhere looked just a little the worse for wear, half wondering what had put him in such a bad mood, when really he should be feeling quite light-hearted. Everything had gone very well the night before and the fee for the job was not to be sneezed at, not that that ever seemed to make a scrap of difference as far as Victor was concerned. He never seemed to alter his attitude according to his client's worth. If he disagreed with a client, then he went right ahead and spoke his mind, regardless of the fact that a disgruntled client might well dispense with his services.

'The house is pretty impeccable, though. Wouldn't you say?'

'He'll have to invest in rather more cleaning help if this thing gets off the ground,' Victor said, neither agreeing nor disagreeing with her. 'I really don't think that Jen and her half-hearted attempts at flicking a duster here and there is exactly going to keep things ticking over nicely when hordes of people are tramping through. With children, and all the attendant empty packets and sticky bits of paper that they generate. Not to mention the fact that only a fraction of the house is used at the moment.'

'He did say that he would get all the professional help that might be necessary.'

Victor turned and faced her, his face stony. 'Ah, but then Claydon looks just the sort who will say anything to appease anyone. He's very generous in his statements about spending money to make some, but I wouldn't put too much money on him keeping to his promise. Would you agree with that or do you have some extra insight into our good lord of the manor?'

Alice stared at him, taken aback.

'W-well,' she stammered. 'I don't suppose there's any reason to think that...'

'Don't tell me that you believe everything everyone tells you, Alice.'

'I'm not saying that!' she flashed back at him, suddenly annoyed that she was being made the butt of his ill-temper. 'I'm merely saying that he'd be stupid to jeopardise the venture through penny-pinching short-sightedness!'

'Not,' Victor drawled smoothly in response to her outburst, 'that it particularly concerns us, does it? We launch the campaign, we ensure that it's good enough to get the crowds along, and then what happens next is up to Master James, isn't it?'

It was obvious that James had thoroughly rubbed Victor up the wrong way. She could see why. Victor would have no time for the playboy type and the fact that James had spent most of his life more or less living off the family fortune would not endear him to a man who worked all the hours that God made for reasons that went far beyond the simple making of money.

But James was still a client, and one who was childish enough to react to Victor's bluntness with petulance and a show of temper. She wouldn't put it past him to take his business elsewhere, even if elsewhere could not offer him nearly the level of success that Victor could. She reluctantly decided that perhaps she had better build up James's more substantial qualities, if there were any, and downplay his frivolity, if that was possible. That might at least ensure a bit more harmony when it came to this particular account.

'I suppose so,' she said, feeling thoroughly damp and discontented and wishing that she were back in Portugal, basking under the hot sunshine and slapping on suntan cream every two minutes. 'Although you do normally follow through most of the campaigns.' He did. He knew precisely where every one of his campaigns succeeded and to what extent. It paid to keep abreast of the competition and to jettison ideas that failed to take off.

He didn't answer. They had now reached the copse, and Alice looked at it, remembering how glorious it used to look when the ground was lush with snowdrops. She could see a couple of the little white flowers here and there, but mostly it was lush with dank leaves and a general air of nature having been allowed to run amok.

They plunged in and memories came rushing out at her. There were several twisted paths running through, and she used to push Henry through on finer days until they found a spot to sit. Then she would perch on a rug on the ground, pull out her pad, and they would spend a couple of hours half working, half lulled by birdsong and the fragrant smell of flowers mixed with earth.

'Doesn't this look completely different in this kind of weather?' she said, without thinking, shaking her feet to free them of some of the moist earth. 'When the sun is out, it's so much more beautiful.'

There was a long silence, and when she looked up it was to find Victor staring at her intently. Then she thought of what she had just said and a slow, revealing colour crept up her cheeks. She literally couldn't think of a thing to say.

'You sound as though you're speaking from experience,' he said, not moving.

'Do I?' Alice tried to laugh that one off. 'I'm only speculating. Anyone can see that this is just the sort of spot that would benefit from kind weather, when you don't have to hurtle through at a rate of knots.'

'Have you come here before?'

'Don't be silly!' She half-wished that she had been completely honest from the start, instead of retreating into her privacy, but it was too late now for any such retrospective wishing.

Victor didn't answer. They spent about fifteen minutes wandering through the trees, while overhead the gathering of dark clouds promised imminent rain, and finally decided to call it a day. They still faced the long drive back to London, and in conditions like these it was better to leave sooner rather than later.

They headed back towards the house, and when they were very nearly there he said in a casual voice. 'What did you get up to yesterday?'

'Yesterday when?' Her mind drew a blank at that. Had he forgotten that they had trooped into the town to buy her clothes and then driven out for a bit of sightseeing?

'After we got back to the house.'

'Oh, nothing much,' Alice said vaguely. 'Why?'

'I had a look around for you. Half-heartedly, it has to be said. Wanted to get a tape transcribed.'

'Oh, sorry about that. Why don't you give it to me

when we get back and I can do it as soon as we get to London?'

James had obviously returned. His car was parked outside the house, and she breathed a sigh of relief that they weren't going to be staying for dinner. She didn't think that she could face any more of his advances and she wasn't inclined to continue lying simply because it was easier to say that she would see him some time rather than stand her ground when Victor was around.

'It can wait.'

They went inside to find James in the hall, sifting through a batch of mail and frowning.

'Had a good walk around?' he asked jovially, looking at Alice who was busy disengaging herself from her jacket and replacing the boots with her shoes, which she had left, conveniently, just inside the doorway.

'It's about to rain,' Victor replied. 'Alice and I should be heading off.'

'What, already, old boy? Thought you might stay for a spot of afternoon tea. Rather passable pit stop twenty minutes' drive away. Why don't we let the lady decide?'

He looked at Alice, and Victor said, with a tight, polite smile, 'Because the lady works for me and I say that it's time for us to be heading back to London.'

'I have quite a bit of work to catch up on,' Alice explained hurriedly.

'You're not going straight to the office when you get back, are you?' James sounded aghast at the idea.

'Oh, absolutely,' Alice said, amused despite herself, feeling Victor's suppressed antagonism even though she couldn't see his face. 'I'll just pop upstairs and fetch my bag.'

'I could come up, give you a hand with it,' James said, moving towards her, and she looked away to hide the alarm on her face at that.

'I can manage,' she said hurriedly. She hoped that he would leave it alone, but just in case he didn't she flashed Victor a quick smile and headed towards the staircase, half running until she reached her bedroom.

It was odd, but when she had thought about returning to Highfield House, returning to a part of her past that she had no desire to revisit, she had always imagined that her feelings would be of anger and bitterness. She had carried them around with her like weights on her shoulders for such a long time that they were very nearly part of her personality. She had dreaded meeting James, because she could not conceive of ever seeing him without the shadow of the past taking over. But it had not been that way at all. She remembered Highfield House with sadness and some nostalgia, and James...well, James was hardly worth her bitterness.

So now the fact that his attraction towards her had been revived didn't terrify her. It unsettled her. She didn't need her life to be cluttered by any unwanted appearances from him.

She arrived downstairs with her bag half an hour later to find Victor in the hall with James. His holdall was at his feet and his arms were folded. He looked as though he was only just restraining the urge to tap his feet, impatient to leave. He looked across as soon as she approached them, and again she was aware of that tight expression on his face. James, she saw, was oblivious. He would be in London the following week, he was saying; he would telephone to arrange a meeting, perhaps at his club in Central London. Before Victor could answer, he turned to Alice.

'And of course I shall no doubt meet you again.' He took her hand and kissed it with flamboyant gallantry, and Alice forced herself to smile, politely pulling her hand out of his grasp. Ever fond of the overdone gesture,

she thought. Once she would have melted at the display
of charm. Now she found it irritating.

'Shall we go?' Victor asked from next to her, and she
bent to retrieve her bag which he immediately took from
her.

'The man,' he said, once they were on their way and
Highfield House had vanished from sight, 'makes me
sick.'

'Why?' Keep the peace, Alice reminded herself. He
would be seeing quite a bit of James in the future, until
the deal was finally done, and she didn't think that she
could endure Victor in a state of semi-permanent irritation, taking it out on her.

'Why do you think?' he asked sarcastically. 'He had
to make a supreme effort to concentrate last night. It's
obvious that any form of work is about as welcome to
him as a bout of flu.'

'I guess it's his background,' she answered in a placa-
tory voice, which made Victor frown darkly. 'Must be
difficult to lead a life of such privilege without it going
to your head somehow. Do you need me to direct you
back onto the motorway?'

'I think I can manage to work it out myself.'

They lapsed into silence, with Alice replaying the past
three days in her head, almost giddy with relief that it
was all over, and, better still, had not been the ordeal
she had anticipated.

'How did you find it, anyway?' he asked, once they
had cleared the small roads and were on the motorway,
heading back to London.

'How did I find what?' Alice looked at him, leaning
her head against the window. It was raining hard now,
and the sound of the rain pelting against the car made
her feel as though she was in a cocoon. Victor was concentrating heavily on the road and his voice was slightly

distracted, as though he was chatting simply for the sake
of breaking the silence.

'Going back to your home town.'

'Fine.'

'Weren't haunted by too many unpleasant memories,
I gather?'

'Nothing that I couldn't handle.' She didn't have to
lie about that. In a strange way, going back there had
been the best thing that could have happened. It had
killed off the monster in her head that had spent years
feeding off her nightmarish memories.

'No. I had every confidence in you.'

Now what was that supposed to mean?

'Am I supposed to ask what you mean by that?' Alice
asked after a pause.

'Am I as transparent as that?'

'You know you're not. But some of your remarks are.'

He laughed, as if amused by her answer, although she
could tell that his mind was really only half on their
conversation. The driving rain was making it almost impossible to see out of the window and although they
were on the motorway they were virtually crawling
along in the middle lane. There must have been an accident further up ahead and five minutes later the local
traffic news confirmed it. At this rate, she thought, they
wouldn't be in London for a good two and a half hours
more.

'They say,' he said, 'that a secretary can end up knowing her boss better than his wife.'

'I really don't think that working alongside someone
and discussing work-related things qualifies as *knowing*
someone.'

'And you do make sure that every subject covered *is*
work-related, don't you?'

Even though the tenor of his voice was that of someone with his thoughts elsewhere, his questions were quite pointed, and Alice looked at him cautiously from under her lashes.

'I think that's the best way. Keeping things on a purely professional level.'

'And you've never felt the slightest curiosity about any of the people you've worked for?'

'Where is this going?'

'It's passing a long journey,' Victor said, seemingly surprised by her response to his questions, which she knew that he wasn't. Not in the least. 'I estimate that we're going to be on the road for another two hours, probably longer, and I'm curious to find out what makes you tick.'

What you mean is, she thought, that you don't like thinking that there are depths to people that you know nothing about. For months, he had not wanted to know *what made her tick*. To him, she had been an efficient, one-dimensional secretary. No more. And she imagined that he was frustrated by what he mistakenly saw as the stirrings of wild undercurrents beneath the calm, placid surface.

'My work. I enjoy reading, going to the cinema, going out for meals. Nothing unusual.'

'How old are you?' he asked suddenly.

'Thirty-one.' She blushed, embarrassed by the admission. Work, reading, the cinema—were those normal likings for someone in her early thirties? It was none of his business, but still, she felt inadequate and she never had before.

The traffic had now come to a virtual standstill.

'We'll never make it back to London at this rate,' she said gloomily.

'Does it matter what time we get back? Have you anything you need to cancel?'

'No, but I'm tired and cramped and we don't seem to be getting anywhere at all.'

'You'd better cancel whatever appointments I have for later this evening,' he said, handing her his mobile phone and electronic diary.

She did, and after half an hour of little progress he said, in the manner of someone stating a fact rather than asking a question, 'I suggest we pull off at the next junction and see whether we can find a hotel for the night. Once we get past this accident, there's sure to be another further up ahead in weather like this.'

'I don't think that's a very good idea,' Alice said quickly, dismayed at this turn of events. 'Chances are there's no rain further down south, and it's only...' She looked at her watch and was startled to see that it was much later than she thought.

'Five-thirty,' he finished for her. 'We've covered fifteen miles in over an hour and frankly the thought of driving in these conditions for another three hours or so doesn't appeal.'

He looked exhausted, and Alice felt a pang of guilt. It was all right telling him that she preferred to carry on, but it was a terrific strain being the one behind the wheel, peering through the windscreen and trying to see through the pelting rain.

'I guess it's not such a bad idea,' she said reluctantly.

'So glad you agree with me.' They continued to creep along in fits and starts and it took them another forty minutes before they reached the junction a couple of miles along, whereupon they swung off the motorway and headed for the nearest town.

'You'll have to keep your eyes peeled,' he told her. 'Look for anything resembling a hotel or a bed and breakfast. Shouldn't be too difficult to find. We're still

close enough to Stratford to be in the tourist catchment
area.'

Or course, with the perversity of fate, it was another
forty-five minutes before they found a pub offering va-
cancies. It wasn't ideal but with no let-up in the rain it
was simply a relief to get out of the car and into somewhere warm.

'You want two rooms?' The landlord looked as
though he found that hard to believe. 'Well, that's a new
one on me.' He led them to their rooms, talking all the
way about couples registering under Smith or Brown and
what that always implied. Then he informed them that
they wouldn't be wanting to eat out, not in weather like
this, but they were lucky, since his good wife made a
mean steak and kidney pie and mash. None of this
packet stuff, he told them.

'I'll meet you downstairs in the bar at eight,' Victor
told her, standing in the doorway while she dumped her
bag on the bed.

'Fine.' The sound of the rain had made her feel sleepy
and she would rather have stayed in her room, read a
book and drifted off to sleep by nine, but under the circumstances she knew that she could hardly refuse his
offer.

She had a bath, switched on the television, rather
loudly to compensate for the pounding of the rain against
the window-pane, and was absent-mindedly standing in
front of the mirror on the dressing-table, combing
through her hair with her fingers, when she saw Victor
in the doorway.

She froze. He had hardly ever seen her in anything
but a dress or a suit. They had never been on a conference abroad, where she might have had to wear a swim-
suit if there had been a pool. She was his starchy, effi-

cient personal assistant, and, until lately, one who had been as interesting as a cardboard cut-out.

Now she stood in the room, with the rain slashing down outside, completely naked in front of the mirror, and her shock made her rigid.

Then she spun around, horrified, desperately trying to cover her unclothed body with her hands. An impossible manoeuvre.

'What the hell are you doing in here?' She was finding it hard to speak coherently.

'I knocked but there was no answer, so I pushed the door open.' He stood there with his arms folded and looked at her. No attempt to look at her face and utterly unembarrassed. The grey eyes swept over her body in an appraisal that made her want to sink through the floor-boards and vanish to the centre of the earth.

'Get out!'

He raised his eyes to hers and said, as though there were nothing unduly disconcerting about the situation, 'I'll be in the bar. See you there in a few minutes.'

Then he was gone, shutting the door behind him, and Alice remained where she was, her whole body trembling.

She hadn't the aplomb to deal with this. She would have been angry and humiliated if it had been any other man. The fact that it had been Victor Temple made it all the worse.

She groaned and began dressing hurriedly, flinging her clothes on, slapping a bit of make-up on her face. She hardly looked at what she was doing. She kept seeing Victor standing there, looking at her, and, nudging treacherously against the horror, she admitted angrily to herself, hadn't there been a swift and frightening stab of excitement?

She closed her eyes and rested her head in the palms of her hands.

She would have to leave, of course. How else could she continue working for him, knowing that there was some strange part of her that had suddenly decided to find him attractive? It was nothing to do with her mind, because she had learnt from past experience. She could only blame it on her body which had infuriatingly responded with a will of its own.

Hard on the heels of that came another thought: if she told him that she wanted to leave, he would be mystified. He would think it a hysterical reaction to a perfectly simple mistake. He had walked in on her while she was naked and had left. Where was the problem? He hadn't touched her, had he? She could picture him laughing as she stammered out a resignation. He was probably laughing now, thinking of her horror at his intrusion.

Between the bedroom and the bar, she vacillated a hundred times over what she would do, but by the time she finally saw him, sitting at a table in the furthest corner of the pub, which was half empty because of the weather, she had already decided to put a brave face on it. If he mentioned the episode, she would simply brush the whole thing aside and act like the mature adult that she was.

He wasn't laughing when she finally sat down opposite him and had a drink in her hand. In fact, he wasn't even smiling. And, thankfully, he didn't mention the little episode at all. It was as though nothing untoward had happened. They chatted about inconsequential matters, mostly the weather, until they were presented with their food. Two plates groaning under the weight of steak and kidney pie.

'They're certainly enthusiastic when it comes to portions,' Alice said, not knowing where to start.

'And obviously unconcerned about cholesterol levels.'
In addition to vegetables, there was also a bowl of
French fries to share.

She began eating, but now that she had admitted to
her own attraction to him she found that she was compelled to keep looking at him, as though making up for
lost time. She hungrily absorbed the hard angles of his
face, the muscular appeal of his body, his whole aura of
sexiness which she had previously acknowledged, but in
a detached way, and which now stirred a response in her
that was simultaneously terrifying and hypnotic.

She couldn't wait to get back to London and back to
the routine of work which would protect her against him.
The past three days seemed to have shut the door on one
thing but opened another door on something else.

He was talking to her and when her brain refocused
she realised that he had been asking her a question.

'Sorry?' She put her knife and fork down, having done
justice to about half of what had been on her plate, and
forced herself to look him full in the face.

'I said,' he told her, frowning, 'that you do realise that
Claydon is going to be on the scene quite a bit until the
project is wrapped up.'

What has that got to do with me? she wanted to reply.
I'll just make sure that I'm not around when he is. Not
terribly difficult.

She booked all of Victor's appointments. She would
simply book James to slot in when she was doing something in another part of the office, or, better still, when
she had already left for home. She had faced her night-
mares and come out the other side. No use in tempting
fate. Repeatedly seeing James might well have the con-
verse effect of eventually stirring up all the old feelings
of anger and bitterness.

'How long do you think the whole thing is going to take?'

Victor shrugged. 'The photographers still have to be arranged, then the layouts. I've told Claydon that we're pretty busy at the moment so we'll just have to slot him in when we can.'

'You told him *that*?' Even coming from Victor, who felt absolutely no constraints when it came to speaking his mind, that was surprising. Surprising because of its sheer level of tactlessness.

'You needn't look at me as if I've taken leave of my senses,' he told her, with no hint of humour in his voice. 'It happens to be the truth. We're inundated with work.'

'Yes, I know, but…'

'But…? What *is* the problem here?'

'Problem? There's no problem.' Alice shot him a puzzled look, and he sat back in his chair and regarded her minutely.

'You seem particularly keen to sign Claydon up.'

'*I* seem particularly keen?' She took a deep breath and counted to ten.

'That's right. You've been blowing the man's trumpet ever since you set eyes on him.'

Alice nearly laughed aloud at that complete misreading of the situation. For someone who considered himself an expert at gauging other people, Victor Temple had spectacularly bombed on this one.

'I'm still not convinced that we're even going to accept this job,' Victor said lazily, not taking his eyes from her face. 'I get the feeling that this man could be trouble in more ways than one.'

Now she was completely lost. He had dealt with difficult clients before and had appeared to enjoy the challenge.

'What kind of trouble?' She took a mouthful of wine, which was lukewarm and tasted horrible.

'Fussy, to start with. In case you hadn't noticed.'

'Well, I'm sure he just wants to make sure that everything's done perfectly. I mean, he must be fairly apprehensive about taking this road, because once he's on it, then there's no going back.'

He ignored her. 'Then,' he said, twirling the stem of his wine glass in his hand, 'there's the little matter of you.'

Alice stared at him open-mouthed. 'Me?'

'Yes, you. It's fairly obvious that he's taken a liking to you.'

She could feel the blood rush to her head. 'I haven't noticed,' she lied. 'Not that it would be any business of yours.'

'Oh, but you see it would be. I don't approve of clients fraternising with my staff.'

'Thank you for the warning, but I can take care of myself.'

She sat back to allow their plates to be cleared away and clasped her fingers together on her lap.

'Can you?' He sounded as though that was open to debate. 'There's no man in your life, is there? And hasn't been for years. Now suddenly James Claydon is on the scene and you two are openly giving each other the come-on…'

'We were *not* giving each other the *come-on*!' Alice retorted indignantly. She didn't know what made her angrier—the mistaken assumption that she had been leading James on, or Victor's assumption that he could interfere in her personal life.

'Oh, do me a favour. I'm not blind, Alice. I saw the way the man was looking at you, couldn't tear his eyes away.'

'And what if he was?' she demanded, keeping her voice low and leaning forward so that she could make herself perfectly clear.

'You're biting off more than you can chew with that man,' Victor returned, leaning towards her as well so that their faces were only inches away from each other. 'Don't tell me that you're so desperate you'd involve yourself with a man like that.'

'How dare you?' *Desperate.* So that was what he thought of her. It turned her anger into sheer fury.

'It's hardly as though you're experienced in the opposite sex, Alice.'

'I'm not a complete country bumpkin!'

'But you haven't had a relationship in years. The last one you had ended in tears. You're vulnerable to the sort of cheap charm that Claydon has on offer.'

Not now, I'm not! she wanted to yell at him.

'And you think that it's your duty to make sure that I don't make a fool of myself, is that it?' she asked, gathering her composure together with difficulty and speaking through gritted teeth.

'All in a day's work.'

'No, it is *not* all in a day's work. I'll do whatever I damn well please outside working hours!'

'Like I said, I won't have you sleeping with a client. Is that understood?'

'Absolutely.' She sat back and looked at him coldly. 'I wouldn't dream of doing that.'

He returned her look with narrowed, speculative eyes. 'I'm not sure I believe that.'

And I'm pretty sure that I don't give a damn whether you do or not, she thought silently.

'That's because you have a suspicious mind,' Alice told him. She forced a smile onto her face. Let him go right ahead and misread the situation. If nothing else, it would distract him from the real danger lying under his nose: that her interest wasn't in James Claydon. Her interest was in Victor Temple, who was a far more worrying proposition, if only he knew it.

CHAPTER SIX

A FEW days later, Alice worked out why she had been feeling so rotten. Partly, it had been because her life seemed to have suddenly undergone a few dramatic and highly unwelcome changes, and partly, she now realised, it had been because she was coming down with flu. She awoke with her head throbbing and her throat feeling as though it had had several layers rubbed off, so that swallowing anything was like sticking fire down her throat. She telephoned Victor at seven-thirty promptly, knowing that he would be at work.

'I'm sorry, but I can't come in today,' she told him. 'I'm in a dreadful way. I think I have flu.'

'Have you been to the doctor?' He didn't sound entirely sympathetic to her cause, she noticed. 'How long do you think you'll be out of action? There's a stack of work to be done here.'

Well, that puts my mind at rest, she thought, lying back against the pillows and fiddling with the telephone cord.

'I have no idea. I'll have a word with my virus and see if we can agree on something, shall I?'

'No need for sarcasm, Alice. But if you're going to be away for the rest of the week, then I'll sort something out with a temp.'

'I'll try and make it in tomorrow,' she told him wearily.

'Fine. See you then.' And she was left with the sound of the dialling tone in her car.

Trust him, she thought, closing her eyes and wishing

that she could muster up the energy to get out of bed and do something rather more constructive than just lying down in a state of misery and inertia.

When she next opened her eyes, it was to find that it had gone twelve o'clock, and so the remainder of the day continued, until seven that evening when Vanessa returned, made her something light to eat and brought it into her room, making huge fanning motions with her hands.

'I can't afford to come down with anything,' she said, gingerly depositing the tray on the bed and stepping backwards, as though afraid of being jumped on by a swarm of unruly bacteria. 'I have a Very Important Date tonight.'

'Steve?' Alice found it hard to keep track of Vanessa's various men.

'Old hat.' She forgot about flapping away the germs and perched on the bed. 'Way too boring, as it turned out. I wanted to trip the light fantastic, and he wanted to stay at home and munch on home-cooked food.'

'Poor chap,' Alice said sympathetically, biting into a cheese and ham sandwich which tasted of cardboard. 'Didn't you tell him that you hated cooking?'

'I must have forgotten to mention it,' Vanessa said glumly, 'or else I didn't mention it often enough. Why on earth do most men hit thirty-five and then assume that night-clubs are no longer appropriate?'

'Because they have sense.'

Vanessa laughed, throwing her head back, and then gathering her long red hair with one hand and pulling it over one shoulder. She was so completely the opposite of Alice that they couldn't fail to get along.

'Skipped work today, I take it?'

'But back in tomorrow,' Alice told her.

'That boss of yours is a slave-driver.' She stood up

and stretched, and then repeated the gesture just for good measure. 'You should give him a piece of your mind.'

'When I do, he ignores it,' Alice said, inspecting the sandwich carefully and wondering how on earth a simple cheese and ham sandwich could metamorphose into something that was practically inedible. Her taste-buds were, admittedly, not up to par, but Vanessa's touch, when it came to anything home-made, did leave an awful lot to be desired. It was strange that she continually attracted the sort of man who was on the prowl for a domestic little soul, the absolute opposite of Vanessa.

'Anyway, wish me luck with tonight's hunk of the month,' she said airily, heading towards the door. 'He's tall, blond and handsome and will probably turn out to be as boring as hell.'

Though, Alice thought later, not as boring as spending the day cooped up in bed, and then finishing such high-level excitement by watching a third-rate detective movie which would have sent an insomniac to sleep.

Not that the rest did an awful lot for her constitution. She awoke the following morning feeling slightly better but in no shape to go into work and, predictably, Victor's response was even more unsympathetic than it had been the day before.

'What do you mean, you can't come in?' he demanded.

Alice swallowed back the temptation to inform him that she hadn't cultivated a virus specifically to throw his schedule out of joint.

'I feel a bit better,' she said in a restrained voice, 'but I don't think that I'll be able to make it in to the office.'

'In which case the office will have to come to you,' he told her, after a moment's thought, and Alice did a

mental double take, wondering if she had heard correctly.

'Excuse me?'

'Don't tell me that your hearing's gone on the blink
as well,' Victor said impatiently. 'Look, I have a meeting
in five minutes so I can't stay to have a lengthy chat
with you on the telephone. I'll be round to your place
after work. Expect me about seven-thirty.'

After she had replaced the receiver, she lay back on
the bed and groaned. Wasn't this just typical of Victor
Temple? She spent the day trying to get herself into a
frame of mind that would enable her to face him when
her defences were down and she felt wretched, not
helped by the fact that Vanessa was going to be out, so
she wouldn't even have the moral support of another
presence in the house.

'You look terrible,' was the first thing he said when
he entered the house, fifteen minutes late. He was carrying a wad of files which he proceeded to deposit on
the table in the living room; then he turned to face her
and gave her the once-over. 'You should be in bed.'

'I *was* in bed, until you called and told me that you
had to come over.' She folded her arms and attempted
to outstare him, which was impossible.

He shoved his hands into his pockets and continued
to scrutinise her, until she became increasingly sensitive
to the fact that her skin was pale and blotchy, her eyes
slightly pink and her hair in need of a wash.

'Can I get you a coffee?' she asked, bustling off in
the direction of the kitchen.

'I don't suppose you have anything to eat?' He followed her and although she had her back to him she
could feel his presence a few feet away. Even though
she did her utmost to relax, she could feel the hairs on
the back of her neck standing on end, and her move-

ments were so deliberate that her body felt as rigid as a plank of wood. She imagined him looking at her in that room in the pub, felt the tingle of forbidden awareness course through her, and immediately blocked the image from her mind.

'I haven't exactly been out shopping,' she said, pouring hot water into two mugs and not turning around to face him.

'Bread and cheese will be fine. A little lettuce if you have any and some mustard and mayonnaise.'

Alice dumped the kettle on the counter and turned around.

'Sure that's all?' she asked with overdone sweetness.

'Oh, yes, I think so.' He raised his eyebrows, aware of her sarcasm and choosing to ignore it. 'Unless, of course, you're too ill. Although it's good to be up on your feet. Too much lying on the bed just makes you feel worse.'

'Thanks for that bit of medical input,' Alice muttered darkly under her breath, concocting a sandwich for him with bad grace, and then proceeding to join him in the living room, where he had taken over the coffee table and was spreading out several files.

He had removed his jacket and absent-mindedly rolled up the sleeves of his white shirt to the elbows. She had to stop her eyes lingering on the strong lines of his forearm, the sprinkling of dark hair, the length of his fingers.

'Thanks,' he said, not looking at her, biting into the sandwich with the enthusiasm of someone who hadn't eaten for several days.

'Ready?' he asked as she sat down opposite him and tucked her legs underneath her. He glanced at her and frowned. 'Shouldn't you have gone to the doctor?'

'Doctors can't prescribe anything for flu,' she told him, doodling on her notepad and looking at him. 'It's a virus. You can't take antibiotics for a virus. Aren't you ever ill?'

'I try and avoid it,' he said, sitting back and clasping his hands behind his head. 'I can remember having chicken-pox as a child and it was such an awful experience being cooped up that I've tried not to repeat it.' He grinned at the expression on her face.

'And I suppose germs would think twice about coming near you,' she said thoughtfully. 'They wouldn't dare.'

He laughed, amused, and then proceeded to open several files, quizzing her on the status of them, firing off a few letters which she transcribed onto her notepad. He had brought a laptop computer with him and he told her that she could type up the letters and then it would be just a matter of printing them the following day.

'Shouldn't be too hectic,' he said soothingly, and she wondered where his definition of hectic came from, because within the hour she had already been briefed on enough work to keep most people busy for the better part of a week.

'You look a bit peaky,' he said as the words accumulated on the ground next to her and a quick glance at the clock on the mantelpiece told her that it was nearly nine-thirty. 'Should you take a couple of aspirin?'

'I suppose so,' Alice said, stretching out her legs and flexing her ankles so that some sort of blood circulation could recommence. Surprisingly, she felt better. She stood up, and he waved her back down.

'Sit, sit! Tell me where they are and I'll fetch them.'

'It's all right. I need the exercise.'

'Nonsense.' He stood up and looked at her questioningly, and she told him that he could find them in her bedroom, second along the corridor, by her bed. She was finding it difficult to adjust to his presence in her flat and she wished that Vanessa were around to provide a distraction. Now that she had acknowledged the way she felt about him, her mind seemed to have opened up to every nuance, every shade of his conversation, every mannerism which she must have noticed in the past and stored up somewhere in her brain for just this moment when she seemed unable to focus on much else. Concentrating on what he was saying took superhuman will-power. Having him here, in her private space, made matters all the worse, she decided. Things would soon revert to their usual even tenor when she returned to work.

He returned with the box of tablets too soon for her liking, and he brought them to her with a glass of water from the kitchen.

'Now,' he said in an infuriatingly paternal voice, 'you just swallow these down. Have you got a fever?'

'No.' She swallowed one tablet and eyed him warily over the rim of the glass.

'Are you quite sure? You look a little flushed.' He reached out and felt her face with the back of his hand, and she almost choked on the second tablet.

'I'm absolutely fine!' she snapped, pulling away. 'Really.' He had squatted down to her level and she tried not to press herself against the back of the chair in an attempt to put some distance between them. When he was this close, she almost felt that she couldn't breathe.

'I hope you've been eating properly.' He didn't move and she had the distinct impression that he had remained where he was with the sole purpose of rattling her.

'Never better.' She produced the best noncommittal smile she could muster, and he stood up and stared down at her.

'Good. And tell me if you're finding this session a little hard and we'll stop.'

'I do feel a bit tired, now that you mention it.'

'Well, there's only a little left to go through, then I'll be out of your hair. Where's your flatmate?' He strolled back to his chair, and Alice released her breath and felt herself relax.

'Out on a date.' She sneezed into a handkerchief and tried to look as exhausted as she could, which wasn't very difficult.

He ignored that and pulled out a few more files, and pressed on with blithe disregard for her tiredness. Victor Temple, she decided, was a law unto himself.

'No need for you to come in to work tomorrow,' he said forty-five minutes later, as he was sifting through what he needed to take away with him. Alice, not looking at him, was stacking her files and wondering whether a relapse might not occur with the amount of work he had thoughtfully left for her to do.

'I'll try and make it in for the afternoon. That way I can spend the morning working and finish on the computer in the office.'

'Oh, no. I insist you stay at home. I can collect these in the evening some time.'

'Oh, no! There's no need. I'll get Vanessa to drop them in. She works quite close by. I'm sure she wouldn't mind.' He was heading towards the door and Alice hurried behind him, panicking at the thought of him being in her house twice in the space of a few days. Once was bad enough.

'No trouble.' He had reached the front door and he stood there now, with one hand on the doorknob and a solicitous expression on his face. 'You just rest. Take it easy. And don't do all the work I've left if you feel that you can't manage.'

'That's very generous of you,' Alice said dryly, and their eyes met with a flash of shared comprehension. If she decided not to complete what he had left, then his generosity would vanish pretty quickly.

'Oh, by the way,' he said as he was turning away to leave, 'Claydon's dropping by tomorrow morning. I'll fill you in when you're at work next week.' He pulled open the door, still not looking at her, only glancing around when he was halfway to his car, and then only to give a short wave of his hand before driving off.

So, she thought slowly, packing up and getting ready for bed, that was why he had been so insistent on her not going in to work the following day. She might have guessed. The man didn't have a compassionate bone in his body. He had merely wanted to make sure that she and James were not thrown together, because he had incorrectly assumed that they were interested in one another and for various reasons, all bad, he had summarily decided that any such liaison would not do.

She almost, perversely, was tempted to show up at eight-thirty promptly for work, simply to see the expression on his face, but the thought only lasted a couple of seconds. The fact was that she doubted she would be up to Victor by the time morning rolled round, and also it suited her to be off work when James showed up. She had no intention of laying eyes on him again if she could possibly help it, and the fact that she was ill was fortuitous.

In point of fact, she felt much better by the following morning, and by eight she had neatly laid out all the files on the kitchen table and was going through them when Vanessa drowsily staggered in for a cup of coffee.

'Oh, God, you're not working, are you?' were her first words as she headed towards the kettle, pulling her dressing-gown around her and yawning. 'How many times do I have to lecture to you on all work and no play…?'

'How did the date go?' Alice looked up, smiling, and Vanessa grimaced expressively at her.

'He has this hobby. He flies in his spare time.'

'Really? How talented of him. Does he grow wings for the purpose?'

'Planes, you idiot.' She sat down and grinned. 'I thought it sounded terribly exciting when he first told me, but you'd be amazed at how boring three hours on the subject can be.'

'Ah.' Alice sighed and shook her head with exaggerated disappointment. 'So you're telling me that it was another of your famous flops. Thanks, I'll stick to the all work and no play routine.'

'I shall never find someone on my wavelength,' Vanessa moaned, sitting back and yawning again. 'I mean, what *is* it about me? Why do I always manage to attract men who look as though they should be exciting but turn out to be as dull as dish-water?'

'Because the exciting ones think that you might be unfair competition?'

'Because the exciting ones have already been snapped up,' Vanessa said in a forlorn voice. 'The only ones left for ageing belles like me are the boring leftovers. It's like arriving at the dinner table only to find that the best bits have gone and all that's left are the Brussels sprouts and lettuce leaves.'

'Poor old you.'

'Less of the old, please.' She swallowed the rest of her coffee and stood up. 'I don't suppose you have any eligible, wildly exciting men stashed away in that closet of yours, have you?'

'If I had, I would be at great pains to keep them to myself.'

'Well, the search continues, though I'm beginning to think that I'd stand a better chance of hitting upon a UFO than someone I get along with for longer than two months at a stretch. Anyway, work calls. Not all of us can sit at home with a basket of files kindly delivered by our boss and put our feet up for the day.' With which she vanished in the direction of her bedroom, only resurfacing half an hour later on her way out.

'Back early!' she said, from the kitchen door. 'For once!'

Alice gave no more thought to that for the rest of the day. She buried herself in her work, enjoying the fact that she had something to do, and only remembered that Vanessa was returning early when the doorbell rang at six that evening.

She didn't even pause to ask herself why her flatmate didn't just let herself in. Vanessa was famous for forgetting to take her key with her if she happened to leave before Alice.

So when Alice pulled open the door she was expecting to see her, and the sight of James, lounging against the door-frame, brought her to a complete standstill.

'Flowers,' he said, whipping them out from behind his back like a third-rate magician performing a fourth-rate trick.

'What are you doing here?' Alice looked at him coldly and ignored the offering of flowers. The man was obviously deranged if he seriously believed that he could show up here, unannounced, uninvited and unwelcome, and expect her to fall at his feet at that old, tired routine of his, of flowers, meals out and boxes of chocolates. Hadn't he got the message when she'd seen him at Highfield House?

'I've come to see you,' James said, stating the obvious and adopting a wounded expression.

'Well, you've seen me. Now please go away.'

'You said that we could get together when I was up in London!'

'I lied.' She folded her arms and firmly remained where she was, blocking the door.

'Why would you do that?'

'Because it was the easiest thing to do at the time.' She sighed in frustration. 'Look, James, it was pure co-incidence that we met after all this time...'

'Call it fate...'

'*Coincidence*. But I don't want you back in my life.' She paused and looked at him. 'You really hurt me back then.'

'I was a fool. I have,' he continued with awkward sincerity, 'changed. Divorce, growing older, who knows? Look, can't we discuss this inside?'

'There's nothing to discuss!'

'Then let's just all have a drink and discuss nothing!' They both looked around to see Vanessa, who was openly appraising James and was clearly pleasantly grat-ified by what she saw. 'I thought you said that your closet was empty of eligible males.' James looked back at her, taking in the long hair, the fun-loving expression, the attaché case, while Alice clicked her tongue in an-noyance at the bad timing of Vanessa's arrival and thought, sourly, that this was worse than Piccadilly Circus at the height of the tourist season.

'And you are...?' James produced the flowers once again. 'Would you believe,' he continued, not giving Vanessa time to reply, 'that I had a premonition that I would bump into a gorgeous redhead, and came prepared with a bunch of wildly expensive flowers?'

'No, as a matter of fact, I wouldn't!' Vanessa threw back her head and laughed. And before Alice could en-gineer a way of letting Vanessa get past whilst continuing to keep James very firmly out all three found themselves inside, and she found herself a bystander as James pulled all his charm out of his box and Vanessa responded in kind.

They seemed to click immediately. Vanessa was utterly immune to James's attempts at charm, which she laughed at, and he plainly found the response bewitching. They positioned themselves on opposite chairs in the room, but even so anyone with the mental IQ of a cretin, could see from their body language that they were revelling in each other's company.

At the end of an hour, Vanessa stood up and announced that she had to leave.

'Away for the weekend,' she said airily, and James followed her out with a hangdog expression on his face.

'Any chance I could come?'

'No chance. But if you're a very good and very, *very* persuasive little boy you might ask me out for dinner at a very expensive restaurant next week, and I might actually consider going.' She laughed at her own outrageous proposition and James laughed as well.

'Monday onwards is good for me,' he said.

'But not for me,' Vanessa informed him, her eyes gleaming. She placed her hands on her hips and frowned thoughtfully, and Alice looked at James, noting how every pore in his body seemed to respond to the unspoken sexual invitation in Vanessa. 'I can meet you next Tuesday at eight-thirty. Promptly. Here. And,' she threw over her shoulder, 'don't be late. I hate men who don't show up on time.'

After she had left, James looked at Alice and let out a long, low whistle.

'You share your house with a sex goddess,' he said in a dumbstruck voice.

'And there I was, thinking that the flowers and charm

had been laid on specially for me.' She felt giddy with relief that this additional complication was not going to materialise after all.

'Well...' He shot her a sheepish look.

'Would you like a cup of coffee before you go?' she asked, and he nodded and followed her out to the kitchen, trying to prise information out of her about Vanessa the whole way. What did she do for a living? Was there a man in her life? Had she ever been married? What sort of girl was she? *Really?*

Alice answered as evasively as she could, making them both a cup of instant coffee to hurry along his departure, and they sat at the kitchen table in a spirit of companionship which she would never have imagined possible.

But hadn't she always liked him? Why shouldn't Vanessa? And maybe he *had* changed. It was a hurtful thought, but perhaps he just hadn't been captivated enough by *her*. He had thought that he had wanted a different type, but maybe he had just needed a different *person*. Unanswerable questions, she thought wearily.

When she heard the doorbell ring fifteen minutes later, he jumped up and said gleefully that it might be Vanessa.

'Couldn't bear the thought of a weekend away now that she's met me, the man destined to be her lifelong partner.' He said that in a joking voice, but there was an element of seriousness underlying it that Alice wasn't even sure he had noticed himself.

It wasn't Vanessa. It was Victor. With all the unexpected turn of events that had been taking place for the past couple of hours, she had completely forgotten that he had told her to expect him that evening to collect the work. She had no idea where James was, but she stood at the door, not budging.

'How are you feeling?' he asked, looking at her, his masculinity filling her senses like incense.

'Better. Much better. Thank you!'

'Are you going to let me get by?'

'No need for you to stay,' she returned quickly, praying that James would not materialise out of the woodwork. 'If you wait right here, I'll just go and fetch the work. I've managed to get through the lot and I'm happy to come in tomorrow morning and update the computer.' She still hadn't moved. If anything, she had narrowed the gap in the door.

'It can wait until Monday.' He paused. 'I get the impression that you don't want me in the house.'

Alice gave a laugh which sounded fairly manic to her own ears. 'Just want to save you time. I know you're probably in a rush to get back to…wherever it is you're getting back to. I'll just dash and get the files.' She gently shut the door, leaving only a tiny gap, and sprinted towards the kitchen where she frantically bundled all the paperwork, glancing around to make sure that there was nothing lurking on a chair or on a counter anywhere. She headed back towards the front door to find him inside the house, looking around him.

She thrust the files into his hands and he looked at her wryly.

'That was quick. You must be on the mend if you can m—'

He stopped in mid-sentence and Alice didn't have to look around to know that James had appeared.

'Claydon!'

Alice turned around to see James grinning at Victor, moving forward with his jacket now on, looking every inch a man who was satisfied with life.

'Didn't think we'd be meeting up quite so soon,' James said, half turning to look at Alice. 'Forgot to mention in all the excitement that I was at your headquarters today. Nice little place you have there.'

'Oh, were you?' Alice said faintly, not quite daring to look in Victor's direction and hating herself for the weakness, because after all it was *her* territory and she could do just as she pleased in it, whatever Victor Temple had to say on the subject.

'Excitement?' Victor looked between them, his eyes cold. 'Have I disturbed you two?'

'Not in the least!' James said cheerfully. 'We were just winding down with a cup of coffee. In fact, I'm on my way out.'

Which, Alice thought, just left her and Victor. Her and the man-eating ogre.

'No need to hurry off just yet,' she heard herself saying, because between James and the man-eating ogre James won by a small margin.

'Don't you worry!' He winked at her, pausing. 'We'll be seeing quite a lot of each other in the future, if I have my wicked way.' He laughed, delighted at the prospect of that, and Alice shut the front door behind him, reluctantly turning around to finally face Victor.

'It's not what you think,' was the first thing she said when she found him staring at her, with a thunderous look on his face.

Why am I doing this? she wondered angrily. Why am I rushing into an explanation for something that doesn't concern him?

'And you know what I think, do you?'

'It doesn't take a genius to read your mind.' She moved into the sitting room, resigned to the fact that he wasn't going to simply leave without some kind of explanation from her, and he followed her. It was like being followed by a prowling tiger on the look-out for its next meal.

She sat down and waited until he had sat down as well. 'I have no idea how James got my address, but he just arrived here unannounced...'

'Remarkable turn of events. And such a surprise following on from your less than private goings-on at Highfield House.'

'Excuse me?' Her voice was cold.

'When we went into that little forest, I could have sworn that you had been there before. I have my answer.'

'You are *not* my keeper. Sir. You are my employer.'

'And as such I feel I should tell you that consorting with clients is against company rules and as such will result in instant dismissal.'

They had had mild disagreements in the past, there had been times when she had felt pushed to the absolute limit, but those instances had been, thankfully, few and far between. To have this ultimatum delivered now was like a blow to the stomach, and especially since it had been based on a totally inaccurate assumption. She stared at him, dumbfounded, and he stared right back at her, although there was a dark flush on his face.

'Well?' he asked aggressively.

'Thank you for being so blunt,' Alice said with a blank expression and in a perfectly modulated voice. 'Now, perhaps you might care to leave? I'm still very tired with this flu.' She stood up and folded her arms, and eventually he stood up as well, although he didn't spin around and head towards the door. Instead, he remained where he was, as though incapable of turning his back on a situation he had created.

'Look, Alice...'

'I got your message loud and clear. Sir. There's no need to repeat it.'

'I may have sounded harsh...'

'Not at all,' she replied coldly. 'I quite understand your position and it's only fair that you warn me in advance of what the consequences would be, should I decide to start a passionate fling with James Claydon. Which, of course, I'm quite likely to do since I'm little more than a desperate, inexperienced has-been, just the sort who would fall head over heels in love with anyone with a bit of charm who might pay me a moment's attention.'

'I never said anything of the sort,' Victor told her, but she could tell from the way he looked away that her accusation had found its mark.

He had no idea of the reality of the situation, but, even so, she found it insulting that he had automatically assumed that anything between herself and James would be sexual. The thought of friendship had never crossed his mind, and of course James's parting words had only thrown wood on the fire.

'If you're quite finished? *Sir?*'

Victor shook his head impatiently and muttered, 'Will you stop calling me Sir?'

'Would you rather "Boss"?' Alice asked politely. 'That way we can make sure that we both know precisely who lays down the laws, whatever the laws might me.'

'I wouldn't allow anyone else to speak to me like that...'

'Then,' she said, walking towards him, hands on her hips, and thrusting her chin out, 'sack me.'

'Sack you?' She hadn't realised quite how close they were, but she did now. 'Right now, that's not exactly what I had in mind.'

Part of her had known what he intended to do, but the thought had seemed so incredible that she had not allowed the idea to filter through to her consciousness. So

when he bent his head towards her she was totally un-
prepared.

She felt his mouth against hers and it was like being
suddenly given a huge electric shock. His lips crushed
hers, forcing her mouth open so that his tongue could
explore, a hungry, urgent exploration that sent an explo-
sion of excitement through her body.

When he pulled away, she almost staggered back.

'Don't go near him, Alice,' he murmured. 'I'm warning you.'

She didn't answer. She couldn't speak. She remained
where she was until she heard the front door slam, then
she sank onto the chair like a puppet whose strings had
suddenly been cut.

CHAPTER SEVEN

ON TUESDAY morning, Alice was amazed, at seven o'clock, to find Vanessa in the kitchen before her, fully dressed and gulping down a cup of coffee by the sink.

'You look full of it,' she said, trying to inject some enthusiasm into her voice.

'And you look like a wet rag.'

'Thanks very much.' She grimaced and then threw Vanessa a watery grin. 'Nothing that several years in cold storage wouldn't cure.'

'Still suffering?'

'Oh, no. I've completely got over my little bout of flu.' She eyed her flatmate thoughtfully. Impossible to explain why she was feeling miserable.

The day before had been long and draining. She and Victor had worked alongside each other in an atmosphere of monosyllabic politeness. Enough had been said for work to be done, but beyond that was an abyss of things unspoken. He'd barely looked at her and she'd felt the loss more than she could ever have imagined possible. She had never realised just how accustomed she had become to his ways and how enjoyable she had found their familiarity.

Did he remember that kiss? She would never have asked him the question in a million years, nor would she ever have told him quite how affected she had been by it. In fact, she had barely thought of anything else over the weekend. She had replayed the scene a thousand times in her head, cursing herself for her momentary weakness while feeling a treacherous thrill of excitement at the memory of it. It had been like a banquet of food given to a starving man. She had known that he attracted her, but she was shocked to discover that attraction was a mild term for what she had felt, which had been a wild, abandoned hunger, something so powerful that it had swept over her like a tidal wave, pulverising every ounce of common sense in its path.

'Have you got a few minutes before you leave?' she asked, and Vanessa nodded and sat down at the table with her cup. 'I think you should know that James and I used to go out together once. A long time ago.'

'What?'

'Yes, I wasn't always a dreary stay-at-home,' Alice replied irritably, and Vanessa immediately looked contrite.

'That's *not* what I meant. I wasn't expressing surprise at the going out, I was expressing surprise at the *who* you were going out with. How on earth did you meet him...? You dark horse!'

'I worked for his father for a while, and that's how we met.'

'Am I treading on toes? Is that what this talk is about?'

Alice laughed. 'Not in the least. In fact, you couldn't be further from the truth!'

'Then what?'

'I just want you to be careful, that's all. James can be very charming when he puts his mind to it...'

'But in fact he's a complete cad.'

'No...' Alice admitted slowly.

'What happened?'

'It ended rather badly, I'm afraid. Or, at least, rather badly from my point of view. He threw me over because I wasn't good enough and promptly took himself off and married someone who was.' She paused. 'No, I'm not being quite truthful. James hurt me because I allowed myself to be hurt. I read everything into a relationship when in all fairness he had never let me believe that marriage was the eventual resting place. I just assumed...' She had tried for years, and largely succeeded, in blaming everything on James. It had made it easier to accept her pain. Now she looked at Vanessa, the complete opposite of her, and wondered whether the man she'd sought and failed to find had perhaps always been there, but there for someone else. Someone like Vanessa.

'Let me get this straight. You're telling me that he left you and now he's married?' Vanessa's expression changed from one of sympathy to fury, and Alice waved her hands up and down.

'Not now, he isn't. But what I'm trying to say is that you should watch your step. I wouldn't like you to be hurt.'

'Thanks for the warning, Ali. It's appreciated but—' she grinned slowly '—James Claydon is the one who needs to watch his step. I intend to step on any phoney charm he might throw my way, just in case he makes the mistake of thinking that it stands a hell's chance of working. I don't intend to be taken for a ride,' she continued, and then added in an apologetic voice. 'Not that I'm implying...'

'It doesn't matter.' Alice shrugged. 'Like I said, it was an awfully long time ago and I've changed a lot since then.' Now, she thought, I make sure that I fall for the *really* dangerous type. Why be a little bit hurt when you can go the whole hog and be totally demolished? 'What do you think of him, anyway?' she asked curiously.

Vanessa stood up, rinsed her cup, set it on the draining-board and then said pensively, 'I think he has a tendency to be full of himself. He's probably been spoiled rotten since birth and given half a chance would prob-

ably ride roughshod over some poor, unsuspecting female. Fortunately he's met his match in me. In fact—'
she walked towards the door and turned to look at Alice,
with a little smile '—I suspect he might well be a very
pleasant challenge. He'll certainly be a very pleasant
change from my usual sort, who can't wait to play hus-
bands and wives and take out a mortgage on a nice little
property, with a nice little patchwork of green around it,
somewhere half an hour out of the city.'

'In that case—' Alice smiled back '—why on earth
did I ever worry about you? You'll have to tell me how
it went.'

'In all its gory detail!' Vanessa laughed loudly, and
twenty minutes after she had gone Alice let herself out
of the house and headed to work.

She arrived to find that Victor was nowhere around.
Instead, there was a note on her desk, informing her that
he had gone to see a client in Wimbledon, and wouldn't
be back until some time towards the middle of the afternoon.

She breathed a sigh of relief. Reprieve, at least temporarily, from the uneasy tension that had hung over the
office the day before, and maybe by the time he waltzed
in later on she might have undergone a remarkable personality change which would enable her to confront him
as though nothing had happened. Maybe she would
come down with selective amnesia and her memories of
the past few weeks would be eradicated, leaving her a
free person. And if neither was possible, then maybe she
could get her act together and persuade her brain to start
behaving itself. That wasn't asking too much, was it?'

She worked steadily until twelve-thirty and in fact
didn't notice the time at all until she saw a shadow looming over her and looked up to find James standing in

front of her desk. He beamed at her and Alice sat back
in response, eyeing him warily.

'What a warm welcome,' he said, unnervingly cheerful, and perched comfortably on the edge of her desk,
rearranging several files in the process. He adjusted his
tie, which bore an expensive label, and was, she suspected, rarely used given his lifestyle. 'Actually, I just
dropped in to see your boss.'

'He's out at the moment,' Alice told him, 'but he
should be back around three this afternoon.' She flipped
open the diary on her desk and consulted it. 'He has a
free slot between four and four-thirty.'

'Busy man.'

'James,' she said wryly, snapping shut the diary and
sitting back, 'your average Swiss cheese plant leads a
busier life than you.'

'That's good!' He nodded appreciatively at the sarcasm. 'Time has certainly developed your tongue.' He
leaned forward and said confidentially, 'But as it happens I'm quite busy at the moment. Work, you know.'

'James! You work now?'

'Only a couple of days a week, admittedly, but someone has to be at the helm of Dad's businesses.'

'And you're that person?'

'A man could be offended by some of the things you
say, Ali. Fortunately, it's all water off a duck's back for
me. Anyway, like anyone with a brain, I've managed to
trim my schedule right down to fit in with my out-of-
work pursuits.'

'And how have you succeeded in doing that?' She
pulled a plastic container from her drawer and un-
wrapped a sandwich which was a rather unhappy crea-
tion of cheese and mustard.

'I could tell you over lunch?'

Alice shook her head and contemplated telling him

that lunch with him might well cost her her job. But that would have involved explaining Victor's misguided impressions of their relationship, and now that James was off her hands with Vanessa the less she reminded him of his original intentions towards her the better.

'I don't think so.'

'Oh.' He looked disappointed. 'And I wanted to ask you if there were any topics I should steer clear of tonight when I see your flatmate.'

'I don't really care what you talk to Vanessa about.' Alice shrugged her shoulders and abandoned the sandwich after three mouthfuls. 'I've told her about us, though.'

'You've *what*?'

She watched him as she spoke, saw his expression alter from horror to resignation, to optimism that perhaps not all was lost. Should she be feeling something that the man she had once been so besotted with was now in thrall to her flatmate? If so, she felt nothing, merely relief that at long last the past that had held her so tightly was finally releasing its painful grip.

When she had finished speaking, she realised that her body was no longer tense, and James, leaning closely towards her to hear every word she was saying, was going to topple onto her if he wasn't careful.

'Off my desk, James,' she said, laughing.

And she looked up, past him to the door, to find that they were no longer alone. James, grinning, anything but intimidated by the sudden appearance of Victor, made no move to reposition himself. He remained exactly where he was, perched on her desk, precariously balanced on both hands.

Victor looked at the two of them, his expression cool and unreadable.

'I—I didn't expect you back quite so early,' Alice

stammered, almost getting up. 'I thought that you would be back some time later this afternoon.'

His expression said, And while the cat's away... But he merely said, 'I dropped in to fetch something from the office.' He looked at James questioningly.

'Oh, I just came on the off chance of finding you in,' James said, finally standing up and looking more like someone with a purpose rather than someone who had called round on a social visit. 'Just a few details to discuss.'

Victor flicked back the cuff of his shirt and consulted his watch. 'I have twenty minutes at the most. If you need longer than that, then you'll have to make an appointment through Alice.'

'Oh, twenty minutes is about all I want.' He strolled ahead of Victor, into his office.

Victor watched, and when he was firmly ensconced in the office he bent over Alice and said in a cold voice. 'I believe I've already spoken to you about unprofessional conduct. In case you hadn't noticed, this is an office, not a singles bar.'

'I...I apologise.'

'Tell me, what the hell do you think you're playing at?' His voice was low and controlled and they could well have been discussing work. 'What would I have found if I had walked in ten minutes later? You on the desk with Claydon?'

'That's...that's a despicable thing to say...!' It was simply too much to keep quiet and she knew that her outburst had found its target because mixed with his thunderous anger was the dark, angry flush of someone who suspected that they might have overstepped the mark.

'I'm not finished with this yet,' he told her in the sort of voice that didn't promise a cheerful chat over a pot of tea. 'Not by a long shot. I intend to continue this later—make sure that you're here.'

'And do you have any idea what time that might be?' she asked, surprised that she could actually speak, when the blood was coursing through her veins like hot lava.

'No idea whatsoever, but then you're not paid to clock-watch, are you?' He straightened up, walked into his office and shut the door behind him.

Her attraction to the man, she decided, was utterly illogical. How on earth could she be so powerfully attracted to someone with a Jekyll-and-Hyde personality? In fact, how could *anyone* be attracted to a man with a personality like Victor's? She glared at the computer screen, which stared blankly back at her, and cast her mind back to the two women who had crossed the threshold of his office on the odd occasion when they had clearly arranged to go out somewhere straight from work. He didn't make it a habit to bring his personal life into the work environment. He could have had thousands of mistresses, two, or several on the go at the same time. Alice had no real idea, because what he did outside work was largely a closed book.

Well, the answer lay there, didn't it? The two women she had glimpsed had struck her as the types on whom a split personality disorder would have had no effect whatsoever. And he probably pulled out all the stops with them anyway. He probably charmed the socks off them. He probably—and her fingers clanged in a sudden fit of jealous passion on one of the letters on the keyboard—*never* subjected them to his foul moods, his sharp tongue and his predilection to lecture. And she doubted that he had ever kissed anyone, *ever*, simply to *see what it was like*!

That was it. She was going out to lunch and hang

Victor Temple if he emerged from this office to find her seat empty. She needed to clear her head.

She spent the next hour seething through various shops in Covent Garden, glowering at anyone who got in her way, and purchasing two ridiculously skimpy outfits which she suspected she would hate just as soon as her temper calmed down and she was back to her normal, unflappable self. Even though she had to admit that her unflappability had adopted a very low profile recently.

She felt much better by the time she made it back to her desk, however. Her brisk walk had helped, as had, surprisingly, her impulsive buys. And Victor was nowhere around, although there was a note on her desk informing her that she had better not forget that he wanted to see her when he returned later that afternoon. Alice read and reread the few scrawled lines, then tore the paper up and chucked it into the bin.

As four-thirty approached, then five, then five-thirty, then six, she was seriously tempted to ignore his command and head for home, but she had a feeling that if she did that he would simply arrive at her house to say whatever it was he had to say. He would, she thought caustically, smoke her out.

By the time he finally arrived, at a little after six-thirty, she was too angry at him for his high-handedness to feel intimidated.

'Still here?' he asked, striding into the room, which infuriated her even more.

'Where else did you expect me to be when you gave me orders to remain at my desk until you got back?' She smiled as pleasantly as she could at him.

'Quite.' He looked as though he had only just remembered his command.

He stared at her speculatively, perching, as James had

done, on the edge of her desk as he did so. There was, she thought, a chair not too far away. Why didn't he use it? It was disconcerting to have him looming over her like this.

'Perhaps we could make a start on whatever work you want me to do?' she asked, still ultra-pleasant. 'I'd quite like to get home.'

'Why? Have you got plans for this evening? Dinner date, perhaps?'

'Only with my microwave lasagne,' Alice said blandly.

'You mean that you and Claydon aren't going to be painting the town red?'

'Not red, blue, yellow or any other colour for that matter.'

'In that case you can have dinner with me.'

Was that an invitation? It had sounded more like a statement of fact and her eyebrows shot up at the implicit arrogance behind the offer.

'I can't possibly,' she said, thinking fast and trying to work out how she could suddenly invent something more interesting than lasagne for one, without sounding utterly implausible.

'I want to discuss work and it'll be a damned sight more comfortable doing that in more congenial surroundings.'

Her heart lurched at that. Discuss work? Was that another way of saying the he wanted to give her the sack?

'Fine,' she agreed, still maintaining an appearance of calm whilst she fetched her jacket from its hook and slipped it on.

She didn't ask where they were going. They made neutral conversation as he drove and she racked her brain to think of what he could possibly say to her that couldn't have been said in the office. 'You're fired' didn't exactly lend itself to congenial surroundings, did it?

She only registered that they weren't at a restaurant when he pulled up outside an extremely attractive mews house in one of the most expensive parts of London.

'Where are we?' she asked, scouring the place for a restaurant sign.

'Outside my house.'

'What are we doing here?' She had never been to his home before and the thought of going inside did weird things to her stomach.

'We're going to have dinner here,' he said, as though surprised that he should have to explain the obvious.

'Here?' The pitch of her voice had risen a couple of shades higher.

'Do you have a problem with that?'

'How am I going to get home?'

'Taxi. I'll call one for you. Anything else?'

Anything else? Did he have a few days to spare?

'No,' she said reluctantly, opening her car door and stepping outside. She lagged slightly behind him, up a few steps to the front door, then into the hallway. He flicked on the light and she looked around her, curiosity overcoming panic. It wasn't huge but it was magnificent. Very pale colours. The off-white carpet was thick and luxurious, the sort of carpet that encouraged you to slip off your shoes and pad around barefoot. The paintings on the walls were mostly modern, exercises in cubism which she felt she should recognise and which were certainly not prints. She divested herself of her jacket and handed it to him.

'Do you want to eat now or later?'

'Now,' Alice said, following him into the kitchen and looking around her as she went. Everything was compact, but the decor spoke of someone to whom money was no object. It was only when they were in the kitchen that the intimacy of the situation struck her, and she walked towards the pine table and sat down, her back straight, her hands resting on the surface of the table.

'What would you like?' He opened the fridge door and peered inside.

'I don't mind,' Alice said, clasping her fingers together. 'Anything.'

'Right.' She watched in silence as he removed several things from the fridge, fetched a chopping board, and then began expertly to cut various vegetables. He had rolled up the sleeves of his workshirt and he looked strangely incongruous standing by the counter with a tea-towel slung over one shoulder, chopping and slicing. Every so often he threw a question at her, and she answered in monosyllables.

'Can I help?' she asked finally.

'You can open a bottle of wine. In the fridge. Just choose whichever takes your fancy. The corkscrew's over there.' He pointed to the window-ledge by the sink, and she obligingly extracted the first bottle that came to hand and opened it, rooting around until she found the wine glasses; then she poured them both a glass and retreated back to her position at the kitchen table. From where she surreptitiously inspected him.

When the meal was eventually in front of her, prepared, cooked and ready in under thirty minutes, she tucked in, and after a couple of mouthfuls looked across at him and said that she would never have expected him to be a gourmet chef but that the food was delicious.

'Hardly gourmet,' he conceded dryly, 'but thank you very much for the compliment. Men are as competent as women when it comes to cooking, and living on your own does rather force you into cultivating the skill.'

'I don't seem to have mastered it,' Alice said, marvelling at how a few ingredients could be tossed together in a pan and emerge onto a bed of pasta with every appearance of something that had been slaved over for hours on end. Admittedly she wasn't as hopeless as Vanessa, but she obviously had a longish way to go.

'Is your flatmate a good cook?'

'Useless.' She twirled some noodles onto her fork and submerged the lot into some sauce. 'She's only just learned how to operate the toaster without burning the bread. She feels that supermarkets are far more inventive at producing meals than she ever could be, so why bother?' She sipped some of her wine and then a little bit more. It was very drinkable and, judging from the number of bottles in the fridge, he obviously bought the stuff by the crate-load. She allowed herself another glass and resolved not to have any more. She hardly ever drank alcohol and she could become tipsy on a remarkably small amount. Which wouldn't do. Not here, not now and certainly not in the company of this man. She needed her wits about her. Especially since the object of this little exercise was work-related.

'Right, then,' she said, once she had finished eating, 'shall we get down to business?' She sincerely hoped that whatever work he had in mind wasn't going to be too complicated. Her brain didn't feel up to much.

'No dessert?'

'Don't tell me that you're capable of whipping up some *crème brûlée* in a few minutes?' Okay, she thought, just one more glass to relax her. She helped herself to some more, cravenly abandoning her decision to keep the alcohol intake to a minimum.

'*Crème brûlée* might pose a problem,' he admitted ruefully. 'Actually my talents don't stretch to desserts. I lost interest somewhere during the main course.'

'That's fine,' Alice informed him airily. 'I don't want

any anyway.' She sat back and was aware that her body felt looser than normal. 'Coffee would be nice, though.' Nice, warm, sobering coffee. Strong and black and un-sweetened. If that didn't clear her head then nothing could.

'Shall we have it in the sitting room? More comfort-able. He began clearing away the dishes and she made a half-hearted attempt to help, although her legs felt wobbly and she found that she had to concentrate so that she didn't drop anything.

Did he notice anything amiss about her? she won-dered. He certainly gave no indication that she was be-having oddly, which must mean that it was all in her head, although she knew that she was smiling just a little too brightly for comfort.

She hovered by the door, watching as he competently washed the dishes, stacking them on the draining-board in such a random manner that it would be a miracle if they all survived intact. Then he began brewing some coffee, asking her about three troublesome accounts which they had been working on over the past few days.

Alice tried very hard to sound knowledgeable on the subject, but she could feel her mind wandering and she continually had to bring it back to rein.

'The sitting room's just beyond the hall, second door on the right,' he told her. 'I'll bring the coffee through, shall I?'

'What a role reversal!' Alice said with gusto.

Ten minutes later, she saw him enter with slightly more than two cups of coffee. There were two small glasses on the tray as well, and a bottle of port. He deposited the lot on the coffee table in the centre of the room, and went to draw the curtains, thick ivory creations that coiled in an artistic, overlong manner on the ground.

'Port?' he said, pouring her a generous glassful, and Alice shook her head feebly.

'No, really, I've already had too much to drink.'

'You've only had a couple of glasses of wine. Surely not.'

He succeeded somehow in making her sound irretrievably drab if she couldn't stomach a couple of glasses of white wine without coming unstuck at the seams, so she took the glass of port from him and delicately sipped at it.

She felt far more comfortable here than in the kitchen anyway, she thought. The light wasn't as harsh, and the huge chair she was sitting on wrapped itself around her like an enormous, well-padded duvet. She kicked off her shoes and tucked her legs underneath her.

'I'm afraid I haven't brought anything to take notes on,' she said.

'That's not a problem. You won't need to take notes for what I want to say.'

That penetrated through her fuddled head and made her sit more upright.

'Are you happy working for me?' he asked, crossing his legs and surveying her over the rim of his port glass.

'It's a very good job,' Alice said in confusion.

'That's not what I asked.'

'Well, then, yes. I am.' Far too happy, she thought, even when I'm in a state of complete and utter panic because you do stupid things to my nervous system.

'Even though some might say—untrue, of course— that I'm not exactly the easiest person in the world to work for?'

'I guess I've become accustomed to...to the way you operate.'

He was staring at her so intently that she shifted in the chair uneasily. In a nervous gesture, she tucked her hair behind her ear and realised that her hand was trembling, although she wasn't certain whether this was because of his presence on the sofa or because of the mixture of wine and port.

'Why?' she asked.

'When was the last time you had an appraisal?'

'I can't remember. I'm not sure whether I've had one since I came to work for you. At least not a formal one.'

'You're a good worker, Alice,' he said, and she went bright red. Occasionally, he had congratulated her on a certain piece of work, or told her that she had done a good job on something, but only in passing.

'Thank you very much,' she mumbled.

'Which is why I've decided to increase your salary.' He named an amount and she gaped at him.

'But that's almost twice as much as I'm getting!' she exclaimed in amazement. 'Why have you suddenly decided to give me a pay rise?' she asked suspiciously. She had thought that her job might be on the line, and after all the fuss over James a pay rise was the last thing she had expected when she had stepped into his car two hours ago. How had she managed to misread the situation so completely?

Victor gave her a dry look. 'You must be the first person in history who gets an enormous pay rise and immediately assumes that there's a hidden agenda behind it. I'm giving you a rise because you're a damned good worker, very committed to your job, and it's a sign of appreciation. Is that straightforward enough for you?'

He sounded amused by her reaction. Amused, too, by any passing thought that there was something suspicious about his action.

'Yes, I suppose it is,' Alice told him doubtfully. She

just couldn't think this thing through. She was certain that if she could she would see that there was more to this act of generosity than met the eye.

'It *has* been quite a while since your salary was reviewed,' Victor said casually, reading her mind. He strolled across to her with the bottle of port in his hand and she didn't even bother to protest when he tipped some in her glass. After all, she was celebrating, wasn't she?

'Was that all you wanted to discuss with me?' she asked, masking a hiccup with a cough.

'Wouldn't you say that it was enough?' He hadn't moved from where he was, deliciously close, even if she *did* have to crane her neck to look at him, which didn't feel altogether good for her head.

'You're making me dizzy, hovering over me like that,' Alice told him, but instead of moving away he stooped down in front of her.

'This better?'

Better? Well, she didn't have to tilt her head now at a ninety-degree angle, but her breathing suddenly took a nosedive. She began reminding herself that she was his secretary, a grown woman and not some silly adolescent, but she lost the thought even before it began.

'I should be going.'

'You haven't got around to drinking your coffee.'

'Oh, no. I forgot.' She giggled a little hysterically at that, and then over-compensated by frowning very hard at him. In the mellow light, she could make out every nuance of his face. Her eyes seemed to be glued to him.

'Are you feeling all right?' he asked, in response, she thought, to her bizarre and inappropriate behaviour.

'Absolutely. Never felt better.'

'You're not accustomed to drink, are you?'

'No. I never drink because I'm terribly boring and

spend all my evenings at home with mugs of hot chocolate, watching television.'

'Don't put words into my mouth.' But he smiled when he said that, a slow, very focused smile.

'I drink now and again, but I always think it's rather sad to stay in on one's own with a bottle of cheap wine for company.'

'It needn't necessarily be cheap.'

That, for some reason, struck her as very profound. 'Yes,' she told him gravely. 'That would make all the difference. It would be quite all right to stay at home with a bottle of expensive wine for company.'

'Ah. Now you've got the picture.' The silence that followed this remark was so pronounced that Alice could almost hear the muscles in her stomach clench and unclench. He was so close to her. Her breathing was shallow and she had to close her eyes in order to avoid passing out altogether.

So she didn't see him as he leaned over her in the chair, supporting himself with his hands on either side. She just felt him, his mouth hungrily on hers, his tongue insistent inside her mouth, pushing her back into the chair. And she sighed and returned the kiss without holding back.

CHAPTER EIGHT

WELL, what the heck? That was the only thought that ran through Alice's head as she slid her arms up around Victor's neck, tilting her body to accommodate his questing mouth. She slid a bit further down the chair and he scooped her up in one easy movement, transporting her to the sofa, with her arms still around him. She had her eyes closed and underneath her shirt she could feel her breasts throbbing in anticipation of his touch.

It had been such a long time since James. In fact, she had forgotten how she had felt with him and whatever memories she had had were jaded now by his reappearance on the scene. It was as though the present had superimposed itself on the past, so that she could no longer remember the thrill of being with him without thinking of the disappointment of seeing him again.

Underneath her, the sofa was as comfortable as a small bed. It was very large and soft and Victor had dispensed with the ornamental cushions, creating more space for them both.

Alice propped herself up at the top, squashing her head against one of the cushions which weren't lying on the floor, hardly daring to open her eyes in case the spell, whatever weird spell it was, was broken.

She did open them, though, when the pressure of his mouth left hers and she became aware that he was looking down at her, his face inches away from hers.

'Are you sure that you want to be here?' he asked, and she half-smiled, thinking what an unfair question that was. How could he now hold out a choice to her when her body was at the point of no return? She drowsily looked at him.

'Here as opposed to where?' she asked.

'As opposed to upstairs, in my bedroom, on my bed?'

'You have a very comfortable sofa. Was it bought with this in mind?'

'As opposed, even, to in a taxi on the way back to your flat, a little worse for wine.'

Alice didn't answer. She pulled him back down towards her, parting her legs on either side of him and having to wriggle a bit to accomplish that because her skirt was not designed for that particular manoeuvre.

She groaned as he began kissing her again, on her lips, her face, her neck, tickling her ear with his tongue. He gently pulled her head back, his hands coiled into her hair, and her breath skipped a beat as he traced the contours of her collar bone with his tongue.

She vaguely thought that this was indeed the wet and slippery path to ruin, but even if her mind was weakly pointing that out her body was way past caring.

Her shirt was done up at the front, and he continued kissing her while he expertly undid the buttons, brushing open the shirt. He tugged it free of the waistband of her skirt, and unclasped her bra at the front.

She hardly needed to wear a bra at all. It wasn't as though her breasts were so big that they needed containing. A memory rose to the surface, something that she hadn't thought about for years. When James had touched her for the first time, he had told her, more with surprise than with criticism, that she was the first woman he had ever been attracted to whose breasts weren't big.

'I'm not exactly a D cup,' she heard herself saying, in an apologetic voice, and Victor raised his head to look at her.

'Since when did that ever matter?'

'You don't mind?'

'I'm not as shallow as you seem to think, when it comes to the opposite sex.' As if to prove his point, he lowered his head and took one nipple into his mouth, teasing it with his tongue, then covering the large, dark area with his mouth, sucking hard until Alice felt that she would faint from the sheer, erotic pleasure coursing through her body.

She felt like a virgin. Every touch, every caress seemed new to her. Except there was nothing shy about her response to him. She wanted him as she had never wanted anyone in her life before. He eclipsed every kiss, every touch she had ever had.

'Take your clothes off,' he murmured raggedly, drawing himself up so that he could remove his shirt, then standing up to free himself of the rest of his clothes.

Alice was mesmerised. There had been such unspoken but defined barriers between them, they had worked for so long together without sex interfering with the relationship, that to see him standing in front of her now was a revelation.

He walked across the room to switch off the overhead light, turning on two table-lamps instead, and she watched the graceful movements of his body, fascinated by the smooth, hard lines of his torso.

The sight of him aroused such an intense response in her that she was almost frightened by it. She dimly recalled that it had been different with James. She had always viewed his arrivals with excitement, but she had not craved him during his absences, although she had missed those feelings of excitement. With James too, sex had tended to be a hurried, sweaty affair, a torrid rush of desire that was over virtually before it began, and because he had been her first lover she had assumed that that was simply how it was meant to be.

There was nothing rushed about this. He approached the sofa, amused by her transfixed inspection of him. She shrugged herself out of her skirt and bra, still looking at him, loving the way his eyes could make her feel vulnerable and wanton both at the same time.

The remnants of her tan were still visible and her breasts were white in comparison with the faint gold of her stomach and legs.

Her skirt, one of her many sensible buys, which could automatically put her in a working frame of mind, now felt like an irritating encumbrance, and she quickly undid the button at the back and pulled down the zip, wriggling to get out of it.

When she began to remove her tights, he pushed her hands away and did the job himself until she was lying there, unclothed apart from her lacy underwear.

The effect of undressing was to dispel any hint of tipsiness. She felt as sober as a judge. But instead of this catapulting her back to the cold light of reason it had the opposite effect. She wanted him. Never mind common sense. Need, desire and curiosity had merged into something over which she made no attempt to have any control. For the past few years, no man had awakened anything remotely resembling sexual attraction in her, and what she felt now was too overwhelming to rise above.

He parted her legs, lowering himself above her, and leisurely explored her body with his mouth and hands, tasting the curve of her breasts, rubbing his thumbs against the sensitive buds, flicking his tongue over them until she wanted to scream. The only evidence that he was as urgently in need of fulfilment as she was was his hardness, which brushed against her as he moved to explore her stomach, down to her navel.

His hands smoothed against her thighs, tracing the elastic of her underwear, and his fingers slid inside, brushing against her. Very gradually, he pulled down her underwear, and she gasped as his tongue sought out her moist feminine nub. She writhed and moaned, finding it difficult to contain her need to be satisfied, and eventually she had to pull him away. He waited until her breathing settled, then returned to what he had been doing, and when she was afraid that she would have to urge him away again he thrust inside her, long, rhythmic movements that brought her to a shuddering climax.

How long was he lying on her before either one of them said a word? It felt like a lifetime, but it could only have been a matter of minutes. The really strange thing was that here, in this room, time seemed to have stopped completely.

She suddenly felt exhausted. 'I think I might go to sleep if I stay here much longer,' she said, suppressing a yawn.

'I hope that isn't a comment on my masculine appeal,' he said softly, with lazy teasing in his voice. He stroked her hair away from her face and regarded her.

'I think it's a comment on the amount I've drunk this evening. It seems to be suddenly catching up on me.' She rubbed her eyes with the backs of her fingers. 'I really must get going.'

'Why?'

'Why?' What kind of a question was that? she asked herself. 'Because my bed is waiting for me.' She began levering herself up and he pushed her back down.

'My bed is far more convenient,' he murmured, nuzzling against her neck so that suddenly visions of a taxi ride back, then her own bedroom and her cold little bed, began to seem unappealing.

'No! Stop!' She laughed and pushed him away, standing up and putting on her clothes in a random fashion.

He sat up and donned his trousers, omitting to buckle the belt, which hung down on both sides and lent him a rakish, appropriately just-got-out-of-bed look. 'It doesn't make any sense your going back to your place when you could stay here,' he pointed out.

But it *did* make sense. Somewhere at the very back of her mind, the thought of staying the night suggested something, to her, that went way beyond the bounds of mere physical contact. It suggested an intimacy that unsettled her. It suggested the laying down of a relationship. At least, to her it did. To him, it suggested, she thought, nothing at all. Nothing beyond convenience.

She ignored further reasoning on his part that the easiest option, especially considering that she was now virtually falling asleep on her feet, was to remain with him. She telephoned a taxi to collect her within the next half an hour, and she then made sure that she stayed on her feet. She didn't want to get too comfortable sitting anywhere because she did not want Victor to persuade her to his way of thinking. He was too manipulative like that by half.

'This is all very unorthodox, isn't it?' she said, nervously drinking the cup of coffee he had made for her and wondering, as her logical thought processes began to filter back into life, what exactly happened now.

'Highly.' He strolled across to where she was standing and leant over her, propping himself up by resting his hands on either side of her on the kitchen counter. 'But pleasurable.' He used one finger to deflect the cup of coffee away from in front of her and kissed her on her mouth. 'I've been wanting to make love to you for a while.'

'I don't believe you,' Alice informed him. If there was one thing she had learnt from James, it was a basic mistrust of what men said when they were under the influence of physical attraction.

'Don't be so cynical,' he murmured.

'I'm way too old for romance.'

'So am I.'

Alice afforded him a long, hard look. 'So, in other words, this is just about sex.'

'*Just* about sex? You make it sound as though sex is no more than a passing bodily function. Like sneezing.' He laughed softly and kissed her again, this time harder but already alarm bells were beginning to ring in her head. He might not have used charm to butter her up, but wasn't the net result the same thing? Bed? He had simply bypassed the courting routine, but that didn't make him any more sincere than James had been.

Not, she thought, that she was looking for anything beyond the physical. She might not be too old for romance, but she was certainly too jaded for it.

'The taxi's going to be here in a minute,' she protested as he shifted his position, moving his hands underneath her jacket to cup her breasts. She reached around to deposit the cup of coffee on the counter and placed both her hands over his. 'Am I going to be able to continue working for you?' she asked flatly.

He rubbed her nipples through her bra and she could feel them hardening in response, could feel her breathing quicken.

'Well, you've just got a pay rise. Why on earth would you want to look for another job?' He unbuttoned the top three buttons of her shirt and slipped his hands under her bra, pushing it up so that her breasts were exposed.

'Victor, please.'

'Happy to oblige.' He lifted her up onto the counter so that she was sitting, and unbuttoned her shirt completely, pushing up her bra further and bending to circle one pulsing nipple with his mouth. She felt the wetness of his tongue and leaned back, arching and pressing his head down. *This isn't what I meant!* The thought struggled against the pleasurable sensation of his teeth, nipping against her aroused breasts. How could she think coherently when he was there, suckling her breasts, while his hand explored her through her underwear?

'We need to talk…' She gasped as his fingers, rubbing against her, began moving harder and faster. 'No…!'

'Yes!' He raised his head. 'Open your eyes and look at me.'

Alice opened her eyes but it was a massive effort. She could feel her body tightening in response to what he was doing. She cupped her breasts with her hands, massaging them, and released a sharp, whistling sigh as he brought her to the brink and beyond.

There was a knock on the door, and she pushed him aside, jumping off the counter and frantically rearranging herself into some semblance of order.

There were questions that she had meant to ask. He had diverted her, and she had allowed herself to be sidetracked, and it was too late now to voice any of them. She grabbed her bag and was about to pull open the door when he put his hand over hers.

'Work as usual,' he said lazily, raising one eyebrow as though anticipating some disagreement on her part.

'As usual.' Alice tilted her head to him, and he bent over quickly, covering her mouth with his, then opened the door to the taxi-driver, who was tapping his feet impatiently and who, as soon as he saw them, gave a knowing grin. Alice decided that she wouldn't leave him a tip.

But things were not back to usual. In fact, over the next fortnight, she felt as though she had stepped out of reality and was floating in some other hemisphere.

On the face of it, they continued to work as efficiently together as they ever had, but there was an electric atmosphere between them. She could feel his eyes on her every time she sat in front of him, with her head lowered, jotting in her notepad. She could feel the current running between them every time his hand brushed against her in passing. And she was sure that he could feel it as well. The days were spent in an atmosphere of restless excitement and the nights were spent fulfilling it.

But where was it all leading? She never asked and he never volunteered a suggestion. Permanence was a topic that she knew, instinctively, she had to skirt around.

And that's fine, she told herself now, sitting lethargically in front of the television. It was the first night of lethargic sitting she had done in a fortnight and she missed him.

I miss him. The thought revolved in her head like a swarm of bees suddenly let loose from their hive. She switched down the volume of the television, so that the dreary soap opera was reduced to silence, and in the silence her brain finally supplied the information which she had been hiding from for weeks, months, for ever.

I've fallen in love, she thought with dismay. She should have seen it coming, but she hadn't. She had been so complacently sure that her emotions were locked away inside her behind some mysterious door which she could open and shut at will that the realisation made her heady with shock.

When had it happened? When had her heart stolen out of its cage and surrendered itself to Victor Temple?

She placed her half-empty mug of coffee gingerly on the table in front of her while her mind grappled with the implications.

To be attracted to Victor Temple was one thing. That was understandable. He was a dynamic, witty, intelligent man. She might well have lacked foresight in letting herself succumb to the physical urges inside her, but she was only human after all.

But love? Well, love was different. Love sent down roots, love required commitment or else it was meaningless, and he didn't love her. He teased her, he talked to her, he made love to her, but he wasn't in love with her. In fact, the word had never once crossed his lips, not even at the very height of passion.

She began to pace through the room with her arms folded protectively across her breasts. She could feel her nails biting into her skin, and forced herself to relax. But she couldn't relax. If she were to take her temperature now, she was sure that she would be running a high fever, because she felt so hot all over.

It had never been like this with James. With James, she had been young, vulnerable, in love with the idea of being in love. But this…this was like a bolt of lightning struck into the core of her. She didn't *want* to be in love, at least not with Victor Temple. She just *was*, and love carried its consequences. She wouldn't be able to retreat from the relationship a little bit dented but more or else in one piece. She would retreat wounded, fatally wounded, and the longer she allowed the situation to continue, the more hurt she was building for herself.

Of course, she could, she acknowledged, continue with things the way they were, and hope that in time, if time was on her side, Victor would eventually be ensnared, just as she was; but the prospect of that happening was so minuscule that it wasn't even worth thinking about.

'I have to do something about this.' She realised that she had actually spoken the words out loud. Thank goodness Vanessa wasn't around. She had always maintained that talking to yourself was the first sign of madness.

There was, she forced herself to admit, only one thing she could do. Leave. It wouldn't be enough to try and wriggle out of the relationship, because he would wonder why and she didn't want him to press her on the subject. She didn't want him to suspect, even for a moment, that she was far more heavily involved than he was. Also, she doubted that any woman had ever walked out on him, and he might just see that as a challenge to be overcome.

No, she would have to get herself sacked, and there was only one sure-fire way to do that, wasn't there? She had seen quite a bit of James recently—he seemed to spend all of his free time in pursuit of Vanessa.

The thought of Victor sacking her because of a false assumption made her feel slightly ill, but what else was there to do? How else could she extricate herself from the situation? She would thank herself for the decision in the years to come, she was sure of it, but just now the prospect of life without Victor was like staring into a bottomless abyss, devoid of light.

She waited up until eleven-thirty, when James and Vanessa returned, even though she had been dying to go to bed hours earlier.

'You're up!' Vanessa had had too much to drink. Alice could recognise that give-away brilliance in her eyes and the over-heartiness of her voice.

'By the skin of my teeth.' Alice yawned broadly and looked at the two of them. No date had been set for a wedding as yet, but it wouldn't be long, she was sure of it. There was already a cosy familiarity between them that spoke of contented domesticity on the not too distant horizon. Wasn't it amazing how things worked out? On paper, James and Vanessa would have appeared hideously mismatched. She had always thought that he would need someone to pamper him and Vanessa was the sort of girl who would guffaw with laughter at the thought of pampering a man, yet here they were, like two drifting souls destined to meet and spend their lives together.

'I wanted to have a chat with the two of you,' she said cautiously. Years of emotional reticence made it difficult for her to pour out her feelings, but she needed to be as straight with them as she could because she needed their help.

'Oh, God.' James sat down on the chair opposite her and stretched out his legs onto the coffee table.

'Off!' Vanessa prodded his feet with hers. 'This isn't a doss-house, James. Put your feet on the ground, where they belong.'

He groaned in a good-natured way and gave her an adoring look from under his lashes.

'Spit it out, Ali,' Vanessa said, sitting down next to her.

'I have a problem.' She paused and thought about what to say next but was saved the trouble by Vanessa asking her whether the problem was in any way linked to all her nights out recently.

'You could say. I've been seeing someone...' she said awkwardly.

'Victor Temple,' James announced smugly. And when she looked at him in surprise he continued comfortably, 'I could tell when I saw the two of you together that there was something going on.' He was virtually crow-ing at this point. 'I am,' he informed Vanessa, 'a very sensitive kind of guy.'

'You're as sensitive as a bag of potatoes,' Vanessa said absent-mindedly, looking at Alice. 'Is that true? You've been seeing your *boss*?'

'And it needs to finish.' Alice lowered her eyes because she didn't want them to see the misery in them at the thought of that.

'Why?' Vanessa sounded truly bewildered at that line of logic. 'He seems a pretty good catch to me.' She looked at Alice and then nodded slowly. 'Ah, I get it.'

'Get what?' James asked.

'I thought,' Vanessa informed him, 'that you were such a sensitive kind of guy?'

'It's a talent that comes and goes.'

'How can we help?'

'It's no good,' Alice said, treading cautiously around the full truth, 'trying to break it off without an explanation. You don't know Victor, but he wouldn't fall for that, and it would be awkward anyway because I work for him.'

'Then just leave,' James told her. 'There are other jobs around. I'm sure I could rustle you up something in one of my companies. You'd be a damned sight better than me.'

'You're telling me,' Vanessa said, looking at him affectionately. 'It's a good thing you were born with a silver spoon in your mouth because you sure as hell wouldn't have been able to put one there yourself.'

'I'll rise above that.' He looked at Alice questioningly. 'So what do you want us to do?'

'Just you, actually,' Alice said, looking at him. A few months ago the thought of James Claydon had been enough to fill her with sickening bitterness. Now here she was, asking a favour of him. Whoever said that fact was stranger than fiction had certainly hit the nail on the head. 'I want him to see the two of us together...'

'And fly into a jealous fit.' James nodded sagely.

Alice gave a short laugh. 'Fat chance. No, I want him to sack me and if he sees the two of us together he'll do just that.' It was a line of reasoning that was clearly way above James's head, but he nodded in an obliging manner.

'I'd have to get the okay from my wife-to-be,' he said, glancing at Vanessa, who told him that she wasn't going to stand in the way of progress, and besides, what was it with this *wife-to-be* remark?

An hour later they had planned the eradication, Alice thought unhappily, of all prospect of future happiness for her. She lay in bed and kept reminding herself that it was for the best, that she'd be a fool to do otherwise, that this was the best and only way out for her.

The plan involved Victor accidentally seeing her and James together in some sort of compromising situation. An embrace of kinds. She knew where he was going to be on what night, because she kept track of his diary, and the date was set for the following evening. He would be taking two clients to a play in the West End. She even knew where he would be sitting because she had booked the tickets. In the morning, she would book two tickets for a couple of seats three or four rows in front of him. All James would have to do would be to sling his arm behind her. Victor's imagination, she knew, would supply the rest.

'You could be making a big mistake,' Vanessa told her the following morning. 'You could have misread the situation entirely. You *could* be blowing the biggest thing in your life.'

'And pigs might fly,' Alice said glumly. She felt close to tears. What was she going to do with the rest of her life now? Exist. Every man who came into her life—and her track record promised few—would be compared and found wanting. She tried to hate him for turning her life on its head and found that she couldn't.

And at work he noticed the difference in her, even though she tried her hardest to act as naturally as she could.

'Okay,' he said at five-thirty, shutting the office door, 'so what's wrong?'

'Wrong?' She raised her eyes to his and smiled innocently. She was logging off the computer, and she looked away and began tidying her desk with slow, exaggerated meticulousness. 'It's the time of the month,' she sighed, hitting on a brilliant excuse with relief.

'Oh, is that right?' He hovered over her, looking unconvinced, and she smiled reassuringly at him. Men, she had always heard, tended to back away from Women's Problems. Ask too many questions and they seemed to think that they would be assailed by all manner of hair-raising details, a bit like being attacked by the contents of Pandora's box. Victor was no exception. He brushed the side of her cheek with his finger and smiled. 'In that case, I hope you're back to yourself tomorrow. I've booked a splendid restaurant in Fulham. If I could cancel tonight, I would. The thought of spending the evening with clients when I could be spending it with you...' He gave a deep-throated, velvety laugh that made the hairs on the back of her neck stand on end.

'I know,' Alice said with a mixture of heartfelt comprehension and sadness. 'Still...' She stood up and they walked together to the lift, taking their separate routes once they were outside the building.

She had under two hours to get back to the flat, get dressed and make it to the theatre in time to take her seat there next to James before Victor arrived. She didn't want to have to run the gauntlet by arriving later than him, and she guessed, anyway, that he wouldn't notice her presence there immediately because he wouldn't be expecting to see her there. He would notice when his attention to what was going on on-stage began to wander.

She put a great deal of thought into what she was going to wear, with a little help from Vanessa, who repeatedly said that she thought it was a stupid plan.

'You're in love with the guy,' she grumbled, sitting on the bed while Alice got dressed. 'Enjoy it for what it's worth and take each day as it comes.'

'I just haven't got that kind of sanguine mentality,' Alice said, slipping on the black dress which was little enough to be provocative, but not so little that nothing was left to the imagination. It clung to her body like a well-fitting glove and, once done up, the zip, which was at the front and ran from neck to waist, accentuated her breasts and the smallness of her waist. She turned to face Vanessa. 'If I stayed with things the way they were, I'd spend the entire time waiting for the axe to fall. I'd torture myself by worrying over every little word he said, wondering if any of it indicated something beyond sexual attraction. I'd be miserable.'

'You're miserable now,' Vanessa pointed out reasonably.

'I'd be even more miserable.' She shoved her feet into shoes which were too high for comfort and thanked the Lord that she wouldn't have to do much walking in them. Then she sat at the dressing-table and very carefully applied her make-up. In the background she could hear Vanessa chatting, but her mind had already leapt forward and she was envisaging how Victor would react when he saw her with James.

She managed to make it to the theatre with time to

kill, and James, who had dressed for the part in such great style that he was very nearly a caricature, arrived five minutes later.

'I know it's all an act, James,' Alice said, standing back and inspecting him, 'but aren't you taking it a bit far?' Dark trousers, red and cream striped shirt, dark bow-tie, cream jacket, and, of all improbable things, a cream hat which she made him promise not to put on.

'Just doing things properly,' he complained. 'Has he arrived yet?'

'No, so we'd better get to our seats quickly before he does. I don't actually want to face him. I just want him to glimpse us together and draw his conclusions without any input from me.'

James shrugged and they made their way through the crowd, which was growing by the minute, to their seats, which were among the best in the house.

As she passed the three seats which she had reserved for Victor and his clients weeks ago, she risked a quick glance. He wasn't there. For a minute she felt a brief surge of panic, thinking that he might not turn up at all, that the charade would have all been for nothing, and then reminded herself that he would be there at the very last minute. Right now, he was probably downing a gin and tonic, talking shop and steeling himself for the musical. He hated musicals but had given in to her advice that Americans loved them and the last thing they would see as great entertainment would be a weighty, depressing play involving two characters and no change of scenery.

She stared fixedly ahead of her, barely answering James, and as the lights were dowsed and the curtain raised she almost jumped when she felt his arm around her at the back of the seat.

'You can rest your head on my shoulder if you like,' he whispered half an hour later. 'Verisimilitude.'

'That's a big word for you, James,' she whispered back. 'When did you reach V in the dictionary?'

'Cute.' He squeezed her shoulder in a brotherly manner and so they remained sitting, right through the interval, because Alice was terrified of standing up and seeing Victor face to face, and through the second half of the play. She would have to face him, of course, in the morning when she went in to work, but at least then she would have had a night to prepare herself for the ordeal.

'I think,' James whispered in her ear as the musical drew to a close, 'that we should leave slightly ahead of everyone. That way he can't fail to see us, just in case he hasn't already.'

'Okay.' But she was so nervous when they stood up and began shuffling their way out to the aisle that she almost fainted. She linked her arm through James's, more as support than as a way of feigning a relationship, and kept her eyes very firmly averted from the seats four rows behind them.

Outside, they parted company with heartfelt thanks on her part and a wry smile on James's, who said, with embarrassed sincerity, that he hoped their slate was now wiped clean.

It can never be clean, Alice thought, but it's a lot less grubby than it once was, and that has only a bit to do with tonight.

She took a taxi back to her place, and spent the night in a state of restlessness, only managing to fall asleep in the early hours of the morning, and, to her horror, completely sleeping through her alarm.

So that when she arrived at work the following morning she was flustered, apprehensive and, as she stepped into her office, gut-wrenchingly sick at the thought of confronting the man who was standing by her desk, hands in pockets and with a look on his face that would have sent hell into a deep freeze.

CHAPTER NINE

'I'M LATE. I'm sorry.' Alice couldn't quite manage a smile, so instead she busied herself hanging up her jacket, while she mentally steeled herself for what lay ahead. Now was the time to find out just how good an actress she was and she kept her fingers crossed that she would be in the Oscar-winning league. She was not supposed to know that she had been seen the evening before at the theatre in the company of James. She was not to know that she would be sacked. Her back was turned, but she could feel Victor's eyes on her, boring through her, and she had an insane desire to remain where she was, standing with her back turned in front of the coat rail, for the remainder of the day.

'I slept through my alarm,' she said, reluctantly turning around. 'I must have been more exhausted than I thought when I went to bed last night.'

The grey eyes that surveyed her were icy cold.

'Could you come into my office?'

'Of course.' She watched as he walked away from her desk into his office, and then followed more fiddling around while she gathered her notepad and pen together, switched on her computer, tried to get herself under control. She could feel her heart thudding against her ribcage, and for the first time she wondered whether she had done the right thing. What if she had carried on, holding her love inside her, waiting and hoping? Too late now, of course.

'Shut the door behind you,' he said, as soon as she walked in, and she clicked the door closed. Her movements felt heavy and laboured and she had to force her legs to carry her to the chair facing him.

'And you can put the notepad away. It won't be necessary.'

Alice stretched out, rested the pad and pen on the desk and then sat back with her fingers on her lap, entwined. Then she looked at him. It occurred to her that she would be seeing him for the last time and once that thought took root it began gnawing its way through her brain.

'You don't seem to be in the best of moods,' she said, because it would have been unnatural not to have commented on what was patently obvious. 'How did last night go with the clients? Did you manage to persuade them to commission you for their advertising campaign?'

'Last night was awful.' He folded his arms and sat back in the chair, a small shift of position that somehow managed to distance him from her even more. Body language could be powerfully informing. She now felt as though she was looking at a stranger, someone who had drawn down the shutters on every personal aspect of himself. 'Where were you last night?'

'Where was…I?' She frowned as though giving the matter some thought. 'Oh, yes. At the theatre. A dreary musical, I'm afraid. What was yours like? You did go to see *The Angel Rising*, didn't you?' She knew that he hadn't. The pretence was beginning to exhaust her and for a moment she just wanted to rest her arms on the desk, bury her head in them, and fall asleep. Preferably for a thousand years.

'No. I didn't. I went to the same show as you did, and don't even attempt to lie to me, because I saw you there.'

Alice allowed silence to speak on her behalf.

'Lost for words, Alice?' His mouth twisted cynically, and Alice could feel herself inwardly flinch. Even though his face was unreadable, she could sense a pool of fury swirling around inside him, kept at bay by the sheer force of his self-control.

The telephone rang, and he snatched up the receiver and told whoever was at the other end that he would not be taking any calls until further notice. All the time, his eyes remained glued to her face.

'I...I...'

'Yes?'

'I suppose you're going to tell me that you saw me with James Claydon.' There. She had said it. There was no point in beating about the bush anyway. She didn't even have to feign the catch in her throat, or the reddening in her cheeks. They were as real as the feelings of nausea coursing through her.

'What the hell do you think you're playing at?'

'I don't feel that I have to explain myself to you,' she said, with an attempt at bravado. She tried to pretend that someone else was sitting in front of her, someone who had no right to question her actions, someone to whom she could respond with self-righteous indignation at an intrusion into her personal life.

'Oh, but you're wrong,' he said, in a menacingly soft voice. 'You're going to explain yourself very fully to me and you're not going to stop until I tell you to.'

'Or else what, Victor? We're not children in a playground. You can't bully me.'

'What were you doing with that man?'

'I told you, we went to the theatre. I didn't see the harm in that and I wouldn't have made the arrangement if you hadn't been occupied yourself.'

'So while the cat's away...? Is that it?' There was contempt in his voice which she pretended not to notice. 'Answer me!' he shouted, when she didn't say anything.

'I don't understand what the problem is! We don't

own one another!' Her own voice had risen as well. She could feel her body trembling and if she could have she would have rushed out of the office, but she had to stick it out.

'Are you saying what I think you are?'

'I realise that you don't approve of James, but...'

'I'm beginning to understand.' He subjected her to a long, scathing look that was full of dislike. 'I think I'm beginning to get the picture. What's the matter, Alice? Did you think that he might have been losing interest?'

'What?' This leap in logic was so incomprehensible that she stared at him in bewilderment.

'There's no need to give me that butter-wouldn't-melt-in-your-mouth look. When did it all start with Claydon? When did you two sleep together for the first time? Was it at Highfield House?'

How ironic, she thought. He was absolutely right, but in a way that he could never have imagined.

'Yes, I've slept with James, and yes, it was at Highfield House.' She heard herself admitting it and the bond between them, which had been unravelling, was now finally severed. She had told him the truth, but the truth was not what he thought.

'I see.'

No, you don't. How can you? If you could see anything at all, then you'd see that I'm hopelessly in love with you, you'd see that I don't want to be sitting here allowing you to believe the worst of me, you'd see that you're the only man I've ever given my heart to.

'What happened, Alice? Did he start losing interest once he'd got you into bed?' He didn't wait for her to answer. He carried on, his voice heavy with undisguised disgust. 'Is that when you decided to cultivate me so that you could make him jealous?'

'What?' The suggestion was so absurd that she wondered whether she was hearing properly.

'Shocked at the accusation, are you?' He leaned forward and even though the width of his desk was separating them Alice still instinctively drew back into her chair. He looked as though he wanted to kill her.

She stared at him speechlessly, knowing that whatever conclusions he reached about her would be wrong anyway, so why try and selectively correct a few of them?

'Or perhaps you're just shocked that I managed to get to the heart of your seedy little game. Because that's what it was, wasn't it? A seedy little game played out by a manipulative little schemer. You must have thought that either way you couldn't lose. If Claydon decided that he didn't want you, then there was always me to fall back on. After all, you were sleeping with two men. Law of averages would dictate that one might turn up trumps.' He banged his fist on the table, and she jumped. 'I could quite happily strangle you!'

'Why? Because your pride's been pricked?' She could feel the tears coming to her eyes and she blinked them back. 'You think that I'm a schemer...'

'Are you going to deny it?'

'What would be the point? You think I manipulated you, but don't tell me that you didn't use me as well! You were more than happy to make love to me, but that was all it meant to you, wasn't it? If you're so keen on the truth, why not admit your own truth? Why not admit that you would have discarded me without a backward glance the minute you got sick of me?' Her face was burning, and she was shouting too. Thank heavens, she thought, that both doors to his office were shut. This sort of argument would be grist to the office mill, They had handled their brief fling discreetly and this shouting match would have been manna from heaven for the office gossips.

'When did you decide to put me in the picture?' He began toying with the pen on his desk.

'What do you mean?'

'I mean—' he tapped the pen forcefully once and dropped it '—when did you decide to rope me into your little game? Was it when I showed an interest in you?'

'Don't be ridiculous,' she muttered under her breath. She was perspiring, as though she'd just finished a long run.

'Was James the catch? Or was it supposed to be me?' He looked at her narrowly and she found that she couldn't meet his gaze. Of course, she thought, he would naturally assume that she was eaten with guilt at the truth of what he was saying, but since she couldn't deny anything she allowed herself to be miserably and helplessly carried along with the tide. It was small comfort to know that, although this might well turn out to be the longest day in her life, a day was still a day in the scheme of things. It would end.

'It's not like you to forget which play I would be going to see,' he mused in a voice that could cut glass. 'Not like you at all. Perhaps I've got it all wrong. Perhaps you'd hoped that I *would* see you at the theatre. See you and react by wanting you more. Was that it?'

'You're wrong.' That much was the truth at any rate, and he must have read the sincerity on her face because he flushed with sudden anger at her denial. 'Look, please could I go now?'

'Go? *Go?*' He made that sound as though she'd asked for a ticket to the moon. 'I'm not nearly through with you yet. You're not leaving here until this thing has been explained. You're not walking away and leaving any unfinished business on my hands!'

'You can't make me stay!' Alice protested, but her voice lacked conviction. If he had any sense at all, she thought, he would realise the power he had over her simply because of that one fact. If he'd meant nothing, she would have walked out. Couldn't he *see* that?

'Where did the lies end and the truth begin, Alice?'

If she hadn't known better, she would have imagined that he was being reasonable. His voice was certainly reasonable enough. But his face, an icy mask, belied the impression.

She didn't say anything.

'Is your mother really dead?' he asked, with insulting calm. 'Was that house really where you lived or was that all part of the sweetness-and-light act you were trying to cultivate?'

She found that she was gripping the arms of the chair. 'How can you think that I would lie about something like that?' she asked huskily.

He ignored her question. 'And were you little Miss Untouched, deep-frozen for years? Or did you just think that I would fall a little harder for that line?'

'I don't have to answer your questions!' Still, though, she remained glued to the chair, agonisingly wounded by the barrage of insinuations but even more agonisingly terrified by the prospect of leaving him behind for ever. She fleetingly wondered whether she should just confess everything, confess how much she loved him, put an end to this ridiculous charade, but the thought of that was even more horrifying. He would strip her of everything if she did that. Besides, at this late stage, who knew? He would probably see it as just another desperate ploy to try and capture his interest. She had burnt her bridges and there was no point in trying to rebuild them. They were beyond salvation.

'There's one thing I absolutely cannot stand and do you know what that is?'

Rhetorical question, Alice thought, not even attempting to formulate a reply. She nervously tucked her hair behind her ears and looked at him.

'Schemers. Women who plot and plan and lie and cheat.' He picked the fountain pen up and tapped it sharply on his desk. 'I just can't believe that I was taken in by someone of your ilk.'

'I'm sorry,' Alice said, apologising for everything, all the things that she couldn't tell him.

'Well, that's all right, then,' he said coldly. 'That makes me feel a hell of a lot better.'

'That's what bothers you most, isn't it?' she asked quietly. 'Not the fact that you won't see me again but the fact that you think that you were duped.'

'*Think* that I was duped?' He leaned forward and she thanked God that the width of the desk separated them. 'Are you going to try and tell me that I was wrong? That I *didn't* see you arm in arm with Claydon? After you admitted that you slept with the man?'

'No, I guess not,' she said on a miserable sigh.

'Well, he's welcome to you. And to think that I was stupid enough to try and warn you about him.'

Without warning me about you in the same breath, she thought.

'You know that you're out, I presume.'

Alice nodded. So they had got there in the end. It seemed to have taken for ever. She knew that she would spend the rest of her life remembering this conversation in all its dreadful detail. Every word, every sentence, every look. Relive it all and for ever wonder what might have happened if she had taken a different turning.

'Will you want me to work out my notice?' It was

asked in a dull voice and simply for formality's sake.
She knew what he would say.

'You can pack your things as soon as you leave this
office. I'll have Personnel forward your outstanding
pay.'

'Fine.' She stood up and realised that her limbs felt
like lead weights and yet were barely able to support
her. She couldn't meet his eyes but she forced herself to
look at him. One last time.

'I know you won't believe me, but you'll never know
how sorry I am that...' She sighed, looked away and
moved towards the door. She almost expected him to
stop her in her tracks. She would have welcomed it,
welcomed the few moments' reprieve from the black
void now awaiting her, but he didn't say anything, and
as she opened the door she could hear him dialling out
on the phone. All things back to normal. Work to carry
on as though nothing had happened. He might think
about her for a day or two, wonder how someone as
experienced as he was with the opposite sex could ever
have found himself outmanoeuvred by her, and then she
would be replaced. In time, the memory of her would
be filled with bitterness and distaste. The same bitterness
and distaste that had filled her after her fling with James
had come to its painful end, except that he would never
let thoughts of her influence his life.

She packed her few belongings quickly and quietly.
On her last birthday, he had given her a paperweight,
which she always kept on her desk, and after a moment's
hesitation she stuck it into her bag. It would be one piece
of proof that he had existed, something to bolster her
memories.

She didn't stop to talk to anyone on the way out. She
knew that her distress was on her face, apparent for all
to see, but she was leaving the place behind and she

found that she didn't care what people speculated about her sudden departure. There would be quite a few who would be thrilled at her sacking. She knew that she had been the object of jealousy amongst some of the older hands, who had been there for a while and had seen her position of trust with Victor as something which they had been denied.

She kept going for the rest of the day, on automatic, or so it seemed. Her body carried on while her mind travelled along a different route.

She thought that she had managed to acquire some of her self-control back by the time Vanessa and James returned to the flat at a little after ten that evening, but as soon as James faced her and asked whether it had worked she burst into tears. Heaving sobs that wrenched her body and were unstoppable. When she next raised her face, it was to find that James had vanished, and Vanessa was sitting on the sofa next to her.

'I'm sorry,' Alice said, sniffing and accepting the paper towel which had been thrust into her hands. 'I've spoilt your evening.'

'You poor, poor thing. Don't be absurd.' Vanessa gave her a weak smile and a brief hug.

'Has James gone?'

'Yes. But don't say a word about being sorry.' She paused. 'Do you want to talk about it?'

'It was a nightmare. He hauled me into his office as soon as I came in.'

'You knew that he would. That was supposed to be the whole pint of it.'

'Yes, I know, but...'

'The reality was worse than you thought?'

'A million times worse, Vanessa.' She closed her eyes and leaned back with her head resting on the back of the sofa, and drew her legs up, tucking them underneath her.

'He implied that I'd lied to him about everything…he said that I was nothing more than a scheming opportunist, that I'd manipulated him… The worst of it was that I couldn't tell him the truth and I couldn't deny a word he said…'

'It's behind you now,' Vanessa said soothingly, and Alice nodded, thinking that behind her was the very last thing it was. It would never be behind her. It would be her constant companion until the day she died. Why was it that she had been destined to have two horrendous love affairs? Or one, at any rate, she thought. James had just been a trial run for this.

'What are you going to do about work? Why don't you take a holiday somewhere? Go off on your own for a couple of weeks?'

'That would be running away.'

'That would be clearing your head.'

'No. I've got to face this down and carry on.' She looked at her friend and smiled wanly. 'Tomorrow I shall go out there, one of the unemployed, and start looking for another job. This paper towel is coming to bits.'

'They don't make 'em like they used to,' Vanessa said with a stab of humour. 'You'd think they could withstand a little bit of heartbreak. Shall I get you something to drink? Tea? Coffee? A good stiff brandy?'

'No. Thanks. I'm going to go to bed now.'

'A little alcohol might hasten sleep.'

'But I'll still have to face tomorrow.' And the day after that, and the day after that. Ever more. She stood up and smiled, feeling a little better, at least for the moment. 'Thanks for listening to me.'

'My accountant will send the invoice through the post.'

Alice laughed and headed towards the bedroom, but it was hours before she managed to get to sleep. She almost wished that she had succumbed and had a few glasses of wine; but the thought of a hangover the following morning wasn't appealing, and besides, she had meant it when she had told Vanessa that she would have to face this thing down. She would have to confront her memories for however long it took and hope that time would eventually bring some kind of peace.

In the meantime, she would fill her hours as effectively as she could.

She spent the following week trudging to various agencies and went to three interviews. Perfectly acceptable jobs, but she turned all three down because the thought of working for someone else was so horrifying. She would accept the fourth. She told herself that ten days later. She wasn't doing herself any favours and sooner or later she would need the money. She had a fair amount in savings, but the rent on the flat needed paying, groceries needed buying, and her money had not been set aside with those things in mind.

She was just leaving the flat for a day of interviews, at the end of which she would have a job come hell or high water, when the telephone rang, and her heart stopped as soon as she recognised the voice on the other end of the line.

'What do you want?' she asked, sinking onto the chair by the telephone. Simply hearing him made her head swim. Thoughts which had been close to the surface of her mind rushed out at her, breaking through the flimsy barriers she had tried to impose like a tidal wave. She had to steady herself by taking a deep breath; then, as soon as she released it, she felt unsteady all over again.

'The Cooper file.'

'Oh.' It took her a few seconds to absorb what he had said, then a wave of bitter disappointment washed over her. So what had she thought? That he had been calling to actually find out *how she was*?

'We've searched through all of the filing cabinets and drawn a blank.'

'We...?'

She hadn't wanted to ask but the question somehow had found its way to her lips of its own accord. She knew that it was stupid to torture herself but she couldn't fight the temptation to hear about her replacement.

'That's right. Now, can you shed some light on the Cooper file?'

Alice felt her eyes smart. So he wasn't going to tell her anything about the woman who had replaced her and she knew that she would spend the next week, if not year, fabricating a perfect image in her head. Tall, leggy, glamorous, yet spectacularly clever and wildly efficient at everything she set her mind to.

'Doug Shrewsbury had it a couple of weeks ago.'

'What the hell was he doing with it?'

'Something had gone wrong with the billing and he had to backtrack over the file to see if he could sort it out.'

'Right.' There was a pause on the other end of the line. 'I take it you've found another job?'

'Oh, yes,' Alice lied, because she would have felt a sorry loser to have told him the truth. 'In the West End,' she continued, thinking of something unbelievably exotic. 'Working for a film producer, as a matter of fact. Incredibly stimulating.'

'Which film producer?'

'I'd rather not divulge,' she said, alarmed at the unexpectedness of his question. Victor knew a huge assortment of people. It wouldn't do for him to find out that she had concocted the whole thing.

'Fine,' he said indifferently, and she could imagine

him shrugging at the other end of the line. What she did with her life was no longer his concern.

'How are you?' She hated herself for asking that, for showing interest, but the yearning to continue hearing his voice was almost painful.

'Good.' He paused and then said coolly, 'This wasn't meant to be a social call.'

'No, of course not.' She could feel herself going red with humiliation and was immeasurably relieved that he wasn't there, face to face, witness to her reaction. 'I'm in a bit of a rush anyway.'

'Of course,' he said politely. 'Can't keep your film producer waiting. Thanks for the information.'

'If there's any...' But she didn't manage to complete the sentence because the line went dead on her and she remained sitting there for a few minutes, holding the disconnected telephone in her hand, as though it might suddenly spring back into life; then she quietly replaced the receiver, stood up and sternly told herself that she was a fool. Hadn't she learnt the stupidity of letting herself feed off bad memories? Of allowing them to rule her life? Yes, of course she had.

She briskly headed out of the flat. It was sunny outside. Still cool, but with the promise of warmth in the air. She told herself that she felt invigorated, and she kept repeating it every time the thought of Victor threatened to drag her down.

It carried her through her interview and very nearly made her overlook the fact that the offices were small and in need of refurbishment, and the director, who would be her boss should she be offered the job, was uninspiring. She asked lots of bright, intelligent questions and feigned interest in the manufacture of automotive parts. She allowed herself to be shown around the department where she would be working and tried very hard not to notice that the carpet was worn and in need of a clean. The entire staff appeared to be much younger than her, apart from two old biddies who were comfortably chatting to one another next to the fax machine and drinking coffee out of mugs with saucy little mottoes printed on the sides.

'Well?' Geoff Anderson, who had insisted at the start of the interview that she call him Geoff because he liked to feel that he and his staff were on the same level, looked at her brightly when they resumed their seats back in his office after their tour of the respective departments. 'What do you think?'

'Super little place,' Alice said with a sinking heart. 'Everyone looks very jolly.'

'Oh, yes. We're one big, happy family here.' He beamed at her. 'I don't have to tell you that we've had a stack of people interested in this post—' he leaned forward confidentially '—but if you want it the job's yours.'

'Oh,' Alice said, taken aback. 'I'm flattered, but I shall need a day or so to think it over if that's all the same to you. I have one more interview this afternoon, and I shall make my mind up at the end of the day.' She stood up and held her hand out, just in case he got it into his head that another quick tour of the office was called for.

'Right.' He engulfed her hand with both of his. 'Look forward to hearing from you.' He reminded her of a teacher she had had in secondary school, a spaghetti-thin man with dusty grey hair who had had the annoying habit of laughing at his own witticisms even though no one else did. She felt sorry for him. How on earth could she possibly work for a man she felt sorry for?

Her afternoon interview was just as hopeless. John Hope, chairman of a company that manufactured paper, was excessively fond of his own voice. He smiled a bit

too much and at the end of the interview held her hand
for just a shade too long to be comfortable. She decided
that she couldn't possibly accept a job there, should it
be offered. He had been a little too glib when she had
asked him about the plight of the trees that went into the
manufacturing of paper products. She couldn't help but
sum him up as utterly unethical. How on earth could she
possibly work for someone who lacked ethics?

When she told Vanessa about the outcome of the interviews later that evening, Vanessa subjected her to an
expression of amused disbelief.

'So let me get this straight, Ali,' she said, folding her
arms. 'Job one…? That place in Marble Arch…?'

'Too small.'

'Job two…?'

'Too big.'

'Job three…'

'Oh, yes, the toy company… Not the right sort of toys.
They looked cheaply made.'

'And job four and five similar lame excuses.'

Alice blushed and shot her a protesting look from under her lashes. 'I know what you're thinking,' she said,
'and you're wrong. Is it my fault that all five jobs so far
haven't been to my liking?'

'Most people would be grateful for *one* job offer,
never mind *five*!'

'I don't know whether I would have been offered the
last job.'

'But then,' Vanessa continued thoughtfully, 'most
people wouldn't have had a job like your last one as a
point of comparison.'

'There's no question of a comparison,' Alice mumbled. 'I just don't believe in rushing into something if it
doesn't feel right. I mean, that wouldn't be fair to my
prospective employer, would it?'

Vanessa's brow cleared and she nodded sagely. 'Ah! So *that's* it! Concern for your prospective employer!' She laughed and slung her bag over her shoulder. 'I'm moved by your consideration, Ali. You're a lesson for us all!' She was still laughing when Alice chucked a cushion at her, missing her by inches as she vanished through the front door.

She made herself a salad and was settling in front of the television to watch whatever happened to be showing on whatever channel her finger chanced to select, when the doorbell rang. She felt a little surge of irritation. She had no idea who it could be, but whoever it was was not welcome. She wanted to be alone with her thoughts. Wrong, she knew, but how tempting to indulge in her unhappiness, how tempting to try and re-create an alternative present.

I'll spare you my bad humour, she thought, by not bothering to answer the door—but after three more rings she reluctantly strolled towards the door and yanked it open.

He was still in his work clothes, minus jacket, but despite that he looked vaguely unshaven and haggard. The top button of his shirt was undone, and his tie was pulled down. Alice stared at him, open-mouthed. She could feel her grip on reality slipping through her fingers like water. It had been bad enough hearing his voice unexpectedly down the end of a telephone line. Seeing him now made her feel as though she had suddenly been deprived of oxygen.

'What are *you* doing here?' Her hand was gripping the door-knob tightly and her body barred his entrance to the flat.

'What do you *think* I'm doing here?' he flung at her. 'Just passing through and thought that I might as well knock on the door and pay a courtesy call?'

'I suppose you've come to quiz me on more office matters,' Alice was fired into retorting by the tenor of his voice and by the fact that the last time he had contacted her it had not been to enquire about her health. 'I would have stayed on to make sure that my replacement knew where everything was. *You* were the one who insisted that I leave immediately and I resent you popping back into my life every two seconds because whoever's working for you can't understand my filing system.' She felt an unnatural stab of jealousy for this mysterious person who was now occupying *her* chair, in *her* office and having daily contact with the man she had fallen in love with. She imagined them conversing, chatting about accounts, having the occasional laugh together while *she* remained lost in her own wilderness, unable to get on with her life without Victor's input. It simply wasn't fair!

'Are you going to let me in?' Victor rasped, staring down at her with such intensity that she could feel herself getting hot and uncomfortable. 'I don't intend to conduct a conversation with you standing at your front door.'

'I might have company,' Alice said, hating him for unsettling her like this and hating herself for not being able to control her response to him. Weak and pathetic, she told herself angrily. That's what you are. Weak and pathetic.

'Have you?' he asked tightly.

'No.'

'Good. In that case, move aside so that I can come in. It's time you and I had a good long talk.'

CHAPTER TEN

ALICE struggled with herself as she watched Victor walk in the direction of the sitting room. She felt like a starving man suddenly confronted by a feast, desperate to dive in and enjoy the food but knowing that each morsel was poisoned. She remained where she was, standing by the front door with her hand on the knob, and only moved away towards him when he turned around to look at her.

If he had come to have a chat about more lost files, then she wished that he would just get on with it. Ask his questions and then leave her to wallow in her misery. There had been no need for him to enter the flat at all.

'Where's that flatmate friend of yours?' He had sat down on the sofa and now he looked at her with a bad-humoured frown on his face.

'Out.' Unfortunately, she thought to herself. A third party might well have helped her rapidly depleting self-control. 'I would offer you something to drink, but I assume you won't be staying long. I *assume* this isn't a social call.'

'I'll have a whisky and soda.'

'I can offer you a cup of coffee.' Take it or leave it, her tone implied, and she folded her arms across her chest, meeting his dark expression with an equal amount of defensive hostility.

'I suppose that'll have to do, in that case.' He loosely crossed his legs and continued to stare grimly at her.

Alice vanished into the kitchen. She could feel her heart thumping in her chest, could feel every pore and muscle in her body stretched taut like a piece of elastic with no more room to expand, ready to snap at any minute.

Her thoughts were a confused blur. She couldn't believe that he had personally come to her flat to discuss work. No, he could easily have done that over the telephone. In fact, he could have got his secretary, the blonde, leggy, efficient bombshell with the mind like a steel trap, to call on his behalf. But if he wasn't here for work, then *why* on earth was he here? To throw a few more accusations at her? To reduce her by a few more notches? What satisfaction could that possibly give him? Days had gone by. His temper would have cooled. She picked up the mugs of coffee and realised that her hands were shaking.

When she handed him his mug, she retreated very quickly to the chair facing his and rigidly positioned her body in it.

'You're trembling,' he said, thereby killing any notion she had had that he might not have noticed.

'I hardly expected you to show up here,' Alice told him tightly. 'Can you blame me? After our last encounter in your office?' Rather than let him answer that, she carried on in a rush. 'Why have you come? Is it to do with work?'

'No. In fact, your replacement is working out far better than I would have expected.'

'Good.' She felt as though her heart had been twisted and then squeezed tightly. Since there was nothing further to say on the subject, she fell silent, and was surprised to find that he had nothing to say either. She looked at him and underneath the accusing glare she saw a shadow of hesitancy on his face.

'How's your job going?'

'What?'

'Your job. The stimulating one with the film producer. How's it going?'

Alice tilted her chin forward. 'There *is* no job, if you must know. I lied.' So there, she thought. Now are you satisfied? The thought of embarking on another tangled network of lies simply to keep her pride afloat was too exhausting. 'But of course I don't suppose you're in the least surprised by that, considering you already think that I'm a liar and a cheat.' She looked away from him and concentrated on drinking her coffee. It was a small distraction.

'But you didn't lie about you and Claydon.'

'Not that again!' The words were dragged out of her. She felt bogged down at the prospect of another pointless argument over this, at her inability to do anything about his assumptions. Why had he come here? Why couldn't he have just left her alone to get on with her life, such as it was?

He placed the mug on the table in front of him, and leaned forward until his elbows were resting on his thighs. He looked down for a minute, shielding his expression from her, and when he raised his eyes the glowering anger had gone, replaced by a sulky defensiveness that she had never seen before. He looked like a child who had been denied pudding for reasons which he didn't quite comprehend.

'I can't get it out of my mind,' he said accusingly. 'I keep thinking about it, over and over again—you two in bed together. Dammit!' He stood up and began pacing the room, hands in his pockets.

Alice watched him and felt a perverse rush of pleasure at the thought of his jealousy. She must have meant *something* to him if he had been jealous. Not love. No, not that, but *something*. It was enough to bring a smile to her lips, and he glared at her.

'I'm so glad you think this is so funny.'

'I don't think it's funny. I just...well, I suppose...' She shrugged helplessly, unable to continue the train of thought. She desperately wanted to remember him just as he was now, his body in half-shadow, his posture stubborn, his expression defiant and sheepish at the same time. She wanted to remember so that she could feed off the memory in the years to come, pick it to bits, analyse and scrutinise and dissect.

'How could you...?' He hadn't wanted to ask the question. She could see it in his face, but it had been wrenched out of him.

'You don't understand...'

'Don't tell me that I don't understand!' He stopped his pacing and moved swiftly to where she was sitting, leaning over her with his hands on either side of her chair, glowering as she pressed herself back. 'There's not much to understand, is there? A man and a woman meet, they have sex. What's there to misunderstand?'

Alice stared at him wordlessly. She badly wanted to confess everything, but somewhere, at the back of her brain, she dimly knew that there were very good reasons why she shouldn't do that. He barely gave her a chance to reach a decision.

'What the hell did you see in him?'

'Why are you so angry, Victor?' she asked quietly. 'Is it because you can't stand the thought of James and me...together? Or is it because you think I betrayed you? Because your manly pride suffered a temporary blow?'

'Does it matter?' He pushed himself away from her and raked his fingers through his hair. 'I haven't even asked myself that question. I just get to the point where you two are in bed, and I see red.'

'You shouldn't.' What were those reasons for not telling him everything? She couldn't recall. She just knew that the past few days had been hell, and things couldn't get any worse than they were at the moment. She took a deep breath. 'I didn't lie when I told you that James and I slept together, but it wasn't quite the full story.' She had all of his attention. He was leaning forward, looking at her intently, so intently that she began fidgeting through sheer nervousness. If he chose to disbelieve what she had to say, then so be it. At least she would have said goodbye with a clear mind instead of tangled up in a network of half-truths. 'James and I had a relationship many years ago...'

'What...?'

'Just let me finish, Victor, then you can say what you have to say and leave.' She couldn't quite meet his eyes when she said this. 'After my mother died I went to work at Highfield House, for James's father. He was writing his memoirs and he needed someone to act as his personal assistant.'

'And you let me think that there had been a man there...'

'Yes, there was. James. I met him a while after I'd started working for his father. I was young and inexperienced and he swept into my life like a thunderbolt.' She stood up, feeling suddenly confined in the chair, and began walking around the room, thinking aloud. 'I had never met anyone like him before. He was suave and sophisticated, and I guess you could say that he went to my head. I fancied myself in love.'

She gave a short, bitter laugh. 'You were right when you said that James was the sort of man to be careful about, but I wasn't careful, you see. I never stopped to read the writing on the wall. I was so caught up in everything that I didn't even see the wall. I thought that what we had...I thought that it was going somewhere.'

She stopped and stared out of the window. 'Eventually I told him that I wanted some sort of commitment from him and that's when he said that he just wasn't ready for commitment. He thought that I'd understood. He was very apologetic, dismayed even. I gathered that I was too lowly for him. I spent a long time torturing myself, thinking how he must have breathed a sigh of relief that he had managed to wriggle away from the nobody down the road with the stars in her eyes.' There was no bitterness in her voice when she said this. She was stating an unpalatable fact.

'Carry on.' His voice was low and tense, but when she looked at him she was unable to read the expression on his face. Sympathy? Pity? Smug satisfaction that his pride was salvaged after all? Like a dog after a bone, he had pursued her to find out the truth, and she was relieved to be telling him.

'I hated him. I hated him because I blamed him for robbing me of my dreams, not to mention three years of my life. Then I saw him again and I faced up to the fact that, yes, he had ended it, and, yes, he probably ended it, at least in part, because he needed to do what was expected of him, find the right wife, but I had had my fair share of the blame to take as well. I had been blind and naïve and stupid enough to think that because I wanted something so did he.'

'I'm sorry.'

'It was a long time ago, Victor.' She turned to face him. 'My only regret is that I let that love affair influence my life more than it should have. I fled to London but I was still haunted by it. That's why when you first mentioned Highfield House it was like being thrown back in time, back into a nightmare.'

'Why didn't you tell me from the beginning?' he demanded tersely.

'Because it was a part of my past that I had grown accustomed to keeping behind locked doors, if you must know.'

'What happened when you met him again?' He tried to make the question sound casual, but didn't quite succeed.

'Nothing. Nothing happened.' She sat back down and curled her legs underneath her, cradling the mug of now tepid coffee in her hands, drawing solace from the warmth it radiated.

'He still wanted you.'

'He was surprised to see me,' Alice said shortly. 'His divorce had been a messy affair. We had both done a lot of growing up and I suppose he vaguely imagined that I might be stupid enough to take up where we had left off, since fate had seen fit to throw us together.'

'And you didn't.' Although that was said as a statement of fact, there was still the ghost of a question behind it.

'No, we didn't. I made that crystal-clear from the start.'

'Then why was he lurking around you?'

'He wasn't *lurking around me*. In fact, he and my flatmate are entwined in a passionate romance. I guess his experience of marriage to someone with the right background finally made him see that a person is a person, irrespective of where they come from, or what their father does for a living. I look at the way he is with Vanessa and I can see that he and I…well, we were never destined for permanence.'

'And do you find it hard to swallow that your ex-lover is going out with your best friend?'

'Does it matter one way or the other? Whether I find it hard to swallow or not?'

'Damn right it does.' He looked at her fully in the

face when he said that and she had to apply the brakes to her imagination, which suddenly threatened to go wildly out of control.

'Why?' She held her breath and waited for his answer.

'Because I can't stand the thought of you having any feelings whatsoever for Claydon. Or for anyone else for that matter.' He paused. 'Apart from me, that is.'

'What are you trying to say?' Alice whispered in a voice that was barely audible. She had stopped trying to control her imagination, and now all the possibilities behind his words were spinning in her head, dangerously out of control, making her breathing thick and laboured.

'Have you nothing stiffer to drink? I can't have this conversation on a cup of coffee.'

Alice would gladly have bolted to the nearest off-licence and bought a crate of whisky, if that was what it would have taken to prolong the conversation. Her head was spinning, and for the first time since she had left his office she felt wildly, passionately alive.

'There's some wine in the fridge.'

'I'll have a tumbler,' he muttered.

She didn't pour him a tumbler. She poured them both a glass each, handed him his, and was about to retreat to her previous position on the chair when he took her hand, stopping her in her tracks. The pressure was gentle but enough to make her freeze.

'I also can't have this conversation with you sitting a mile away from me on the other side of the room.'

Alice sat down on the sofa and immediately felt as though she was going to faint from the sheer force of his presence next to her.

'What was your real reason for coming here, Victor?'

'I didn't *want* to. Don't think that I was jumping for joy at the fact that I had no control over my goddamned emotions. I've been out with women before—dammit,

I'm not green when it comes to the opposite sex—but none of them ever had this effect on me.'

Excitement spread through her like the roots of a plant, shooting out in all directions. She fought to keep it under control.

'I can't just hop into bed with you again,' she said, and what an effort it took to say it, but the future had to be considered. If she was going to end up hurt, then she was doing herself no favours by postponing it.

'Why?' His voice was ragged. 'I want you. No, more than that. I need you. Since you left, I've done nothing but think about you. You've got under my skin and I'm going crazy.' He rested his head against the palms of his hands and raked his fingers through his hair, then looked at her. 'Have you thought about me at all?'

'Of course I have...' That, she thought, has to be one of life's greater understatements. 'But...'

'But...?'

'But I'm not looking for a two-month fling with you.'

'What are you looking for?'

She thought carefully about his question. She wanted to tell him the truth, of course she did, but now that the opportunity was staring her in the face so was the prospect of humiliating rejection. Another repeat of the James Claydon scenario, this time with Victor telling her that long-term commitment was out of the question, that he really couldn't promise anything beyond the temporary, that he was very sorry, that he would be on his way now. She closed her eyes and hesitated, torn between a desire for honesty, whatever the cost, and the need to maintain her pride.

But hadn't she already tried her hand at maintaining her pride? And where had it got her? Weeks of misery.

'I deliberately went to the same musical as you,' she said, taking a deep breath and looking at him unwaveringly. 'I knew that you were going to be there, and I knew where you would be sitting. I made sure that I got tickets for two seats where you couldn't miss me.'

Victor didn't say anything, but she could see his jaw harden.

'I knew that if you saw me with James you would sack me. You'd already told me that that would be the price of going out with him.' She had started down the road to telling him the truth and she felt dizzy as the words gathered momentum.

'I see.'

'Do you? What do you see, Victor?'

'That there's no point to this conversation. I was a fool to come here in the first place.'

He stood up, and Alice said sharply. 'I'm not finished!'

For a split second he looked as though he might tell her to go to hell, but then he said grudgingly, 'What else have you to say? You wanted to get out of my life, and you chose the path of least resistance.'

'Yes, I wanted to get out of your life, Victor,' she answered, watching as frozen shutters snapped down over his eyes. 'And yes, perhaps it was the path of least resistance, but I only wanted to get out of your life because I was...afraid.' There, she had said it, and she found that the world hadn't stopped turning on its axis. She could still breathe.

'Afraid of what?'

'I can't talk to you when you're standing up like that,' she muttered. He sat back down, leaning forward and looking at her. 'You were the first man after James,' she said, admitting the truth reluctantly but determined to spit it all out if it killed her. 'When I first went to work for you, I was aware that you were an...attractive man, but I wasn't attracted to you. Or, at least, I don't think

I was. It's hard to be sure. James had put me off men;
I had become accustomed to seeing right through them.'

She glanced down at her hands, entwined, and nervously fiddled with her fingers. 'I don't know when that
all changed, but it did. I just know that when I went on
holiday with Vanessa I had a good time but I was itching
to get back to England, back to work. Back to you.'

She raised her eyes to his, defying him to laugh at
her, but his face, half in shadow, was deadly serious. 'It
never occurred to me that I might be attracted to you. I
had somehow convinced myself that James had tarnished
all men for ever. It was only when I saw him at Highfield
House that I realised how much I had exaggerated his
hold over me. I guess my memory had turned him into
something far more powerful than he was in reality. It
was as though I had been living in a darkened room,
and then, suddenly, the curtains had been pulled back
and there was light pouring in. I realised that what I felt
for James had been youthful infatuation, nothing more.
Then I slept with you...'

'And...?'

For a few seconds, Alice didn't say anything. She listened to the silence around her, absorbing it, drawing
strength from it.

'And I realised what love was all about,' she told him
simply. 'I slept with you because I had fallen in love
with you, and I walked away from you for the same
reason.' They stared at one another, and eventually she
said, with a small, self-conscious laugh, 'You wanted the
truth. Well, Victor, there it is. Now you can hurry back
to your home and rest assured that you won. Your male
pride is firmly in place; you needn't stoop to pick up
any pieces.'

He sat back and watched her until she wanted him to

yell that she must be crazy. She wanted him to say *something*, anything to break the silence.

'You still didn't answer my question,' he said softly.

'What question?'

'What are you looking for out of me?'

'Are you making fun of me?' Alice asked tightly. 'I've sat here and shown you my sleeve with my heart very firmly printed on it…what more do you want me to say?'

'I take it that you want me to marry you.'

'Oh?' she said, throwing caution to the winds. 'And what if I do?'

'Then I accept.'

Alice stared at him in utter astonishment, and wondered if she had just heard correctly.

'Since you proposed, it does mean that you'll have to carry me over the threshold, of course.' And he smiled, a slow, lingering smile that made her heart sing.

'You want to marry me?'

'As soon as possible.' He crooked his finger, and she slowly edged her way towards him, until their faces were only inches apart. 'Just in case you decide to change your mind.'

'But…why?' she whispered incredulously.

'Because, woman, I'm in love with you.' He covered her mouth with his and played with her lips with his tongue, tracing their full outline. 'When you walked out of that office, it was as though you'd taken a part of me with you. I found that I just couldn't function properly without you in my life. I couldn't eat, I couldn't sleep, I couldn't concentrate on a damned thing. I didn't have to phone you up about that file. It was a ridiculous pretext to hear your voice, but I felt even sicker after I'd hung up, because you sounded so bloody *normal*, when I felt anything but.'

His hands spanned her collar-bone, then cupped her
breasts underneath her shirt. 'I swear to God that I
thought I was losing my mind,' he moaned into her neck.
'You were the last thing on my mind when I fell asleep
at night and the first thing when I got up. I came here
determined to get you back into my life by hook or by
crook. More, I was damned sure that I was going to get
a ring on your finger even if I had to force you.'

So this was what it felt like to fly. She had wings, and
was soaring high above the clouds. As he unbuttoned
her shirt and unclasped her bra, she could feel her
dreams creeping out of their boxes. She groaned as his
hands caressed her flesh.

'I think we should do this in bed,' he murmured, lifting her up. He carried her into her bedroom.

'Yes. We wouldn't want James and Vanessa to walk
in on us.' Her skin was hot against the cool sheets on
her bed, and in the darkness she could hear her own
happiness beating inside her.

Every touch sent the flames of desire raging higher
inside her. His mouth, as he explored her body, sent
electric currents through her, which made her writhe and
twist, groaning. How could she have forgotten the power
of his love-making? She pulled him closer to her as she
neared her climax, until their bodies seemed to merge
into one.

It was only afterwards, as they lay in a tangle of sheets
with the duvet cover half off the bed, that she said lazily,
'There's just one thing I want to ask you about.'

'What's that?' His voice was as warm and languid as
her own. He licked her lips with his tongue as though
unable to resist the temptation of her mouth so close to
his.

'My replacement…?'

'Ah, yes, your replacement. Will have to stay, I'm

afraid. I can't have my wife working for me. Far too much temptation for one man to bear.'

'This wife doesn't approve of anyone tall, blonde, good-looking and devilishly clever.'

'Which means, I suppose, that the replacement will have to go.'

'You mean that she's all those things?' Alice threw him a good-natured scowl of alarm.

'I haven't noticed the good-looking bit...' he nibbled her ear. '...but rumour on the office grapevine tells me that there are quite a few girls after him, so he must be...' He laughed softly. 'I won't be introducing you in a hurry.'

She smiled and stroked his hair with her fingers. 'No fear, my love, you're quite enough for me.'

'At least for the moment,' he replied, 'until we decide to fill our house with a few of our lookalikes.'

'In which case,' she murmured, 'shouldn't we continue practising?'

Business
Arrangement Bride

JESSICA HART

Jessica Hart was born in West Africa and has suffered from itchy feet ever since, travelling and working around the world in a wide variety of interesting but very lowly jobs, all of which have provided inspiration to draw from when it comes to the settings and plots of her stories. Now she lives a rather more settled existence in York, where she has been able to pursue her interest in history, although she still yearns sometimes for wider horizons. If you'd like to know more about Jessica, visit her website, www.jessicahart.co.uk.

Be swept away to a tropical island next month with Jessica Hart in *Destination: Summer Weddings!*

CHAPTER ONE

WHERE had he seen her before?

Tyler watched the woman across the room as she smiled and shook hands with a group of men in suits. He had noticed her as soon as she arrived, and it had been bugging him ever since that he couldn't work out why she seemed so elusively familiar.

It wasn't as if she was the kind of woman who would normally catch his eye. Apart from that luminous smile, there was nothing remarkable about her at all. She had nondescript features and messy brown hair, and she was squeezed into a suit that was much too small for her. Stylish and beautiful she definitely wasn't.

And yet…there was *something* about her. Tyler couldn't put his finger on it and it was making him cross. He was a man who liked to know exactly what he was dealing with, and he was irritated by the fact that his gaze kept snagging on this very ordinary-looking woman who was taking not the slightest notice of *him*.

He had been watching her for nearly an hour as she circulated easily around the crowded room. She obviously had the ability to relate to people that he so conspicuously lacked, according to Julia, anyway.

'You're a lovely person, Ty,' his best friend's wife had told him with her usual candour, 'but honestly, you've got the social skills of a rhinoceros!'

Tyler scowled at the memory.

Unaware that his glower had caused several of the people around him to flinch visibly, he took a morose sip of champagne and surveyed the crowded foyer of his new building. He hated occasions like this. He couldn't be bothered with all the social chit-chat that woman seemed to be able to do so well, but his PR director had insisted that a reception to mark the opening of his controversial new headquarters would be politic. So now he was stuck here in a roomful of civic dignitaries and businesspeople, all of whom seemed to be hovering, hoping for a chance to ingratiate themselves, to lobby for his support for their pet schemes or to suggest mutually beneficial business opportunities. They all wanted to talk to him.

All except her.

She hadn't so much as glanced his way all evening.

Some councillor was boring on about the city's local transport plan, and Tyler let his gaze wander over the room once more, wondering how long it would be before he could decently leave. Why had he agreed to such a tedious PR exercise anyway?

Suddenly he realised that he couldn't see the woman any more, and he felt oddly jolted to have lost her. Frowning, he searched the crowd with hard eyes. Had she gone? Surely she would have—

Ah, there she was! She had found a quiet corner by herself and was easing off her high-heeled shoes. Tyler saw her grimace. Her feet were obviously killing her. If she had any sense she would go soon, and he would never find out who she was. The thought was oddly unsettling.

He could ask someone, he supposed, but the group around him were still droning on about Park and Ride schemes.

Or he could go over and ask her himself.

'Excuse me,' he said brusquely—who said he didn't have social skills?—and, leaving the rest of them in mid bus lane, as it were, he headed across the room towards her.

In her quiet corner near the lifts, Mary was surreptitiously wriggling the toes on her left foot and wishing she had the nerve to take off her right shoe as well.

The shoes had seemed a good idea when she'd put them on too. The news that Tyler Watts, the North's very own bad boy made good, was moving the headquarters of his phenomenally successful property company out of London and back to York had riveted the business community, while his construction of a cutting edge building on the river front had divided opinion across the city. It had outraged conservationists and delighted others who claimed it as stunning proof that the city could not only hold on to its historical heritage but also stake a claim as being at the forefront of architectural design in the twenty-first century.

Either way, the champagne reception to celebrate its opening was certain to be the networking opportunity of the year, and Mary was determined to make the most of it. She wouldn't be the only one lobbying for a contract with Watts Holdings, and she might make some useful contacts even if she didn't get the big one.

So she had chosen her outfit carefully. This was her first public outing as a professional woman since Bea's birth, and she wanted to look elegant and…well, professional. A smart suit and stylish shoes would create the perfect impression. Mary knew; she had read all the magazines.

Sadly, the magazines didn't tell you what to do when you realised, five minutes before you were due to go out, that you were a good two sizes larger than you had been the last time you put on your best suit. Nor did they remind you what agony it was standing around on high heels, and that was before you tried walking on what some bone-headed architect had decided was cutting edge flooring, apparently forgetting that a glassy sheen was more appropriate to an ice rink than an office building.

Mary sighed and switched shoes, giving her right foot a break. As so often in her life, she reflected glumly, there was a huge gap between imagination and reality. She had pictured herself charming the assembled employers of York, so impressing them with her professionalism that they were queuing up to get her to solve their recruitment problems, but it hadn't worked out like that. Oh, everyone had been very pleasant, but they had all wanted to talk about Tyler Watts, not business, and while no one had been rude enough to point out that her jacket was straining across her ample bust, no one had offered her any work either, and she had been burningly aware that professional was the last thing she had looked.

All she had got out of the evening was pinched toes and a sore back.

Mary took a slug of champagne, put down her glass and squeezed her poor foot back into its shoe. She would make one last effort to meet the Human Resources director of Watts Holdings, she decided, and then she would give up.

It was at that point that she detected a ripple of interest around her and looked up from her shoe to see none other than Tyler Watts bulldozing his way across the room, groups parting and stepping back sycophantically to make way for him.

Not that he noticed or acknowledged them, Mary noted

sourly. That was typical of him. In her brief meetings with him in the past he had struck her as the most arrogant and ruthless person she had ever met and she was in no hurry to renew her acquaintance with him. She might want a contract with Watts Holdings, but she had no desire to deal with the man at the top, thank you very much.

Extraordinarily, he seemed to be heading straight towards her. Mary glanced around her, in case there was someone interesting standing behind her shoulder, but she was momentarily isolated.

If she didn't do something about it sharpish, he would be on top of her and there would be no avoiding him.

Picking up her glass from the table beside her, Mary turned to slink behind the group on her left, but she was too hasty and hadn't reckoned on the slippery floor. The next thing she knew, one of her wretched heels was skidding out from beneath her and she pitched forwards.

There were indrawn breaths around her as everyone anticipated an almighty crash, but she never hit the floor. A hard hand caught her under her elbow, swivelling her up and round until she was upright once more. More or less upright, anyway. One of Mary's arms was still flailing madly as she tried to regain her balance, and the polished floor wasn't helping at all.

Mortified, she managed to stand on two feet once more. 'Thank you so—' she began breathlessly, and then the words died on her lips as she looked up and found herself staring into Tyler Watts's glacial blue eyes.

Her first thought was that he must have moved at the speed of light to reach her in time, her second was that he was incredibly strong. She was not exactly a lightweight, but he had caught her and hauled her upright with a single hand.

It was only then that she noticed the stain on the front of his shirt. Somehow, in all her skidding and flailing, she must have knocked the glass in his hand.

'I'm so sorry,' she said nervously.

She didn't want to be nervous, but there was something about Tyler Watts that made you feel edgy. You had to admit, the man had presence, and it wasn't anything to do with looks, although the dark, beetling brows and grim lines of his face were intimidating enough on their own. He exuded a restless, driven energy that reverberated around him and left people half thrilled, half mesmerised by a mixture of awe and apprehension when he was around.

Not a man you would choose to knock drink all over.

Good move, Mary, she thought with an inward sigh. She had thought her aching feet were the low point of the evening, but apparently not.

Tyler's fingers were still gripping her arm just above the elbow, but as Mary's eyes dropped to them he released her.

'Are you all right?' he asked brusquely.

'Yes, I'm fine. Thank you.' She managed a nervous laugh and resisted the urge to rub her skin where he had held her. Her whole arm was tingling and throbbing from his grip and it was making her feel a bit odd.

'This floor is lethal in heels,' she tried to explain in case he thought she'd been over-indulging in the free champagne. 'But that's trendy designers for you,' she said, conscious that she was babbling but too rattled by his nearness to think sensibly. 'What clot thought a floor like this would be a good idea?'

'That would be a clot like me,' said Tyler Watts with a sardonic look.

If a black hole had yawned at Mary's feet at that moment, she would gladly have jumped into it and disappeared. How

could she have said anything so stupid? Criticising the design
of the building that marked the culmination of a spectacularly
successful career to a man whose business she desperately
needed was *not* a good move.

'You've obviously never tried walking on it in high heels!'
she said, deciding that her only option was to make a joke of
it, but Tyler was unamused.

'The other women seem to be managing to stay upright,'
he pointed out. 'Perhaps it's your shoes that are the problem,
not my floor?'

They both looked down. The shoes were Mary's favour-
ites—or had been until they had started hurting so vilely—
and she had chosen them deliberately because they reminded
her of her days in London when she had been slim—well,
slimm*er*—and sharp and successful. They were black with
white polka dots, so you could get away with wearing them
with a suit, but the peep toes and floppy bow were fun when
you didn't want to be *too* serious.

Maybe the heels *were* a bit high, Mary conceded to
herself, but what kind of office floor was designed without
stilettos in mind?

Tyler looked down at the shoes, noticing in passing that
she had surprisingly nice legs, and shook his head at their
impracticality.

'I suggest you wear something more sensible next time.'

Mary opened her mouth to say that being sensible was good
advice coming from a man who had chosen a floor like an ice
rink, but she managed to stop herself in time. She was supposed
to be drumming up business, not alienating potential clients.

'I'll do that,' she said instead, and if there was a suspicion
of gritted teeth about her smile, she didn't think Tyler Watts
would notice.

She hadn't really wanted to talk to him but, since he was there, she had better make the most of the opportunity. Somehow she had to convince him that she was a competent businesswoman and not just a tactless idiot in silly shoes. If he were to be impressed enough to recommend her to his Human Resources director, her problems would be over.

Her most pressing ones, anyway.

Summoning a bright professional smile, Mary held out her hand. 'I'm Mary Thomas,' she said.

The name didn't ring a bell with Tyler, but then it wasn't a particularly memorable one. In fact, there was nothing particularly memorable about her now that he had a chance to study her more closely. She had beautiful skin and intelligent grey eyes, but her round face was quirky rather than pretty, with eyebrows that didn't quite match and features that all seemed to tilt upwards, giving her a humorous look.

None of which explained why she seemed so familiar.

Irritated by his inability to place her, Tyler took her hand and shook it. 'Tyler Watts,' he introduced himself briefly.

'I know,' said Mary, acutely aware of the feel of his fingers closing around hers and pulling her hand away rather sharply.

'You do?'

'Everybody knows who you are,' she told him, nodding around the crowded lobby. 'You're famous in York. Everyone here wants to talk to you and do business with the new expanded Watts Holdings.'

'Including you?' he asked.

'Including me,' Mary agreed. 'Except that I was hoping to meet Steven Halliday rather than you.'

The dark brows snapped together. 'What's wrong with me?' he demanded.

'There's nothing wrong with you,' said Mary hastily, more

intimidated than she wanted to admit by his frown. 'I just thought it would be more appropriate to talk to Mr Halliday. I understand he's your Director of Human Resources?'

More appropriate and a lot easier. Mary didn't know what Steven Halliday was like, but he had to be a whole lot better to deal with than the glowering Tyler Watts, who famously gave his staff a mere thirty seconds to make their point. She would really rather talk to someone with a bit more patience, not to mention a few listening skills.

To someone who wouldn't insist on looming over her with that ferocious frown and those unnervingly pale, polar-blue eyes that seemed to bore into you. It was hard to keep your cool when faced with that mixture of arrogance, impatience and sheer force of personality.

'He is,' Tyler admitted grudgingly. 'What do you want to talk to him about?'

'I'm in recruitment.'

This was the perfect time to produce one of those cards she had had printed at such expense. Mary had been dishing them out all evening, though, and she just hoped that she had some left.

Digging around at the bottom of her bag—really, she *must* organise it—her fingers closed around a card just as the pressure of her hand snapped the fragile chain and the whole thing lurched downwards, spilling most of the contents over the floor, where they skidded merrily over the glossy surface.

Mary closed her eyes. Excellent. Fall over, knock drink over him, insult his design taste and tip her handbag all over the floor... Could she look any more of a fool, and in front of the man with the power to make or break her precious agency, too?

Pink with embarrassment and irritation with herself, she

stooped to gather up keys and lipstick and business cards—
there were plenty left, it appeared—plus a sundry collection
of pens, safety pins, tissues, scraps of paper with scribbled
lists, a couple of floppy disks, an emery board and a plastic
baby spoon.

A biscuit left in an opened packet ended up at the tip of
Tyler's perfectly polished shoe and Mary scrabbled to retrieve
it. That explained all the crumbs in the bottom of her bag
anyway. It must have been there for ages, and the wonder was
that she hadn't eaten it.

Tyler bent and picked up a spare nappy, which he handed
to Mary with an expressionless face.

'Thank you,' she muttered, shoving it into the bag along
with the rest of the stuff and straightening.

She was amazed that he was still there, and couldn't think
why he hadn't walked off in disgust long ago. Why had he
come over in the first place, in fact? she thought with a trace
of resentment. She had been perfectly all right, minding her
own business and not doing anything stupid, and then he had
turned up and transformed her into a blithering idiot.

But Tyler showed no sign of walking off. He just stood
there, looking daunting, and waited for her to explain what
she was doing there.

Tyler was, in fact, bitterly regretting having come over to
talk to her. He had moved instinctively to catch her when she'd
fallen, not realising how heavy she would be, and he was
lucky she hadn't taken him down with her. As it was, she had
managed to knock the champagne he'd had in his free hand
all over him. Always fastidious, Tyler was very conscious of
the stain on his shirt and, as for his tie, it was probably ruined,
he thought crossly.

Not content with that, she had criticised his floor, and he

didn't take kindly to criticism from anyone, let alone someone who wore ridiculously inappropriate shoes and evidently possessed a handbag as messy as the rest of her. Everyone had turned to look as the contents scattered over the floor, and they had probably noticed him there too with a nappy—a nappy, of all things!—in his hand and a spreading stain on his shirt, and no doubt looking a fool.

If there was one thing Tyler hated, it was feeling ridiculous.

Actually, there were lots of things that he hated, but looking stupid had to be way up there at the top of his list.

He wished he had never been sucked into Mary Thomas's chaotic orbit, but now that he was here he couldn't think of a way to leave. If they'd been in a meeting, he could just have told her that her thirty seconds were up but, as it was, she was looking pink and flustered and he didn't feel able to turn on his heel and walk off, no matter how much he might want to.

'What sort of recruitment?' he asked after a moment, deciding to pretend that the whole bag incident had never happened.

Mary only just stopped herself from sighing in time. She had been willing him to make an excuse and leave, at which point she could have slunk off home and enjoyed her humiliation in comfort.

This was a fantastic opportunity for her. Half the room would give their eye teeth to be in her position, with Tyler Watts's apparently undivided attention. She should be making her pitch and sounding gung-ho, but it was hard when your feet were aching, your toes pinched, your jacket was gaping and you had just humiliated yourself three times in as many minutes in front of the man you had to try and impress, and when you would really much rather be stretched out on the sofa in front of the television with a cup of cocoa.

But lying on the sofa wouldn't get her agency off the

ground. It wouldn't get her a home of her own, or make a new life for Bea.

Lying on the sofa wasn't an option.

Mary took a deep breath and, mentally squaring her shoulders, handed Tyler a business card and launched into her carefully prepared spiel.

'I understand you're expanding your operation in the north now that you're making York your headquarters, so if you need people with accountancy, clerical, computer or secretarial skills, I hope you'll think of my agency. I can find you the best,' she told him with what she hoped was a confident smile.

'I don't deal with junior staffing decisions,' said Tyler, frowning down at her card.

'I'm aware of that, which is why I was hoping to meet Steven Halliday here.' Mary kept her voice even and hoped that she didn't sound as desperate as she felt. 'I have worked for Watts Holdings in the past myself, so I understand the company ethos and how it operates,' she went on. 'That's a huge advantage when it comes to finding suitable staff, as I'm sure you are aware.'

But Tyler wasn't listening. 'You've worked for me?' he said, a very faint light beginning to glimmer.

'It's nearly ten years ago now, so you won't remember me,' said Mary, a little unnerved by the way the pale, polar-blue eyes were suddenly alert as they rested on her face. 'I worked in Human Resources here in York. Guy Mann was director then.'

'Ah…!' Tyler let out a hiss of satisfaction. He had it now. Mary Thomas… Of course.

'I do remember you,' he said slowly. 'You were the one who spilt coffee all over the conference table at some meeting.'

Of course, he *would* remember that. Mary bit her lip and

averted her eyes from the stain on his shirt. 'I'm not usually that clumsy,' she said.

'And you stood up to me over that guy... What was his name?' Tyler clicked his fingers impatiently as if trying to conjure the name out of thin air.

'Paul Dobson,' Mary supplied, since there was no point in pretending she didn't know.

'Dobson...yes. You told me I was wrong.' He eyed her with new interest. Very few people dared to tell him he was wrong about anything.

It was all coming back. He could remember the shocked silence around the table as Mary Thomas had spoken out, the scorn in her voice, how taken aback they had all been, as if some gentle kitten had suddenly puffed up to twice its size and lashed out without warning.

'I hope I put it a bit more diplomatically than that,' said Mary, her heart sinking. He would never give her work if he associated her with trouble.

'There was no diplomacy about it,' said Tyler. 'You told me flat out that I was wrong and should be ashamed of myself.'

He had been furious at the time, Mary remembered, marvelling now that she had ever had the nerve, but when she risked a glance at him she was sure she detected a gleam of something that might even have been amusement in the chilly blue eyes. It had a startling effect, lightening the grimness of his features and making him seem suddenly much more approachable.

'You told *me* I was a bleeding heart,' she countered, emboldened.

'So you were,' he agreed. 'But a bleeding heart who got her own way, I seem to remember.'

Mary nodded. 'You were fair,' she acknowledged.

That was one thing you could say about Tyler Watts. He

might be rude and impatient, and the most difficult and demanding of employers most of the time, but he was straight
and he didn't ignore or manipulate facts that didn't suit him.
Irritated he might have been, but he had listened to what she
had had to say about Paul Dobson. The upshot had been a
special inquiry, and Tyler had been prepared to reconsider his
decision when he knew more.

Well, that explained why she had seemed so familiar,
anyway. Tyler felt better. He didn't like being puzzled or uncertain. Having solved the mystery, he could move on, but he
was remembering something the HR director had once told
him: 'Mary Thomas may be young, but she's got an instinctive understanding of human relationships.'

And, if that were still so, maybe Mary Thomas could be
of some use to him after all.

'Why did you leave Watts Holdings?' he asked her.

Mary, trying to relaunch into her sales pitch, was thrown
by the abrupt question. 'I wanted to work in London,' she said,
puzzled by his interest. 'I grew up in York and I was really
lucky to get a job with you after I graduated, but after three
years I was ready to spread my wings.'

'You could have got a job with us in London.'

He sounded almost peeved that she hadn't. She hadn't
realised that joining Watts Holdings was supposed to be a
lifetime commitment. Mind you, there had been some fanat-
ically loyal members of staff who probably thought of it that
way. There tended to be a very high turnover amongst the rest,
though, most of whom were terrified of Tyler Watts. Mary had
only managed to survive three years by not being important
enough to have much to do with him.

Still, better not tell Tyler that. She had been tactless enough
for one evening.

'I wanted to broaden my experience,' she said instead.

'Hmm.' Tyler's hard eyes studied her with such intentness that Mary began to feel uncomfortable. 'And now you're back in York?' he said.

'Yes. I've been back a few months now,' she told him, relieved that he seemed to be getting back to the business in hand, which was about winning some work.

'I've recently set up a recruitment agency,' she went on, ready to launch back into her spiel and wishing that her feet didn't hurt so much. 'I offer a complete headhunting service for junior staff. Companies tend to spend a lot of money recruiting senior members of staff and skimp on employees at lower grades, but it's a false economy in my view.

'A financial investment in finding exactly the right person, however lowly the job, pays dividends,' she said. 'If all your staff, from janitors to chief executives, are doing the job they're best suited to, your entire company will function more efficiently.'

Tyler was unimpressed. 'Sounds expensive,' he commented.

'It's more expensive than accepting anyone who happens to have the skills to do the job,' Mary agreed. 'But less expensive than realising you've appointed someone who doesn't fit into the team or who doesn't work effectively with their colleagues.'

She was beginning to perk up a bit now. Tyler's expression might be unresponsive, but at least he was listening. 'Before I look for the right person for you, I need to understand the company culture, and that means working very closely with your human resources department. It's important to know exactly what the job entails and what sort of personality would fit most comfortably into the existing team.

'I see my job less as matching skills and requirements, and

more about forging successful human relationships,' she finished grandly. She always liked that bit.

Relationships, the dreaded R word! Tyler was sick of hearing about them. He had recently spent a weekend with his best friend and his wife, and Julia had spent her whole time banging on about 'relationships' and making free with her advice.

'For someone so clever at business, you're extraordinarily stupid when it comes to women,' she had told him bluntly. 'You've got no idea how to have a relationship.'

Tyler had been outraged. 'Of course I do! I've had loads of girlfriends.'

'Yes, and how many of them have lasted more than a few weeks? Those are encounters, Ty, not relationships!'

Tyler was fond of Julia in his own way, but her comments had caught him on the raw, especially after that reunion he had gone to with Mike where all his peers seemed to be measuring their success suddenly in terms of wives and children rather than share value or racehorses or fast cars.

'That's what being really successful is nowadays,' Mike had said, amused by Tyler's bafflement. 'You're going to have to get yourself a wife and family, Tyler, if you want to be the man who really does have it all!'

'And you won't be that until you learn how to have a relationship,' Julia added. 'If you want to be the best, Ty, you're going to have to get yourself a relationship coach.'

It was all rubbish, of course, but her words had rankled with Tyler. He liked being the best—*needed* to be the best, even—and he wasn't prepared to accept that there was anything he didn't do well, even something as unimportant as relationships. He didn't do failure, in any shape or form.

Now here was Mary Thomas going on about relationships too.

'What is it with all this relationship stuff nowadays?' he demanded truculently. 'Why is it no one can just do the job they're paid to do any more? Why do they all have to spend their time *forging relationships*?'

'Because unless they *do* form relationships, they won't work effectively,' said Mary, who was wishing Tyler Watts would stop talking and let her get out of these shoes. 'You know, it's not a big deal,' she told him when he made no effort either to move on or to hide his scepticism. 'It's not about hugging each other or sitting around chanting. It's just about understanding that different people have different approaches, different needs, different expectations. It's about being aware of other people, of what they do and how they do it.'

She attempted a smile, although they tended to be rather wasted on Tyler from what she could remember. 'Like any other relationship, in fact.'

To her surprise, an arrested expression sprang into the cold blue eyes that were boring in to her. 'Do you think you can teach that?'

'Teach what?'

'All that stuff you were just talking about…you know, understanding, being aware of people…' Tyler waved a dismissive hand, clearly unable to remember any other alien concepts.

'Of course,' said Mary, surprised.

This was one area she really did know about, thanks to Alan. He had been running a coaching course when she'd met him, and she had been bowled over by his psychological insights and grasp of the complexities of human relationships.

Of course, it hadn't helped when their own relationship had fallen apart, but that was experts for you.

'I've run a number of courses on workplace relationships in the past,' she went on, thinking there would be no harm in bigging herself up a little. 'It's an interesting area, and it's amazing what a difference tackling problems like this can make to a company's productivity.'

'Do you do other kinds of coaching?' Tyler asked.

'Yes.' Mary was really getting into her stride now. 'I can help people identify their goals at a personal level and work out a strategy to achieve them.'

Now she was talking his language. Tyler looked at her with approval. He might not have a clue about relationships, but he understood goals and strategies all right.

'In that case, I might have a job for you,' he said.

Mary was taken by surprise. 'I thought you weren't involved with staff recruitment?'

'This isn't about staffing,' he said. 'It's about me.'

'Oh?' said Mary, puzzled but polite.

'Yes.' Characteristically, Tyler went straight to the point. 'I want to get married.'

CHAPTER TWO

MARY laughed. 'Well, this is very sudden!' she said, entering into the spirit of the joke and pretending confusion. She pressed a hand to her throat as if to contain her palpitations. 'I don't know what to say. I had no idea you felt that way about me.'

'What?' Tyler stared at her.

'Still, it's a good offer,' she said, putting her head on one side as if giving it serious consideration. 'I'm thirty-five, and a girl my age can't be picking and choosing. I'm up for it if you are!'

Looking down into her face, Tyler realised with a mixture of incredulity and outrage that she was *laughing* at him. The grey eyes were alight and a smile was tugging at the corner of her wide mouth.

'I'm serious,' he said, glowering.

The smile was wiped off Mary's face and it was her turn to stare. 'I thought you were joking!'

'Do I look like the joking type?'

'Well, no, now you come to mention it, but… No, come on.' She laughed uncertainly. 'You *are* joking!'

'I can assure you,' said Tyler grimly, 'that I am not in a humorous mood.'

'But…you don't want to marry me, surely?'

His expression changed ludicrously. 'Good God, no!' he said, appalled at the misunderstanding. 'I don't want to marry *you*.'

Charming, thought Mary acidly. She knew that she wasn't beautiful and, OK, she was a bit overweight at the moment, but she wasn't *that* bad, and Tyler was no George Clooney, when it came down to it. He had no call to look as if he would rather pick up slugs than touch her.

'Well, you know,' she said, leaning forward confidentially, her smile a-glitter with defiance, 'that's what the princess in the fairy tale always says to the frog, and you know what happens to them!'

Tyler's fierce brows were drawn together in a ferocious scowl, and if Mary hadn't been so cross with him by this stage she would have been quailing in her heels. As it was, when he demanded, 'Do you want a job or not?' she only looked straight back at him.

'I'm not at all clear what this job of yours involves,' she said. 'Or, to put it another way, I haven't a clue what you're talking about!'

A passing waiter, seeing that they were without glasses, approached with a tray, only to falter as Tyler waved him away irritably, but as the man made to retreat Mary gave him her best smile.

'Thank you,' she said. 'I'd love one.'

Ignoring Tyler's glare, she helped herself to a glass of champagne. She didn't care what he thought anymore. It was late, she was tired, her feet hurt and she was fed up with Tyler Watts looming over her. She didn't know what he wanted, but it didn't sound like it was anything to do with recruitment, and that meant he was wasting her time.

'I think you'd better go back to the beginning,' she told him coolly and took a sip of champagne.

Tyler drew a deep breath and counted to ten. If he was the kind of man who was prepared to admit that he had made a mistake, he would have to accept that he might have made a big one in approaching Mary Thomas.

When the idea had first struck him, she had seemed ideal. She had been talking about coaching and he needed a coach. More to the point, he didn't want to spend time finding a suitable coach, and here was one, right in front of him and anxious for work, it seemed.

Her ordinariness had been appealing too, if he was honest. While accepting in principle the idea of a relationship coach—it was just one step in his strategy, after all—Tyler hadn't been looking forward to the prospect of discussing his private affairs with anyone too smart or sophisticated. He had every intention of remaining in control of the whole process, and Mary Thomas had looked suitably meek and deferential. All he wanted was for her to offer him a few pointers and then fade into the background.

But the closer he looked, the less ordinary she seemed. Take away that ill-fitting suit and those ridiculous shoes, and you would be left with a lush figure and an impression of warmth that made an intriguing contrast with the direct grey gaze and the slight edge to her voice. Mary Thomas, he had realised already, was not going to do meek or deferential.

It was annoying, Tyler admitted. He had decided that she was the person he needed, and once he had made up his mind he liked to go straight for what he wanted. His ability to focus on a goal and his refusal to be diverted had been the secret of his business success and he wasn't going to change a winning strategy now. He didn't have time for doubt or hesitation. He needed to get Mary Thomas on side, and get the job done.

'All right,' he said. 'I'll start again. I want a wife.'

There was a pause while Mary tried to work out what was going on. He sounded utterly clear and utterly serious but she couldn't see how this could be anything other than a very elaborate joke at her expense. People just didn't *say* things like 'I need a wife'.

Although, perhaps, people like Tyler Watts did.

'I think you've misunderstood what I do,' she said after a moment. 'I'm not a dating agency. I can find you a secretary or a computer operator, but not a wife.'

And then she offered a smile, just in case he turned out to be joking after all.

Tyler looked down at the empty glass in his hand, made an irritated gesture and put it down. He was getting frustrated. Mary Thomas didn't seem to be taking this seriously at all.

'I don't want you to find me a wife,' he said in a taut voice. 'I'm just trying to explain. Getting married is my goal. I just need a bit of coaching to get there.'

'Coaching?' said Mary, trying to look willing but still confused about where she came into all this.

'Yes, you know…relationship coaching.'

Tyler couldn't quite hide his distaste of the term, although Mary wasn't sure whether it was relationship or coaching that was the problem for him. There was a very slight tinge of colour along his cheekbones and he looked faintly uncomfortable.

Mary's interest sharpened. The Tyler Wattses of this world would normally only discuss emotions if they were listed on the stock exchange, so it must be costing him a lot to even mention the word *relationship*, let alone with the implication that he needed some help on that front. Men like Tyler Watts didn't do asking for help any more than they did talking about their feelings. Things must be pretty bad.

She had only ever thought of Tyler as an employer, but of

course he was a man too. And not an unattractive one, Mary had to admit. He projected such a forceful personality that it was hard to get past that and look at him properly, but if that cold blue stare didn't have you trapped like a rabbit stuck in headlights, it was possible to see that he had a face that was dark and strong rather than handsome.

The fierce brows, jutting nose and forceful jaw were familiar, of course, but she had never noticed his mouth before, she realised. It was rather a nice mouth too, now she came to look at it. They might be set in a stern line right now, but his lips looked cool and firm, and it would be interesting to see what they would be like if he smiled.

Or feel like if he kissed.

Sucking in an involuntary breath at the thought, Mary caught herself up sharply and stamped down firmly on the little tingle that was shivering its way down her spine.

What was she *thinking* of? This was *Tyler Watts*, of all people. He was a hard man, and she didn't envy the woman he was planning on marrying. It would be like cuddling up to a lump of granite.

On the other hand, she would know what it was like to kiss him.

Enough. Mary pulled her wayward thoughts sternly to order.

'Relationship coaching isn't really my field,' she said carefully. 'If you're having problems with your fiancée, there are plenty of organisations that offer counselling and will be able to help you. I could put you in touch with them, if you like.'

'I don't need *counselling*,' said Tyler, outraged at the very idea. This was all proving much more difficult to explain than he had anticipated. 'I haven't got any problems. I *haven't*!' he insisted crossly when Mary just looked at him.

'What does your fiancée think?' she asked.

'I haven't got a fiancée, that's the point,' he snapped, goaded by the needle in her voice.

'But you said you wanted to get married,' said Mary, puzzled.

'I do.'

'Then who do you want to marry?'

'Anyone—anyone except you,' he added hastily.

'Anyone?'

'Well, not *any*one,' Tyler amended. 'Obviously I'd want my wife to be beautiful and intelligent and sophisticated, but the point is, I don't have anyone particular in mind yet.'

Incredible. He actually meant it, thought Mary. It was an oddly old-fashioned attitude for a man who had built this extraordinary twenty-first century building, but there wasn't so much as a glimmer of laughter in his voice, and she could only conclude that he was serious. Anyone would think he was some stiff-necked earl planning a marriage of convenience in a Regency romance.

'I'm sorry, but I still don't see where I come in,' she told him, looking around for somewhere to put her empty glass.

Tyler raked a hand through his hair in frustration. 'Look, finding a woman isn't a problem,' he said with unconscious arrogance.

Mary would have loved to have contradicted him, but she was afraid it was all too true. Tyler was in his early forties and had built his company up from nothing to be listed in the top hundred in the country. He was extremely wealthy, undoubtedly intelligent, apparently straight and even attractive if you liked the ruthless, hard-bitten type—and let's face it, lots of women did, even when the toughness wasn't accompanied by loads of dosh.

No, Mary could see that acquiring a girlfriend wouldn't be too difficult for Tyler.

'Then what *is* the problem?'

'Keeping her,' he said. 'I want to get married, but my relationships aren't lasting long enough to get engaged.'

'Maybe you just haven't met the right woman yet,' Mary suggested mildly, but he dismissed that idea.

'It's not that. No, there've been several suitable women, but I'm doing something wrong. That's where you come in.'

'I don't see how,' said Mary frankly.

'You said that you ran coaching courses where you helped people identify and achieve their goals.'

'Well, yes, but in a work context,' she said. 'I help people with their careers, not their love lives.'

Tyler brushed the distinction aside. 'It's the same process, surely? I've identified my goal—to get married. I need you to help me with my strategy.'

'Relationships aren't like business plans,' said Mary. 'You can't have a strategy for emotions!'

'Everything's a strategy,' said Tyler. He dug his hands into his pockets and hunched his shoulders. 'I'm obviously getting something wrong,' he conceded. 'You work out what that is and tell me what I should be doing instead. I apply what I've learnt to my next relationship, the relationship works, I get married and achieve my goal. That's strategy.'

Mary sighed. 'I can tell you now what you're getting wrong,' she said. 'Your attitude.'

'What's wrong with my attitude?'

'Relationships just don't work like that. I can understand wanting to get married, but first of all you need to fall in love and that's not something you can plan for. You can't predict when you're going to meet the right person. It's not like interviewing for a job, you know. Falling in love isn't about mugging up a few notes, drawing up a list of criteria and finding someone who more or less fits your requirements!'

That was exactly what Tyler had planned to do. 'I think you're over-romanticising,' he said stiffly. 'The goal here is to get married. It's not about falling in love.'

'But if you want to get married, that's exactly what it should be about,' said Mary, appalled.

'You don't really believe that love is the only reason people get married, do you?' he asked, raising his brows superciliously, and Mary lifted her chin.

'Yes, as a matter of fact, I do!'

'You're a romantic.' He didn't make it sound like a compliment. 'My own view of the world is a little more practical…perhaps realistic would be a better word,' he added after a moment's consideration.

'I'm prepared to accept that some people do indeed get married because they're *in love*, whatever that means,' he went on, putting sneery quotation marks around the words, 'but you're a fool if you think it's the only reason, or the only good reason. There are plenty of equally valid reasons to marry.'

'Like what?' she demanded, profoundly unconvinced.

'Like security…stability…comfort…fear of loneliness… financial incentives…status…convenience…'

'Oh, *please*!' Mary rolled her eyes. 'Marriages of convenience went out centuries ago!'

'I disagree,' said Tyler. 'I think the idea of settling into a routine where you don't have to think about making the effort to go out and impress someone new is very appealing for a lot of people. Knowing that there's someone else to do the cooking and cleaning, or change the plug, or pick up the dry-cleaning, is a lot more convenient than having to think about everything for yourself. I imagine there are a lot more happy marriages based on comfort and convenience than on bodice-ripping passion.'

Mary opened her mouth to disagree, then thought about her

mother's second marriage. Her mother had been open about the fact that she was settling for comfort this time round, and she had been very happy with Bill. Until Bill had decided that comfort wasn't enough, of course, but that was another story.

'Perhaps,' she allowed, 'but I don't see you as someone who's short of comfort and security and all that stuff. You certainly don't have any financial incentive to get married! So why get married unless you are in love?'

'Because I've decided that's what I want to do,' said Tyler curtly. He didn't have to explain himself to Mary Thomas. 'You're not concerned with the goal, only with how to achieve it.'

Mary shook her head. 'I'm not concerned with any of it,' she corrected him. 'I'm sorry, but I can't help you. You're not talking about the kind of goals and strategies I want to be associated with.'

His brows drew together in the familiar frown at the flatness of her rejection. 'I thought you were looking for work?'

'Not that kind of work,' she said. 'Recruitment opportunities, yes.'

'And if I tell Steven Halliday I don't want your agency considered if any recruitment contracts come up?'

Mary's eyes narrowed dangerously. 'That's blackmail!' she said, and he shrugged.

'That's business. I want something from you, you want something for me. Why should I give you what you want if I don't get what I want in return?'

'That's not *business*,' said Mary, her voice shaking with fury. 'I'm offering you an excellent service. If you choose to use that service, you pay me for what I do. *That's* business.'

Tyler merely looked contemptuous. 'That's not the deal that's on offer here.'

'Then you can keep your deal! I may be desperate for work, but I'm not that desperate!'

'Sure? The recruitment contract will be a lucrative one.'

'I'm sure,' said Mary distinctly. She took a firmer grip of her bag and got ready to leave. 'You know, I'm not surprised that you have problems forming relationships if your first response to rejection is bullying and blackmail,' she told him, too angry by now to care about alienating him, his company or the entire business community if it came to that.

'What makes you think that I'd want to be involved in your pathetic strategies?' she went on in a scathing tone. 'I can think of better goals to work towards than seeing some poor woman trapped in a loveless marriage with someone so emotionally stunted! Frankly, the whole idea is offensive.'

A muscle was jumping furiously in Tyler's jaw and there was a dangerously white look around his mouth. It was some satisfaction to know that he was as angry as she was.

'I may be emotionally stunted, but I don't need any lessons from you about business,' he retorted. 'I've got an extremely successful company,' he said, pointing a finger at his chest, and then at her for emphasis. '*You've* got a piddling recruitment agency with no clients. Which of us do you think understands business better?'

He shook his head. 'I would moderate your ambitions, if I were you, Ms Thomas. You'll never get your agency off the ground if you're going to get all emotional and upset about every opportunity that comes your way.'

'I'll take my chance,' said Mary with a withering look. 'You're not the only employer in York, and if I'm going to be in business I'd rather deal with people who don't resort to blackmail as a negotiating technique!'

She turned to leave, wishing the floor didn't prevent her

stalking off in her heels. 'Now, if you'll excuse me,' she said, 'I've wasted enough time tonight. My feet are killing me and I'm going home.'

'How's she been?' Mary tiptoed over to the cot and rested a protective hand on her baby daughter's small body, reassuring herself that she was still warm and breathing. She knew it was foolish, but she had to do it every time she went out, had to see Bea and touch her to reassure herself that she was all right.

She had asked her mother if she would ever get over the terror at the awesome responsibility of having this tiny, perfect, miraculous baby to look after, and her mother had laughed. 'Of course you will,' she had said. 'When you die.'

'She's been fine,' Virginia Travers said quietly from the doorway. 'Not a peep out of her.'

Reluctantly, Mary left her sleeping daughter and hobbled downstairs, collapsing on to the sofa at last with a gusty sigh. 'Thanks for looking after her, Mum,' she said as she rubbed her poor feet.

'It was no trouble,' Virginia said, as she always did, which always made Mary feel even guiltier. 'How did the reception go?'

Mary made a face. 'Not good,' she admitted. Disastrous might have been a more accurate reply, but she wanted to sound positive for her mother, who had enough to worry about at the moment.

Absently, she rubbed her arm where Tyler had grabbed her to stop her falling. It felt as if his fingers were imprinted on her flesh and it was almost a surprise to see that there were no marks there at all.

'It was a waste of time, really,' she told her mother.

'Oh, dear.' Virginia's face fell. 'It sounded such a good opportunity to make contacts too. There's no chance of a contract with Watts Holdings?'

Mary thought about Tyler's expression as she'd walked off. 'Er, no,' she said. 'I don't think that's at all likely.'

'Mary, what are you going to do?'

Her mother sounded really worried and Mary felt guilty about having blown her one chance to make an impression on Tyler Watts. At least, she had probably made an impression, but it wasn't the right one.

'Don't worry, Mum, something will come up,' she said, forcing herself to sound positive. 'There are still one or two companies I haven't approached yet, and I've placed a few temporary staff.'

All of whose contracts were up at the end of the next week.

Deciding to keep that little fact to herself, Mary found a smile of reassurance that she hoped would fool her mother, but when she looked closer she saw that Virginia was plucking nervously at the arm of the chair and avoiding her eye.

Mary straightened, suddenly alert. 'Mum?'

'Bill rang this evening,' Virginia told her a little tremulously. 'He wants to come home.'

'Oh, Mum…' Mary went over to sit on the arm of the chair and put her arm around her mother's shoulders.

Virginia had been distraught when Bill had suddenly announced that he was leaving earlier that year. His decision had coincided with Mary's unexpected pregnancy, and coming back to York to have the baby had seemed the obvious solution.

Mary had needed somewhere to live and Virginia had needed the company, and in many ways it had worked as planned. Thirty-five was really too old to be living with your mother, and the house was too small for the three of them, but they had been rubbing along all right. Mary had even begun to think that her mother might be ready to move on. She had served Bill with divorce papers only the week before.

'What did you say?' she asked Virginia gently.

'I said I'd meet him tomorrow and we'd talk about it.'

Mary heard the wobble in her mother's voice and hugged her tight. 'You want him back, don't you?' she said, and Virginia's eyes filled with tears as she nodded.

'I know I ought to hate him after he hurt me like that, but I just miss him so much,' she confessed.

'Well, you need to talk about what happened, but you're still married,' Mary pointed out. 'If you decide you want him back and he wants to come back, there's no reason you shouldn't just get on with being married again.'

'He can't come back yet,' said Virginia, still a bit tearfully. 'There isn't any room for him now.'

'Bea and I will move out. It's time we were doing that anyway, and you certainly can't sort things out with us around.'

'But you can't afford your own place,' her mother objected.

'I'll work something out,' said Mary confidently, giving her mother's shoulders a final squeeze and getting to her feet. 'Don't worry about us, Mum. You concentrate on sorting out things with Bill and I'll find somewhere to live.'

But where? Mary asked herself wearily as she started the long climb up the stairs to her office the next morning.

She liked her attic office in the city centre. Dating from the seventeenth century, the building had higgledy-piggledy rooms, sloping floors and dangerously low beams. It was charming but there were times, like now, when she had Bea on her hip and two bags to carry, that she wished for a few more modern amenities. Like a lift, for instance.

Plodding upwards, Mary made it to the first landing and hoisted Bea higher on to her hip as she pondered her accom-

modation problem. Her mother was happy for the first time
in months, and if she and Bill had some space and some time
on their own, Mary was sure that they could work things out.

If only Alan would release her money from the house,
there wouldn't be a problem. As it was, Mary was beginning
to wonder if she would ever get her money back. She had put
the savings that she had into renting this office and getting the
agency off the ground, but the only way that she had been able
to afford that was living with her mother. She couldn't borrow
while Alan was being so obstructive, and her income from the
agency was sketchy, to say the least.

She had thought it was such a good idea to set up her own
business when she moved back to York. It had seemed her best
hope of generating an income while still giving her the flexibility to look after Bea herself, but perhaps she would have
to think about applying for a job after all.

That wouldn't solve her immediate problems, though. It
would take too long for her mother and Bill and, anyway, she
would have to find a job that earned enough to cover childcare costs. What she needed right now was some money to
put down as a deposit on a flat and cover the first few months
rent until she had some proper income from the agency but,
short of robbing a bank, Mary couldn't think where she was
going to get it.

Her thoughts were still circling worriedly as she puffed up
the last flight of steps and rounded the landing to stop dead
when she saw who was waiting outside her office door.

'Oh,' she said. 'It's you.'

Her heart had lurched violently at the sight of him, leaving
her breathless and a little shaken. Tyler Watts was the last
person she had expected to see this morning.

He looked as grim as ever and his massive presence was

overwhelming on the cramped landing. Mary was suddenly very conscious of the fact that her skirt was creased, her hair unwashed and she hadn't even had time to put on any lipstick.

She had overslept after a broken night and had fallen into yesterday's clothes as she hurried to get Bea ready for the day. Normally her mother would look after her, but Virginia was preoccupied with her coming meeting with Bill. Bea wasn't sleeping well at the moment and Mary would have been exhausted even if she hadn't had her own worries to keep her awake long after she had got the baby back to sleep.

She had spent half the night replaying that conversation with Tyler and wishing that she hadn't lost her temper. His attempt at blackmail had been outrageous, of course, but it wasn't as if he had been trying to force her into white slavery, was it? All he wanted was a bit of coaching.

Would a few tips on how to make a relationship work have been so hard to do? Mary asked herself. It was only what she would discuss over a bottle of wine with her girlfriends, after all. They were all relationship experts now. And, in return, she could have had an introduction to Steven Halliday and a chance at a contract that would save her agency.

But no, she had had to get all righteous and uppity because he unnerved her. The way he was unnerving her now.

'What are you doing here?' she demanded rudely.

Tyler was looking from her to Bea. 'You've got a baby.'

'My, he's a quick one.' Bea got very heavy after three flights of stairs and Mary shifted her to her other hip. 'We can't fool him, can we, Bea?'

'Is she yours?'

'She is, and before you ask, no, her father's not around.'

Mary pulled her bag round and fished one-handedly for the key. Having already accused him of being a bully, a blackmailer and being emotionally stunted, it seemed a bit late to try sucking up to him, and she was too tired and fed up with her whole situation to make an effort any more.

'What do you want?'

'To see you,' he said and then looked at his watch. It was half past nine. 'Do you always start work this late?' he asked disapprovingly. In Tyler's world, everyone was at their desks at eight o'clock on the dot, and he was probably at his even earlier.

'No, not always,' said Mary, still searching for the key. 'It's been one of those mornings.'

Where was that key? She sucked in her breath with frustration. Of course, she hadn't had time to transfer the contents to a different bag so she was still carrying the one that had broken so inopportunely last night, and the muddle at the bottom was even worse than usual. She had managed to knot the broken strap together, but it hardly made for a professional image.

Still, it was too late for that.

This was hopeless, thought Mary, rummaging fruitlessly. She glanced at Tyler, still waiting for her to open the door. Her unwelcoming greeting didn't seem to have put him off, but then she guessed he was a man who didn't go until he had said what he was going to say.

'Look, would you mind holding her a moment?' she said, handing Bea over to him before he had a chance to answer. 'I'll just find my key.'

Appalled, Tyler found himself holding the baby, his arms extended stiffly so that she dangled from his hands. He stared at her nervously and the baby stared back with round eyes that were exactly the same grey as her mother's.

'Ah…here it is.' Mary produced the key from the depths of her bag and inserted it in the lock. She opened the door on to a room that was surprisingly light as the autumn sunshine poured through the two windows set into the sloping roof, and she waved a hand with a trace of sarcasm. 'Come into my luxury penthouse,' she said.

CHAPTER THREE

TYLER was left literally holding the baby as Mary went in. He followed hastily and stood waiting for her to take it back, but instead she went over to the desk and switched on the computer.

'Er…Mary?' he said to remind her and she glanced up from her keyboard.

Good God, you'd think the man had never held a baby before! Mary smothered a smile. She had never seen anyone look so awkward with a small child. He was holding Bea at arm's length and his expression, normally so grim, was distinctly alarmed.

Who would have thought that a baby was all it took to put the ferocious Tyler Watts at a disadvantage? Pity she hadn't taken Bea with her last night. Things might have been very different.

As Mary watched, the alarm changed to horror as Bea's little face crumpled and, terrified that she was going to start crying, Tyler jiggled her up and down a bit. To his surprise, the baby paused, as if unsure how to react. For a breathless moment she looked extremely dubious and it was touch and go until, just as Tyler was convinced that she was going to bawl after all, she dissolved into a gummy smile.

Absurdly flattered, Tyler jiggled her up and down some more. Apparently deciding that this was a good game, Bea gurgled triumphantly. 'Ga!' she shouted, smiling, and, succumbing to that irresistible baby charm, Tyler smiled back.

Mary froze over her keyboard. She had never seen him smile before and the effect was startling, to say the least, lightening the grim lines of his face and making him look younger and more approachable.

And disturbingly attractive.

Swallowing, Mary straightened. She had wondered what he would look like if he smiled, and now she knew. Amazing what a mere crease of the cheek could do. Watching him smile was making her feel quite…unsettled. She wasn't sure it wasn't easier to deal with the grimly formidable Tyler than a Tyler who smiled like that.

'Coffee?' she asked in a bright voice and, reminded of her presence, Tyler stopped smiling abruptly. He flushed slightly, embarrassed at having been caught out playing with the baby.

'Thank you,' he said curtly, reverting to type.

Mary went over to fill up the kettle and tried not to feel put out that he would smile at Bea but not at her. She knew that he could do it now, so there was no excuse.

While the kettle boiled, she spread a rug on the floor and retrieved Bea from Tyler at last. The brush of their hands as he passed the baby back made her nerves leap alarmingly and she busied herself settling Bea on the rug and finding some toys for her to play with, and willing the heightened colour in her cheeks to fade.

'Sit down,' she said to Tyler, but without meeting his eye. 'I won't be a minute.'

Tyler nodded, but chose to walk around the room instead. It was very simply decorated in cream and the furniture she had chosen was simple and unfussy. Clearly a start-up operation, he thought.

He made himself think about the likely overheads of a business this size and not about the warm feeling Bea's smiles had given him, or the way Mary's top shifted over her curves as she stretched up to retrieve some coffee filters from the cupboard. Picking up a calendar from her desk, he pretended to study it, but he was very aware of Mary moving around, rinsing mugs, bending to find milk in the little fridge or chatting playfully to the baby, who was banging happily on the floor with a bright plastic ring.

The presence of the baby had thrown him, Tyler decided. He hadn't been expecting her or how warm and heavy she would feel between his hands. Mary Thomas seemed to have a very odd idea about how to conduct business. He just needed a few minutes while she was making the coffee to collect himself and remember what he was doing here.

Mary studied him out of the corner of her eye as she waited for the coffee to drip through the filters. Tyler was probably used to freshly ground coffee, but that was too bad. He was lucky that he was getting coffee at all after last night!

What was he doing here anyway? She had been dismayed to see him, but what if there was a chance that she could somehow make up for the mistakes of last night? It seemed too good to be true, but why else would he be here?

She mustn't mess this up if she got another chance, Mary told herself sternly. With her mother so anxious to get back together with Bill, now was not the time to be taking high-minded stands on jobs. If she were to earn enough to get her and Bea somewhere to live, she would need to take anything she could get.

Tyler came back when the coffee was ready and took one of the easy chairs Mary used for interviewing. She would have preferred to sit behind her desk where she would feel more in control, but Bea might protest if she lost sight of her and, anyway, she reminded herself, she wouldn't give him the satisfaction of suspecting that he made her feel nervous.

So she sat opposite him and picked up her mug of coffee. 'What can I do for you?' she asked him.

Tyler was glad that he could get straight to the point. 'I want to offer you a deal,' he said.

'We discussed your idea of a deal last night,' Mary reminded him, cautious about getting her hopes up yet.

'I'm making a new offer.'

'Oh? Some new form of blackmail, perhaps?' she couldn't resist saying.

Tyler's eyes narrowed but he restrained his temper. Only the tic in his jaw indicated how difficult that was.

'No,' he said evenly. 'I'm prepared to offer you the recruitment contract for all junior staff in the York office if you will agree to give me some relationship coaching.'

Mary considered what he'd said. 'That's the same blackmail as before,' she pointed out.

'No, it isn't. Last night I said that I wouldn't give you the contract if you didn't agree. That was a threat. Now I'm saying that I'll give it to you if you do. That's an incentive. It's quite different.'

He paused. 'I'll also give you a lump sum—let's say ten thousand pounds—when I embark on a successful relationship, and if your advice leads to an engagement soon after that there'll be a further bonus.'

Mary stared at him, hardly able to believe what she was hearing. Ten thousand pounds! Plus the income from that lucrative contract! Moving its headquarters back to York would make Watts Holdings one of the biggest employers in the city. The company was expanding dramatically and most of the new jobs would be at junior level. This would make her agency, she thought excitedly. She might not even have to rent. If she could get Tyler hooked up with someone nice, she could think about buying a small place for her and Bea.

And all she had to do in return was to teach Tyler a bit about how to keep a woman happy in a relationship. It wasn't what she had imagined herself doing, but it wasn't as if he was asking her to do anything immoral or unethical, was it? You could even say that there was something admirable about a man like Tyler putting so much effort into making a relationship a success.

'You must want this coaching very badly,' she said slowly, still hardly daring to believe that there wasn't a catch somewhere.

'I do.'

'But why do you want me? You could easily find someone with much better and more appropriate qualifications.'

Why *did* he want her? Tyler had been asking himself that all night. Because she was there, he had decided in the end. Because she seemed to know about coaching. Julia's words had been rankling and coming across Mary had seemed like the perfect opportunity to solve a nagging problem. Tyler wasn't a man who had reached the top by not grasping an opportunity when it came along.

Because he had decided that Mary was the coach he wanted, and he always got what he wanted.

Or it might have been because he hadn't been able to get her face out of his mind. He had kept hearing the scorn in her voice, remembering the directness of her grey gaze, and the way her eyes had danced when she had had the temerity to laugh at him.

'Because you're not afraid of me,' he told her in the end.

'I wouldn't be too sure about that,' muttered Mary.

'And I don't want to talk about feelings,' he went on, practically spitting out the word. 'I just want practical advice and you seem like someone who could give me that. Plus, you're available and have experience of coaching.'

'I don't have experience of the kind of coaching you mean,' Mary felt she should remind him. 'Not professional experience, anyway. I think most women my age get pretty expert at helping friends through relationship crises, but we tend to do it over a bottle of wine!'

She spoke lightly, but Tyler pounced on her comment. 'Exactly!' he said. 'And you're exactly the kind of woman I'm looking for. Well, not *you*, obviously,' he said quickly as Mary's brows shot up. 'But a woman like you. A bit younger, ideally, but professional and…you know, intelligent…*classy*,' he tried to explain.

Mary looked down at her crumpled skirt and top, which still showed traces of where Bea had gugged up some milk that morning, and boggled privately. She had never been called classy before.

'You said yourself that you talk to your friends about all that emotional stuff, and that means you'd know what women like that want from a man,' Tyler went on. 'At the same time, there's no risk of getting personally involved with you.'

'Why not?' asked Mary.

Tyler scowled, thrown by the directness of the question. 'Well, because you're not…you're not…' Damn it, she knew what he meant!

'Not attractive enough for you?' she suggested sweetly.

'Yes…I mean, no, you're very…' He hated being made to stumble and stutter and look a fool like this. 'Look, you're just not my type, OK? Just as I'm sure I'm not yours.'

'Quite,' said Mary, who was rather enjoying his discomfiture. It made up a little for being told that he found her completely unattractive. Not that she cared, of course, but still, a girl had her feelings.

'Besides, you've got a baby,' he said, indicating Bea, who was thoughtfully sucking the leg of a stuffed elephant.

'Does that mean I can never have another relationship?' she asked innocently. 'I'm a single mother, yes, but I might be on the lookout for a father figure for Bea.'

She was only teasing, but a wary look sprang into Tyler's eyes. 'I'm not looking to take on another man's child,' he warned. 'I want my own family, not someone else's.'

'Well, that's us rejected, Bea.' Mary heaved a soulful sigh. 'It looks like it's going to be just the two of us.'

At the sound of her name, Bea took the elephant out of her mouth and beamed at her mother. Her smile was so sweet that Mary's throat tightened with such a powerful rush of love that she felt almost giddy. Reaching down, she smoothed the baby's hair with a tender smile.

When she glanced up once more, she saw Tyler watching them with a strange expression. 'It's OK,' she said patiently. 'I was just joking!'

'The condition of the deal is that our relationship is strictly a business one,' he said gruffly, more disconcerted than he wanted to admit by the sight of Mary leaning down to her baby. For a moment there, she had looked almost beautiful, her face soft and suffused with love and, when she'd looked up, the grey eyes had still been shining.

That luminous look was fading as she studied him, and he was vexed with himself for even noticing. What had he been expecting? That she would look that way at *him*?

'Fine,' she said. 'But what makes you think that I will agree this time?'

'I asked around last night,' he told her. 'Your business is in a bad way. You've got no long-term contracts.'

There was no point in lying about it. 'No,' Mary agreed, getting up to find some biscuits. She was starving, having skipped breakfast, and she couldn't concentrate properly without something to eat.

'I am prepared to consider your offer, but I need to know exactly what you want,' she went on, offering the packet to Tyler, who shook his head with a touch of disapproval.

Defiantly, Mary helped herself to two biscuits. They might be the last thing her figure needed, but a girl had to have *some* indulgences and, anyway, what difference was a pound or two going to make? She had already been told this morning that she was fat and unattractive and absolutely not Tyler's type. A biscuit here or there wasn't going to change that.

Not that she wanted it to change, of course.

'I've told you,' Tyler said with a trace of impatience. 'I want to get married.'

'But why?' she asked, brushing biscuit crumbs from her skirt. 'If you said you wanted to marry X or Y, I could understand it, but you're just talking about "a wife" as if it doesn't really matter who she is. Why would you want a wife?'

'Because everyone else has one,' said Tyler. 'Because being successful now means having a wife and family, and I haven't got that.'

'There are other ways to be successful, though,' Mary pointed out. 'People who use their talents, people who are happy and contented with their lives…you can argue that they're the most successful people. You don't have to measure success against what others have.'

'I do,' said Tyler grimly. 'It was easy when it was just a

question of having a bigger annual bonus or a faster car, but it's different now.'

'In what way?'

There was something disconcerting about the luminous grey eyes that were fixed on him and Tyler looked away, only to discover that the baby seemed to be watching him too. She had eyes exactly like her mother, he noticed.

Irritably, he got to his feet. He wanted to make Mary understand why it was so important to him to get married, and he couldn't do that with the baby distracting him.

'Last October I went to a reunion,' he said, marshalling his thoughts. 'We'd all done an MBA together a few years back.'

He hadn't wanted to go at first, but Mike had talked him into it. 'Jack'll be there,' he had said. 'And Tony. They've both done incredibly well,' he'd added cunningly, knowing how competitive Tyler was. 'You'll be able to compare Porsches.'

So Tyler had gone along and it hadn't been too bad at first. Jack and Tony had indeed done well for themselves, but neither could rival the success of Watts Holdings.

'So your Porsche was bigger and better after all?' said Mary, following so far but not overly impressed. It was hard to care very much about the rivalry men felt over the size of their various toys.

'That's just it. No one was interested in talking about cars.' Tyler sounded so baffled that for a moment there Mary almost felt sorry for him.

'What were they talking about?'

'Babies.' He made it sound like aliens.

Mary couldn't help laughing. 'Really? I bet they were all still being competitive, though?'

'Oh, yes.' Tyler's mouth turned down. 'Who has the biggest/happiest/highest achieving family, who cried most when they saw their first child being born, whose child is most advanced—one was taking A levels in the womb, apparently.'

He stopped and looked down at Bea from his considerable height. 'I suppose yours is a super-achiever too?'

'No.' Mary smiled and retrieved the elephant that Bea had thrown at her feet. 'She's just a baby.'

She glanced back up at Tyler, who was looming over them both. 'It sounds as if it was a pretty boring evening,' she commented, 'but, other than that, what was the problem?'

What *had* been the problem? Tyler asked himself. It wasn't that he'd felt excluded. There was nothing new there. He was always the outsider.

And it wasn't that he'd been jealous. He had never wanted children.

But he didn't like not having what everyone else had. It had been easy before. Work until you could buy the biggest house, the best car, the fastest yacht. Now it was as if the rules had been changed when he wasn't looking. Success couldn't be measured by what you had bought any more. Suddenly it was all about families and children and relationships, areas in which he couldn't compete. He didn't even know the rules of the game.

Tyler didn't like that feeling.

But he sensed that if he was going to get what he wanted, he was going to have to be honest with Mary Thomas.

'The problem was realising that the game has changed. It's not about working hard and getting what you want any more. It's about being a different kind of person and I don't know how to do that,' he confessed in a burst of honesty.

'I thought it would be easy. If everyone was getting married and having a family, I could do that too.'

'It's never as easy as you think it's going to be,' said Mary, thinking of Alan.

'No,' Tyler agreed morosely.

The truth was that he couldn't bear the thought of being considered a failure. He knew that was how the other men had looked at him. His wealth, his spectacular success, had counted for nothing when compared with squatting in a birthing pool or changing a nappy.

Tyler had no intention of being a failure. If a family was what he needed to be considered a success, a family he would have.

He would have the best family ever. He would have the most beautiful wife, the most blessed of children. He would have it all.

That would show them.

But it wasn't proving as easy to acquire a wife as he had thought.

'I worked out a strategy,' he told Mary. 'First, I'd find someone to marry.'

'Good plan,' she said, her voice heavy with irony. 'It's always a good idea to choose a mother before you start the business of actually having children.'

Her sarcasm made Tyler shoot her a sharp look, but he decided to ignore it and get his story told so that could get out of here and back to work.

'I decided what kind of woman I was looking for,' he went on, determined to outline his careful strategy, but Mary interrupted him again.

'Let me guess!' she said, holding up her hand. 'You want someone young, beautiful, sexy, charming…what else? She probably needs to be intelligent—but not too clever, of course—feminine, but not too needy…am I close?'

Tyler eyed her with dislike. 'I wanted her to be good with children too.'

'Of course!' Mary snapped her fingers. 'How could I have

forgotten? Naturally you'd need her to be a good mother as well as someone you can show off to all your colleagues.'

'Is that too much to ask?' he demanded, provoked.

'Have you met this paragon yet?' she countered.

'No,' he had to admit. 'That's the problem. I had plenty of girlfriends, but none of them were the kind of girls you'd want to marry, if you know what I mean.'

'No,' said Mary. 'What *do* you mean?'

'They were all young and pretty enough, but they were just out to have a good time, and that suited me. They were happy with being wined and dined and bought expensive presents. I want my wife to be classier than that,' Tyler explained haughtily. 'I want someone special.'

'We all want someone special,' said Mary.

Tyler ignored that. 'I started dating different women—attractive, professional women who had that kind of classiness and style. They're not hard to find.'

Mary could believe it. She had lots of wonderful, warm, intelligent, attractive friends who were finding it harder and harder to find a boyfriend.

And she was one of them, she realised with a shock. Well, not the attractive bit, according to Tyler, anyway. It was true that she was having trouble shifting the weight she'd put on when she was pregnant, and she was too tired most of the time to look stylish—witness her current outfit—but she had lots of friends who wouldn't hesitate to describe her as wonderful too.

She rubbed absently at the stain on her top, turning over the idea that she was once again a single woman. She had been with Alan for five years, and since then her world had been entirely occupied by Bea. There hadn't been time to think about whether she would ever find anyone else. Meeting a new man was right at the bottom of her priority list at the moment.

Which was just as well. Otherwise, it might have been mortifying to realise that she would never figure on Tyler Watts's wish list. Not that she would want to. Her own preference was for men with a little more warmth.

And then, for some reason, she found herself remembering how he had looked when he'd smiled at Bea, and a little *frisson* travelled down her spine.

OK, he had a nice smile. And a good body, she'd give him that. And, if she was being absolutely truthful with herself, there had been something about those big strong hands holding Bea that had given her a bit of a quiver too, but that was *it*, she reassured herself firmly. It wasn't enough to make him her type.

Not really.

Mary didn't like the way her thoughts were heading on this one, and distracted herself with another biscuit. 'With all this choice, why aren't you waltzing up the aisle right now?' she asked him indistinctly through the crumbs.

'I don't know, that's the problem.' Tyler sounded frustrated. 'It's always fine at first, but just when I begin to think that I might have found someone suitable, they start complicating things,' he complained.

'Complicating how?'

He hunched an irritable shoulder. 'They want me to *communicate* more, so that we can talk about our relationship, but it never seems to me that there's anything to say,' he said, sounding puzzled. 'I don't understand what the big deal is. We're sleeping together, we're going out to nice restaurants, we're having a nice time… What's the problem? But they get disappointed because I can't see the problem, and next thing there's a tearful scene and, before I know what's happening, they've gone and somehow it's all my fault!'

Tyler glowered. 'What am I doing wrong?' He started

pacing again. 'This whole relationship thing is a mystery dreamt up by women, if you ask me,' he grumbled. 'Why does it always have to be so complicated?'

'Because people are complicated,' said Mary, handing Bea the elephant again.

'Well, I want the simple version,' said Tyler.

Mary sighed. 'The whole point about a relationship is that it's not just about what *you* want. You need to think about what your partner wants too—and maybe what she wants is for you to talk about how you both feel.'

'Right, that's the kind of thing I need to know.' Tyler swung round, relieved that they were getting somewhere at last. 'If I have to go through a whole lot of emotional mumbo-jumbo, I will. Everybody else seems to be able to do it, so there's no reason why I can't learn it too, is there?'

'You know, if you're going to think of my advice as mumbo-jumbo, I'm not sure we're going to get very far,' said Mary in a dry voice. 'It doesn't sound as if you're going to take it very seriously.'

'But I am,' he insisted. 'I'm deadly serious. I'll do whatever I have to do. You just have to tell me what women really want from a man, and I'll put it all into practice.'

'It sounds very easy when you put it like that,' she said.

'It will be easy,' he said confidently. 'I can't imagine an easier way to win a contract and ten thousand pounds, can you?'

Mary couldn't. 'No,' she admitted.

'So you'll do it?'

'On two conditions.'

Having got her agreement in principle, Tyler was prepared to negotiate. 'Which are?' he asked, sitting back down and then regretting it as Bea squawked with delight and promptly started crawling towards him.

'First, that we put a time limit on the exercise. I suggest two months,' said Mary coolly. She had been thinking while Tyler talked, and she hoped she could carry her plan off. 'A month for intensive coaching and a month for you to put it into practice, with my advice and feedback available if you're having problems.'

Tyler considered that. He didn't want to be spending months and months on this either. 'Fair enough,' he said, one eye on Bea, who had reached his shoes but had stopped there, to his relief. He had been afraid she'd want to get up on his lap.

'I'd want five thousand pounds at the end of the first month, regardless of whether you're in a relationship or not,' Mary went on, crossing her fingers. 'The other five thousand would be payable only if you were still in a relationship by the end of the second month.'

The pale blue eyes sharpened. 'My offer was ten thousand if I was settled in a relationship,' he reminded her.

'I know.' She met his eyes squarely. 'But that's my condition. Take it or leave it.'

Tyler studied her with new interest, unaware that Bea was pulling at his shoelaces. Take it or leave it was very much his own negotiating style, and very successful he had found it, but you needed to be in a strong position to carry it off. He wasn't sure that applied to Mary Thomas. Her business was clearly on a very shaky footing and she couldn't afford to risk losing the contract he was offering. He could beat her down easily.

On the other hand, he couldn't help admiring her guts. He liked people who were prepared to take a risk to get what they wanted. Mary was well aware that he had taken a risk in telling her as much as he had about himself, and he approved of her determination to make the most of her slim advantage. Besides, what was ten thousand to him?

'Agreed,' he said. He saw Mary's shoulders relax slightly as she let out a tiny breath of relief, and he very nearly forgot himself and smiled. 'What's the other condition?'

'That Bea and I move in with you for the first month.'

That did take him aback. 'Move *in*?'

'You've got a spare room, haven't you?'

'Yes,' he agreed cautiously, thinking of his ten bedrooms. 'But I don't see why we can't have our sessions in the office.'

'Because you can't treat it like learning a language or woodwork,' said Mary, who was wondering when he would notice that Bea had managed to undo both his shoes before crawling away to find her elephant again. 'Relationships are complex things. You can't divide them up into neat little segments, no matter how much some people, especially some men, would like to think that you can,' she added with a trace of bitterness. 'The only way for you to learn about relation-ships is for us to have one.'

Tyler immediately looked wary. 'I thought we'd agreed…?'

'Oh, not a physical one,' she interrupted him. 'I think we've established neither of us wants *that*.'

'Right,' he said, but not with quite as much relief as he would have expected.

He'd been honest when he said that she wasn't his type. He liked his women tall and blonde and elegant. Mary Thomas was none of those. She was on the short side of average and her curvaceous figure was…not fat, no, but def-initely…*luscious* was the word that came to mind, and once it had lodged there it was impossible to shake it.

Her clothes were awful, true, and her hair needed a cut, but there was a softness and a warmth about her that contrasted intriguingly with the sharpness of her tongue and the quirki-ness of her face.

So, while she might not be his type, there was something unnatural about the thought of going home to her every night and having to be relieved that he wasn't sleeping with her.

'I don't see why it's necessary,' he said, looking away from her.

Mary leant forward in her chair. Her mother needed this time alone with Bill to rescue her marriage and Mary was determined to make sure that she had it. That meant finding somewhere to go, and Tyler's house was the best option she had.

'Look,' she said, 'we've both got work to do during the day. Most relationships take place in the evening, and they're not just about sex. They're about learning to live together, to be aware of each other, to compromise. If I move in with you, you'll have to learn to do all those things and you can use me to practice your new skills.

'Of course it won't be an intimate relationship,' she went on persuasively, 'but it doesn't sound as if the physical side of things is your problem! What you need is practice communicating and listening and anticipating what the person you're living with really needs. Does that seem reasonable?'

'I suppose so,' said Tyler reluctantly.

'Living with me will mean that you have to do all of that, and if you *don't* do it it'll be my job to tell you. And, unlike in a real relationship, I won't get upset if you get it wrong because I won't have an emotional investment in you.'

It *could* work, Tyler admitted grudgingly to himself. There was even a bizarre kind of logic to it.

'What about the baby?' he said.

'She comes with me, of course.'

He eyed Bea dubiously. Having Mary in the house was one thing, but a baby…?

'I don't think my house is very suitable for a baby,' he said.

'What do you mean, *not suitable*?' demanded Mary. 'It's not as if she's a toddler who might break some of your ornaments. She's only just crawling!'

'It's not that.' Tyler didn't like being on the defensive, and he got restlessly to his feet, only to almost trip. *'What—?'*

Looking down, he saw that his shoelaces had been neatly untied and, with a muttered exclamation, he sat back down and did them up, knotting them with a savage yank.

Oblivious to his hostile glare, Bea batted her arms up and down with a crow of delight and would have set off towards him again if Mary hadn't intervened, scooping her up into her arms and trying not to laugh.

'She'll be a distraction,' Tyler said crossly, getting up once more and prowling over to one of the windows. It looked out over a cluster of rooftops to the Minster, its towers soaring proudly against a vivid blue autumn sky. He turned back to Mary. 'If I'm paying you all this money, I want you to concentrate on the job in hand.'

Unperturbed, Mary settled Bea on her lap and tried to distract her with her elephant. 'The job is to teach you how to have a relationship,' she reminded him crisply. 'And the first lesson you're going to have to learn is compromise.'

CHAPTER FOUR

'COMPROMISE?'

'Yes. You know what it means, don't you?'

Tyler scowled. 'Of course.'

Mary doubted if he had ever done it, though. Tyler Watts was not the compromising kind.

'Here's the deal, then,' she told him. 'I'm not going anywhere without my daughter, so you're going to have to decide whether you want me or not. Now, you may not want a baby around, but it's not just about what you want any more, is it? If our relationship is going to work, you've got to think about what I need and, in this case, I need to have Bea with me.'

'Why can't you be the one to compromise?' Tyler grumbled.

'Because my daughter isn't something I can compromise on,' said Mary. 'I can compromise on other things that don't matter to me so much, like how much time we spend together in the evenings, say, or when our deal starts.'

'It feels like it's started already!'

'Quite, which is why your first test is an important one.' She saw that he was looking mutinous, and sighed. Coaching a man like Tyler was going to be hard work. 'Look, imagine I'm your perfect woman,' she said, trying to make him understand. 'How much are you prepared to compromise to get me to live with you?'

'My perfect woman doesn't have a baby,' he pointed out, and Mary rolled her eyes.

'OK, what if she has a dog? Would you want a dog in your house?'

'No,' he said without hesitation.

'But what if this woman is perfect in every other way? She's gorgeous, talented, loving, clever…everything you've ever wanted, in fact. She adores you and makes you feel ten feet tall. Are you really going to give her up because she loves her dog?'

'If she adores me that much, she could give the dog up,' said Tyler facetiously, although he was secretly rather taken with the idea of someone adoring him.

'You can forget that,' said Mary. 'If she's a dog lover, there's no way she'll be giving up her dog for a man. No, it's down to you. What's the problem with a dog, anyway?'

'It'll make a mess.'

'So will children, and you say you want a family,' she pointed out. 'You're going to have to think very carefully about what really matters to you. I know what matters to me—my daughter—and that's where I'll refuse to compromise. What matters more to you than anything else? Your home? Your independence? Money?'

Tyler thought about it. 'Success,' he said at last.

'Right.' Mary suppressed another sigh. It was becoming clear why his previous relationships had never come to anything. 'If success means having this fabulous woman by your side, don't you think it's worth giving way on the dog thing if it means you get what you really want in the end?'

'I suppose so,' said Tyler grudgingly.

'That's compromise,' she said. 'It's all I'm asking you to do now. This is good practice for you, in fact.'

'Oh, all right,' he grumbled. 'Bring the baby—but keep her away from my shoelaces!'

Mary laughed. 'Honestly, you won't even know we're there most of the time.'

Tyler doubted that very much.

'Well, now that we've established that I do all the compromising and you get your own way,' he said a little grumpily, 'when do we start?'

Mary thought about it. 'Why don't we say Monday? That'll give me the weekend to get myself organised. Or is that too soon for you?'

He shook his head. 'The sooner we get started, the better, as far as I'm concerned.'

He was pleased that she didn't want to hang around. Once he had a goal in mind, he liked to focus on it. The two month thing sounded good too, Tyler thought. He would pick up some tips the first month, and start a relationship the second. He did a quick calculation. If he applied himself, he could be engaged by Christmas.

Golden leaves swirled down like lazy confetti as the car spluttered up an avenue of lime trees and emerged at last in front of a beautiful Georgian mansion, its mellow red brick warm in the late afternoon sunshine.

Mary switched off the engine with a sigh of relief. Her car was on its last legs—or should that be wheels?—and the fifteen miles from York along winding country roads was about as much as it could cope with.

She just hoped it would be up to the journey every day. She couldn't think why Tyler didn't have an apartment in the city.

It would be much more convenient, but then again, it wouldn't have the showy value of a house like this.

Mary had to admit that it was lovely. A flight of stone steps led up to a stately front entrance that in a more mundane house would be called a front door, and the tall windows were typical of Georgian grace and elegance. Mary had sometimes pressed her nose to exclusive estate agents' windows and seen houses like this, where no prices were ever mentioned. The implication was that if you had to ask, you couldn't afford it. It was the sort of house you visited on a Sunday afternoon, but not the kind of place you could imagine actually living in.

Unless you were Tyler Watts, of course. Mary wondered if he'd bought it because he thought it was beautiful, or because it was the biggest and best available.

'Ms Thomas?' A pleasant-looking woman had appeared at the door, and came down the steps to meet her as Mary lifted Bea out of the car. 'I'm Susan Palmer. I'm housekeeper here.'

Housekeeper, eh? Of course. Mary might have known Tyler would surround himself with flunkies to show how far he had come. He probably had a butler too, and an array of footmen and maids to tug their forelocks and say 'yes, sir, no sir' as required.

Freeing her hand, she offered it with a smile. 'I'm Mary,' she said, 'and this is Bea.'

'Welcome to Haysby Hall. Mr Watts said you would be coming.'

'He isn't here?' asked Mary, unaccountably put out.

'He doesn't usually get back until after I've gone,' Mrs Palmer explained. 'I leave a meal for him in the kitchen and he heats it up when he wants it.'

'Oh,' said Mary, digesting this. 'So you don't live here?'

'I live in the village. Mr Watts prefers being on his own. He values his privacy.'

So much for imagining Tyler surrounded by servants. It looked as if she'd been wrong about that.

It wouldn't be the first time, Mary reflected wryly, reaching into the car for the bag full of Bea's stuff.

Now she was going to have to think about the fact that she would be spending the next month out here alone with Tyler Watts. When she'd thought about it before, she'd just assumed that there would be other people around.

She would have to decide how she felt about that later.

'Is it OK if I use the kitchen when you're not here?' she asked Mrs Palmer as they walked towards the house. 'I need to prepare meals for the baby, and I like cooking for myself too.'

'Of course,' said Mrs Palmer. 'Mr Watts said you were to the treat the house as your own.'

She helped Mary carry all her things inside and showed her to a lovely bedroom with its own bathroom and smaller room next door for Bea.

'Is there anything else you need?' she asked Mary at last.

'No, I don't think so.' Mary was a little embarrassed at all the clutter she had brought with her. Most of it was Bea's and looked absurdly out of place in the gracious rooms. 'You've been very kind.'

'I'll be off then.'

Mary had secretly been longing for her to go so that she could explore properly. She and Bea spent a happy hour poking around the house, which was impeccably decorated. Clearly, a very expensive designer had been at work and no expense had been spared, but the final effect was rather like a show home for potential stately home owners. Mary couldn't find a single room that had an individual touch to it.

It was quite a relief in the end to go back to her bedroom, even if the floor was covered with a cot, packs of nappies, feeding bottles, bibs and all the rest of the baby paraphernalia.

She had tidied most of it away, bathed Bea, fed her and put her to bed, and still there was no sign of Tyler. Beginning to feel distinctly peeved at his absence, Mary had a bath and changed into a loose skirt with a camisole worn under a dusky pink wrap-over ballet top.

She was just putting on some lipstick when she heard the crunch of tyres on gravel. It was dark by then, but the light pouring out of the downstairs windows was enough for her to see a silver Porsche park next to her battered old car. The next moment, Tyler got out and strode towards the door, disappearing out of Mary's sight.

There was the sound of the door closing and then silence. No call to find out where she was, or if she was all right. No honey-I'm-home. If Tyler was anxious to see that she had arrived safely, he was concealing it very well.

Mary's lips tightened. It was nearly half past eight and she had been here four hours. Stalking out on to the landing, she leaned over the elaborate balustrade. Tyler had found the letters waiting for him on the magnificent marble table in the hall and was leafing through them, apparently unaware of his duties as a host.

He must have heard her, because he glanced up. 'Oh, there you are,' he said, pushing the letters together and turning towards the room Mrs Palmer had pointed out as his study. 'I just need to make a couple of calls, then I'll be with you, OK?'

'No,' said Mary.

Tyler stopped, looking up over his shoulder with a distracted frown. 'No, what?'

'No, it's not OK,' she said and came down the stairs towards him

'What's not OK?' he asked, taken aback.

'Your behaviour,' said Mary succinctly.

'My *behaviour*?' he echoed incredulously. 'I've only been in the house a matter of seconds! How can I have done something wrong in that time?'

Mary surveyed him coolly. 'You weren't here to greet me when I arrived,' she told him, 'which means that I've been hanging around for nearly four hours, waiting for you to deign to come home. Now you want to come in and *ignore* me while you finish your business!

Tyler's face tightened with exasperation. 'You were the one who wanted to come out here,' he pointed out.

'And *you* agreed that the best way for you to learn about relationships was to pretend that we had one,' said Mary, reaching the bottom step. 'That relationship isn't going to last long if you think a few phone calls are more important than making me feel welcome. How do you think a real girlfriend would feel if you disappeared into the study as soon as you arrived without bothering to say hello?'

'I'm sure she would understand that I was probably busy,' said Tyler. 'As I *am*,' he added meaningfully but Mary refused to take the hint.

'I think it's more likely that she would think you rude and unfeeling,' she said. 'Why would she want to marry a man who would treat her like that?'

Tyler's jaw clenched with the effort of keeping his temper. 'Look, I'm only going to be five minutes,' he said. What could be more reasonable than that?

'That five minutes could be the kiss of death on your relationship,' said Mary and he scowled.

'Aren't you being a little overdramatic?'

'Tyler, do you want to learn how to have successful relationship with a woman or not?' she asked through gritted teeth.

'That's why you're here.'

'Quite, so I suggest that you listen to what I'm saying! What's the point of paying me to be your relationship coach if you're not going to take my advice?' she asked, exasperated. She put her hands on her hips. 'Let's start again. Imagine you're in love with me,' she ordered him. 'Go on!' she added as his jaw set in a stubborn line.

Tyler blew out an irritable breath, but turned obediently back to study her.

She looked different tonight, he realised, looking at her properly for the first time. Her hair was a soft cloud around her face, and she had abandoned that tight suit and was wearing instead a floaty sort of skirt and a top with a plunging neckline that emphasised her generous cleavage. Beneath it she wore a lacy camisole, the discreet glimpse of which hinted deliciously at hidden delights and made Tyler's head spin suddenly with images of sexy lingerie and silk stockings.

He swallowed. 'All right,' he said, 'I'm imagining.'

The odd thing was that the more he looked at her, the more he *could* imagine it. Not the whole being in love thing, obviously, but it wasn't that difficult to imagine wanting to kiss her, wanting to discover if those lips were as sweet as they looked, wanting to unwrap that top and see what that lace was concealing…

'I'm ready,' he said, annoyed to find that his voice was a lot huskier than it should have been.

'OK, now imagine how *I* feel,' she told him. 'We're deeply in love, remember. We can't keep our hands off each other and

I haven't seen you since last night. I've spent all day looking forward to seeing you again. I've counted every minute.'

Getting into the part, she let a little wobble creep into her voice. 'I've come out to see your home for the first time, but you're not here to meet me when I arrive. I thought you loved me?'

Tyler was getting confused, not least by the way he couldn't rid his mind of the picture of not being able to keep his hands off her. It was disturbing to realise quite how vividly he could imagine it right now.

'I don't love you,' he said. He was on fairly sure ground there, surely?

Mary tsked. 'Not *me*, you idiot! We're pretending, remember?'

'Remind me why,' he said, weary of all the confusion.

'So that you can learn how to do it right when you come home to someone you really *do* love,' she told him. 'Now, I'm the love of your life and I'm feeling disappointed and unloved. What can you do to make me feel better? And here's a clue,' she added, not without a certain sarcasm. 'Disappearing into your study to make phone calls the moment you arrive is not the correct answer!'

Tyler rolled his eyes. 'All right, I need to pay you—her!— a bit more attention when I come home.'

'Exactly!' said Mary, pleased that he had got the point at last. 'I want to feel that you've been counting the hours too, that you're thrilled to find me here, that you can't wait to take me to bed…' She paused, listening to her words echoing uncomfortably around the hall. 'That is, *I* don't want that, of course,' she clarified carefully, 'but if I was in love with you, I probably would.'

'I see,' said Tyler dryly, not entirely sure that he did but unwilling to admit it, and distracted in any case by the idea of taking her to bed.

What would it be like to come home and find Mary waiting for him? he wondered. How would it feel if she were smiling, not criticising? If she opened her arms and let him kiss her? If he could run his hands over her warm curves, unwrap that top, slide off the silk and the lace and pull her upstairs to his room, so that they fell together on to his bed and he could lose himself in her softness and her warmth?

'Now, go outside and do it again.'

Tyler gulped and jerked back to attention. 'What? Do what?' he asked distractedly.

'Come in and greet me as if I'm the woman you want to marry,' said Mary patiently. 'Think of this as lesson one.'

'I thought compromising was lesson one?'

'OK, lesson two, then,' said Mary, rolling her eyes. 'This time, though, you've got a practical test. You've got to show your girlfriend—that's me—that you're thrilled to see her.'

'What am I supposed to say?'

'Make me believe that you love me,' she said. 'Starting with an apology is always a good move too.'

Still shaken by the vividness of his fantasy, Tyler let her push him outside, where he took some deep breaths of the cool autumn air. It smelt of damp leaves and woodsmoke, helping him pull himself together.

This was what he had wanted, he reminded himself. He had wanted practical advice on what to say and do in this kind of situation, and that was what Mary was giving him. He just hadn't counted on her being quite so distracting.

A few more breaths and Tyler had himself under control once more. This wasn't difficult. He should treat it as a challenge, and go in there and show Mary exactly what he could do.

Pushing open the door once more, he saw Mary at the foot of the stairs, looking so warm and inviting that all Tyler's fine speeches immediately went out of his head.

'Mary…' he said and stopped, realising that his lungs had forgotten how to work.

'Hi.' She smiled and came towards him. 'I was beginning to think you were never coming.'

Tyler managed to inflate his lungs. 'I'm sorry I'm late,' he said awkwardly. 'You look…gorgeous,' he said, and Mary paused for a moment.

'That's good,' she said. 'Very good, in fact.'

'No, I mean it.' Tyler stepped to meet her and took both her hands in his. 'I've been thinking about you all day,' he said. 'I was thinking about that suit you wear, and thinking about taking it off you, and now I come home and find you looking wonderful, and I still want to take it off you.'

'Yes, well, that's fine,' croaked Mary, trying, and failing, to tug her hands out of his, but Tyler ignored her.

'I've been thinking about touching you all day,' he said, his voice dropping until it seemed to reverberate in Mary's very core. 'I've been thinking about tonight and how it's going to be. Just you and me and a big bed.'

Mary gulped. 'Um, Tyler, I think that's probably—' she began, managing to pull her hands away at last, but he had released them only so that he could take her by the waist and pull her towards him.

'I've been thinking about this,' he said, bending his head and, although Mary opened her mouth, she had no idea either then or afterwards of what she was going to say. And, anyway, by then it was too late. Tyler's lips came down on hers and he kissed her.

Mary's heart seemed to stop with the shock and excitement

that jolted through her at the first touch of his mouth. Her first thought was that Tyler was a great actor, her second that he was a great kisser and her third… Well, after the second she stopped thinking at all.

It was so long since she'd been kissed. She'd forgotten how good it felt to be held against a hard male body, to have strong hands sliding over you, round you, to pull you closer. His lips were cool and firm and very sure on her. They teased and tasted and tested her resistance, which wasn't very strong, it had to be admitted.

There was something so seductive about being kissed like this. It was a game, a pretence, but shockingly intimate too, or that was how it felt to Mary. It didn't matter that Tyler Watts was practically a stranger, or that she didn't even like him that much. Right now, he was just a man and he was making her feel like a woman for the first time in a very long time.

Mary could have pulled back easily enough, but she didn't want to. She was tired of being sensible. Ever since Alan had thrown down his ultimatum she had held herself bottled in. She had focused on Bea and refused to let herself think about her own needs. Life was about being practical and getting through the day. It wasn't about yearning to be held or wanting to be touched.

But now she was being held and being touched, and Tyler's kiss was like the first breach in a dam, where everything she had been keeping suppressed was building into a wave of sensation inside her, so powerful in its intensity that Mary would have been frightened if she had allowed herself to think about it. Instead, she gave herself up to the sheer pleasure of kissing and being kissed, of leaning into a strong, solid body and feeling her senses uncurl and shiver with delight.

And it was OK, because it didn't mean anything. It was

just Tyler. It was just a pretence. They were playing a game, that was all.

Except perhaps they should have agreed on some rules before they started, like when they would stop, or how they would stop, and what they would say to make sure the other understood that it hadn't meant anything at all, that it was just a game…

In the end, it was Tyler who broke the kiss first. It took a huge effort of will for him to still his hands and loosen his hold on her warmth. Lifting his head slowly, reluctantly, he looked down into Mary's face.

Her eyes were dark, almost dreamy, her lips parted and he could see the heat flushing pink beneath her skin. It was all he could do not to kiss her again.

He felt ridiculously shaken. He hadn't really been thinking. He had walked in all ready to pretend, and in the end it had been easy enough to imagine how he would react if he had been waiting for her all day, how good it would be to see her, to be able to touch her and then… Well, dammit, he was only doing what she had told him, wasn't he?

Imagine you're in love with me, she had said. So he had.

He just hadn't expected how warm and soft and *sexy* she would be, how sweet she would taste, how she would melt like fire in his arms. He hadn't expected it to feel so good, so alarmingly *right*, to kiss her, and now all he could do was look down into her face, unable to think of a single thing to say, other than to wish that he could kiss her again.

Mary found her voice first.

'Very good,' she said. Her voice was a bit squeaky but, under the circumstances, she didn't think it sounded too bad. She cleared her throat. 'That was really quite convincing.'

Tyler felt a stab of something—relief that she had just been pretending too, he told himself.

At least he hoped it was relief. It had felt perilously close to disappointment and he didn't want that.

Belatedly realising that he was still holding her, he let Mary go and stepped back. 'I'm glad you approve,' he said.

'I certainly do.' Mary was relieved to hear herself sounding positively composed, which was quite something when her blood was still thrumming and her heart thumping and every nerve in her body was screaming at her to leap into his arms and cling on to him until he promised to kiss her again and not stop, ever.

'Go to the top of the class,' she said.

Tyler Watts might be useless at emotions, but he clearly wasn't useless when it came to the physical side of a relationship. Somehow she hadn't thought anyone so brusque would be such a good kisser. She would have expected him to be rough and as careless of feelings as he was at work, but he hadn't been like that at all. He had been slow and sure and sensuous. If he kissed like that, what would it be like when he made love?

Mary swallowed as an image of Tyler making love to her presented itself with uncomfortable clarity. He must be really, *really* bad at the emotional stuff, she thought, for all those ex-girlfriends to walk away.

'Can I go and make those phone calls now?' he asked.

A bucket of cold water dashed in her face could hardly have been a more effective return to reality. Tyler was back to business.

Mary thought she had done pretty well just to stay upright, and at least she had managed to keep *some* grip on the fact that the kiss had just been part of the pretence, but Tyler made her efforts look absolutely pathetic! He had probably been thinking about his phone calls all along.

Good, Mary told herself. That made it easier for her to stay cool and professional, the way they had agreed.

And the sooner he went, the sooner she could sit down. Her legs were trembling so much she was afraid that she would crumple to the floor any minute, and how cool and professional would that look?

'I think you've done enough of the devoted lover bit for now,' she agreed. 'Mrs Palmer left a meal which just needs heating up,' she added as he turned towards his study once more. He wasn't the only one who could do practicality. 'When do you usually eat?'

'When I'm ready.' Tyler looked at his watch. 'There are a few things I want to catch up on. Let's eat about half past nine.'

Something in the quality of Mary's silence made him look at her. 'What?'

'A better reply would have been, Are you hungry?' she said. 'Or, When would *you* like to eat? Just a suggestion,' she added sweetly. 'Something for you to bear in mind when you have someone you want to impress here.'

'Oh. Yes.' Tyler grimaced at having been caught out again. Clearing his throat, he tried again. 'When would you like to eat, Mary?'

'About nine would be nice,' she replied, equally polite. 'I'll see you in the kitchen then, shall I?'

In fact, it was just before nine when Tyler made his way to the kitchen. It wasn't that he didn't have lots to do, but he hadn't been able to concentrate with Mary in the house. She wasn't making a noise, but just knowing that she was there was a distraction.

He'd been trying to read a report at his desk, but it was hopeless. The words kept shimmering in front of his eyes and he'd end up thinking about that tantalising glimpse of lace, about how soft she had been beneath his hands, about how good it had felt to kiss her.

This was ridiculous, Tyler reminded himself irritably. Mary Thomas was not part of his strategy, or only in an advisory role. She wasn't his kind of woman. He was looking for someone gracious and elegant, not a chaotic single mother, no matter how good she might feel.

It had probably been a mistake to kiss her, but he had only been proving a point, he managed to convince himself at last. It clearly hadn't meant anything to Mary, anyway. She had been cool as a cucumber afterwards. Tyler glowered down at the page he'd been trying to read for the last twenty minutes. There was no reason for either of them not to be cool. They had both been pretending.

Hadn't they?

Of course they had.

Tyler closed the report and slapped it down on to the table with an irritable exclamation. It was hopeless trying to read this now. He would go and have something to eat, remind himself of all the reasons he wasn't interested in Mary Thomas, and then come back and work.

He found Mary in the kitchen and paused in the doorway, astounded at the transformation in the room. He only ever came into the kitchen to use the fridge or the microwave, and it had never struck him as a room he would spend any time in. But Mary had pulled the blinds and switched on the concealed lights under the cupboards so that the kitchen looked positively cosy. The table was laid for two, with glasses and a candle, and an appetising smell wafted from the oven.

And then there was Mary herself. Wrapped in Mrs Palmer's striped apron, she was measuring vinegar into a little bowl and humming happily to herself and her presence seemed to suffuse the room with a warmth it had never had before.

Tyler cleared his throat and she jerked round, breaking off

in mid-hum. 'Oh…hi,' she said after the tiniest of pauses. It took a huge effort to keep her voice neutral when every nerve she possessed had sprung to attention at the sight of him and her heart was blundering around in her chest, bouncing off her ribcage and generally behaving like a hyperactive puppy.

She turned back to the dressing she was making. 'You don't mind eating in the kitchen, do you?' she asked, super-casual. 'I thought it would be cosier than the dining room.'

'Here's fine,' said Tyler, coming into the kitchen. 'I usually take a plate back to my study and eat while I work.'

'Really?' Mary glanced at him in surprise. 'I imagined you dining in solitary splendour in that wonderful dining room, having a five-course meal served by a butler!'

'No.' He hunched a shoulder in what Mary was coming to recognise as a characteristic gesture. 'I'm not comfortable with servants. I prefer to have the house to myself.'

'Mrs Palmer said you valued your privacy.' She hesitated. 'Is that why you didn't want us here?'

'Partly,' said Tyler, although he wasn't sure that was strictly true. He couldn't admit that he'd been afraid that she would change things just by being here, and of course that was exactly what she had done. She'd only been here a matter of hours and already the house felt subtly different.

'But you're not here as a servant,' he went on. 'I don't like being waited on. It makes me realise I don't know the right knife and fork to use, or which way I should be passing the port.'

It was a surprising glimpse of vulnerability from such a hard man, thought Mary. She wouldn't have expected him to give a toss about what other people thought of him.

'Don't you have to do a lot of entertaining?'

Tyler's mouth turned down at the thought. 'I get a cook in

and extra staff to serve if that happens, but I try to avoid all that as much as I can.'

'It's a shame,' said Mary lightly. 'It's a perfect house for parties.'

'I can't stand all that socialising and chit-chat,' he grumbled. 'I never know what to say.'

'You didn't seem to have any trouble talking to me the other night,' said Mary, grinding salt and pepper into her dressing.

'That was different,' said Tyler, although he wasn't sure how. He just knew that it had been.

'Perhaps you should try blackmailing all your party guests,' she suggested mischievously. 'That seemed to be a good way to keep the conversation going!'

'It seemed to work with you anyway,' Tyler agreed, and to Mary's dismay he smiled, the same startlingly unexpected smile as before. She wished he wouldn't do that, just when she'd got her breathing under control again.

She busied herself searching in the cupboards for mustard and honey and willed her heartbeat to slow.

'It's a big house for one person. Don't you ever get lonely here?'

Tyler shrugged. 'I'm used to being on my own.'

Mary located some mustard and straightened. 'Well, I'll try not to disturb you too much while I'm here.'

She could try, but Tyler doubted very much if she would succeed. She'd only just arrived and she was already disturbing him far more than he wanted to admit.

CHAPTER FIVE

'YOU'D better get used to having other people in the house,' Mary went on, determinedly cheerful.

'Why's that?' asked Tyler warily.

'If you're going to have a wife and children, you'll soon fill up all those rooms,' she told him. 'You'll have to wave goodbye to your peaceful life then!'

He didn't look as if he found the prospect very appealing.

'I suppose so,' he said, with a marked lack of enthusiasm.

He tried to imagine being married. There would be another woman in the kitchen then, but when he tried to picture her, all he could see was Mary, with her cloudy hair and soft curves and dancing grey eyes.

Searching around for a change of subject, he spotted the glasses on the table. 'Would you like me to find a bottle of wine?'

'That would be lovely,' Mary answered.

'I'll just go and find one.'

He was back a few minutes later, blowing dust off a bottle with an eye-popping label. Of course, she should have known that he would have a fully stocked wine cellar, because that was what you had when you'd made it. He probably had a

string of racehorses too, although Mary was prepared to bet
he never took time off to go the races.

'I was thinking more of a bottle of plonk,' she said when
he showed her the bottle.

'I haven't got anything cheap,' he said haughtily. 'We may
as well have this.'

Mary put the salad on the table and watched him out of the
corner of her eye as he found a corkscrew and opened the
bottle. He moved with a lightness surprising in one of his
rocklike build, and there was an economy and a control to his
movements that Mary could only envy.

He was a complicated man, she thought. Complex and difficult; it was easy to be overwhelmed by his forbidding personality and miss the vulnerability underneath. Who would
have thought that he would be a man who ate his meal alone
at his desk, for instance, or who cared if people noticed that
he was using the wrong knife?

Who would have thought that he would be such a good kisser?

She wasn't supposed to be thinking about that kiss, Mary
reminded herself sternly and busied herself putting the salad
together and taking Mrs Palmer's lasagne from the oven.

But the more she tried not to think about it, the more her
eyes kept snagging on his hands, deft as they spun the bottle,
twisted in the corkscrew and eased out the cork with a deliciously soft pop. She couldn't help remembering how warm
they had felt through her top, how insistent against her spine,
how sure cupping her breast.

Wrenching her eyes away, Mary set the lasagne on the
table, where it made an absurd contrast with the expensive
wine that Tyler was pouring into the two glasses.

'Try it,' he said, and she paused to take a sip. It was like no wine she had ever tasted before, velvety soft and smooth and utterly delicious.

It was nearly as good as kissing him.

Stop it, Mary scolded herself furiously. Stop it at once. He's your client, that's *all*.

Taking another sip of wine to steady herself, she sought around for a subject of conversation that would take her mind off Tyler, sitting solid and formidable on the other side of the table.

'Do you mind if I do some cooking while I'm here?' she asked at last, helping herself to lasagne and trying to keep her eyes off his hands.

'No,' said Tyler. 'But there's no need if you don't want to. Mrs Palmer is a perfectly adequate cook.'

'I know, but I love cooking and it would be a real treat to use a kitchen like this. Mum's only got a tiny galley.' She looked around her enviously. 'This is a wonderful kitchen. It's an amazing house, in fact. It'll be a great place to bring up a family. There's so much space here, and the house is just crying out to be full of people and noise and laughter. You're very lucky,' she told him.

'I'm not lucky,' said Tyler flatly. 'I've just worked hard to get what I want.'

'Maybe the luck is in having the personality to stay focused on what you want,' Mary suggested. 'Half the time I don't even know what I want. I'm too busy just getting from day to day.'

'You must have some kind of goal.'

'I suppose I do, but it's not a very grand or ambitious one,' she said. 'I'm not like you. I don't have to be the best.' She sipped at the wine reflectively. 'I just want a little house I can call my own where I can bring Bea up and…well, just be happy.'

'Aren't you happy at the moment?'

Mary sighed a little as she picked up her fork and tucked into the lasagne. 'I think I've been too worried about money recently to be really happy,' she said, aware that the wine had loosened her tongue, but too tired of keeping it all to herself to care.

'I've been living with my mother since I came back to York,' she told Tyler. 'She's been fantastically supportive, and I don't know what I would have done without her, but the house isn't that big, especially with all the clutter you accumulate with a baby. We do get on top of each other a bit.'

Putting down her fork, she took another sip of the wine, which was slipping down very nicely indeed. She was feeling better already.

'I'm desperate to find my own place but I haven't been able to afford to buy, or even rent. Until now, that is,' she said, smiling at him. 'I'm hoping that will all change now that I've got the contract with Watts Holdings. I'll start to get some income from the agency—and of course my coaching fee will help too!'

Her smile had an odd effect on Tyler, and he tried to hide it with a reproving look. 'An agency is a risky thing to start up if you don't have any capital.'

'I realise that now,' she said ruefully. 'But it seemed like a good idea at the time. I thought that it would be a good way to use my personnel experience but still keep my independence.

'Childcare is so expensive nowadays,' she said with a sigh. 'It wouldn't be fair of me to rely on Mum, and I'd have been lucky to have got the kind of salary that would have enabled me to pay someone to look after Bea while I was at work. And if I *had* got a well-paid job, I'd have had to work so hard I wouldn't have enough time with Bea. I didn't want that. I thought the agency would give me some flexibility. I could take Bea with me sometimes, or work from home if I had to.'

Her glass was empty and Tyler reached over with the bottle to top it up. 'I don't understand why you're having to do everything on your own,' he said. 'Where does Bea's father figure in all of this?'

'He doesn't,' said Mary, and her face closed.

Tyler cursed himself. What was it Julia had said? The social skills of a rhinoceros. At times like this he wondered if she was right.

'Sorry,' he apologised gruffly. 'It's not my business. I shouldn't have asked.'

'It's OK.' Mary's expression relaxed slightly. 'You're showing an interest and asking me about myself and, as your relationship coach, I approve of that! And I don't mind talking about Alan, not really. For a long time I couldn't talk about anything *but* Alan.'

'Alan being Bea's father?'

She nodded. 'I met him in London. He's a psychologist by training. My company sent me on a coaching course that he was running, and I thought he was brilliant.'

Her face softened, remembering how dazzled she had been. 'Alan's one of the cleverest people I've ever met. And he's got a kind of charisma... It's difficult to explain,' she said. 'He really understands people and what makes them tick, and he's got a fantastic ability to help people think clearly about what they want and how to realise their dreams. You'd get on well with him.'

Tyler didn't think so. The man sounded a complete wimp to him.

'I was incredibly flattered when Alan suggested I train as a coach myself and go and work with him,' Mary went on, unaware of Tyler's mental interjection. 'He wanted to expand his company to offer a wider range of courses, and I could be part of that. It was a really exciting time for me.'

'But it wasn't just a professional relationship?'

'No.' Mary gave a self-deprecating grimace. 'I know it's hard to believe now!'

Tyler frowned. 'Why?'

'Well, you know…' She gestured at her hair and then down at her clothes. 'I'm such a mess. Mum says I've let myself go since having a baby, and I suppose it's true.'

He had thought she looked a mess at the reception, Tyler remembered. And when he had been to see her at her office she hadn't looked any better groomed. It was true that her hair could do with a good cut, and she didn't have the kind of style he usually admired in a woman, but she looked different tonight. He couldn't put his finger on why.

It was that damned bit of lace, Tyler decided. He was too distracted by it to think analytically.

'You don't look a mess now,' he said abruptly. 'You look…' *Warm. Sexy. Alluring.* '…fine,' he chose in the end.

Mary paused with the glass at her lips and looked at him over the rim. Her eyes were wide and a lovely shimmering grey, and Tyler found his gaze caught in them for a long jangling moment.

'Thank you,' she said, putting the glass down a little unsteadily. 'That was kind of you, but you really don't need to be polite. It's only me!' She felt ridiculously shaken by that meeting of their eyes, and that was stupid because he was, after all, a man who could kiss her until her bones melted and then calmly walk off and make phone calls.

The only way to deal with it was to make a joke of it, she decided. 'For future reference, though, no woman ever wants to hear that she looks "fine",' she told him in her best teacher mode. 'When your fiancée asks you how she looks, try and think of a different adjective—and not "nice"!'

'What should I say?' asked Tyler. 'Beautiful? Gorgeous?' His eyes dropped to the lacy camisole. 'Sexy?'

His voice seemed to reverberate down Mary's spine in the fizzing little silence that followed. This is a lesson, she told herself with an edge of desperation. It's not real. He doesn't really think you look gorgeous or sexy. How could he?

Inhaling slowly, she pinned on a smile. 'Any of those would do perfectly. Where were we?' she added brightly.

'You and Alan were having a relationship,' he reminded her in a dry voice.

'Oh, yes. Well, I was madly in love with him, of course.'

Tyler stabbed a piece of lettuce. 'Why "of course"?'

'Because Alan's like every woman's dream,' she said simply. 'He's good-looking and witty and clever—he's one of the most intelligent people I know. He runs a very successful business, he knows about food and wine, he's well-travelled and cultured…'

Mary's smile was twisted with sadness as she remembered how dazzled she had been. 'But the best thing about Alan is that you can *talk* to him,' she said. 'He really listens to what you say. You've no idea how rare that is in a man,' she added wryly.

He was listening to her, Tyler wanted to say, but Mary was still going on about the perfect Alan.

'I couldn't believe that someone like Alan would be interested in me,' she said. 'When he told me that he loved me and asked me to move in with him, I was over the moon, and it seemed like the obvious solution for both of us. He was struggling to pay his mortgage after the divorce, so it was easier for me to contribute to the running costs and put a bit towards the mortgage myself.'

She could see Tyler looking disapproving already at the idea of such a casual financial arrangement.

'It meant that I could live in a nice house, but it was about more than that,' she tried to explain. 'Paying towards the mortgage felt as if I had a real stake in his life, and that we were committed to each other, even though it was too soon after his divorce to think about getting married. All I wanted was to be with him.'

'So what put an end to this idyll?' asked Tyler grouchily.

'I got pregnant.' Mary turned her glass between her fingers, her eyes on the ruby liquid. 'It was an accident. Alan had made it clear right from the beginning of our relationship that he didn't want children.'

'Why not?'

'He's a bit older than me and he's got three children in their late teens from his marriage. He said he thought three was enough, and that he was too old to deal with all the broken nights and toddler tantrums again. And I was fine with that,' said Mary. 'Having children had never been something I'd dreamed of, and I was so in love with him then that I didn't care about anything as long as I could be with him.'

Tyler made a sound somewhere between a snort and a grunt. He was getting a bit sick of hearing about how much Mary loved Alan.

'So what happened?'

'I was thirty-four. It wasn't exactly my last chance to have a baby, but I had a real sense that it was now or never, and I realised then that I didn't want it to be never.'

She lifted her shoulders slightly, apparently unaware of how the movement deepened her cleavage and revealed a bit more of the lacy camisole. Tyler made himself look away.

'Alan didn't see it my way,' she said. 'He said that he had always made it clear that he didn't want any more children, and that was true, he had. He told me that I would have to choose.' Mary swallowed, remembering the painful scene. 'It was him or the baby. I couldn't have both.'

'And you chose the baby?'

'Yes,' she said, letting out a long breath. 'I chose Bea. And I've never regretted it, not for a second.'

'Even though she cost you the love of your life?'

Mary looked sad. 'Yes, even though it meant I lost Alan. I'd hoped that once the baby was born he'd change his mind, but he's refused to even acknowledge her.'

'He's still obliged to support her,' Tyler pointed out, but she shook her head.

'I don't want any support from him. It was my choice to have the baby, and I'll support her by myself. I wouldn't take maintenance from Alan, even if he were to offer it, which he won't. He said he didn't want anything to do with her.' Her voice quavered at the memory.

Tyler was unimpressed. 'If he felt that strongly about having children, he could have had a vasectomy,' he pointed out. 'Bea's his daughter whether he likes it or not, and he ought to provide you with some financial support at the very least.'

'I don't want it.' Mary's mouth set in a stubborn line. 'Alan said I wouldn't be able to manage on my own with a baby, and I'm going to prove him wrong.'

'Maybe,' Tyler allowed, 'but it sounds as if you're struggling.'

'Only because Alan's quibbling about the money I put into the house and the company.'

She couldn't believe that she was telling him all this. It must be the wine, Mary decided. It was so mellow and delicious that she had got to the bottom of another glass without even noticing. She had better not have any more.

'I didn't just lose Alan,' she told him. 'I lost my job and

my home and my savings, although I'm hoping I'll get some of those back eventually.'

Tyler was appalled. 'You lost your *job*? Even I don't sack staff when they get pregnant!'

'I wasn't exactly sacked,' said Mary, amused in spite of herself. The 'even I' spoke volumes! 'But it would have been too difficult carrying on working with Alan under the circumstances. It's one of the disadvantages of sleeping with the boss,' she added with a dry look.

'What's happened about your money?'

'Nothing as yet. Alan agreed to buy me out of the house—it was his home before I came along and he needed somewhere his children could go and stay, so that seemed fair—so I moved in with a friend, but it was clear that I couldn't stay there for ever and I wasn't sure how I was going to cope after the baby was born. I didn't have any income so I would have to go back to work as soon as I could.

'It was about then that my stepfather left my mother. She was distraught, and it seemed to make sense for me to come back to York and be with her. I'd be company for her, she could help me look after the baby, and if nothing else it would be cheaper than London, but I think it may have been a mistake. Once I had somewhere to go, Alan stopped feeling guilty and it allowed him to drag his feet about buying out my share of the house.'

Tyler was looking very disapproving by now. 'You should have a legal claim on the house. Didn't you have a proper contract drawn up?'

'I should have done, but I didn't,' said Mary. 'It was stupid of me, but we were so happy together that it never occurred to me that I would need it. Alan says he will repay my share, but first he has to have the house valued, and he's quibbling about how much money I actually put in…'

She sighed. 'I know he's angry but I never thought that he would be so petty and so mean. It's not as if we're talking about a huge amount of money but it would have helped me get a place of my own here. As it is, I'm reduced to forcing myself on you for a month,' she said with a wry smile.

'I'm hoping my mother and stepfather will be able to sort out their problems, but they need to be able to do that without Bea and me sharing the same very small space. Moving in here seemed like my best option, but I didn't take into account the fact that you'd prefer to be on your own. I'm sorry,' she finished apologetically.

'It's not going to be a problem,' said Tyler gruffly. 'In fact, I think you're right about it being the best way to coach me. I feel as if I've learnt a lot about relationships already tonight.'

'Good.' Mary smiled, glad to be able to lighten the atmosphere and shift the conversation away from the sorry mess she'd made of things lately. 'Well, that's what I'm here for! You're going to be so clued up on relationships by the time I leave, the next woman you date will be a very, very happy woman!'

And if Tyler made love the way he kissed, she would be a very lucky woman too.

Mary swallowed the last of her wine in a gulp and pushed that thought aside. She was lucky too, she reminded herself sternly. She had Bea, and by the end of the month she would have five thousand pounds to put down on a flat of her own. What more could she want?

Mary's mind flickered towards Tyler and she was revisited by a sharp, shivery memory of that kiss before she wrenched it determinedly away. She wasn't even going to *go* there. A healthy baby and somewhere to live. She would be perfectly content with that.

* * *

Mary lifted her baby daughter out of the bath and wrapped her in a warm towel. She loved this part of the day. Bea was always sweet-smelling and smiley, squealing with delight at the games Mary played with her.

It had been a busy day, but a productive one, and Mary felt pleasantly weary. It felt good to know that things were happening at last.

Tyler had been long gone by the time she and Bea had made it down to the kitchen to find some breakfast. They'd found Mrs Palmer there, very concerned that Mary had cleared up the night before.

'You should have left everything,' she protested.

'It was only a matter of stacking the dishwasher,' said Mary. 'Honestly, it was no trouble. I wouldn't have felt comfortable leaving the kitchen in a mess.'

Anyway, there hadn't been anything else to do. Tyler had disappeared back to his study and Mary had been left wishing that she hadn't drunk the wine so quickly, or told him quite so much about her muddled affairs.

She had sat in a beautifully decorated sitting room for a while, but she'd been unable to settle. Normally time to read a book was an unimaginable luxury and it had been frustrating to find the type dancing before her eyes. She'd kept imagining what it would be like if Tyler was sitting there with her.

Perhaps she should have suggested that? After all, if it were a real relationship he wouldn't spend his evenings working. They would be curled up together on the sofa in front of a fire. She would be able to slip her arm over that broad chest and feel the hard, masculine solidity of him, and then her face would be at just the right angle to press into his throat and smell his skin.

She could kiss that pulse below his ear and then feather her lips along his jaw to his mouth, teasing and tantalising until she felt his mouth curve in a smile beneath hers, and then *he* could tip her abruptly beneath him, pulling her down into the softness of the big sofa and running his hands up from her ankle, tracing delicious patterns behind her knee, sliding beneath her skirt and drifting upwards in insistent exploration, and she would unbutton his shirt with unsteady hands and all the time they would be kissing, kissing the way they had kissed in the hall, but this time there would be no reason to stop and he would—

Mary had shut her book with a snap. This had to stop, and right now.

Think Mary, she'd told herself. This is a man who is looking for a leggy, slender, well-groomed blonde with no children and a hard-headed attitude to marriage, a man who has told you quite frankly that he doesn't find you attractive. He's a ruthless, arrogant workaholic with all the charm and sensitivity of a bulldozer.

A man who kissed you until you were weak at the knees and then went off to talk business on the phone.

On a scale of one to ten, she'd asked herself, how sensible is it to start fantasising about him making love to you on a sofa?

Minus three hundred and forty-two, at least.

You're here to do a job, Mary had reminded herself sternly. And that's *all*.

Which was all very well, but a pain when you had to spend your entire time remembering to remember. Too often during the day, Mary had been aware of a small fizzy feeling deep inside at the thought of seeing Tyler again that evening. Whenever she caught her mind drifting that way, she would sit up with a start and make herself get back to work, but it was exhausting having to be constantly vigilant with her own thoughts.

Still, when she hadn't been wasting time trying not to think about Tyler, it had been a good day. Most of it had been spent in a flurry of activity, contacting prospective staff and arranging interviews. Bea had been obliging. She had either slept or been happy to play with her toys, and at lunchtime Mary had pushed her to the Museum Gardens to enjoy the autumn sunshine while it lasted.

'I don't know what I'm going to do with you tomorrow, though,' Mary told her as she dried her little toes. She had a meeting with Steven Halliday at Watts Holdings to talk about the new contract and assess their requirements, and it would be hard to strike the right professional note if she had Bea with her. Her mother was the obvious fallback position, and Mary didn't really think that she'd mind, but when she'd rung there had been no reply. 'Your granny isn't answering the phone.'

Bea squealed and batted her arms in reply. She loved being part of a conversation.

'Do you think she's out gadding around with Bill?'

'Ga!'

'I've asked her to ring me back, but if she doesn't get home until late I'm just going to have to take you with me, and it would be very, very good if you felt like having a sleep then.'

'Ga, ga, *wa*!'

Kneeling beside her, Mary smiled down at her daughter, who was kicking her legs on the towel. Lucky Bea, who didn't have to worry about childcare or contracts.

Or how to achieve just the right balance between friendliness, professionalism and nonchalance when Tyler came home.

Mary glanced at her watch. If yesterday was anything to go by, she had nearly three hours to calm the pathetic butterflies in her stomach. He wouldn't kiss her again. They had done greetings yesterday.

And that was a good thing, of course.

'A very good thing,' she said out loud to Bea, tickling her feet and making her crow with laughter.

'What do we care, anyway?' she asked her, as Bea squirmed with pleasure. 'We're going to find a lovely flat just for us, and we'll have fun there, won't we?'

Talking nonsense, she dusted Bea with powder and played with her, kissing her tummy until she giggled and clutched at her mother's hair, and squealing so loud that Mary didn't hear Tyler until he cleared his throat and she spun round, her heart jerking frantically.

He was standing in the doorway, tall and solid and somehow definite, and all the air seemed to have whooshed from her lungs as she sat back on her heels, one hand to her throat.

'Hi,' she said, and her voice sounded abnormally high. 'I didn't realise you were back.'

'Sorry, I didn't mean to startle you.'

Tyler felt lumbering and awkward hanging around in the doorway, but he was reluctant to intrude into the happy scene in the bathroom. Mary's back had been to the door and he had watched her laughing with her baby, moved in a way he couldn't quite identify. She was pink and flushed still, her hair all messy where Bea had been clutching it in her tiny fists.

'That's all right. I just wasn't expecting you back yet,' she said. 'You're early tonight.'

'I thought I should follow up on lesson one,' said Tyler, 'and spend more time at home now you're here.'

It was impossible not to feel pleased, even though she knew that he was just playing a part.

'Very good,' she approved. 'We'll have to teach you about communication next. An email or a text during the day would be just the thing to let me know that you're thinking of me!'

Tyler was still trying to decide if she was joking or not when a phone started ringing in the other room.

Mary got to her feet, brushing baby powder from her hands. 'That's my mobile. It'll be my mother. I'm hoping she'll be able to look after Bea for me tomorrow.' She glanced from the baby to him and hesitated. 'Would you mind keeping an eye on her for a second while I answer it?'

'Er…all right.'

Left alone with the baby, Tyler was conscious of a moment of panic. Bea didn't like being abandoned by her mother and her small face darkened ominously. Terrified that she was going to cry, Tyler moved into the room and squatted down beside her on the floor.

They eyed each other dubiously. Tyler couldn't remember being this close to a baby before and he studied her with a kind of reluctant fascination. She was perfect in miniature, he thought, with ten tiny fingers and ten tiny toes. When he stretched out his hand tentatively, she clutched at his finger with surprising strength, a determined look on her face.

She had a round little tummy, chubby legs and plump arms that ended in a fold at the wrist, and her round eyes were not only the same luminous grey as her mother's but seemed to Tyler to hold an identically critical expression.

Ridiculously nervous, he tried a smile but that seemed to be a mistake. Bea's expression changed and for an appalling moment he thought she was going to burst into tears.

'No, no, don't do that,' he said hastily and tried to distract her by reaching out to prod her tummy.

To his huge relief, the stormy look vanished from her eyes and she dissolved into one of her gummy smiles instead. Encouraged, Tyler tried it again and she chuckled, so he tickled her feet next, making her giggle and try to grab her toes.

'One step, two steps…' he began, his fingers marching up her arm. It was obviously a game that she recognised because she squealed with excitement. She was enjoying herself so much that Tyler couldn't help laughing.

'She likes you,' Mary said from behind him, and Tyler turned to see her watching them with a curious expression in her eyes.

Feeling a fool, he got to his feet. 'I thought she was going to cry,' he said to explain the uncharacteristic lapse into playfulness.

'She looks pretty happy to me,' said Mary, moving into the bathroom, and Tyler caught a waft of her perfume as she passed.

She knelt down next to the baby and reached for a nappy. 'Did you like playing with Tyler?' she asked Bea, who chortled and waved her arms and shouted.

Mary laughed and Tyler felt an odd tightening in his chest as she looked up at him.

'I think that means yes!' she said.

CHAPTER SIX

HE COULD go now. He had done his bit coming to say hello, but something held Tyler in the warm, light bathroom.

Mary glanced at him. 'Would you like to have a go at putting on a nappy?' she asked, and suppressed a smile at his visible recoil.

'No, thank you!'

'It would be very good practice for you,' she pointed out. 'You're the one who wants to have a family, so you might as well get used to babies.'

'I'm not changing a nappy,' he said firmly, but he was watching as Mary fastened Bea's nappy and deftly buttoned her into a Babygro.

'You know, being good with babies is a very attractive trait in a man,' she teased. 'It would be a big plus when you've found the woman of your dreams and are trying to impress her.'

'I'm hoping that the woman of my dreams will be more impressed by where Watts Holdings figures in the Dow Jones Index,' said Tyler austerely

'But think how handy the experience will be when you have children of your own!'

'I won't be changing their nappies,' he said, half suspecting that she was making fun of him and eyeing her suspiciously. 'I'll be at the office, working to support them.'

'Well, it's your loss,' said Mary, picking Bea up. 'They're gorgeous at this age. Why would you want to miss out on this?'

Holding Bea above her head, she blew raspberries against the baby's stomach. Convulsed with laughter, Bea grabbed at her hair.

'Ouch!' said Mary playfully and brought the baby back to her shoulder for a cuddle, kissing her downy head as Bea bumped her forehead against her mother's nose.

'Show Tyler how well you can kiss,' Mary said, laughing, and Bea banged her open mouth against Mary's.

Mary melted the way she always did, and hugged her little daughter to her. 'You won't want to be in the office when you have children, Tyler,' she said. 'You'll be lost the moment your baby gives you a slobbery kiss like that.'

Tyler couldn't imagine it. He had been holding on to the idea of a wife and family, but he hadn't considered the reality of it. He hadn't thought about nappies or slobbery kisses or baby chuckles. What would it be like to have his own child? he wondered. The thought kindled a tiny glow deep inside him.

The tight feeling in his chest wouldn't go away. Tyler badly wanted to think that it was irritation, but he was very much afraid that it might be jealousy. He wasn't jealous of the baby—Good Lord, how pathetic would that be? Just because all Bea had to do was stretch out her arms and Mary was there, to pick her up and kiss her and cuddle her! Of course he wasn't *jealous*.

Or maybe he was a little bit jealous, but only of the bond between Mary and her daughter. He was prepared to accept that he might feel that. He could see how completely they loved each other, how openly they laughed and kissed, how easy it was for them to show tenderness. Tyler recognised it as love, but it wasn't an emotion he had ever felt, and he didn't think that he ever would.

He looked away. 'Is she going to bed now?'

'Not yet. She needs some supper first.' Hoisting Bea up, Mary got to her feet. 'I got some shopping in the market today, so I'm going to make us a meal too. You did say that it was all right, and I think Mrs Palmer's grateful for the break.'

'Fine by me,' said Tyler, still feeling awkward and uneasy for some reason. 'Thank you.'

'When would you like to eat?'

He opened his mouth to reply before remembering his lesson from the night before. 'When would suit you?'

Mary laughed. 'You're a quick learner, I'll give you that! Would eight o'clock be too early for you?'

'Eight's fine.'

'I'm just going to be putting Bea to bed and pottering around until then if you want to do some work,' she said.

'Oh. Right.' It sounded like a dismissal to Tyler. 'Good,' he said and cleared his throat. 'I'll be in my study then.'

Tyler switched off the phone and tossed it on to his desk. There was a whole pile of papers waiting for his attention and he reached for the first one before dropping it back with an irritable sigh.

This was ridiculous. It had been hard enough trying to concentrate last night, but tonight was even worse, and the slow tick of the clock on the mantelpiece only emphasised the silence.

He wondered where Mary was. In the kitchen probably, he thought, humming away and chatting to Bea, filling the room with warmth and light and laughter.

He could go and see what she was doing. The thought

lodged in Tyler's brain, unsettling him, and he drummed his fingers on the desktop uncertainly. There was no need for him to find her. She wasn't a guest, and anyway she probably wanted time on her own. And it wasn't as if he didn't have plenty of work to do here.

On the other hand, he realised, it would be thoughtful to go and see if she needed anything. He could offer to make her a cup of tea or something. *Imagine you're in love with me,* she had said. He was supposed to remember to be attentive for the next time he brought a real girlfriend here.

Tyler tried to picture his next girlfriend. She would be tall and willowy, probably, because that was the kind of woman he found attractive. She would be sensible and well-groomed and she wouldn't clutter up his house with baby paraphernalia, or tick him off for not paying her enough attention or tease him about changing nappies. She would be sweet-natured and beautiful and…

Boring? a subversive voice in his head suggested before Tyler could stamp down on it.

Nice, he substituted instead.

She would be perfect.

And, in the meantime, he might as well work on his relationship skills. He could go and find Mary with a clear conscience. Pushing back his chair, Tyler got to his feet.

He found her, as predicted, in the kitchen. Bea was banging a spoon on the tray of her high chair and shouting while Mary tasted a spoonful of her supper to check the temperature.

'All right, all right, I'm coming,' she said to Bea, pulling out a chair with her foot. Catching sight of Tyler, she grimaced. 'I wouldn't come in unless you've got a strong stomach! Bea loves her food, but watching her eat isn't a pretty sight!'

'I'll risk it,' said Tyler. He watched her scoop up a spoonful of purée and offer it to Bea, who grabbed the spoon with both hands and proceeded to smear it over her face. He saw what Mary meant now.

Averting his eyes, he went over to the kettle. 'I was going to make a cup of tea,' he said stiltedly. 'Would you like one? Or something stronger?'

Mary would have killed for a gin and tonic just then, but it wasn't quite six yet and she had downed half a bottle of wine in double-quick time last night. She didn't want Tyler thinking that she had no control.

'Tea would be lovely,' she said.

She studied him under her lashes as she fed Bea. He was leaning back against the counter, legs crossed at the ankle and arms folded, while he waited for the kettle to boil. He'd rolled up his sleeves and loosened his tie, but somehow those signs of relaxation only served to make him seem tougher and more formidable than ever.

He was so solid, so self-contained, so *definite*, thought Mary. She always felt as if she was unravelling at the edges, but there was a steadiness to him that was insensibly reassuring. You felt as if you could hold on to him and be safe, no matter what else was happening.

And now she knew how it felt to hold on to him, the image was impossible to dislodge. She remembered the hardness of his body, the strength of his arms, the sureness of his lips, so that she only had to look at him, like now, and feel the heat flare through her, rushing along her veins and flushing her skin and tying her entrails into knots.

Gulping, she concentrated fiercely on loading another spoonful of purée for Bea.

'What *is* that?' Tyler asked with distaste.

'Chicken with carrot and leek.'

'It looks disgusting!'

'Oh, dear, and I made extra for you specially. *Now* what are we going to eat tonight?' Mary was doing her best to keep a straight face, but Tyler could see the corner of her mouth twitching.

'Right,' he said, and then he smiled that smile that made Mary's stomach do a spectacular somersault and land again like a fat quivering jelly. That didn't feel quite so damn funny.

Unaware of the effect of a single grin, Tyler nodded in Bea's direction. 'She seems to be enjoying it, anyway.'

Mary was glad of the excuse to look at her daughter instead. Bea was a messy eater, even allowing for the fact that she was only seven months old. Purée was liberally daubed over her face and there were bits of carrot and chicken stuck in her hair, up her nose and over her ears, and she chortled as she busily smeared any droppings over her tray.

'It'll be a while before we can take her to tea at the Ritz,' she agreed. 'I'm hoping she'll sleep after this. She's had a busy day.'

The kettle had boiled and Tyler turned to pour water into two mugs. 'Did you take her to the office with you?'

'Yes, she was really good.' Mary scraped the bowl for Bea. 'I just hope she'll be as good tomorrow.'

'Why, what's happening then?'

'I've got a meeting with Steven Halliday at eleven to talk about the new contract. I'd been hoping to leave her with Mum, but I don't think I can ask her now.'

'Was that her on the phone earlier?'

'Yes, but she's preoccupied with sorting out things with Bill at the moment, and she said something about meeting him tomorrow. I don't want to complicate things by mentioning Bea, because I know she'd say yes, and I think she needs to concentrate on herself at the moment.' Mary shrugged as she got up to rinse the bowl in the sink. 'I'll just have to take her with me.'

Tyler was holding the milk over her mug, his brows raised in query, and she nodded. 'Thanks,' she said, and smiled at him as she took the mug. 'Do you think Steven will mind?'

'Not if I tell him not to,' he said.

'You can't do that!'

Tyler lifted his brows. 'I can do what I like,' he said with a return to his old arrogance. 'It's my company.'

'Well, yes, but your employees *are* the company. You've got to take their feelings into account.'

'It's a business, Mary. The only thing I have to take into account is profits. If Steven doesn't like the way I run the company, he can go and work elsewhere. I don't see any reason for him to object to Bea's presence, but you might find it difficult to concentrate on the meeting yourself if she's there.'

'That's true.' Mary bit her lip worriedly. 'I've left it a bit late to ring any of my friends, though.'

'Someone in the office will be able to look after her for an hour or so,' said Tyler. 'I'll ask Carol. She's my PA and, before you say anything, no, I don't think she'll mind.'

'I think *I'd* mind if somebody dumped a baby on me without warning when I was trying to work,' said Mary doubtfully. 'Well, I'll see how it goes. With any luck Bea'll sleep through the whole meeting and I won't need to ask anyone to look after her.'

But at five to eleven the next morning, Bea was wide awake. She had slept in the car on the way in and was looking refreshed and alert and not in the least in need of a restorative nap any time soon.

'Typical,' Mary said to her with a sigh.

She couldn't help remembering the last time she had been

in the Watts Building, when her shoes had been killing her and Tyler had come up with the preposterous suggestion that she do a bit of relationship coaching on the side.

It seemed a very long time ago now. Mary was finding it hard to reconcile the ruthless businessman she had met then with the Tyler who had squatted down by her daughter and tickled her tummy until she laughed. She hadn't even liked him when she'd met him then and now… Mary didn't want to analyse too closely exactly what she felt now. All she knew was that her entrails jerked themselves into a knot every time she saw him.

She had been careful to wear more sensible shoes this time, and it made walking on the floor a lot easier. Without the crowds of people, the foyer seemed vast and impressive.

The receptionist looked askance at Bea, but promised to let Steven Halliday know that she was waiting. Mary carried Bea over to the glass wall that ran along the riverfront and pointed out a solitary rower sculling past.

It was a still, bright day and the river was like a mirror, reflecting the range of buildings that lined its banks, representing centuries of development from the medieval Guildhall to contemporary bars with their glass walls and decking. Amongst them all, the Watts Building stood out. It made no concessions to its historic backdrop. It didn't try to blend in with its neighbours, but demanded that you took it on its own terms.

A bit like Tyler, in fact.

'Mary?' A man in a suit was coming towards her, his hand outstretched. 'I'm Steven Halliday. How nice to meet you.'

Mary shook his hand mechanically, but her attention was riveted on the man beside him, a man whose appearance had made her heart lurch into her throat and lodge there, hammering frantically.

'I didn't know that you were going to be in on the meeting,' she blurted out, and then felt stupid.

'I'm not,' said Tyler calmly. 'I came to see if Bea was sleeping, and if not to see whether you'd like me to find someone to look after her.'

As Bea had recognised Tyler and was holding her arms out towards him with a crow of delight, there seemed no point in pretending that she was on the point of falling asleep. Meekly, Mary found herself handing her daughter over to him.

Their hands brushed as Bea was passed over, and Mary was mortified to feel the colour rise in her cheeks.

'Thank you,' she said stiffly. 'But if your PA is busy, will you promise to bring her back to me?'

'I'm sure it won't be necessary.' Tyler looked at Bea, who beamed back and fastened her little fingers around his nose, making him wince. 'Do you want to come with me, Miss Thomas?'

'Ba!'

Bea let herself be carried off without a backward look at her mother.

Mary couldn't help thinking that having Bea with her might have been less disturbing in the long run than Tyler's intervention, but was going to have to think about that later. For now she had a meeting to attend.

In the end, her discussion with Steven Halliday was extremely productive. Steven himself was not exactly obsequious, but he clearly thought she had a much closer relationship with Tyler than was in fact the case. Mary couldn't tell him that she was just providing a service like any other consultant without betraying Tyler's confidence and, anyway, he wasn't likely to believe her, having seen his boss so obviously at home with her baby.

At the end of the meeting, Steven escorted her personally

to Tyler's office on the top floor with a fantastic view over the city. Carol, his PA, was a cool and elegant blonde who immediately made Mary feel fat and crumpled, but she smiled from behind her desk.

'Are you looking for Bea?' she asked.

'Yes.' Mary looked around the pristine office. 'I was rather expecting her to be with you. Is she here?'

For answer, Carol put a finger to her lips and walked over to a door, opening it noiselessly and beckoning Mary over. Through the open door, they watched Tyler pacing around his office, Bea in one arm and a report in his free hand.

'Five billion sounds excessive to me. What do you think?' he was saying.

'Ga! Ba ba ga!' said Bea and he nodded with apparent seriousness.

'I couldn't agree with you more. But the environmental impact assessment sounds promising, eh?'

'Ya!' shouted Bea, pulling at his earlobes with her small fingers.

Mary and Carol exchanged a look. 'He cancelled two meetings,' whispered Carol. 'He's had her the whole time. I think he's smitten!'

Mary's answering smile was just a little bit tight as she knocked on the door to attract Tyler's attention. Uh-oh, she thought, appalled at her reaction. It smacked suspiciously of jealousy, and of her own daughter too!

'Am I interrupting?' she asked brightly. Too brightly.

'I was just trying to keep her amused,' said Tyler, sounding faintly defensive. He looked so guilty, and Bea looked so content, that Mary felt her sudden tension melt in a rush of warmth that was perilously close to tenderness, or even love, but which she decided in the end was affection.

Yes, affection. It was a good neutral word. She could legitimately feel affection for Tyler, even if he was a client, Mary decided. He had just spent the last couple of hours looking after her daughter. He could be a friend.

Just not a lover.

'Absolutely,' she agreed, straight-faced. 'Business plans do it for me every time too.'

Tyler shifted a little uncomfortably. 'I didn't have anything more interesting.'

'Bea doesn't care,' Mary reassured him, rather touched by the rare glimpse of uncertainty. Bea had squealed with delight at the sight of her mother and was clamouring for her notice, so Mary held out her arms as Tyler passed her back. 'She doesn't know what you're reading. All she wants is your attention and the sound of your voice. Don't you?' she added to Bea, tossing her in the air. 'How are you at analysing business plans, anyway?'

'She's been great,' said Tyler, trying, not that successfully, to disguise his disappointment at having to hand Bea back. 'She never criticises or argues back, and she thinks all my ideas are great. She's the perfect companion!' he added, unable to resist tickling her hand with his finger, which looked enormous in comparison.

Bea immediately put on a fit of shyness, burying her face in her mother's neck, but then spoilt the effect entirely by peeping a glance at him under her ridiculously long lashes, smiling and then hiding again as soon as he smiled back.

'Stop flirting,' Mary said to her with mock sternness, but she couldn't help laughing too, which was a mistake as her eyes met Tyler's in what was supposed to be shared amusement but which turned instead into something infinitely more disturbing as their smiles faded and the air tightened between them.

It was extraordinary how that pale glacier-blue gaze could burn into her and make her feel so…hot. Warmth was tingling through her and she was horribly afraid that Tyler would see the colour staining her cheeks, but when she tried to look away she found that she couldn't.

Snared in the blueness of his eyes, Mary felt the breath evaporating from her lungs and for a long, long moment she could only stare helplessly back at him while the silence spun round them until there was only the unsteady thump of her heart and the slow, shaky simmering in her veins.

And then, as if sensing that she had lost their attention, Bea squawked and batted her mother on the nose in a peremptory reminder of her priorities. Startled, Mary managed to jerk her eyes away from Tyler's and gulp a breath at the same time.

Swallowing, she wondered if she were capable of stringing a sentence together. 'Thank you for looking after her, anyway,' she said at last, squirming at how high and strained her voice sounded. 'It was very kind of you.'

Tyler made a dismissive gesture. 'Did you have a successful meeting?' he asked after another awkward little pause.

'Very, thanks to you.'

The stilted politeness was awful.

Bea was clutching her hair and bumping her head against Mary's throat, which at least gave her an excuse to leave. Mary tilted her jaw out of head-butting range and produced another bright smile.

'I must take Bea out of your way and let you get on with some work,' she said. 'What time do you think you'll be back tonight?'

That sounded awfully domestic, she realised belatedly. 'I mean…obviously, just come back whenever you want,' she explained. 'We're fine without you.'

Oh, God, that didn't come out right either.

'That is, we'll just be doing our usual routine,' she tried again, miserably aware of the deepening colour in her cheeks.

Not that Tyler seemed to care. He was already turning back to his desk. 'I'll aim for about six,' he said indifferently.

Mary did her best to pretend that she was similarly indifferent but, in spite of all her efforts to the contrary, she ended up watching the clock as six o'clock approached. She rationed the number of times she could look but, no matter how long she tried to spin it out, barely a minute would have crawled past. Had something happened to the rotation of the earth? she wondered wildly. If time went any slower it would start going backwards, and then where would they be?

As long as it didn't rewind too far, it might not be a bad thing, Mary reflected. Say, to a week ago, when Tyler Watts had been no more than a fading memory of a demanding boss.

Having taken its time about getting there, six o'clock came and went in a blur with no sign of Tyler. In the kitchen, Mary was furious with herself for being so disappointed and set about chopping an onion with savage concentration. It was nearly half past by the time she heard the front door bang.

He was here. The realisation sucked the air out of Mary's lungs and she made herself inhale very slowly and very carefully. There was a sick butterfly feeling in her stomach and every nerve in her body seemed to be jangling and jitterbugging in a frenzy of awareness.

Oh, for heaven's sake, Mary told herself, exasperated at last. Pull yourself together!

'Sorry I'm late,' said Tyler, appearing at the kitchen door a few moments later. 'There was a bit of a crisis in the London office.'

'Not a problem,' said Mary brightly.

She was utterly horrified by how much she wished she could go over and lean against him. Where had it come from, this urge to feel his arms close around her, to lift her face for a kiss? She needed to get out of here—and quick.

'I'm just about to put her to bed,' she said, lifting Bea out of the high chair. 'Is eight o'clock OK for supper again?'

'Fine,' said Tyler, quelled by her brisk manner.

He had been looking forward to coming home all afternoon, and to sitting in the warm kitchen and watching her with Bea, but she seemed to be making it clear that his presence wasn't required, so he could hardly hang around.

'I'll go and do some work,' he said.

Wonderful smells were drifting from the kitchen when Tyler made his way along the stone-flagged hall at eight o'clock. Mary was there, slicing tomatoes and looking round and rosy in a red jumper and soft trousers, but her smile seemed to him to hold a hint of brittleness.

'Can I do anything?' he asked.

'No, it's fine. Supper's nearly ready.'

Mary had given herself another stern lecture while she'd been putting Bea to bed. She had to stop being silly and remember what she was doing here. Tyler was a client, and she needed to keep their relationship on a professional level. Yes, it was hard when they were living together like this, but that was the part of the job.

Moving in with him had been her idea, Mary reminded herself. She was getting very well paid for it and it was time to stop messing around and earn her five thousand pounds. And that meant not thinking about how nice it would feel to lean against him or wondering what it would be like if their relationship was real after all. It wasn't real. It was a pretence, and she had better not forget it.

'This is very different from what I'm used to,' said Tyler as she set the dishes on the table.

'What is?' she asked in surprise.

'All of this.' He gestured at the table. 'Sitting in the kitchen, eating home-cooked food...'

'What do you usually do with your girlfriends in the evening?' asked Mary, and then could have bitten her tongue out. What a stupid question! 'I mean, you know, when you're not...'

'Not what?' asked Tyler, raising an eyebrow.

'You know,' she said crossly.

They couldn't spend their whole time in bed, surely? But then maybe they did. A real girlfriend wouldn't be faffing around making tomato salad. She would be lying warm and naked beside Tyler, arching beneath him as his hands drifted and curved and demanded, shuddering luxuriously at the feel of his lips against her skin. Or she would be leaning over him, her hair tickling him as she explored the lean, hard body and found a way past the tough, driven exterior to the real man underneath.

'Ouch!' Mary burnt her finger on the roasting dish and sucked it furiously as she tried to steady her breath. Served her right for letting her imagination get carried away. She could really have done with a bucket of cold water, but the burn had done a good job of shocking her back to reality.

'I tend to take girlfriends out to eat,' Tyler answered her question at last. 'Mrs Palmer might leave a meal sometimes, I suppose, but we never did this.' He watched as Mary lifted the rack of lamb from the roasting dish and set it on a board, slicing it into chops, her burnt finger held at an awkward angle. 'I've never had food like this before.'

'What, you've never had roast lamb?'

'In a restaurant, or heated up in a microwave. Never

cooked in the oven and then put on the table so you can all eat together.' Tyler couldn't explain how strange it felt. How strange and how nice.

Mary divided the lamb between two plates and set them on the table. 'Not even when you were growing up?' she asked. 'Didn't your mother cook for you?'

'She may have done. I certainly don't remember if she did. She died when I was six so my father brought me up.' Tyler's voice was quite expressionless. 'He wasn't what you'd call a domesticated man. He'd open a tin of beans or something oc-casionally, and he'd buy takeaways when he remembered about eating, but he would certainly never have dreamt of cooking a meal.'

Mary's heart ached for the little boy who had lost his mother. 'He didn't marry again?'

'No. I don't think he really wanted to get married the first time round, to tell you the truth. I suspect they only did it because my mother got pregnant, and it wasn't as easy to be a single mother then as it is now.'

'I wouldn't describe it as easy now,' said Mary ruefully, 'but I know what you mean.'

'He wasn't a particularly attentive father but, after my mother died, he was the only parent I had,' Tyler went on. 'I yearned for his approval, but he didn't give it easily. I'd take pictures for him home from school, but he'd just toss them aside and say they were scribbles and, looking back, I suppose that's exactly what they were.'

Mary flinched. She couldn't wait for Bea's first pictures. She would be proud of every scribble and stick them on the fridge for the world to admire. What had it been like for a lonely little boy to have his offerings tossed aside with contempt?

'But sometimes, if I did something really well, he would

be pleased with me and a casual "good boy" from him was worth any amount of gold stars from a teacher,' Tyler confessed, his mouth twisted with self-mockery.

No wonder Tyler was so driven to succeed now, thought Mary. No wonder he found relationships so hard. He had never had one to use as a model. He had never seen that a man and a woman could live happily together and talk and laugh and love each other and be friends. He didn't know what it was to be unconditionally loved, so he didn't know how to love himself.

It explained a lot.

She wanted to reach out and hug him, to reach the little boy he had been, but she couldn't do that.

Because professionals don't hug their clients, do they, Mary?

CHAPTER SEVEN

MARY let Tyler pour her some wine instead. 'It must have been very lonely for you growing up.'

He shrugged. 'Maybe. It was normal for me, whatever it was.'

'I'm an only child too,' she offered. 'My father died when I was nine, but my experience was very different from yours. My mother was always loving, and she married again when I was twenty and had left home.'

'How did you feel about that?'

'I was a bit jealous at first,' she confessed. 'But when I saw her and Bill together, I realised how lonely she had been all those years. She deserved to be happy.'

'I'm not sure how I would have got on with a stepmother,' said Tyler. 'As it was, my father died when I was sixteen, and since then I haven't had to worry about what anyone else thinks. When you're only accountable to yourself, you can take risks you wouldn't otherwise be able to take. I built up my first company from scratch, made a million and lost everything, so then I had to start all over again. I wouldn't have been able to do that if I'd had to think about someone else.'

'You're going to have to think about someone else if you get married,' Mary pointed out.

'I suppose so.' Tyler didn't sound particularly enthused at

the prospect. 'Not that my wife will be concerned with the business side of things.'

'Why not?' said Mary. 'You can't divide life into neat little compartments.' She could see his jaw setting mulishly, and she sighed. 'The whole point of marriage is that the two of you share everything,' she told him patiently. 'I'm not suggesting your wife is in on every business decision, but she'll certainly want to know if you're worried about work, just like you'll need to know if there's anything *she's* worried about. You're going to have to learn to talk to each other.'

'Why are women so obsessed with talking?' said Tyler with a return to his old irritability. 'All they ever say is, "We need to talk," when what they mean is, "I need to tell you what you're doing wrong"!'

Mary took a reflective slug of her wine. 'If you'd ever listened to what they had to say, you might not be in a position where you have to pay me five thousand pounds to say much the same thing,' she pointed out with deceptive mildness. 'Anyway, it's not just about discussing problems. You shouldn't marry anyone you're not happy just to sit and chat to, without ever having to think of something to say. A fulfilling relationship is about a lot more than sex, you know.'

'Are you suggesting that we don't have sex until we're married?' asked Tyler, lifting his brows derisively.

There was a short pause while they both listened to his words echoing into the silence.

'When I say "we", of course I don't mean you and me,' he added, his colour slightly heightened. 'I mean a future fiancée.'

'Of course,' said Mary, pleased to be the one who could sound smooth and understanding for once. 'I'd certainly agree that sex is an important part of most relationships, but when you do meet someone, you should bear in mind that she's not likely to consider marrying you if she thinks that you're only interested in her for sex.'

There, listen to her talking coolly to Tyler about sex. She sounded positively professional.

It was just a pity she didn't *feel* cool and professional.

'So you suggest that I spend the evenings sitting and talking to her instead?'

'There are worse ways to spend an evening,' said Mary dryly, but Tyler was unconvinced.

'I should think it would get pretty boring,' he said, firmly suppressing the realisation that he hadn't been bored at all sitting and talking to Mary.

'It's not boring if you're with someone you love,' she was saying, her words overlapping his thought with an unintentionally disturbing effect. 'No, don't roll your eyes,' she went on as he did his best to disguise his reaction. 'I'm serious.'

'Is this the old you-should-only-marry-for-love argument, by any chance?' he asked, leaning over the table to refill her wineglass.

Mary's lips thinned. 'You seem to think that marriage is something you can acquire, like a car or a boat,' she said. 'It's not like that. It isn't about having a wife you can show off to your friends. It's about being with the one person who can light up your life and make you feel better just being near her, and she needs to feel the same way about you.'

'Is that how you felt about Alan?' he asked, his voice hard, and she looked away.

'Yes,' she said sadly. 'It was like that and it didn't last, but that doesn't mean I don't believe that what I'm saying is true. Your wife, whoever she is, shouldn't just be that. She needs to be your rock, your anchor, the only one who can make the rest of your life make sense. When you find someone like that,

Tyler, then *that's* when you should get married, because you'll know in your heart that she's the one.'

'But what if she's *not* the one?' he argued. The idea of Alan being the one who lit up Mary's life was annoying, like an itchy little insect bite. 'It's all very well saying you'll know, but people change. They fall out of love as easy as they fall into it. You only have to look at the statistics for divorce nowadays to realise that. Sometimes they don't even make it as far as the altar. Look at you and Alan,' he said, which perhaps wasn't fair, but he wasn't feeling particularly fair this evening.

Mary winced, but she met his gaze squarely. 'It's true that my relationship with Alan didn't work out,' she said quietly, 'but it wasn't because we fell out of love. It was because we couldn't find a compromise when it came to having a baby.'

She paused. 'My experience only proves the point I'm trying to make, which is that if you want a successful relationship—and you say you do—then you both have to be prepared to work at it and learn to compromise. If you don't, then chances are that you'll end up as a statistic like me, and I'm sure you don't want that.'

Tyler didn't. He wasn't prepared to contemplate the prospect of failure on any front.

He drained his glass and set it down on the table. 'If it's going to be that hard work, I think I'd rather skip the whole lighting up my life bit,' he said with an air of finality. 'My marriage is much more likely to succeed if I choose someone with the same practical approach as mine.'

'Well, OK, if that's your attitude,' said Mary, giving up with a shrug.

It was almost a relief to be reminded of Tyler's cold-blooded approach to marriage, she reflected. There had been times when he had come perilously closely to seeming like the kind of man it would be all too easy to fall in love with, she had to admit. When he smiled at Bea, or held her in his big square hands, she was in danger of forgetting that he was also a man who focused ruthlessly on his goal.

Right now, his goal was to get married and he certainly wasn't thinking of a woman like her. And that was just as well, Mary reminded herself. Her heart was still raw from Alan's rejection and the last thing she needed was to get involved with a man like Tyler who didn't believe in love and wanted very different things out of life. Her job was to help him make a success of a relationship with someone else entirely.

'In that case, though, it's even more important to make sure that you've found the right woman and spend time getting to know her rather than just falling into bed, isn't it?' she said in resolutely professional mode. 'Remember, you're going to be spending the rest of your life together, so if you've used up all your conversation on the first date, that's not going to be a good sign. Surely you want to marry someone who's going to be a good companion over the years, who's interesting and intelligent and doesn't bore you?'

'Of course I do,' said Tyler, although he couldn't think of a single woman he knew who fitted that particular bill. Except Mary, of course, and he had already decided that she wasn't the kind of wife he wanted.

'You're going to have to work hard to convince an interesting, intelligent woman that the kind of marriage you've got in mind is one that she might want,' Mary warned, and he scowled.

'That's what you're here for,' he reminded her.

Quite. Better not forget that, Mary.

Pushing back her chair, she gathered the empty plates and carried them across to the dishwasher. 'Talking of why I'm here, it's time to move on to your next lesson,' she said brightly.

'*Another* one?'

'You've only had three!' she pointed out. 'The first one was about the importance of compromising,' she went on, counting them off on her fingers. 'The second was about making a prospective wife feel welcome and wanted and the third was showing that you can be good with babies. I'd have to give you full marks on that one after the way you looked after Bea this morning,' she finished.

'So what's lesson four?'

'Communication,' said Mary succinctly.

'Communication?'

'See? You don't even know what communication is!'

'Of course I do,' snapped Tyler. 'I just don't—'

'Understand why it's so important in a relationship?'

'No,' he said, gritting his teeth. 'I was going to say, before you interrupted me, that I don't see the difference between communication and talking, and we've already done that.'

Mary set a plum tart on the table and went to the fridge for some cream. She shouldn't really, but she had already had half a packet of biscuits today, so it was a bit late to worry about the diet. She would start that tomorrow.

'They're related, of course,' she told Tyler, 'but I'm thinking about communication more as keeping in touch. With your previous girlfriends, did you ring them during the day at all?'

'Not when I'm at work,' he said, sounding appalled at the very idea.

'Did you send emails, perhaps? A text now and then?'

'I go to the office to work,' said Tyler pointedly, 'not waste my time on personal calls.'

Mary tutted as she sat back down at the table. 'Right, so you're a compartment man. You close the door in the morning when you leave the house and put all thought of everything except work out of your mind until you get home again at night.'

'How else am I supposed to concentrate on my business?' demanded Tyler, remembering uncomfortably how hard he had found it to put Mary out of his mind today. 'I like to focus on one thing at a time.'

That figured, thought Mary. 'I can see multi-tasking isn't your strong suit,' she said, cutting him a slice of the tart, 'but you can't run a relationship like a business, whatever you think. When you're building a relationship with a woman, you want to make her feel that she's special, and you can do that by making contact when you're apart during the day.'

'I can't spend all day on the phone,' he said irritably. 'I'd never get anything done.'

'I'm not suggesting long conversations, but a spontaneous call to let her know that you're thinking about her would make a big difference. You don't have to talk for long.'

Tyler had his stubborn look on, she saw. 'Look,' she said, 'what have we just been saying about having to work hard if you want the right woman? It's not that difficult to send a text, is it? And an email only takes a few seconds. What's the problem?'

'I wouldn't know what to say,' he admitted grudgingly.

'Just say "I'm thinking about you", "I miss you"… You could even go the whole hog and say "I love you",' said Mary, and then stopped. 'Oh, except you aren't going to do love, are you?' she said, not without a touch of sarcasm. 'Scrap that one. "I like you" or "I respect you" don't have quite the same ring to them, so I'd avoid them too, but otherwise I don't think it matters what you say. It's just a way of letting her know that she's part of your life.'

She poured cream over her tart. 'I'll give you my mobile number and you can send me a text tomorrow,' she told him.

'It'll be good for you to get in the habit of it so, by the time you meet someone, you can do all this sort of thing as second nature. I'd better have your number too,' she added, pointing inelegantly with her spoon, her mouth full of tart.

'What for?' asked Tyler.

Mary swallowed her mouthful. 'I might need it,' she said. 'I might want you to pick up some extra milk on your way home or something.'

He bristled. 'I'm not a shopping service!'

'We're living together to all intents and purposes,' she said. 'The idea was that we do everything normal couples do.'

'Except sleep together,' said Tyler, and she flashed him a startled glance before dropping her eyes back to her plate.

'Except that,' she agreed.

'Mr Watts?'

'Hmm…what?' Startled out of his reverie, Tyler jerked round to see his PA standing in the doorway, watching him with a curious expression. 'What is it, Carol?' he asked gruffly, disliking being caught at a disadvantage.

'Are you ready for your eleven-thirty meeting?'

Meeting? What meeting? Tyler felt oddly disorientated this morning. Instead of working, he had spent the last twenty minutes spinning mindlessly in his chair, drumming his fingers on the leather arm and wishing he could get Mary's face out of his mind.

The thought of her had been distracting him all morning, and his two earlier meetings had been positively embarrassing. Tyler had seen the furtive glances the others around the table had exchanged on more than one occasion when he had had to have his attention recalled. He was famous for his sharpness and his focus, but both seemed to have deserted him today.

Tyler couldn't understand it. It wasn't as if Mary was beautiful. She wasn't even that pretty. The grey eyes were lovely, but her mouth was too wide, her nose too big and her chin too stubborn. As for those quirky eyebrows, they were plain odd. Somehow, though, the humour and intelligence in her face meant that you didn't really notice her features, and the more Tyler looked at her, the more he found himself deciding that she was really very attractive.

You want an interesting, intelligent woman, she had told him, and Tyler agreed. What he wanted was a woman like Mary, in fact, but without a baby or those ridiculously sentimental notions of love and marriage.

He wanted someone better groomed too, he reminded himself. Mary always seemed to be spilling out of her clothes and, if she was wearing something nice, ten to one she would have dropped something down her front. She was clumsy and critical and she had a sharp tongue. She was the last kind of woman he wanted to marry.

It was just that he liked watching her talk, liked watching the way her expressive face lit up as she gesticulated, liked the gleam of fun in her smile and the way she could keep her expression perfectly straight sometimes while her eyes brimmed with laughter.

'Mr Watts?' Carol prompted him. 'Is everything all right?'

'Of course,' snapped Tyler, humiliated by the open curiosity in her stare, and more than a little embarrassed at having been caught with his thoughts drifting yet again. 'Send them in—no, wait!' He changed his mind at the last moment. 'Give me five minutes.'

Carol nodded an acknowledgement and withdrew, closing the door carefully behind her as if humouring an eccentric, and Tyler was left alone. He picked up his mobile from his desk and then put it down again, staring at it as if it were a strange and unpredictable beast.

This was silly. He didn't do texting or schmaltzy emails, and he didn't want to start now. He was too old and too busy for that kind of thing.

On the other hand, it would only take a minute and if it made the difference Mary said it did, it was a technique he could—perhaps should—learn. Abruptly, he picked up the phone and, using his thumb, typed in 'thinking about you', which was true, after all. He signed it T and, after a moment's hesitation, put an X after it. He wasn't completely clueless, whatever Mary thought. Then he pressed 'send' before he could change his mind.

'That was all that was required,' said Mary approvingly that evening when he got home. 'It wasn't so hard, was it?'

The hard bit had been waiting for her to reply. God knew what had gone on in that meeting! Tyler had spent the whole time trying not look at the phone, and when it had finally lit up to indicate that a message had been received it had been all he could do not to snatch it up. It had taken immense will-power to wait until he had hustled the meeting to a close before he'd let himself read her reply.

Ridiculously, he had even been conscious of a tiny thrill when he'd seen that it was indeed from Mary, although as a message it was hardly one to treasure. 'V good' she had written. 'Go to top of class. M XX'

The worst thing was that he had actually counted how many x's she had included. Tyler couldn't believe that he had actually noticed, let alone wondered what they had meant. Were two 'X's the equivalent of flirting?

Not that there was anything remotely flirtatious about Mary's manner when he got home. He had managed to leave the office by six again, and even the security guard had commented on his changed routine.

'You're not usually out of here much before nine, Mr Watts. There isn't a problem, is there?'

No, there wasn't a problem, Tyler reassured himself. There was just…Mary. And she was just doing what he had asked her to do. What he was *paying* her to do. There was no reason for him to feel that everything was changing. He was exactly the same as he had ever been. He was just applying himself to his course.

He sat in the kitchen with Bea on his lap, watching Mary cook while the baby explored his face with inquisitive little fingers, tugging at his lips and twisting his ears curiously.

'What's the lesson tonight?' he asked, wincing at a pinch. Those little fingers could give quite a nip.

'I've been thinking about that.' Mary turned from the worktop and wiped her hands on her apron. 'Keeping in touch the way you did today is good, but you also need to think about other ways you can show that you're aware of her needs.'

'Couldn't you be a bit more specific?' said Tyler, lost already.

Mary chewed a thumb absently as she tried to think of a way to explain. 'It's about being thoughtful and sensitive and putting yourself in her shoes,' she tried slowly. 'Maybe one day she'll need some comforting, and another one she'll want you to boost her confidence. Or she might want to be surprised.'

It all sounded very vague to Tyler, and he said so.

'Most women just want to feel loved and desired and appreciated,' said Mary. 'OK, so you're not going to make her feel loved, but you can at least try not to take her for granted.

Don't get so wrapped up in your work that you forget to tell her that she's beautiful, or how much she means to you.'

'Right,' said Tyler, filing all this away. 'I'll try to be more thoughtful.'

Looking back later, Mary was surprised at how quickly she got used to living with Tyler. It was odd the way she could be so uncomfortably aware of him, and yet feel so comfortable when they were together. Most of the time, she had herself under pretty good control, and then it seemed perfectly natural that she should be living in a mansion or sitting at the kitchen table telling Tyler Watts, of all people, about her day.

But there were other times when it wasn't so easy. She would look at him tossing Bea into the air and her entrails would tangle themselves into a knot that left her feeling hollow and slightly sick. Or her eyes would get stuck on his hands or the crease in his cheeks and a wave of heat would catch her unawares, pushing the air from her lungs and setting her senses afire.

Mary couldn't understand it. True to his word, Tyler was trying to be thoughtful, but clearly it didn't come easily, and most of the time he reverted to his usual abrupt manner. He was brusque, impatient and irritable, with a sardonic turn of phrase and no charm whatsoever. There was absolutely no reason to feel breathless and giddy whenever he walked into the room.

But she still did.

Bea adored him. She crowed with delight when he walked in, and Tyler kept most of his rare smiles for her. Without either of them being quite aware how it happened, they fell into a routine where he fed Bea while Mary cooked supper. Mary would watch him out of the corner of her eye and marvel that the tough businessman she knew could be so patient and gentle with a baby. He managed to remain immaculate too. When she fed Bea she ended up with half her supper down her front, but Tyler sat fastidiously at arm's length and never got so much as a drop on his expensive Italian suit.

When Bea was thoroughly wiped down she was allowed to sit on his lap, which she loved, and if she was crying he grew quite adept at distracting her, walking around the room with her in his arms or tickling her until she giggled. He drew the line at changing a nappy, though, which Mary supposed was fair enough. Bea wasn't his baby, although sometimes it was hard to remember that.

Once Bea was in bed, they would have supper together and Mary found herself looking forward to that time with him far more than she ought. It was all too easy to forget that she was supposed to be a coach and he the client. Every now and then, one or other of them would recall that they should be discussing relationships, but usually they just talked.

They disagreed on most things, and as often as not they would end up arguing, but Mary even enjoyed that. Their arguments were always stimulating and she felt mentally alert in a way she hadn't done since Bea's birth. For the first few months as a mother, she had been consumed by worry: about Bea and Alan's attitude to her, about money and her mother, about finding somewhere to live and getting the agency off the ground and just getting through from one day to the next.

Those worries hadn't disappeared, but for the first time Mary felt able to shelve them for a while. She couldn't think about Alan or the need to find somewhere to live just yet. This month with Tyler felt like a time out of time. She was content to live for the moment, and if she was conscious of feeling more vibrant and alive than she ever had before, Mary chose not to question too closely why that should be.

So the arguments were fine. The times when they ended up laughing together were altogether more disturbing. Mary would lie awake those nights, tossing restlessly while Tyler's smile burned behind her eyelids, and remind herself that there was no point in liking him, let alone loving him.

She had absolutely no reason to suppose that he had changed his hard-headed attitude to marriage, or changed his mind in the slightest about the kind of woman he wanted for his wife. He had brought her flowers once, and he sent the odd email, but only when he remembered that he was supposed to be thoughtful. None of them meant anything. Lovely though they had been, the flowers weren't for her. They were just practice.

Tyler was very careful about touching her, she had noticed, and avoided where he could even a mere brush of their hands. It was usually he who ended their supper-time conversations. He would get up—often quite abruptly—and shut himself up in his study to work. It was clear that he had no interest in spending the whole evening with her, no matter how easily they had been talking.

And why should he? Mary asked herself bleakly. Face it, she was fat and frumpy and clumsy and untidy and probably boring too. Her life revolved around Bea and the agency, and she had no energy for anything else. She had spent an evening with her mother, and had been for a drink with an old school friend, but it wasn't exactly a high old social life. Glamour-puss she would never be. There was no use in fooling herself. She just wasn't the kind of woman Tyler wanted to show off to his peers, and that was all there was to it.

Not that she should care, Mary reminded herself, but it was getting harder and harder to remember why not.

The fine weather lasted for over two weeks until one morning

Mary woke to gusty rain splattering against the windows. She dragged herself out of bed, rubbing her eyes wearily. It hadn't been a good night. Bea seemed to have picked up a cold from somewhere, and Mary had been up with her four times.

Bea's screams had woken Tyler too. At one point he had appeared bleary-eyed in the bedroom door and asked if he could help.

Bea had just been sick all over her, and you would have thought that she would have other things on her mind, but Mary had still found time to notice that he was wearing only a pair of pyjama bottoms. Tyler was always immaculately turned out and she had got used to seeing him in his pristine shirt and tie and his crisp suit. He looked very different in the middle of the night, with bare feet, a piratical stubble and his hair slightly tousled from his pillow.

Very different and very, very attractive.

His skin had looked smooth and warm and firm, and she could see the flex of muscles in his powerful shoulders. Impossible not to wonder what it would be like to reach out and lay the flat of her hand against his flank.

Mary had shivered at the thought. The dangerously enticing thought.

The shiver had been followed almost immediately by a wash of shame. What kind of mother was she? What other woman's pulse would kick up a notch at the sight of a broad, bare male chest when she had a sick child in her arms?

'I don't think there's anything you can do, but thanks anyway,' she said, firmly averting her eyes from him. 'Sorry we disturbed you.'

Tyler's unsettlingly pale gaze rested on her for a moment. 'I'll leave you to it, then,' he said abruptly, levering himself away from the doorframe and disappearing.

Probably horrified by the sight of her without her make-up on, thought Mary glumly as she cleaned Bea up and buttoned her into a fresh Babygro. Either that or he hadn't liked being scoped out by a middle-aged mum with piggy eyes and baby sick in her hair.

She was wearing her oldest, baggiest pyjamas too. They happened to be her most comfortable ones too, but they could hardly be said to be flattering. Mary felt enormous in them and, oh, look, the buttons down the front were all done up the wrong way too. *Not* a good look.

'Oh, well, what does it matter what I look like?' Mary sighed to Bea, picking her up and cuddling her close. 'I'm never going to be slender and glamorous.'

Unlike Tyler's wife. She might not have a name yet, but Mary was quite sure that she would be the kind of woman who could look beautiful at four in the morning. Her hair would be blond and slightly dishevelled and she would look like an angel leaning over the cot in some seductive, slithery silk nightgown that Tyler wouldn't be able to keep his hands off and that would never, ever be stained by baby sick.

'Why should I care?' Mary demanded of her sleepy daughter.

There was no answer to that. Mary just knew that she did.

The miserable weather reflected Mary's spirits and she felt oppressed all day. There was no other reason to feel down, she kept reminding herself. Business was booming at the agency, her mother had finally settled things with Bill and was happier than Mary had seen her for a very long time, and she would be leaving Haysby Hall next week with five thousand pounds in her pocket. She could think about looking for a flat soon. She ought to be ecstatic.

The fact that she wasn't, Mary put down to the murky rain and the lowering grey cloud that squatted over the city. It had nothing to do with the prospect of leaving Tyler next week, she decided as she gave up on an unprofitable day early and headed home in the car. He probably couldn't wait for them to be gone, she thought drearily. Especially after last night.

Bea's mood was no better than Mary's. She was grizzling in the back seat and, between her and the frantic slap of the windscreen wipers, it took some time before Mary realised that the car was making funny noises.

To her dismay, it started coughing and steaming, until it spluttered to a halt a good five miles from Haysby Hall. Naturally, it picked the most isolated section of the narrow country road in which to stop.

Mary dropped her head on to the steering wheel and let out a long groan of despair. This was all she needed. The rain was driving against the windscreen and the wind buffeted the car and howled through the trees as if auditioning for Hammer House of Horrors.

In the back, Bea set up a wail, not liking the noise, and Mary gritted her teeth. There was no point in just sitting here. It was a struggle to push the door open into the wind, but she managed to get out and push the car further away from the dangerous bend, which was something.

By the time she got back into the car and switched on the hazard lights she was sodden through to her skin and she wiped the rain from her face. Now what? She had Bea's pushchair, but she couldn't walk her five miles in this. Thank heaven for mobiles. There was nothing for it but to ring for help.

Afterwards, Mary thought of all sorts of people she could have called. Her mother was at home and could have arranged a taxi, or Bill would doubtless have come out to rescue her, but at the time she didn't even think. There was only one person whose voice she wanted to hear just then. She rang Tyler.

CHAPTER EIGHT

'WATTS,' Tyler barked into the phone, and just hearing him made Mary want to cry for some reason.

'It's me,' she said. 'Mary.'

'I'm in a meeting,' he said. 'What is it?'

'I've broken down in the middle of nowhere,' she said, fiercely swallowing the wobble in her voice. 'And I haven't got any cash. Can you ask Carol to get someone to come out and pick us up?'

Tyler didn't waste time on commiserations. He asked Mary where she was, told her to stay in the car until help came, and rang off.

Resigning herself to a miserable wait, Mary huddled in the back seat with Bea and tried not to think about how cold and wet she was, but it wasn't in the end that long before a knock on the window made her jump and she saw Tyler himself peering into the car under an umbrella.

'Come on, let's get you out of there,' he said.

Mary stared at him. 'I thought you were in a meeting,' was all she could think of to say.

'They're finishing it without me,' said Tyler. 'Hurry up, I'm getting wet out here,' he added when Mary just sat there as if stunned. 'And Bea looks as if she wants to go home, even if you don't.'

Chivvying her as if she were a recalcitrant child, Tyler got the two of them into his Porsche, which was wonderfully warm and dry. He took charge of her car, organised a mechanic to come and tow it away and then drove them home with a brisk competence that made Mary feel treacherously weepy. It was bliss to be looked after for once, to drop her head back against the leather seat and simply put herself in Tyler's capable hands.

She was dripping all over his luxurious leather upholstery and her wet clothes clung unpleasantly. 'I'm sorry about this,' she said as he put the car into gear and pulled out. 'I didn't mean to drag you out of your meeting.'

'It doesn't matter,' he said without looking at her.

He didn't seem to want to talk, but there was something so uncomfortable about the silence that Mary felt as if she had to persevere.

'You got here awfully quickly,' she said. 'You must have left straight away.'

He had, in fact, barely paused to make his excuses to the meeting, Tyler remembered. As soon as he had learnt that she was alone and in trouble, his one thought had been to get to her.

'There was no point in hanging around,' he said tersely, not sure if he was cross with her for putting him in the situation where he abandoned meetings at the drop of a hat, or with himself for feeling so anxious until he had seen that she was safe.

The truth was that he had been irritable all day. He hadn't slept at all after Bea's crying had woken him in the middle of the night. He had lain in bed, unable to get the thought of Mary in those ridiculous pyjamas out of his mind. He could have understood if she had been spilling out of some sexy little number, but they had been faded and shabby and shapeless. And all he had been able to think about was how warm and lush she had looked, about how much he would have liked to be able to undo those buttons and lose himself in her luscious flesh and her soft curves, to—

But there Tyler pulled himself up short. The baby hadn't been well. Mary had been worried. It was downright perverse of him to be noticing how soft and warm and *touchable* she looked, with her brown hair all tousled and her grey eyes blurry with sleep.

Perverse and pointless. Mary, he reminded himself for the umpteenth time, had no part in his plans for the future. Thinking about what it would be like to make love to her was unprofitable, to say the least, and profitability always had to be the bottom line. He was a businessman, wasn't he?

It exasperated Tyler that somewhere along the line over the last three weeks he had lost his focus. He was famous for his workaholic tendencies and for his ability to concentrate his energy on a single goal, but that had all gone by the board too. He couldn't work if Mary was in the house, no matter how firmly he shut himself up in his study, and he couldn't work if she was out either. One night she had gone to see her mother and the house had seemed cold and empty and lonely until she'd breezed back after ten.

Tyler felt as if he were losing control and it wasn't a feeling he liked. He was going to have to do something about it, he decided. Things couldn't go on like this. Mary was too distracting.

Look at her now. He glanced sideways to where she sat shivering in the passenger seat. Her hair was hanging in damp tendrils. Her nose was red. She looked wet and miserable and downright plain, but he felt a tightness in his chest that he couldn't explain just looking at her, and he was conscious of an absurd desire to stop the car, gather her into his arms and warm her with his body until she stopped shivering.

As it was, all he could do was reach forward and turn the heater on to full blast.

He had to get a grip, Tyler reminded himself fiercely. Keep an eye on his goal, remember his strategy. There was no reason why he shouldn't think of Mary as a friend, he decided, but not as anything more than that. That would be his new strategy, in fact.

That was his justification for sending her off to have a bath as soon as they got in, anyway. 'I'll look after Bea,' he said. 'You'd better get those wet clothes off.'

Mary sank into the bath with a long grateful sigh. The miserable day suddenly didn't seem quite so bad.

It was wonderful to feel warm again, but she had a nasty feeling that not all of the heat was due to the hot bath. There was a dangerous little glow inside her at the knowledge that Tyler had come to her rescue himself. He had even left a meeting early for her, which was unheard of in the history of Watts Holdings! He could easily have sent someone else, or had Carol sort out the whole sorry mess, but he had chosen to come himself. Mary hugged the knowledge to her.

Was this how all those fairy tale princesses felt when their knight galloped up on his charger? Tyler Watts made an unlikely knight, it had to be admitted. He was irascible rather than chivalrous, and he had been brusque and uncommunicative in the car, but that hadn't stopped her being agonisingly aware of him.

There was a solidity and a self-contained strength to him that was almost overwhelming at close quarters. His brows might be drawn forbiddingly across his nose, and his mouth might be set in a grimmer than usual line, but his stern presence was incredibly reassuring.

Mary had been seized by an almost uncontrollable desire

to reach out and touch him. He had been so close. It would have been so easy to lay a hand on his thigh, to lean across and press her lips to his throat, to cling to that hard body. The urge had been so strong that her fingers had twitched and tingled, and she had clasped them in her lap, her heart hammering madly in her throat at the very thought of it.

She wouldn't have done it, of course. Having a lustful woman crawling all over him would have been far too distracting for Tyler when he was driving.

Wrong reason. Mary sat up so abruptly that water sloshed perilously close to the edge of the bath. The right reason for not throwing herself at him was because she would have looked an utter fool.

How many times did she have to remind herself that she and Tyler were headed in quite different directions? She wasn't part of his plan and she could hardly complain. He had been clear about that right from the start. *You're just not my type*, he had said. *Anyone except you.*

So, no more fantasies about kissing him, all right? No more dreams about touching him, feeling him, tasting him, letting her lips drift over the lean, muscled length of his body...

Mary swallowed and stood up, shaking that last thought aside. 'Idiot!' she chastised herself as she reached for a towel. Instead of keeping a careful guard over her emotions, she had let herself fall for that time out of time nonsense, and what was the result? She was halfway in love with Tyler Watts.

You would have thought that she would have known better. Her heart was still raw after the break-up with Alan. She should be cosseting it with some tender, loving care, not tossing it at the feet of a ruthless workaholic whose ambitions were fixed on a loveless marriage and a trophy wife. If she wasn't careful, her poor heart would get trampled all over again, and she would have no one to blame but herself. Tyler had made it very clear what he wanted right from the start, and it didn't include her.

She had to keep her heart safe from now on, Mary realised. For her own protection, she needed to remember just what she was doing here.

But it was hard when she went along to Bea's bedroom and found Tyler stretched out on the floor beside her daughter, patiently retrieving the toys she was throwing. He seemed to have done a very good job of cajoling her out of her bad mood, and she squealed happily and pointed when she saw her mother in the doorway.

Tyler turned his head quickly to see Mary in a skirt and the same soft top she had worn that first night, her hair still damp from the bath. She was smiling but there was a certain wariness in the lovely grey eyes, he thought.

'Better?' he asked, getting to his feet.

'Much, thank you. I feel like a new woman,' she told him. 'Thanks for looking after Bea,' she went on. Bending to pick up her daughter gave her a good excuse to avoid his eyes. 'Come on, you,' she said with an 'ouf!' as she hoisted her up. 'I've had my time off. You'll need changing.'

But there was no tell-tale whiff from the nappy when she sniffed cautiously. Puzzled, Mary glanced at Tyler, who shrugged and looked awkward. 'I had a go,' he admitted.

'*You* changed her nappy?'

'You were in the bath,' he said almost defensively.

Mary's throat was so tight that she couldn't speak. Tyler had been so resolute in refusing to deal with nappies before that it had become something of a joke, but he had done it tonight, and her heart told her that he had done it for her.

'Thank you,' was all she could manage. Still holding Bea

in her arms, she reached up and kissed him quickly on the cheek before she could change her mind.

His skin was rough beneath her lips and he smelt clean and masculine and, after the realisation that she would only have to turn her head a fraction to find his mouth, time seemed to freeze. Their bodies were very close. It was as if two magnets were being pulled irresistibly towards each other, and the yearning to press herself into him was enormous. Temptation yawned as Mary felt Tyler stiffen and his hands lift and for one thrilling moment she thought that he was going to pull her close. Dizzy with longing, she waited, until in the end he just let his arms fall back to his sides.

Only then, and much, much too late, did she remember her poor battered heart and make herself step away.

There was an awkward pause. Mary wanted to say something light, to pass the whole thing off as a joke, but there didn't seem to be enough oxygen to speak and the lack of it was making her breathless and giddy. It was as if the kiss had happened after all, and the air between them was twanging with what might have been.

For Mary it was as if she were standing on the edge of a cliff. It would be so easy to fall in love with him, so easy to succumb to temptation, to trust him with her heart and step out into light and space and glory. But what if she couldn't trust him? What if she fell and he didn't catch her and lift her up?

She couldn't risk it, Mary thought with the sudden panicky realisation of just how close she was to the edge. Perhaps she would have taken the chance if she only had herself to consider, but she had Bea to think about. She couldn't run the risk of falling apart if Tyler didn't love her back.

And he wouldn't. She knew that. No, Mary reminded

herself, she had to be sensible. She had to remember the terms of their agreement, and the fact that she would be leaving soon.

She felt curiously detached. 'You know, now that you've changed a nappy, I'm not sure there's anything more I can teach you about how to have a successful relationship,' she said, meeting his eyes with careful composure. 'I think it's time you did something about putting all those lessons into practice. The month is nearly over.'

Tyler frowned. 'What do you mean?'

'Perhaps you should think about going out and meeting someone,' said Mary, turning casually away and rummaging in a drawer for a clean vest and top for Bea. 'There's not much point in us carrying on like this, is there?'

She had her back to him, and Tyler was glad that she couldn't see his face. He suspected he looked as if she had slapped him suddenly. That quick kiss had nearly undone him. Her lips had been soft, and he'd been able to smell the shampoo in her clean, damp hair. She'd been standing so close, he'd felt quite heady with it.

He had so nearly made a monumental fool of himself, Tyler realised. Without thinking, his arms had come up to pull her close, baby or no baby, and then where would they have been? His careful strategy of sticking to a friendly relationship would have looked a bit foolish then, wouldn't it? As it was, only a supreme effort of will had forced his arms back to his sides.

'No,' he said. 'No point at all.'

His head had still been reeling from her nearness when she had calmly reminded him of their professional arrangement. Tyler had been taken aback by the depth of his disappointment, but really, wasn't she suggesting what he himself wanted? It was easier this way. They were both going to be friendly but professional. It would be fine.

'I'll start dating again,' he promised, ignoring the hollow feeling deep inside him at the prospect. 'I'll meet someone soon.'

Perhaps inevitably, Mary inherited Bea's cold and her soaking the day before brewed it into a real humdinger. So now she had a thick head, red eyes and a streaming nose to add to her charms. Regarding her very unlovely reflection in the mirror that morning, Mary decided to stay at home.

She didn't have a car anyway, she remembered. There were buses, of course, but it would be a long walk to the nearest stop and there was no point in spreading her germs around. She might be committed to her agency, but there were limits.

Tyler rang her on her mobile at lunchtime. 'You're not answering your email,' he accused her. 'Where are you?'

'At home,' Mary croaked. 'I look disgusting and I feel worse.'

'Why didn't you let me know?' he demanded crossly.

'I thought I'd disrupted you enough at work yesterday,' she said through a fit of coughing. 'Anyway, there's nothing you can do. It's just a cold.'

Tyler grunted. 'Well, I'll be back early, anyway,' he said. 'I've got something for you.'

'All I need is a bottle of cough medicine and a barrel of paracetamol,' said Mary as best she could with her blocked nose.

'I'll bring that too,' said Tyler and rang off.

True to his word, he was back before five that evening. He found Mary on the sofa, within easy reach of a wastepaper basket overflowing with tissues, watching a chat show on television with a glazed expression.

'How do you feel?'

'Better than I look, actually,' she said, sitting up and pointing the remote control at the television to switch it off.

She had had a whole day to realise that she had made the right decision yesterday. There was nothing to be gained from falling in love with Tyler, while being sensible, as she *was* being, would leave her with her heart, her pride and her bank balance intact. 'Did you bring any cough medicine, though?'

'I did. I brought something else too,' said Tyler. 'Do you think you could manage a quick trip outside?'

'Outside?'

Puzzled, Mary hauled herself to her feet, managing no less than four enormous sneezes in the process, and trying not to notice how trustingly Bea lifted her arms to him to be picked up. Her daughter would miss Tyler as much as she would when the time came to go.

Next week, Mary reminded herself sternly. Not some hypothetical, misty future. Her departure was only a matter of days away, and she had better get used to the notion.

'What is it?' she asked as Tyler opened the front door.

At the bottom of the steps sat a brand-new BMW. 'It's for you,' said Tyler.

'For me?' she said blankly.

'I had a word with the garage this morning. Your car's pretty much a write-off.'

Her face fell in dismay. There was no way she could afford another car at the moment. 'Oh, no.'

'So you can have this one,' Tyler went on. 'It's been insured in your name, and there's a car seat fitted for Bea.'

'That's a very expensive car to drive a baby around in,' said Mary, eyeing it doubtfully. 'Wouldn't it be better to hire something cheaper?'

'It's not hired,' he said haughtily. 'I bought it for you.'

Her jaw dropped. 'You're not serious!'

'Of course I'm serious,' said Tyler. 'Why wouldn't I be?'

'But that's...that's far too extravagant!' she protested. 'I'm only here for another ten days.'

His eyes flickered at the reminder, but then he shrugged carelessly. 'Keep it when you go.'

'I couldn't possibly accept an expensive car from you!'

'I thought you were short of money,' he said, frowning.

'I am, but I'm not reduced to charity just yet,' said Mary touchily. 'I can hire a car for this week, and I won't need one so much when I'm back in town.'

Tyler made an exasperated noise. 'Why can't you just take this one? Think of it as a bonus, or part of your coaching fee.'

Mary shook her head firmly. 'Look, it's very generous of you, and I do appreciate the thought, but I can't take it. Quite apart from anything else, I could never afford to run it!'

He eyed her in frustration. 'We're supposed to be acting as if we had a real relationship,' he reminded her. 'If you were my girlfriend, there wouldn't be any problem about giving you a car.'

'Yes, but I'm not your girlfriend, am I?' said Mary a little tartly. 'And, even if I was, I wouldn't let you give me a car!'

'Why not? I thought women liked expensive presents— jewels and cars and trips to Paris and all that stuff.'

She sighed. 'I can't speak for all women, but personally, a present as expensive as that makes me uncomfortable. It just makes it obvious how unequal our incomes are. I don't want to feel that I'm being bought. A present is lovely if it's given in the right spirit as a romantic gesture.'

'What, like a diamond ring or something?'

'Exactly, but even then it doesn't have to be the biggest, showiest diamond around. I'd much rather have a ring that you'd chosen because you loved me—that *someone* had chosen because he loved me,' Mary corrected herself hastily.

'A thoughtful gesture means so much more than an ostentatious one.'

Ostentatious? Was that what she thought he was? Tyler scowled. 'I *am* being thoughtful,' he said crossly. 'I'm thinking that you're stuck out here in the country and you need transport to get to work.'

'Yes, but—' Mary bit her lip. 'I know you're being thoughtful,' she tried again, 'but saving me the trouble of hiring my own cheap little hatchback would have meant just as much, and not nearly as much as the fact that you changed Bea's nappy yesterday when I know you must have hated every minute of it!'

A muscle was jumping in Tyler's jaw. 'So you won't take the car?'

'No.'

He couldn't understand it. What was a miserable BMW to him? He couldn't imagine a single one of his previous girlfriends batting an eyelid about him giving them a car. Why did Mary have to be different? He'd imagined her screaming with excitement when she saw the car, had looked forward to watching her face as she sat behind the wheel and smelt the luxurious interior. He'd wanted her to be thrilled. Not for a minute had he thought that she would turn it down.

'At least use it while you're here,' he said grouchily, shutting the front door again with a bang.

Mary judged it time to give in gracefully. She could tell that she'd offended him, but honestly! What did he think she would do with a BMW? She didn't even have anywhere to live when she left here yet, and her mother's street was notorious as a route home from the city centre pubs. Cars were always having their wing mirrors snapped off, or being scraped by vans just too wide to squeeze through the narrow gap between the vehicles parked on either side of the road. A brand-new BMW wouldn't last a minute, and Mary didn't suppose they were cheap to repair. Tyler didn't seem to realise that not everyone had a garage or a stately home well away from passing yobs.

'All right, I'll do that,' she said. 'Thank you. I'll leave it here when I go next week. Who knows?' she said, trying to cajole him out of his bad mood. 'Maybe you'll meet someone perfect soon, and you can give her the car.'

'I hardly think my wife is the type to appreciate second-hand goods,' snapped Tyler.

More disappointed by her reaction than he wanted to admit, he thrust Bea back to Mary. 'I'll be in my study,' he said, and stomped off.

Why couldn't she have been delighted with the car? Tyler thought morosely. Why couldn't she have jumped up and down and kissed him gratefully? Why couldn't she be slim and sweet and elegant?

Why couldn't she be the wife he wanted? He wanted a wife who would impress his peers, a woman so beautiful and stylish that every man would envy him. Who would envy him a plump, messy single mother?

It was just that whenever he tried to imagine his immaculate bride-to-be, her perfect face kept dissolving into a round one with big grey eyes, her smooth blond hair would be transformed into chaotic brown curls and her slender figure would swell until it was voluptuous and inviting.

She would turn into Mary, in fact—the same Mary who was going on and on and *on* about the fact that she was leaving soon. Anyone would think that she couldn't wait to go.

Supper that night was a tense meal, but Mary exerted herself to be chatty and as normal as possible, although it was hard when all she wanted was to kiss his bad humour away and coax him into a laugh.

Or she would have done if she wasn't being so resolutely sensible.

'Oh, I forgot to tell you,' she said as she sat down. 'I had a letter from Alan's solicitor today. It seems they're ready to agree to a valuation at long last. I don't know why they've suddenly got their act together, but at least it means that I should get my money soon.'

'That's good news,' said Tyler, who had already heard it from his own solicitors. He had charged them with putting a metaphorical boot up Alan's backside and it seemed they'd been effective.

'Isn't it?' Mary smiled brightly. 'I can think about finding somewhere to live now. I might have to rent at first, but that's all right. It means I can look around for a little house to buy without any pressure. In fact, I might go and register with some estate agents tomorrow,' she added, and produced another fixed smile. 'You'll have your house to yourself again in no time.'

That would teach him to be helpful, thought Tyler. He had only got in touch with his solicitors because he was outraged at the way Mary was being treated. He had thought a quiet intervention might be useful—showing that she had powerful friends prepared to flex a little muscle wouldn't go amiss.

Funny how he hadn't made the connection that helping Mary get her money would mean helping her to leave.

Still, it was just as well that she was thinking of moving out, he reasoned. It was bound to happen some time and better sooner than later. It would be easier to concentrate on his marriage strategy without her here, anyway.

'That's great,' he said, and then because it didn't sound that

convincing first time round, he cleared his throat and said it
again more forcefully. 'Great.'

In spite of this mutual insistence on the advantages of
Mary moving out as soon as possible, it was not a particularly
happy household. Far from being elated at having a seemingly
intractable problem solved, Mary was tense, snappy and unaccountably depressed. Tyler was even worse. His normal
irascibility seemed positively jolly compared to his mood
over the next couple of days. Picking up on the strain in the
atmosphere, Bea was fractious and grizzly.

Still, her cross little face dissolved into its usual beam
when Tyler walked in that Friday evening, but his answering
smile was cursory and he barely accorded her a pat on the
head before he turned to Mary, tossing an embossed card on
to the table between them.

'Carol reminded me about this today,' he said.

'What is it?'

'An invitation to a black tie reception in the Merchant Adventurers' Hall next Wednesday.'

Taking off his jacket, Tyler hung it over the back of a chair
and loosened his tie. 'I need to go, and it looks better if I've
got someone with me, so you'd better come along. I can
practice being out with a partner, and who knows? I might
meet someone new there and you can give me tips on how to
make a good impression on her.'

Mary turned from the sink, wiping her hands on a tea
towel. 'Do you want to try that again?' she asked with deceptive mildness.

'What do you mean?'

'Or shall we go over it step by step and work out all the
ways you went wrong in one simple speech?'

Tyler had unbuttoned his cuffs and was rolling up his

sleeves, and he glanced up from his task with undisguised irritation. 'I'm inviting you to a party, for God's sake!'

'Oh, that was an invitation, was it?' said Mary furiously. '*"You'd better come along"?* My, you sure know how to sweep a girl off her feet, don't you?'

'Come on, Mary,' he said tetchily. 'We had a deal.'

'Yes, and the deal was that you treated me as you would a real girlfriend,' she said. 'And if you think any woman is going to be bowled over by having a card tossed towards her and informed that she'd better go along as you need someone with you, the implication being that you've got no one better to take, then you'd better think again! I might have other plans for next Wednesday.'

Tyler gave an exasperated snort. 'Have you?'

'As it happens, no,' she conceded, 'but you weren't to know that. And what were you thinking I would do with Bea? Just leave her here on her own?'

'Of course not. I assumed you'd be able to find a babysitter for her.'

'Don't *assume*,' said Mary, secretly relieved that she had a legitimate outlet for her bad temper over the last few days. '*Ask!*'

She hung up the tea towel and reached for a knife and a chopping board. 'Now, if you still want me to go to this reception, I suggest that you try that so-called invitation again—and I'd omit the part where you tell me that you're hoping to meet someone to replace me while I'm there, if I were you!'

'It's not about *replacing* you,' shouted Tyler, goaded. 'In case you've forgotten, you're not in fact my girlfriend!'

Mary's expression froze. 'There's no chance of me forgetting that, I can assure you,' she said icily—and quite untruthfully. She had been in serious danger of forgetting it until a few days ago.

'Well, then! I can't see what all the fuss is about!'

'You're still supposed to be practising your relationship skills, such as they are, on me,' said Mary in an acid voice. 'And that doesn't include treating me like the hired help, even if that's what I am.' She met his furious blue gaze squarely. 'So if you want me to go, ask me nicely.'

Tyler gritted his teeth. He had a good mind to go without her, but he needed her there. The logical part of his mind did ask why, given that he had attended plenty of functions on his own before, but she had made him so angry that he was beyond thinking rationally just then.

'Very well,' he said tightly. 'I'll start again. Are you doing anything next Wednesday, Mary?'

Mary put her head on one side as if flicking through a mental diary. 'I don't think so. Why?'

'I was wondering if you'd like to come to a reception at the Merchant Adventurers' Hall with me,' he ploughed on, only to break off as she held up a hand to stop him.

'Do you know, I think it would be a nice gesture if you told me how much you wanted me to go with you,' she suggested, sugar-sweet.

The muscle in Tyler's jaw was working overtime tonight. 'It would mean a lot to me if you came with me.'

'Hmm.' Mary considered. 'A bit stilted, but a vast improvement on your first attempt, anyway,' she pronounced.

Tyler stuck grimly to his role. 'Would you be able to find a babysitter for Bea?'

'I could ask my mother.'

'Can I take that as a yes?' After putting him through all that, she couldn't even be bothered to give him a straight answer!

Mary smiled graciously. 'If my mother's OK with looking after Bea, then yes, I'd love to come,' she said.

CHAPTER NINE

TEETERING a little on unfamiliar heels, Mary walked along the corridor to Tyler's office. She couldn't help remembering the heels she had worn the night of that reception, and how he had caught her as she fell. Sometimes she could swear her arm still tingled where he had gripped her.

It was hard to believe that had been only a month ago. Tyler had been a virtual stranger then, no more than her disagreeable ex-boss, and now...now he was part of her life. He was more than part of it, in fact. He was stuck smack in the middle of it, and in spite of all her strictures about staying sensible and protecting her heart, Mary was dismally aware of what a gaping hole he was going to leave in it when he had gone.

She had been doing her best to think positively about the future, and had even been to view a few flats, which turned out to be all that she was in a position to buy. Property was much cheaper than in London, of course, but nonetheless her options were still limited. Anything she could afford was going to seem very cramped after Haysby Hall. Luckily Bea was too small to notice or to miss the space.

Or Tyler.

Mary would, though. She was going to miss him terribly. She might have caught herself before she fell too deeply in love—she hoped—but it had been touch and go, and there was still a simmering physical attraction that she was doing her best to keep under control. But she was bearing up pretty well, she thought. Several stern conversations with herself had convinced her of the need to be sensible here. There was no chance of a future with Tyler, so one way or another she was just going to have to move on.

Moving on meant getting a grip on herself on more than just the emotional front. Mary had taken a good hard look at herself the night before and she hadn't liked what she saw. If she was going to have to go to this reception and watch while Tyler scanned the room for a prospective date, she wasn't going to look fat and frumpy while she was at it.

That morning she had blown half a month's rent on having her hair cut and coloured, and then she had bought the kind of dress that credit cards were invented for. There was no way that Mary could justify spending so much on a simple outfit but once she had made the mistake of trying it on, she had had to have it.

For such a tight-fitting dress it was surprisingly flattering, clinging to all the right curves and falling in a lovely swish of heavy silk to disguise the wrong ones, and it had a daring neckline that managed to be sexy without being tarty.

Or so the girl in the shop had assured her. Looking down at the expanse of her cleavage on show, Mary wasn't so sure.

Still, it was too late to change now, and after spending all that money on the dress and matching shoes and a bag, because if you didn't have the right accessories you might as well not have bothered, she would just have to keep her chin up and pretend she didn't realise half her bosom was on show.

The building was eerily quiet at this time of night. Everyone had long gone and the offices were dimly lit, except in Tyler's office where a single reading light burned brightly.

Tyler was at his desk, frowning down at a draft contract, when Mary reached the open door and the breath dried in her throat at the sight of him. The lamp threw the severe lines of his face into sharp relief, and in his formal dinner jacket and bow-tie he looked dark and very formidable.

Intent on what he was reading, he hadn't heard her approach on the soft carpet. Mary smoothed her palms down the sides of her dress, swallowed and knocked lightly on the door.

Tyler looked up, briefly at first, and then he stared, the contract forgotten in his hand.

'Ready?' she asked.

'You've...you...you look different,' he said, so taken aback by the transformation in her that he could hardly get the words out.

'I've had my hair cut. What do you think?' She gave a self-conscious twirl.

Tyler couldn't think. She looked incredibly sexy in that dress that was clinging to all the right places, and proving that everything he had been imagining when he had seen her in her baggy layers or those shapeless pyjamas was all too true. He couldn't take his eyes off her.

And her hair... Tyler wasn't sure what the hairdresser had done, but she looked younger and more stylish, almost glamorous.

Almost beautiful.

His chest was so tight that he could hardly breathe. Belatedly, he dropped the contract on to the desk and pushed back his chair.

'You look...very...nice,' he said inadequately as he got to his feet.

Mary's brows rose slightly and he remembered one of their lessons. 'No, that's not right, is it?' he said. What was it she had told him once? *No woman ever wants to hear that she looks 'fine'.* 'If you were my girlfriend I would have to do better than that.'

'Indeed you would,' said Mary, glad to find that she had a voice after all. There had been a moment there as Tyler sat and simply stared when all the air had been sucked out of the room and she had wondered if she would ever breathe again. And now look at her! Not only could she string a few words together, she could even sound quite brisk and unperturbed while she was at it. Which was amazing, really, when you considered that her nerves were fluttering frantically beneath her skin and her pulse was booming in her ears.

'Your girlfriend will want to feel that the effort she's made is appreciated,' she went on, in the same cool voice that seemed to belong to someone else entirely. 'You should make her feel loved and desired.'

'As if I can't keep my hands off her?'

'Exactly.'

'As if I can't wait to take her home and make love to her? That I need her right here, right now?'

Mary lost her breath for a moment. 'That kind of thing, yes,' she said, retrieving it on a gasp.

'I see.' Tyler came round the desk towards her and took both Mary's hands in his, holding her still in his warm clasp so that he could study her face with those penetrating blue eyes. Mary was sure that he could see deep inside her, that he could tell that her entire body was thrumming with awareness, that he could hear the slow, painful thud of her heart.

His gaze dropped at last, but only to follow the curves of her body, and he inspected her all the way down to her peep-toe shoes in a silence that seemed to wrap itself around them until there were only the two of them in the whole world.

'There's only one word to describe you,' he said at last, and his voice was so deep that Mary felt it reverberate at the base of her spine.

She managed a nervous laugh. 'Fat?' she suggested, but Tyler shook his head.

'Gorgeous,' he said. 'You look absolutely gorgeous.'

Ridiculously, Mary blushed. 'Thank you,' she muttered.

'And if you were my girlfriend, I'd probably kiss you now, wouldn't I?' he went on. 'Just to prove how incredible I think you look.'

'You might do,' she agreed, her voice all over the place, 'but since I'm *not* in—'

'Why don't we pretend that you are?' Tyler interrupted her, his voice as deep and dark as treacle. 'After all, we might as well see the lesson through, and make sure I get it right next time.'

The trouble was, he realised later, that he wasn't thinking clearly. Somewhere at the back of his mind was the idea that he would give her a brief kiss to show Mary how great she looked. It would be a courtesy, no more than that, but that got lost the moment his eyes dropped to her mouth, so lush and inviting, and he forgot everything else but the need to possess it.

Bending his head, he captured her lips with his own, but the first touch of her mouth sent a great crashing wave of something that was far from mere politeness surging through him, and before he had thought properly what he was doing, he had yanked her in to him and was kissing her properly.

In his arms, he felt Mary stiffen for a moment, but the next her resistance had gone and she was melting into him, returning his kiss hungrily, almost angrily. It felt as if they were punishing each other, but at the same time it was out of their control, and there was nothing but taste and touch and feel and churning pleasure as the heat surged between them, searing, scorching and unstoppable.

Tyler's hands were hard on her, sliding demandingly down her back and pulling her closer, closer, and Mary clung to him, arching in to his body, gasping for breath between deep, deep kisses, heedless of anything but the wild, wicked pulse of need. He felt so strong, so solid, so *good*, and his lips were so sure.

She could feel herself dissolving in the sweet swirl of sensation, and the sense of losing herself was so powerful that she clutched harder, holding on to him as if he were the only fixed point in the universe, and when she felt him start to lift his head she murmured deep in her throat in protest, not wanting to face the moment when she had to let him go.

Tyler was so shaken by the loss of control that for a long moment after he broke that long, long kiss he could only stare at her, his heart jerking madly as he struggled for breath. He couldn't believe what had happened, how utterly he had been carried away, intoxicated by her softness and her sweetness and her warmth.

Mary looked totally shocked, he realised, appalled. What had he done? Her grey eyes were dark and dilated, and no wonder. Tyler remembered kissing her once before and how dangerously seductive that had been, but it had been nothing like this.

It was the worst thing that he could have done. He didn't want to know that kissing Mary could be like that. She was leaving and their paths were diverging, and what was he going to say when she asked him why he had grabbed her like that? What *could* he say? God, how could he have been such a fool?

Losing control, being stupid, looking a fool... It was Tyler's nightmare scenario, and somehow Mary was the cause of it all, he thought, half baffled, half resentful. She had turned his life upside down, changing everything, making him behave in ways he couldn't explain, even to himself.

'I'm sorry,' he said raggedly at last, turning away from that great grey gaze and raking a hand through his hair. 'I got a bit carried away there. I wasn't thinking. I forgot it was you.'

Translation: I didn't mean to kiss you at all. I didn't *want* to kiss you.

With an enormous effort, Mary managed to pull herself together. Her body was still throbbing, every sense pulsating, and she wanted nothing more than to throw herself back into the arms of a man who had forgotten who she was, and who wouldn't have wanted her if he had remembered in time.

'Don't worry about it,' she said a little shakily. 'I'll take it as a compliment to my dress. And it's just the thing you ought to do when your real girlfriend turns up so, all in all, I'd give you full marks.'

There, that ought to show him that she hadn't taken that shattering kiss seriously, but her legs were trembling as she escaped to the Ladies, and her hand shook horribly as she tried to repair her lipstick.

Tyler had arranged for a driver to take them to the Merchant Adventurers' Hall, and Mary didn't know whether to be glad or sorry. On the plus side, she would have been struggling on her heels, even if her legs had been functioning normally. As it was, her bones seemed to have melted and were doing a remarkable impression of cotton wool. It was a miracle she managed to stay upright in the lift, let alone contemplate a trek across the river and through the cobbled streets.

So a lift meant that Tyler wouldn't have to abandon her halfway, crumpled in a boneless heap in some alleyway, and that was something. On the other hand, she was going to have to sit in a dark, enclosed space with him in the back of the car, and Mary wasn't sure if that might not be worse.

Once there, she decided that it was. She was desperately aware of Tyler next to her in the darkness. He was like a stranger, remote and forbidding, and he was very careful not to touch her, but the space between them vibrated with tension. Mary clutched her hands together in her lap and stared straight ahead, while every nerve in her body strained towards Tyler. She wanted to crawl over him, to kiss the grim set of his jaw until he smiled. She wanted to press her lips to the pulse in his throat, to feel his rough masculine skin and breathe in the scent of him.

It was a huge relief when they got to the Merchant Adventurers' Hall and she could put some distance between them. Mary practically fell out of the car in her haste and when Tyler made to take her by the elbow as they walked through the narrow stone gateway and across the courtyard she stepped quickly out of reach.

'We don't want to look as if we're together,' she said without looking at him.

'I thought that was the whole point,' said Tyler, exasperated. He was in a foul mood, and having to keep his hands off Mary in the back of the car hadn't improved matters. 'I'm supposed to be practising on you.'

'I thought you were finding someone to date?'

He hesitated, confused now about what the hell he was doing there at all. 'That, too.'

'You don't want me hanging on your arm if you're trying to chat somebody up, do you?' Mary pointed out. 'That would just cramp your style.'

What style? Tyler wondered as they made their way into the medieval hall with its spectacular timber roof. He scowled.

He loathed occasions like this, as Mary knew perfectly well. It had obviously slipped her mind that he was paying her to be here. Instead of supporting him discreetly, she took the first opportunity to leave his side and was soon chatting animatedly at the other end of the hall.

There was a whole group around her, mostly men, Tyler noted grimly, watching her through the crowd, and he couldn't really blame them. She looked fantastic tonight, warm and sexy and alive, her face alight with intelligence and humour. It wasn't her fault that he wished she would go back to being the dowdy, mumsy figure she had been a month ago.

He didn't like the way those men were looking at her. He liked being the only one who noticed how warm and soft she was. Now everybody knew and everybody wanted to talk to her and she couldn't spare him so much as a glance.

Morosely, Tyler accepted a drink and reminded himself of his objective. There must be loads of women here. Surely he could find one who would like to go out? But he was soon buttonholed by men in suits who wanted to talk business to him, while over their shoulders he could see Mary laughing and flirting and apparently having a good time. She seemed to have forgotten that she came here with him, he thought jealously.

But no, here she came, tucking her hand into his elbow, smiling charmingly at his companions. 'Would you excuse Tyler a moment?' she said to them. 'There's someone I want him to meet.'

How come he could never extricate himself from situations like that? He was either stuck or had to go for the brutally rude option and simply walk away. Feeling inadequate, Tyler glowered.

'For God's sake, lighten up,' said Mary out of the corner

of her mouth. 'No one's going to want to go out with you looking like that! Remember what I told you about smiling.'

But Tyler didn't feel like smiling. He glanced at Mary, determinedly tugging him across the room. Obviously that kiss hadn't meant anything to her, because she hadn't lost sight of the business in hand. And he shouldn't either, he thought glumly.

'Who am I meeting?'

'Her name's Fiona. I think you'll like her. She's very pretty, very stylish—blond, of course—and intelligent too. She's something in insurance, I'm not sure what. Perfect for you, anyway,' said Mary briskly. 'I thought she was rather nice, *and* she told me that she's recently split up with a long-term boyfriend. I reckon she's in her late twenties, so probably ready to think about settling down and having children soon.'

'Who turned you into my pimp?' Tyler demanded grouchily. 'You're supposed to be advising me on relationship matters, not trawling for prospective partners.'

Mary stopped and faced him in exasperation. 'You're the one who said you wanted to start dating again!'

'I do, but I can find my own girlfriend, thank you.'

'You won't find one talking business with a load of middle-aged men,' she pointed out. 'You've got to circulate. You haven't moved for half an hour. What were you talking about that was so fascinating?'

'The exchange rate,' Tyler admitted.

'Boy, you really are in the right frame of mind for romance, aren't you?'

'No,' he said. 'So we might as well not waste any more time here.'

He made to turn to the door, but Mary pulled him back. 'At least come and meet Fiona,' she said. 'I've told her about you and you might as well since you're here.'

So Tyler let himself be dragged over and introduced to Fiona, who was, annoyingly, everything Mary had said she would be. Mary stood chatting with them for a while before she excused herself unobtrusively and left them to it.

She seemed very anxious to fob him off on someone else, Tyler thought crossly. It was all very well introducing him to someone else, but how could he concentrate on what Fiona was saying when she was standing only a few feet away letting some man practically fall down the front of her dress?

Turning his back, Tyler did his best to make conversation with Fiona, but he was acutely aware of Mary, and every now and then he would hear her laugh above the hubbub.

Fiona didn't draw attention to herself like that. She was much more discreet. As Mary had said, she was very pleasant. Tyler made himself focus on her advantages. She was intelligent, elegant, *classy*…just what he was looking for, in fact, he reminded himself. She was wearing a perfect little black dress, not a scene-stealer with a plunging neckline that had all the men cross-eyed. She wasn't laughing too loud or flirting or drinking too much champagne.

Mary was doing all three.

Mary wasn't classy. She wasn't beautiful. She wasn't elegant. She wasn't even blond. She was the last kind of woman he'd want for a wife. He was very glad she was planning to move out soon. Only a few more days and he would have his life back, and what a relief that would be.

Tyler made laboured conversation with Fiona for as long as he could, and they exchanged business cards. As Fiona handed hers to him, he was assailed by the memory of Mary giving him her card a month ago. Dammit, did everything have to remind him of her?

What was it going to be like when she was gone?

Empty, a voice inside him answered immediately. Lonely. Desolate.

Tyler pushed the voice aside. What rubbish. He had managed perfectly well without Mary Thomas for forty-three years. He hadn't been lonely before and there was no reason why he should start now His life had been a lot easier and more under control, and he had got a lot more work done. Everything would go back to normal. Except he'd have someone like Fiona living with him instead of Mary.

Tyler wasn't any good at circulating. He couldn't ease himself in and out of groups the way Mary seemed to be able to do. He bumped into his Financial Director though, so they talked work for a while, and then somebody buttonholed him about city parking charges, and all the while he was aware of Mary, smiling and chatting to everyone except him.

At length he could stand it no longer. Muttering a brusque excuse, he went over and took her by the arm. 'I think it's time we went,' he said pulling her away from a very disappointed-looking man in mid-conversation.

Mary was furious. 'I was talking to him!' she said, shaking her arm free.

'Talking?' snarled Tyler. 'Is that what they call it nowadays?'

'Oh, for heaven's sake! You can't just drag someone away from a conversation.'

'You did when I was talking earlier,' he pointed out, and she rounded on him.

'*I* was polite and acknowledged the other people and apologised and made an excuse! You just grabbed. I didn't even have time to give him my card. He's got a small business and I could have had some work from him, which is lost now, thanks to you!'

'You're supposed to be working for me,' said Tyler grimly.

The grey eyes flashed with temper. 'I am working for you, but you're not my only client,' she pointed out in an icy voice. 'I've got a business to run, and I need to make contacts. As it happens, it's been a very useful evening—or it was until you interfered!—and I picked up a lot of potential clients.'

'I'm not surprised, wearing that dress!' he said unpleasantly. 'I just hope you're prepared for exactly what kind of contact all those "potential clients" are interested in!'

'At least none of them will have to blackmail me into a job!' Mary snapped back. 'It's a nice change talking business with people who are happy to keep things on a professional level.'

'Oh, so you're not going to insist on moving in with everyone who offers you a recruitment contract then?'

Mary's eyes narrowed at his snide look. 'No, I won't be making that mistake again,' she said pointedly. 'As a matter of fact, I met a nice estate agent tonight who says he's got some great properties to show me. I'm going to have a look tomorrow.'

'Well, I'm sorry to break up your successful evening schmoozing,' said Tyler, scowling at the thought of Mary looking at places to live, 'but it's half past ten. I thought you'd be anxious to go and make sure that your daughter was all right.'

'She'll be fine with Mum,' huffed Mary, but in truth she wasn't that sorry to have to leave.

It had been an exhausting evening. Sparkling and being vivacious was hard work when you had been kissed to shattering effect by a man who hadn't meant to kiss you at all, and when you had to spend the rest of the evening trying to convince him that you hadn't taken it seriously. Mary was tired and tense, unable to decide what she wanted most, to thump Tyler, to throw herself into his arms, or to burst into tears.

Stalking off wasn't an option either. They still had to pick up Bea, and then the chauffeur was driving them back to Haysby Hall. Mary was dreading the journey, alone in the dark with Tyler. The only way to get through it was to stay bolshy. If she reminded herself enough of how difficult and disagreeable he was being tonight, there would be less temptation to slide over the back seat towards him.

'So,' she said brightly as they waited on the pavement for the car to appear. 'How did you get on with Fiona?'

'Fine,' he said tersely.

'Didn't you think she was pretty?'

'She's very attractive, yes.'

'Did you ask her out?'

'I said I'd give her a call,' said Tyler, resenting this interrogation.

'Well, you'd better try harder to make a better impression on the phone than you did tonight,' said Mary frankly.

He glared at her. 'What do you mean? What was I doing wrong?'

'Let's see,' she said, casting her eyes upwards in a parody of deep thought. 'You were in a foul mood, you were remote and unfriendly, you didn't seem the slightest bit interested in her... Shall I go on?'

'I *was* interested in her,' Tyler insisted, not entirely truthfully. 'I said I'd call her, didn't I?'

'I bet she won't be expecting you to get in touch,' said Mary, turning down her mouth. 'You weren't giving out any of the right signals.'

'Rubbish!'

'I'm serious. I didn't see you smile once! If you'd wanted her to think that you were really interested, you should have been asking her questions, making eye contact, mirroring her body language, even touching her very lightly. You just stood there and looked grim.'

'It worked, didn't it?' said Tyler, annoyed. 'She gave me her card.'

'It's a big step from getting a business card to getting married,' Mary pointed out as the car purred to a halt beside them at last. 'You're going to have to make a lot more effort next time you see her—and you've got to persuade her to go out with you first! If I were Fiona, I'd be hanging out for someone a lot more fun!'

Of course, the trouble was that she *wasn't* Fiona, and she didn't want anyone more fun. The truth was that she wanted Tyler, and no one else would do.

But she couldn't have him, largely *because* she wasn't Fiona, so she was just going to have to get over it, Mary told herself. Still, she couldn't help secretly hoping that Fiona would refuse Tyler's invitation.

Sadly, Fiona didn't refuse. Tyler came home from work the next day and reported that he would be taking her out to dinner on Friday night. Stung by Mary's comments, he had rung Fiona that morning. He was annoyed to find that, just as Mary had predicted, Fiona was surprised to hear from him, but he was able to tell Mary that she had sounded delighted by his invitation.

'That's good,' said Mary, busy at the hob and glad of the excuse not to face him. 'You won't be needing any supper tomorrow night, then.'

That was it, concentrate on the practicalities. It was easier that way.

'No.' Tyler bent down to Bea, who was holding her arms up to him imperatively and demanding his attention in no uncertain terms.

Her little body was warm and solid as he picked her up, and her face was wreathed in smiles the instant she had got her own way. She beamed at him and bumped her head against his in an attempt at a kiss, and Tyler's heart twisted painfully at the realisation that he wouldn't be here to pick her up tomorrow night. He wouldn't be coming home to a warm kitchen and a smiley baby and to Mary.

Joggling Bea in his arms, Tyler glanced at her mother. At least Mary wasn't wearing that dress tonight, which was a lot easier on his blood pressure. Instead she had on loose trousers and some kind of fine-knit cardigan, neither of which were in the least sexy or provocative, but with her new haircut she looked unusually stylish.

Tyler wished she would go back to her baggy layers. He wished that she would turn round and smile at him. He wished he wasn't taking Fiona out to dinner tomorrow night.

Quite suddenly, Tyler felt cold and rather sick. He was making the most terrible mistake, he realised.

'Mary—' he began urgently, but she had turned at last and had started speaking at exactly the same time.

They both stopped and there was an awkward pause. 'You first,' said Tyler, who hadn't really known what he was going to say anyway.

'I was just going to say that I saw a great flat today,' she said a little stiltedly. 'It's perfect for us.'

'Us?' he echoed without thinking, and she looked at him strangely.

'Bea and I,' she explained.

'Oh. Yes.' Of *course* just Bea and her, you fool! Tyler burned with humiliation. You didn't think she meant to include you, did you?

Mary had reminded him of the reality of the situation just

in time. She was leaving anyway. There was no point in
blurting out that he had changed his mind like some big kid,
or telling her that he would rather stay in with her and Bea
than go out with Fiona. She would just raise those odd brows
of hers, remind him that he was paying her a lot of money to
get to this point, and make him feel like an idiot.

Tyler didn't like feeling stupid.

'Are you going to take it?' he asked.

'I think so.' Mary dipped her wooden spoon in the sauce
she was making and tasted it cautiously. 'It's a good price, but
the current tenant's still there. I wouldn't be able to move in
for another couple of weeks.'

'You can stay here until then, if you want,' said Tyler, ul-
tra-casual, but inwardly aghast at how much wanted her to
agree. 'It would suit me. After all, now I'm dating, this is when
I'm going to need your advice most.'

Mary stirred her sauce, not meeting his eyes. 'I'll think
about it,' she said.

She was giving Bea her breakfast when Tyler appeared on
Saturday morning. He was normally long gone before she got
downstairs, even at weekends, but perhaps he made an exception after a heavy date, she thought drearily.

'Hi.' She managed to greet him casually enough, even
though her heart had given a sickening lurch at the sight of him.
'There's coffee in the pot if you want it. It should still be hot.'

'Thanks.'

Tyler might be uncharacteristically late down to breakfast,
but otherwise he was as taciturn as usual. He went over to pour
himself some coffee, and Mary watched his back with a kind
of resentment. He was arrogant, impatient and grumpy and
he had spent the whole of yesterday evening romancing

another woman. It wasn't fair that he could still melt her bones just by standing there.

Yesterday had been the longest evening Mary had ever known. Even when things had been at their worst with Alan, she hadn't felt this dreary and hopeless. She had eaten a lonely supper and looked in vain for something to watch on television, but when she had tossed the remote away in disgust and had gone to have a bath, not even the determined listing of all the great things about the new flat could distract her mind for long from the fact that Tyler was out with Fiona.

Fiona would be sitting across the table from him in some intimately lit restaurant. It was Fiona whose eyes would settle on his mouth, Fiona who would see the way his cool eyes warmed and the crease deepened in his cheek when he smiled. Fiona, whose hands Tyler might reach across the table to hold, Fiona who would wonder what it would be like to kiss him.

Mary could have told her. Mary had tortured herself by imagining what Tyler was doing, what he was thinking. Would he just say goodbye at the end of the date, or would he kiss Fiona? If he thought she was right for him, he wouldn't waste any time pussyfooting around. Mary knew him too well to believe that.

No, Tyler had set out very clear specifications for the wife he wanted, and Fiona fitted them perfectly. She was the kind of woman any man would be proud to have on his arm. Tyler might not have seemed very enthusiastic when he first met her, but Mary knew how completely he focused on his goal. With terrier-like persistence, he wouldn't change his mind once it was made up, and he wouldn't give up until he had got exactly what he wanted.

And that wasn't her. She had known that a long time, but it wasn't getting any easier to accept. It had become plain to

Mary that long, dismal evening that she couldn't stay here. She might understand why Tyler wanted to date other women, but that didn't mean she had to like it, and she didn't have to bear it if she didn't want to. The more his relationship with Fiona developed, the harder it was going to get. Better to go now, Mary had decided.

'More coffee?' Tyler asked, lifting the pot enquiringly in Mary's direction.

'Thank you.' She pushed her mug across the table towards him and took a breath. 'So,' she said brightly, 'how was your date last night?'

'Fine,' said Tyler. His favourite adjective.

'Is that all? Fine?'

'No, it was more than fine,' he said, but it hadn't felt fine. It had felt all wrong to be out with Fiona when Mary was at home, putting Bea to bed, cooking in the warm kitchen.

And then *that* had felt all wrong. After all, Tyler had told himself, he was sitting in the best restaurant in York with a beautiful woman who was interested, friendly, intelligent and everything he could possibly want in a bride. He ought to be pleased with himself, not wishing that he was sitting in the kitchen with a baby on his lap, his tie loosened, having his nose pulled by inquisitive fingers, and watching Mary move around, the intent expression on her face as she tasted a sauce, her smile as she lifted Bea out of the high chair, the way she rolled her eyes if he said something she disagreed with.

Fiona didn't disagree with him. She didn't point out his faults or make him take back something he'd said. She wasn't astringent, and she didn't make him cross, but she didn't make him laugh either. She didn't knock over her wine.

She wasn't Mary.

But she *was* what he was looking for, Tyler had reminded

himself doggedly as the evening dragged past. Mary wasn't what he wanted.

He wasn't what Mary wanted either, judging by the businesslike cross-examination he was getting about his date.

'Well, go on,' she said. 'You've got to tell me a bit more than that. What was she wearing?'

Tyler searched his memory, which was unhelpfully blank. 'A dress, I think.'

So informative. Mary rolled her eyes. 'Did she look nice?'

'Yes.' He was sure about that at least.

'Did you tell her that?'

'I can't remember,' he said irritably. 'What does it matter?'

'It matters if you wanted it to be a successful date and wanted her to look forward to another one,' said Mary. 'You should have been making an effort to make *her* feel as if you were really pleased and proud to be out with her. She won't be telepathic. She won't know you like her unless you give her all those little signals I told you about—touching her lightly, making eye contact, being really open with each other. Did you do *any* of that?'

'She agreed to come out to dinner again next week,' Tyler said, aware that he was sounding on the defensive, and avoiding the question. 'So I can't have got it that wrong.'

'I hope you're going to call her today and say that you enjoyed your evening and that you're looking forward to seeing her again?'

'Look, Fiona's a sensible woman. She won't expect me to jump through those kind of hoops.'

'Showing that you appreciate someone and have been thinking about them isn't a *hoop*,' said Mary, exasperated. 'Haven't I taught you anything?'

'Why do you care?' Tyler demanded abrasively.

'It's my job to care,' she reminded him. 'And I want my second five thousand pounds,' she added, cucumber cool. 'We agreed I wouldn't get that until you were settled in a relationship, and one date hardly counts as one of those, does it?'

'Oh, yes, your money,' he said, tossing back his coffee and getting to his feet. 'We don't want to forget what you're doing here, do we? I shouldn't worry, though. It looks as if you'll be getting your extra five thousand. I think Fiona's going to be perfect.'

CHAPTER TEN

THERE was a tiny pause.

'So…that's good news for both of us, then, isn't it?' said Mary.

'Very good,' Tyler agreed. 'Well, I'm off,' he went on after a moment's silence while they both reflected on just how good the news felt.

Or not.

'Where are you going?'

'To the office. I've got some reports to read.' He could have brought them home to read at the weekend, but there was no use pretending that he would be able to concentrate. Besides, he couldn't hang around Mary and Bea all day and he couldn't think of anything else he wanted to do.

Mary was biting her lip. 'I didn't realise you would be going out this morning,' she said. 'I'd better say goodbye now then.'

'I'll be back later,' said Tyler, checking that he had his wallet.

'I won't be here,' said Mary. 'Bill's coming to pick us up this morning.'

'Pick you up?' He looked up sharply. 'What for?'

'I'm moving out.'

Tyler felt as if he'd been kicked in the stomach. 'I didn't think your flat was going to be ready for a couple of weeks.'

He'd been *counting* on it not being ready. For some reason he didn't feel able to face right then.

'We can stay with Mum and Bill until then.'

'What's wrong with here?'

How could she tell him that she couldn't bear seeing him and Fiona together?

'I…just think it would be better if I go now,' she said carefully, not meeting his eye. 'After all, my work here is done,' she added, trying to make a joke of it. 'You've started a relationship with Fiona. I know it's only at the very early stages, but you'll do better without me around all the time. What if you want to bring her back here? It wouldn't be very romantic if she found your relationship coach making cocoa in the kitchen!'

Tyler frowned. He couldn't imagine Fiona here. This was Mary's kitchen. 'We're nowhere near that stage yet.'

'Well, you never know… Anyway, I'm ready to move out.' She mustered a bright smile. 'It's been great being here and giving Mum and Bill some space for a while, but it'll be good to get back to town. This is a lovely house, but it's not exactly convenient, is it?'

That was it, focus on the disadvantages and not on how much she was going to miss the space and the quiet and the beautiful kitchen and having Tyler come home every night.

His expression hardened. 'If you want to move out, I suppose there's nothing I can do to stop you,' he said curtly. 'I trust you'll remember that we still have an agreement, though? Two months, you said.'

'I haven't forgotten,' said Mary with dignity. 'Naturally, I'll be available for feedback and advice if you need it.'

Feedback! Tyler was furious, and not even sure why. 'I'd better make sure you have a cheque now then, as the first instalment of your account,' he said.

'There's no need to do it straight away,' she said uncomfortably.

But Tyler was already striding off to his study. Scrawling out a cheque, he ripped it out of the book so savagely that it tore and he had to write a fresh one, which did nothing to improve his temper.

'There you are,' he said, dropping it on to the table. 'The first instalment of your fee.'

So it had come to this. Mary felt sick. 'Tyler—'

'I'll be in touch before my next date with Fiona,' he overrode her. 'You can help me prepare for that.'

What could she say? 'You know where to find me,' she said quietly.

Tyler hesitated, his anger draining out of him suddenly. 'Well…goodbye, then,' he said.

Mary tried a smile, but it wavered so much that she had to compress her mouth into a straight line. 'Goodbye,' she managed.

There was a horrible silence while they just looked at each other, and then Tyler roused himself and headed for the door. He hadn't made it before an outraged squeal from Bea made him turn instinctively. She had never taken kindly to being ignored and was bouncing indignantly up and down in her high chair, chubby arms stretched out towards him.

How could he walk away from her? Setting his jaw, Tyler went back.

Bea beamed with pleasure and demanded to be picked up. Unable to resist the iron will of an infant, he lifted her and held her close for a moment, careless for once of her smeary mouth or her sticky hands on his shirt. As she cuddled happily in to him, Tyler breathed in her clean baby smell and closed his eyes against the crack of his heart.

He kissed the soft, fine hair once. 'Bye, Bea,' he said, and his throat was so tight that it was hard to get the words out.

Passing her to Mary was one of the hardest things he had ever done. 'She'll miss you,' said Mary, the luminous grey eyes shimmering with tears.

Tyler didn't trust himself to speak. He nodded abruptly and turned on his heel.

That wasn't what Bea wanted at all. Her face puckered and she started to cry, straining after him so desperately that Mary had to struggle to hold her.

Her wails followed Tyler down the corridor. He slammed the front door against them, but they were still ringing in his ears as he got into the car, and he dropped his head on to the steering wheel, squeezing his eyes shut for a long moment. Then he straightened, took a deep breath and switched on the ignition, and he drove away along the long avenue without looking back.

It was nearly dark before Tyler came home that night. The beam of his headlights lit up the BMW parked under the spreading cedar, and his heart leapt. Mary was still here!

But as soon as he opened the front door, the emptiness of the house settled around him like a stone. There was a note on the kitchen table.

Thank you for everything. I'm leaving the car, but we've taken out the baby seat. Fiona didn't seem like the kind of girl who would object to a car that's only been used for a week, so perhaps it will find another grateful driver. Let me know when you're ready for more coaching. I'm always available for consultation—or to help with any recruitment problems you may have! Good luck with Fiona.

Love, Mary. PS Casserole in fridge. Have rung Mrs
Palmer and she'll start cooking for you again next week.

Love, Mary? Tyler crumpled the note in one fist and swore
as he threw it at the wall. *Love*, Mary! She didn't love him. If
she'd loved him she wouldn't have left him alone in this great,
empty house with a *casserole* to console him!

The kitchen felt desolate without them. Tyler looked
around him, as if unable to believe that the high chair had
gone, and Bea with it. She wasn't there, banging her spoon
on the tray and shouting for attention. Mary wasn't at the
hob, wrapped in Mrs Palmer's apron. There was only the
empty room and the background buzz of the fridge to empha-
sise the silence.

Setting his jaw, Tyler went over to the fridge and took out
the casserole. He wasn't hungry, but he wasn't about to go
into a decline. He had faced worse times than this, and he had
learnt that the only way to get through them was to keep his
head down and plough on. Giving up wasn't in his vocabu-
lary. There was no point in sitting around moping. He would
just have to get on with it. It was high time he got back to
work anyway.

But, as he sat at his desk, he found himself listening for
the sound of Mary's footsteps upstairs, of Bea protesting at
having her nappy changed. The house echoed with their
absence. Tyler stared unseeingly down at the budget he
was supposed to be reading and for the first time in years remembered how he had felt as a little boy when his mother had
died.

He threw the papers down and pushed back his chair. God,
he'd be crying next! It was time to pull himself together.

Defiantly, he pulled out Fiona's card and dialled the

number to ask her out for a drink the next evening. See, he was getting on with his life already. He would be back to normal in no time.

He woke on Sunday morning with a sick feeling in the pit of his stomach that he dismissed as a bug of some kind. He would ignore it the way he ignored every other bug and eventually it would go away. The day stretched interminably. When Mary and Bea were around there never seemed to be enough time, but now it yawned joylessly before him, day after day without them.

His date with Fiona that evening was all that kept him going, reassuring him that he was sticking to his strategy, but the drink was not a huge success. Tyler made an effort to remember everything Mary had told him, but he hadn't counted on the fact that every time he tried to put some of her advice into practice, he would end up thinking about her instead of Fiona. *Make eye contact*, Mary had said, but whenever he met Fiona's beautiful blue gaze he would hear Mary's crisp voice and the blueness blurred before the memory of grey eyes that danced with teasing laughter.

Still, he persevered, because giving up wasn't an option. It was a relief to say good night and go their separate ways at the end of the evening, but that didn't stop Tyler asking Fiona out to dinner the following weekend. He wasn't prepared to admit that the invitation had given him the perfect excuse to contact Mary, but it probably *would* be a good idea.

After all, he was paying her for her advice, Tyler reasoned, and he was quite used to her being gone. He was back in his old routine. It was nonsense to think that he might still miss Mary and Bea. That kind of thing was just sentimental twaddle. His goal hadn't changed, and nor had his strategy.

He waited until Wednesday—any earlier would look as if he couldn't wait to see her again—and surprised Carol by telling her that he would be taking a lunch break. He didn't want to make an appointment. He would just turn up at Mary's office and have a chat with her, maybe take Bea out for a walk. It didn't need to be a formal meeting, did it? He just needed to see her.

For coaching, Tyler added hastily to himself.

Feeling ridiculously nervous, he climbed the rickety stairs and knocked on the door.

'Come in!'

Tyler took a breath and opened the door. Mary was sitting behind her desk and she looked up with a smile that froze at the sight of him.

For a long, long moment they just stared at each other, then Mary got numbly to her feet and came round the desk.

'Hello.' Her voice was thready with shock. She had dreamt of this, without ever letting herself believe that it could happen.

The last few days had been wretched. Leaving Tyler might have been the sensible thing to do, but she hadn't realised that missing him would hurt so much. Time and again, she had picked up the phone to ring him, just needing to hear his voice, before she made herself put it down again.

Be sensible, her head would remind her firmly, while her heart cracked with the need to see him again, to be near him. And now there he was, standing in the doorway, and Mary was almost afraid to move in case he turned into a chimera that she had conjured up with the power of her longing, and that would vanish cruelly if she got too close.

'Are you busy?' Tyler asked stiltedly.

'I've got an appointment at two o'clock, but I've got a few minutes now,' she said, hardly able to believe that she could carry on an apparently normal conversation. She swallowed. 'Come in.'

She gestured Tyler towards the easy chairs and took one herself. They sat facing each other as the silence lengthened uncomfortably.

Mary tried desperately to get a grip, but she felt suddenly overwhelmed. It was like being in a tumble-dryer of emotion at the moment, missing Tyler, longing to see him, dreading seeing him, and now the sheer joy of simply being near him again, on top of Alan's unexpected phone call, which had thrown everything into question once more.

She couldn't look at Tyler properly. She was afraid that she might do something stupid, like blurting out how much she had missed him or how good it was to see him again, so instead of meeting his gaze calmly like a professional meeting one of her clients, her eyes skittered nervously over his face and away in panic whenever they met his pale blue ones.

Tyler broke the awkward silence. 'You're looking good,' he said.

She was, too. It had taken him a little while to get used to it, but her hair really suited her like that, and she was wearing a scoop-necked top with a long skirt and boots that made her look businesslike but approachable.

'Thanks.' Mary smiled briefly. 'How are you?'

'Fine, fine.' He looked around the office, not wanting to think about how he was without her. 'Where's Bea?'

'She's with my mother today. I had several interviews arranged, so I thought it would be easier without her.'

Tyler wanted to ask Mary if Bea missed him, if *she* missed him, but he didn't know how to without looking pathetic.

There was another agonising pause.

'Well,' said Mary at last. 'What can I do for you?'

Time to get down to business, obviously. 'I'm having dinner with Fiona this Saturday,' he said. 'I wondered if you'd have time for a bit of…preparation.'

'Now?'

Tyler felt like a fool. 'Unless you'd prefer a drink tonight?' Funny how he had never felt the slightest bit awkward until he met Mary, and now he seemed to be blundering around getting everything wrong all the time.

'I can't tonight.' She bit her lip. 'Alan's coming up from London.'

'Alan?' He stared at her, his heart sinking. 'Bea's father?'

'Yes.' Mary swallowed. 'He rang a couple of days ago. He's been thinking about Bea, he says. He wants us to get back together.'

There had been months when Mary would have given everything she possessed to hear Alan telling her that. It was ironic that he should ring when she had realised just how much she loved another man.

A lead weight was settling heavily inside Tyler. He hadn't been expecting this. He had thought that Mary might be distant, preoccupied with work or her new flat, but he had never imagined that Alan would reappear. He remembered her face when she had told him how desperately she had loved Bea's father.

'What are you going to say?' he heard himself ask.

'I…don't know,' said Mary truthfully. 'I have to consider it at least. He's Bea's father.'

'He hasn't been much of a father so far.'

'No, but he's the only father she has. If there's a chance of her growing up with two parents, I can't dismiss it out of hand. It's not as if Alan and I didn't love each other. We could love each other again.'

'Sure he hasn't just decided that it would be cheaper to take you back than pay you the money he owes you?' asked Tyler snidely, and then regretted it when he saw her face change. 'Sorry,' he said. 'That was uncalled for.'

Mary dropped her head into her hands and rubbed her temples wearily. 'I just don't know what to do,' she admitted. 'I suppose part of me is hoping that the old magic will come back when I see him, but it's been such a long time, I don't know what it will be like. All I know is that I have to do what's best for Bea.'

'I see,' said Tyler.

'Anyway,' said Mary, lifting her head, 'that's my problem. I shouldn't be bothering you with it.' She summoned a smile. 'I'm the one who's supposed to be the relationship expert around here, after all!'

There was such a curious expression in Tyler's eyes that her smile faded slightly. 'When do you want to meet?'

But his expression had shuttered abruptly and he was getting to his feet. 'You'd better sort things out with Alan first.'

'Are you sure?' she asked, puzzled. 'I haven't forgotten the terms of our deal.'

'I'm sure.'

'All right,' said Mary gratefully. 'Thanks. I must admit, it would be easier to concentrate then. Perhaps we could arrange a session in a couple of days?'

'Fine,' said Tyler, thinking that in a couple of days she might be back together with Alan. 'Ring Carol and make an appointment when you're free.'

'Ms Thomas is here for her two o'clock appointment.'

Tyler's heart lurched uncomfortably. He wasn't sure if he had been longing for this moment or dreading it. 'Thanks, Carol. I'll be out in a moment.'

Swallowing hard, he put down the phone. This was un-
charted territory for him. He knew now what he wanted. It had
meant admitting that he had made a mistake, which hadn't
been easy for him to do, but this time he was absolutely sure,
and a goal was always a reassuring thing to have in mind. Only
this time, for the first time in his life, Tyler had absolutely no
idea of his strategy, or whether he would be able to get what
he wanted after all.

In the next few minutes, he would know.

Outside, in Carol's office, Mary was gently rocking the
pushchair as she chatted to Carol. She was swathed in a
tweedy blue coat and a gaudily striped scarf, and Tyler
decided she looked a bit like a scruffy robin, all round and
pink-cheeked and bright-eyed. She looked glowing, he
thought heavily. Had she sorted things out with Alan?

She broke off as Tyler appeared, but Bea had spotted him
at the same time and gave a cry of delight. Crouching by the
pushchair, he offered her a finger and, as she grabbed it, the
tight feeling that had gripped him ever since he had said
goodbye to her eased a little.

He glanced up to see Carol watching him indulgently,
while Mary quickly lowered her lashes before he could read
her expression.

'Mum's busy this afternoon,' she said, 'so I had to bring
her with me.'

'I don't mind,' said Tyler. 'It's nice to see her again.' And
that was an understatement, he thought, looking at the little
fist gripping his finger so firmly.

'I wondered if you'd mind if we took her for a walk while
we talked? She'll never stay in her pushchair in your office.'

He straightened. 'A walk sounds good to me.' He didn't
want to hear Mary tell him about Alan in the office anyway.

Carol would be able to see his face afterwards, and Tyler wasn't sure that he would be able to bear that.

'Have you got a coat?' said Mary, nodding at his shirt-sleeves. 'It's cold out.'

'I'll be all right in my jacket.' Quickly buttoning his cuffs, Tyler retrieved it from the back of his chair and shrugged it on.

They took the lift down to the ground floor in silence and walked down to the river front, the pushchair juddering over the cobbles. A weak November sun was doing its best to brighten the day, but it was having little effect on the temperature and it was as cold as Mary had warned. She stopped to put Bea's gloves on, and Tyler was glad to shove his own hands in his pockets as they walked.

A chill wind was gusting along the river, ruffling the surface of the water and swirling the drifts of fallen leaves. Tyler was content to walk beside Mary and let himself look at her properly for the first time. Having admitted to himself at last how much he loved her, he had somehow imagined that she would look different now that the scales had fallen from his eyes, but she didn't. She looked just the same. She was just Mary. His throat tightened painfully as he watched her. It was difficult to believe that he had ever thought her ordinary. When had he realised just how beautiful she really was?

The silence lengthened, until Mary tripped over an uneven paving stone and broke the tension.

'I'm as clumsy as ever,' she said ruefully.

Tyler's arm had shot out to catch her instinctively, but the pushchair had stopped her from falling and he put his hand back in his pocket before he did anything stupid like taking one of Mary's.

'How did you get on with Alan?' he asked abruptly. It wasn't his business, but he had to know.

'It was all right,' said Mary. 'I thought it would be really emotional, but actually, when I saw him, I felt quite calm and we had a good talk. He told me how he'd felt when I left. He was very angry and bitter, he said, and he didn't really want to admit that it had happened, that's why he was so unpleasant about the money.'

She glanced at Tyler, walking grim-faced beside her. 'Why didn't you tell me it was you who made him come to an agreement about my share of the house?'

'I didn't do anything,' he said evasively. 'I just got my solicitors to give him a bit of a fright. I didn't think it was fair that you were in a position where I could blackmail you into accepting a job.'

Mary smiled. 'I'm not sure of the logic there, but thank you anyway. Your intervention made Alan realise that he was going to have to do something if he did want me back.'

Great, thought Tyler, the old leaden feeling growing heavier by the second. Why had he interfered?

'So he *does* want you back?'

'He says that he does,' said Mary carefully. 'He says that he missed me, and that he made a mistake. He said that he wanted me to come home.'

'You're going back to London, then?' He looked straight ahead, not wanting to see her smile and nod.

'No,' said Mary, and Tyler stopped abruptly. 'London's not home anymore,' she explained when he stared at her. 'This is home.'

'But…what about Bea?'

'It's because of Bea that I'm staying. Alan is prepared to accept her to have me back, but she deserves better than being tolerated. I'm sure she'll want to get to know him later, and he did say he would acknowledge her and have her to visit when she's older, but he doesn't want to share in her day-to-day care.'

'His loss,' said Tyler, thinking of the feel of Bea on his lap, of her gummy smile and the tight feeling in his throat when she reached out her chubby arms to him.

Mary couldn't help smiling as she remembered his insistence that he wouldn't be a hands-on father. 'You've changed your tune,' she reminded him, and he looked straight at her.

'Yes,' he said, 'I have.'

The silence fizzed quietly for a moment before Tyler looked away.

'But what about you? You said that you loved Alan.'

'I did,' said Mary. 'I loved him terribly, but I don't anymore. I realised that when I saw him. He wasn't there for me when I needed him most, and I'm not sure I would ever be able to forget that. Besides—'

She stopped abruptly. She had been about to say, Besides, I'm in love with you, and how awkward would *that* have been? They were only meeting so that she could give Tyler advice on how to pursue his relationship with Fiona.

'Besides what?'

'Oh…only that it made me wonder whether I had ever truly loved him,' she improvised quickly. 'Alan was like a dream. He was the kind of person I wanted to be with, and he had the kind of life I longed to have, but we never had a truly equal relationship. He was older, more experienced, and I was dazzled by him. I'm not dazzled anymore.'

Her words flooded Tyler with relief. He didn't know if he could make Mary love him, but at least she hadn't chosen Alan. That was a start.

'So what are you going to do now?' he asked.

'What I was always going to do,' said Mary. 'Move into that flat, bring Bea up, make a new life for myself.'

Try to forget you. She kept that one to herself.

They had reached an empty bench, and she parked the pushchair so that Bea could look at the dogs trotting, scampering or snuffling past on their afternoon walks, their owners huddled into bulky jackets.

'Shall we sit down for a bit?' she suggested. 'Or are you too cold?'

Oddly, Tyler didn't feel the least bit cold. Just being next to her kept him warm. 'I'm fine,' he said.

'Fine…your favourite word,' she teased him as she sat down and pulled up the collar of her coat against the wind. The Scarborough train rattled over the bridge, and in the distance the towers of the Minster looked almost pink in the wintery afternoon sunshine.

It felt so good to be with Tyler again. Mary was happy to simply sit next to him and let the reassurance of his solid presence seep into her, and it was hard to remember that this was supposed to be a consultation.

'Tell me how things are going with Fiona,' she said, rousing herself. 'And don't say fine!'

'I won't do that,' said Tyler, 'because they're not fine. In fact, they're going very badly.'

'Badly?' She looked at him in dismay. 'Why, what's happened?'

'Nothing's happened,' he said. 'That's the point. There's been no spark. Fiona's a nice woman, but I don't know how to talk to her.'

'I've told you, you just have to talk to her the way you talk to me.'

'But she's not you,' said Tyler. 'And that's the problem.

Nobody's ever going to be you. I rang Fiona after I'd seen you on Wednesday and cancelled our date.'

Mary was struggling to take in what he was saying. *She's not you*, he had said. 'What…what did she say?' she asked, although what she really wanted to know was what he meant by *Nobody's ever going to be you.*

'She was great about it. I think it was a relief to her too. She told me that she'd only agreed to go out with me because she wanted to make her ex jealous, so we were being equally stupid and refusing to acknowledge that we were both in love with someone else. She still loves her ex-boyfriend and, as for me,' said Tyler casually, 'well, I'm hopelessly in love with you.'

'With m-me?' stammered Mary.

'With you,' he confirmed. 'It turns out,' he said, 'that you're the one I want, Mary.'

Her heart was beating so fast that it was hard to breathe, but Mary couldn't let herself believe it yet. 'You don't want me,' she said shakily.

'Don't I?' Tyler turned on the bench to take her face between his palms, and his smile made the last gasps of air evaporate from her lungs. 'I hate to contradict such an expert on relationships as yourself, Mary,' he said, 'but I think you're wrong about that. I think I'm going to have to show you just how wrong you are.'

He kissed her then, a long, slow, irresistible kiss that left Mary's head reeling and her body thrumming and exhilaration dancing and pirouetting along every vein, as she melted joyfully into him, winding her arms around his neck and kissing him back. The kiss deepened and deepened, so intense that Tyler's hands fell from her cheeks to unbutton her coat, pushing his hands beneath the heavy fabric to slide around her and pull her closer.

'Now tell me I don't want you,' he challenged her breathlessly when they broke apart for air at last, his hands still roaming possessively over her lush curves.

'But I'm nothing like your ideal woman,' said Mary, but in spite of her protest she didn't move away. Well, it was a cold day, and it was wonderfully warm with his arms around her. No point in wasting body warmth, was there?

'I know,' Tyler agreed. 'It's ironic, isn't it? I was so fixed on the idea of someone blonde and elegant and sophisticated that I nearly missed what was right in front of me.'

Tilting her face up, he looked down into shining grey eyes. 'I've missed you,' he said. 'I've missed you more than I can say. I hate going home because you're not there, and Bea's not there. It's not home anymore, it's just a place where you're not.'

He kissed her warm, lush mouth. 'I didn't even know I loved you when you left, Mary. I did everything I could to tell myself that I didn't. I'd never been in love before, and I didn't want to accept that it had happened to me at last, but when I came to see you in your office and you told me Alan was back in your life, I couldn't deny it any longer. It was as if a great black hole had opened up in front of me.' His mouth twisted at the memory. 'I thought I'd lost you before I'd had a chance to tell you what you meant to me.'

'Why didn't you say anything then?' asked Mary, remembering how his face had closed and, clinging closer, still hardly able to believe that he loved her after all.

'I knew you would want to see Alan first,' said Tyler. 'I thought you would choose him because he's Bea's father, and because I knew how much you'd loved him. I thought that I'd left it too late. It was my own fault for being too stupid to understand that I'd been falling in love with you right from the start.'

'You told me you didn't believe in love,' Mary reminded him.

'That's because I'd never been in love before. How was I to know what had hit me like a truck, turning my life upside down and calling into question everything I used to be so sure of?' Tyler kissed her again, very tenderly, on the lips. 'I know what love is now,' he said. 'You were the one who taught me. You told me exactly what it should be.'

'I did? What did I say?'

'You said that I needed to marry someone who could light up my life and make me feel better just by being near me. That's what you do to me,' he told her. 'You're my rock, Mary. Without you, nothing makes sense, and everything I used to think was so important just seems worthless.'

Her arms tightened around him and he rested his cheek against her hair, breathing in her fragrance, his heart swelling at the feel of her. 'You told me I shouldn't marry anyone unless I couldn't live without them,' he said, his voice very deep and low. 'I can't live without you, Mary. I know you're not blond and you're not elegant but you're *real*. Yes, there are slimmer women out there, women who are more graceful and elegant and better dressed, but they're not you. None of them will make my heart lift when I'm near them. None of them will make me count the hours until I can go home and hold them again. I never felt at home until I met you, Mary,' he said. 'And home's not home without you and Bea.'

'Oh, Tyler…' said Mary tremulously. 'Tyler…' Her heart was so full she didn't know where to begin, and the tears were spilling out of her eyes.

'Mary!' Tyler tightened his arms around her. 'Don't cry.'

'I can't help it,' she said tearfully. 'I'm so happy.'

A smile that started deep in his eyes spread slowly over Tyler's face, and his expression made Mary fizzle with joyful anticipation. 'I've missed you too,' she said. 'Bea has too. We both love you,' she told him, and their lips met in a long, sweet kiss that dissolved the memories of the last miserable days and left them with an intoxicating glow of happiness.

'Tell me you'll marry me,' said Tyler urgently at last.

'What about your goal?' asked Mary mischievously. 'You wanted a wife and a family you could show off to your peers.'

'I'm going to have them,' he said, smiling. 'I'm going to have a wife I adore and who loves me, and a beautiful daughter... Who wouldn't envy me? No, I've got a new goal,' he said confidently.

'Oh?' she said. 'What's that?'

The smile faded from his eyes and his expression was very serious as he looked into her eyes. 'To make you happy,' he said simply. 'To love you for the rest of my life.'

Mary blinked back the tears that were shimmering on the end of her lashes. 'That sounds like a pretty good goal to me,' she said.

'I'll need some help on my strategy, though,' he said. 'You know I'm not very good at relationships.'

She laughed a little shakily. 'Obviously, you're going to need some intensive coaching to make sure you get it right,' she agreed.

'That's what I thought,' said Tyler. 'I was hoping I could persuade you to take on that role.'

'Persuasion, not blackmail?' Mary applauded. 'Very good!'

His smile deepened. 'Do you think you'd be prepared to take it on?'

'Well...' She pretended to consider. 'It would take a very long time. We'd have to make it longer than a two month contract.'

'What sort of time scale are you thinking of?'

'A lifetime would be best,' said Mary, her lips curving into a smile as she kissed the corner of his mouth. 'Just to be sure. We'll both have to work at it, and we'll learn from each other, but as long as we look after each other, we'll get there.'

Tyler smiled. 'Sounds like a good strategy to me,' he said, and kissed her again, a kiss that went on and on until Bea realised that she had lost their attention and objected with a shout.

Laughing, Mary lifted her out of the pushchair and sat her on her knee. 'What do you think, Bea?' she asked. 'Shall we go back and live with Tyler and let him change your nappies?'

Tyler grinned. 'I'll even do that if it means you'll come home!'

'Gosh, you *have* missed us!'

'I have,' he said, suddenly serious. 'I never want to miss you like that again.'

'You won't need to,' said Mary softly. 'We'll all be together from now on.'

Bea was straining to get to Tyler and he took her from Mary, holding her out at arm's length and jumping her up and down on his knee while she dimpled and smiled and flirted her lashes at him, delighted to have his undivided attention once more.

'It looks like you've got the deciding vote, Bea,' he said. 'Are you going to let me marry your mum and look after you?'

Bea bounced excitedly on his knee. 'Ga!' she shouted, and Tyler smiled, settling her on his knee and putting his other arm around Mary to draw her close.

'I'll take that as a yes,' he said.

Dirty Weekend

SUSAN STEPHENS

Susan Stephens was a professional singer before meeting her husband on the tiny Mediterranean island of Malta. In true Modern™ style they met on Monday, became engaged on Friday, and were married three months after that. Almost thirty years and three children later, they are still in love. (Susan does not advise her children to return home one day with a similar story, as she may not take the news with the same fortitude as her own mother!) Visit Susan's website: www.susan stephens.net – she loves to hear from her readers all around the world!

For all the fabulous characters I've met and have
yet to meet in the countryside around 'Hawkshead',
from a very grateful if mud-splattered townie!
Hugs and happy reading, everyone!
Susan

CHAPTER ONE

As MUD landed on her windscreen the steering wheel jerked out of her hands and Caz Ryan slammed on the brakes. The new silver Mini lurched and slid sideways into a ditch. Everything went black and there was just sound, bad sound, brambles and stone sloughing off showroom-pristine paint and the catastrophic wrenching sound of metal giving way. The car was dead. And now everything had gone eerily quiet.

Careful not to move, Caz conducted a full physical inventory. Everything seemed to be present and correct: no broken bones, no blood dripping on the carpet, she was intact, and, apart from being wedged between her seat and the door with her overnight bag seemingly welded to her head, she was fine. It was a miracle, no thanks to the Neanderthal driving that mud-slinging tractor.

Where was he, by the way? By craning her neck she had a great view of a muddy bank and a road that belonged under her wheels, not over her head. Her own fault. She should have stayed in London where men knew to get out of her way.

In London things were different. She wasn't Caz Ryan, currently shivering so hard her teeth were threatening to chip, but Cassandra Bailey Brown, the *über*-confident alter ego Caz had created in order to get ahead.

Finding the name had been easy. Cassandra because her mother had had a romantic streak—at least, she had before dumping Caz in a children's home prior to running away to 'find herself'. Bailey Brown came out of the phone book. There were only two listed, which confirmed the surname's exclusivity and made it the perfect choice.

The reason for the change of name? After leaving school she hadn't been able to get a job. Her accent had been a give-away; likewise her manner. She had known she had to do something and inspiration had come from the television—newscasters with their approved English pronunciation were the perfect people to copy. She had watched, learned and listened until she'd felt ready to re-launch herself as Cassandra. The tactic had worked. Doors that had slammed in Caz Ryan's face were held open by doormen for Cassandra Bailey Brown.

But Cassandra couldn't help her now. Wriggling furiously, Caz tried to achieve a better position, but only succeeded in proving that, whereas Cassandra walked tall in the city, she couldn't see over the hedge in the country.

However, this was no time for humour. She was shaking so hard she couldn't concentrate. The shock was getting through to her and with it the fact that she was trapped in a car at night and there was no one to help her other than the man she had so rashly overtaken, and who had now disappeared. She couldn't even reach her phone to call for help.

She tried shouting.

The silence was unrelenting and her bravado was being pushed out by fear. Silence in the country was very different from silence in the city; it was all-enveloping, and apart from the wind blowing a horror-movie soundtrack through the trees there was nothing to suggest another human being existed within miles of her.

What if the man drove away? This wasn't London with cars passing every second, this was Hawkshead, last bastion of civilisation before the harsh moorland conditions had deterred even the cavemen.

Caz tensed as a dark shadow loomed over her. 'Don't just stand there! Do something!'

The man didn't move. Maybe he was evaluating the situation, and maybe she was going to pieces. The only certainty was Cassandra's confidence hadn't survived the trip. The man's footsteps crunched away. Brisk and purposeful, they were growing fainter every second. 'Come back here! Don't leave me!'

For a moment she had felt warm beneath his shadow, but now she felt worse than before. She should be appealing to his better nature and not yelling at him. She had caused the accident, after all.

By almost dislocating her neck Caz managed to see out of the car window, but the angle was so acute the most she saw was that the man was some distance away. Although she did notice how tall and lean he was, with powerful shoulders that packed out his rugged jacket. Her body responded with a very different shiver, but had he any intention of helping her?

She had to stay calm. Cassandra never lost control. Cassandra was never lost for direction, let alone in London where everything was so well signed. But here in Hawkshead, miles from her comfort zone, Cassandra was no use at all.

So it was just Caz and the dark and an unknown man. Hugging herself Caz continued to shudder uncontrollably. This was bad news for Cassandra. Cassandra would never shudder. Cassandra was strong. She had recently been appointed a director of Brent Construction in Leeds, one of the top five hundred companies in the country. Cassandra would have to be back all guns blazing in the office on Monday morning when the new chairman was due to take inventory of his board.

Her new boss, Brent junior, had taken a cosy family business and turned it into a world class concern, and rumour said he moved fast to weed out weak links in his chain. Caz accepted business had no heart and didn't expect any favours, but having reached the top of the greasy pole, she had no intention of losing her grip on it.

It was thanks to her alter ego Cassandra that she was here in Hawkshead at all. Cassandra never turned down an opportunity to advance her career, and so Caz had thrown aside the familiar bustle of London for the promise of a better job and a large country house in Yorkshire.

The house in Hawkshead, twenty minutes outside Leeds, was a bonus, a complete surprise, an inheritance from an aunt she'd never met. She'd never been given a thing in her life before, and now a house. Just the thought of it propelled another yell out of her. She couldn't wait to see it; that was why she had come straight from work in Leeds to Hawkshead…

She couldn't hear a thing, other than owls hooting. The feeling of helplessness was new to her, and she hated it, plus she didn't need this aggravation with Monday morning looming large on the horizon.

Twisting her neck again to try and see out of the car, she gasped to see the man was back. He was standing over her holding a giant-sized pair of cutters. For some reason her shivers stopped at the sight of him and a warm throbbing replaced them.

'I've called the emergency services.'

His voice was deep and husky and vibrated

through her. 'Thank you.' Was that her voice shaking?

'And now I'm going to get you out of there…'

She was confident he would, and excitement at the thought flooded through her. She was going to be free. She was going to be freed. *By him.*

As he continued to murmur reassurances there was something in his voice that made her feel younger than Cassandra had felt in a decade.

Caz was only twenty-eight, but she felt eighteen and reckless again, and was glad she'd come straight from the office where Cassandra always dressed to kill. She was still wearing her ridiculously high heels and a too-tight short skirt. Sadly her make-up had endured a long working day followed by a car ride, but she was tearful and vulnerable and ready to be rescued.

She listened intently as he told her how brave she was. She was anything but. She'd spent her whole working life in Human Resources soothing others, bolstering them up, persuading them to take the next step on the ladder, but quite suddenly the tables were turned, and it was she who was floundering. Thanks to her driving the man had assumed she was generally incompetent and was explaining everything he was doing in that low, sexy drawl as if he knew she was on the brink…

Not that she minded listening to him. No…that was like a vocal caress touching every part of her. She was so at ease he made her start when he moved to adjust his position. There was something elemental about him…something he threw off in warm, musky waves. She couldn't even see him properly, but whatever special powers he had, they were curling round her like a seductive cloak.

After a while she relaxed again; the tone of his voice helped. It made him sound like a hero in a film and what was wrong with being the grateful heroine for once, rather than the hard-nosed businesswoman with an attitude towards men?

It took Cassandra to remind Caz that she hadn't battered her way through the glass ceiling to go soft now.

'We're nearly there…'

Caz refocused fast, and as the man dipped his head to speak her body quivered. Her cheeks were tingling too, and she was sure she could feel his warmth brush her face. Every part of her was on full alert, trying to pick up anything she could about him—his accent, his tone, his intentions towards her…

'Are you all right? Not lost your voice, have you?'

There was something warm and humorous in his tone. Caz made a sound to signal her acknowledgement that the man had spoken, but she was soon soothed into silence again by the easy rhythm of his movement. There was an air of purpose and confidence about him, which reassured her. He was probably a builder or a farmer, she guessed. A man used to working with his hands…a man who knew what to do with his hands…a man who would be good with his hands…

She gulped her guilty thoughts back as moonlight streamed in. He had peeled back the roof of the Mini like the lid off a tin of sardines.

'Did you have to do that?' She exploded without thinking. Money was tight, what with the move to Leeds and now her inheritance to lavish luxuries on. She thought back frantically, trying to remember the level of insurance she had taken out on the car.

'Have you got any better suggestions for getting you out?'

The man's tone put her back up. 'You don't know it's safe to move me.'

'You sound well enough to me.'

That sexy drawl could turn hard in a moment, which was quite a turn-on but was he mocking her?

She had to remind herself that up here on the moors the man would come from a traditional community where women knew their place. And that was almost certainly in the kitchen, or his bed… She needed a big gulp of air to consider this.

'There's petrol leaking from your car. I can get you out, or I can leave you here to fry. Your choice—'

What? 'Get me out!' She could smell the petrol now. 'Please!'

'Can you reach your seat belt?'

Before she had chance to reply he had sliced it through with the cutters. His hand brushed hers, an

incendiary device carrying with it a thousand messages…strong, warm, dry, smooth, capable being
just a few of them.

Her heart was behaving oddly, the rest of her too.
She wasn't used to raw masculinity, that had to be
it. She was accustomed to boardroom pallor and
sandwich bellies. This man's mid-section would be
hard and tanned, and banded with muscle…

Caz flinched as a powerful leg clad in well-worn
denim brushed her face. He was planting his feet,
she realised, straddling the bank above the car,
readying himself to lift her out. He manoeuvred with
care for such a big man. She caught a glimpse of
boots, scuffed and workmanlike, as he lifted her out.
And now her face was millimetres from the mud.
She recoiled, desperate not to land in it. But then a
hand reached around her waist, and she was safe.

'Don't be frightened…'

She was too grateful to be frightened, but her
heart was thundering a tattoo. 'Thank you.' He had
taken an incredible risk.

'Save it,' he said brusquely, tightening his grip on
her.

She could have been cosy in his arms without the
tension, but she could feel the sense of danger in
him, feel his awareness of it. The car might explode
if there was petrol leaking and his desire to put
distance between them meant he had no time to
waste on superficial courtesies.

She liked that. She liked him. It was an instinctive reaction. She liked being weightless in his arms, and letting him take control. But this feeling of release, of letting go, of allowing someone else to take control, was very new to her. Her job demanded that she was the one who took charge, and as for her life, well, that was the most tightly controlled of all.

Maybe that controlling part of her had got a little out of hand recently, but it stood no chance with this man. She'd never felt like this before, never felt the need to writhe and tangle in a man's arms.

She was allowing her imagination to run away with her, Caz realised and to counteract temptation she immediately went as stiff as a board, which the man answered with some disturbingly intimate pressure in her belly.

'I can't carry you if you're going to turn into a plank of wood.'

Such charm! Such grace! She was right about him being a Neanderthal. But lying in his arms wasn't all bad. She could feel the power in each purposeful stride he took, and, gazing back, she could see the lethal spikes of metal through which he'd threaded her.

They reached a clearing where the moonlight was a little brighter and she could make out the shape of his jaw now. It was strong, firm and black with stubble, which insanely made her long to rub her face against it.

Shock, Caz reasoned, relaxing again. But her gaze crept upwards to study surprisingly sensual lips, set, however, in a grim line that didn't invite fantasy. He was an iron man, she concluded, too primitive for steel, but he was clean. Fresh from the shower, she guessed, he smelled warm and spicy like a hot cinnamon muffin, which reminded her how hungry she was. It was a long time since she had last eaten.

He set off again, carrying her, walking with the poise and natural grace of a man who worked close to the land. She was an expert in people, so she knew. Her new Human Resource director's position meant it was her job to sort out the wheat from the chaff. Cassandra Bailey Brown had made her name sniffing out a candidate's career path before their CV had even landed on her desk. Well, she'd struck lucky this time, Caz thought, because in Cassandra's world it was unusual to find a man who could lift anything heavier than a ring binder, and then only when it was empty.

She was just drifting off into shock-induced torpor again when he suddenly changed his grip.

'Did I hurt you?' he demanded as she exclaimed.

No, but his hand had just connected with her naked butt. Commando was the only option in this skin-tight designer suit. She managed to dredge up enough of Cassandra's *sang-froid* to assure him coolly that she was fine as he set her down.

'Hardly dressed for the country though, are you?' he observed disapprovingly.

Was there a prescribed outfit for landing in a ditch?

With difficulty she held back on the invective that sprang to her lips, making allowances because he had saved her. And she was prepared to admit on this occasion that he was right. Her suit was out of place. But to a workaholic a weekend away meant staying at her desk till the last flicker on her screen. Nevertheless, knickers would have been an advantage tonight. She could still feel his touch branded on her bottom like a quality control stamp.

Caz's heart juddered, and then began to race, as a shaft of moonlight hit her rescuer full in the face. The fading light had robbed the scene of colour, but his eyes seemed to possess a generator all their own. Ocean-green, they were extraordinary against his tan, and his stare was wolf-keen as it rested on her face.

When she stopped quivering enough to think she had to admit that his tan threw her for a moment. Perhaps she'd made a mistake about his profession? No, she thought, reconciling it instead with his outdoor life. She had to have some confidence in her abilities—they had landed her a six-figure salary with the fastest-growing building company on the planet. Trouble was, she'd never met a man like this before. She would have to open a new file at the office marked Miscellaneous Man Hunks.

Caz continued her investigations down long, lean legs and then up again to the somewhat enormous bulge in his jeans.

'Feeling better now?' he said, distracting her.

She quickly refocused, trying to appear calm

when everything inside her was gasping for air. A new kind of shock was setting in, she realised.

The man frowned as he looked at her intently. 'I don't think you're fully recovered yet...'

As he made to pick her up again she backed away. 'No,' she agreed readily, 'I don't think I am, but perhaps if I stand here for a moment...' She fanned herself vigorously to excuse her red cheeks. Her pulse had gone crazy and she had to force her chin to tip to its customary confident angle as he stared at her. Her limbs were trembling beneath his gaze, which was an absolute first for her where men were concerned.

'Don't worry, you'll soon get over it,' he assured her.

She sincerely hoped so.

His long, piercing look was cut short by a call to his mobile. The emergency services, Caz guessed, picking up the command in his tone, which gave her confidence.

'Will they recover the car?'

'I'll keep you updated, don't worry.'

She wasn't sure whether to worry or not at the thought that he intended to keep in touch. Perhaps it would help if he'd just look away while he spoke on the phone, which would give her the chance to reorder her thoughts and reconnect brain synapses that were drifting aimlessly.

Why couldn't she summon up Cassandra when she needed her? This man could be useful, and

Cassandra could spot a promising employee at fifty
paces. A competent handyman would be a welcome
addition to her staff at Stone Break House, the
country seat Caz had inherited. According to her
aunt's solicitor it must be somewhere close by, and
if this man was local he could show her the way.

She looked at him hopefully as he snapped his
phone shut. She felt better just knowing she had the
makings of a plan. This might work out for the best,
after all. And if it did she would forgive Hawkshead
anything…almost anything, Caz amended, cursing
fiercely as the heel broke off her shoe.

'Why don't you snap them both off?'

She stared at the man incredulously.

'You'd find it much easier to walk.'

Did he have any idea what these shoes had cost?
And if that was humour in his eyes… Caz forced
herself to take a few deep breaths. She had to
remember what the man had done for her, and what
he might still do for her. She couldn't expect him to
know the value of luxury products stuck out here in
the sticks.

As he held her gaze with a suggestion of amusement in his Cassandra was forced to take a back seat,
leaving Caz Ryan to squirm alone. And the squirm
started in a place that was normally closed for
business as far as men were concerned.

She wasn't used to such directness, Caz reasoned.
She wasn't used to men answering her imperative
stare with a lazy smile. She wasn't used to lazy

smiles setting off quivers down her spine that put some extraordinary thoughts in her head: Lady Chatterley and the gardener; Cassandra and the handyman... Why not? It had a certain ring to it. No one knew her here in Hawkshead; she could do what she liked. But then Cassandra reminded her that there was no time, no place in her life for men.

Which was a shame, Caz thought wickedly, but there was nothing wrong with allowing her fantasies to run free on a country lane. A country lane? In the dark? With a man she didn't know? Nothing wrong? Was she going mad? She would never dream of doing something like this in London or in her new home town of Leeds. So what was different about Hawkshead? What was different about this man?

Drawing herself up to what with her heels should have been an imposing five feet eight, but without them had shrunk to a lopsided five feet three, Caz found herself staring at the third button down on a chequered shirt that was stretched tight over chiselled abs seemingly made out of rock. Maybe if she added some formality to the mix her heart would stop pounding. 'Thank you for your assistance, Mr...?'

'Galem,' he said.

A touch ungraciously, she thought. So was Galem his first name, or his last?

She didn't need to get to know him, Caz reminded herself. Galem was just fine. 'Thank you, Galem. Now, you don't happen to know the number of a local taxi firm, do you?'

He didn't answer her right away, so she took the hint and started digging inside the ridiculously impractical pocket in her jacket where she kept her small change. She breathed a sigh of relief, having found a few coins and a screwed up five pound note. 'Please take this for your trouble,' she said in Cassandra's best ruling class tones.

He ignored her outstretched hand and asked her a question instead. 'And what do they call you in the big city?'

The drawl caught her somewhere between the shoulder blades and then travelled the length of her spine at least twice. 'My name is Cassandra Bailey Brown.' She said this in her best self-tutored voice, and just hearing Cassandra's familiar tones ring out made her feel more confident.

The man looked at her as if she were a species from another planet, then something else crept into his gaze. Was it a spark of recognition? That had to be impossible. Where would their paths ever cross? Cassandra's life was sophisticated, high-tone and fast-paced. This man couldn't even begin to imagine. And now she'd shown her gratitude and her patience was exhausted. For one thing she didn't like being stared at in that faintly mocking way. Wasn't money supposed to be a universal language?

Not here in the country, apparently.

She tried one last time. 'Go on, take it…'

'What for?' he said, frowning.

With a sound loaded with impatience and frustration, she stuffed the money back into her pocket, breaking the last of her acrylic nails as she did so. *Ching!* Her internal till rang again; another fifty pounds down the drain.

'Cassandra Bailey Brown... That's quite a mouthful,' he observed.

As Galem repeated her name Caz noticed how easily a curve of humour found its way to his mouth. He was mocking her again. Cassandra's confident smile evaporated. And why did the name she had chosen for the workplace sound so ridiculous, suddenly?

Maybe because she was plain Caz Ryan?

She couldn't allow him to rattle her. The best employer/employee relationships were based on mutual respect, and first impressions were crucial. 'You haven't told me your second name yet,' she reminded him.

'That's right,' he said unhelpfully. 'My name is Galem. That's all you need to know. And you'll get no taxi here, Cassandra, so what are you going to do?'

Charming! Plus he'd drawn her name out so that Cassandra sounded like some trollop in a porn film. 'Where can I get a taxi then?' she pressed, refusing to be flummoxed.

'Not here...' Slouching on one hip, he looked unhelpful.

'Well, I'll just have to take my chances, and go back to the car. Maybe I'll sleep there,' she said stubbornly, lifting her chin defiantly.

'No, you won't.'

He stepped in front of her. His lazy movements had deceived her. He could move like lightning when he wanted to. 'Are you going to use brute force to stop me?' Even as she suggested it she felt excited.

'If you're daft enough…' He stepped aside.

But as she went to move past him, he nimbly stepped in front of her again. 'I can't let you do that, Cassandra,' he said with the same mocking emphasis on her name. 'In fact, I won't let you do it until the fire service tell *me* the car's safe.' Folding his arms across his chest, he looked down at her, waiting.

'And what am I supposed to do in the meantime?'

'Take a lift with me,' he suggested, easing his massive shoulders in a shrug.

She was certain his dark gaze was mocking her and was equally certain her insides were dancing a tango. She wasn't going anywhere in a car with him; she hadn't lost her marbles altogether.

'Don't worry,' he said with a betraying curve of his lips. 'I'll willingly give you a hand up…'

I bet you would. Her eyes narrowed as she stared back at him, but in truth her options were shrinking.

'Ready?' he said. As he glanced at the tractor and she let out a breath as if she'd been hit in the stomach.

'A lift on your tractor?' she said incredulously.

'Well, I didn't mean on my back.'

The thought of clambering up him without knickers on had to be blanked immediately.

'Are you coming, or not? I promise not to look,' he added dryly.

It was that, or start walking, she realised.

'By the way, you do know this road is a dead end?' he said as she bent down to take off her ruined shoes. 'Where were you going?'

'Of course I know about the road.' She wasn't even sure which road she was on.

'There's only one house down here...'

Her heart leapt. Could this be the right road? Her late aunt's solicitor had told her that Stone Break House was the most substantial house in the village of Hawkshead, and that it stood in solitary splendour at the end of its own road. Solitary splendour, apart from a couple of uninhabited ruins, that was, which she took to mean ruins along the lines of Bolton Abbey, or Fountains Abbey, perhaps with a river running nearby.

Stone Break House represented the pinnacle of Cassandra's aspirations. As far as Cassandra was concerned it said she had arrived. A country seat was what she had been working so hard for ever since Caz had created her. Now Cassandra could keep up, not just with the Joneses, but with the double-barrelled Joneses. The fact that Galem had heard of the house puffed her up even more. Stone Break House...the name alone was enough to thrill her; it had such a ring to it. Caz made a slight, if significant pause before telling him, 'I know it's the only house on the road, because Stone Break House belongs to me now.'

'It does, does it?' He couldn't have sounded more unimpressed.

A tense silence followed.

'Well, come on, then,' Galem said at last in a voice that had lost its charm.

What business was it of his, anyway? Caz thought, wrinkling her brow. Why should he care if she owned the house or not. She shouldn't have told him.

'Shall I leave you here?' he said impatiently.

There were no streetlights in the country, and night had fallen like a smothering black web. The lane was lined with creaking trees and, though she wasn't nervous at night in a brightly lit city, night time in Hawkshead was a very different matter. Stone Break House was sure to be located down some long, impressive drive, and if she missed the gates in the dark and kept on walking into the hills... People had been known to get lost, or eaten by spectral cats, according to some of the magazines she'd read, but, anyway, they definitely disappeared without trace.

'That's it,' Galem said. 'If you can't make your mind up, I'm going.'

'No, wait.' Caz used Cassandra's imperious tones. It was time to re-establish her authority, and Cassandra Bailey Brown had a way with men. In fact one hundred and fifty of them had worked under her in London, something that gave endless amusement to her friends. As they never tired of pointing out, she had one hundred and fifty men working under her, and not one of them had made it on top yet.

'Where men are concerned, you, Cassandra Bailey Brown, are a lost cause…'

And Caz Ryan wasn't much better. As she started to run after Galem, Caz realized this was no time for standing on her dignity. In the city Cassandra might have got her through closed doors that would never have opened for the real Caz Ryan, but in Hawkshead Cassandra was no use to her. It was tempting to think that one day she might put her alter ego in the recycle bin for good. Men had never figured in Cassandra's remorseless drive to the top. So what if she didn't have a private life? She had a blue-chip salary, didn't she? This was the way Cassandra thought. So what if her London chums thought her weird because she didn't date? Truth was one disastrous relationship had been enough for her; it had almost taken her eye off the ball and allowed someone else to be promoted over her head. Cassandra had cut it off without a flicker of remorse long before it had reached the bedroom. The end result? Caz was still a virgin.

'Last chance, townie…'

Slouched on one hip and leaning against his beat-up tractor, Galem was staring at her. 'I'm out of here,' he added, emphasising his point by resting one massive boot on the step of his cab.

'No, wait…please.' She added a plaintive note to her voice, swallowing her pride in the interest of her pedicure. Bare feet and country lanes were a recipe for disaster. 'If you could just drop me off at the gates…'

'The gates?'

'To Stone Break House,' she said as if he should know.

Galem's expression was hidden from her as he came round to help her up. It was this unexpected politeness that stalled her brain for a moment. 'Just as far as the gates will be fine,' she told him, suddenly feeling she maybe shouldn't be alone with him.

'Very well, m'lady,' he said in a way that reassured her.

Perhaps there was hope for him yet, Cassandra approved.

CHAPTER TWO

'THAT'S it?' CAZ peered in horror down the narrow strip of land lit by Galem's tractor beam. This had to be the wrong place. 'You've made a mistake,' she said confidently.

'No mistake.'

'But this can't be Stone Break House. It looks more like a quarry.' She swallowed hard, gazing up at ugly scars carved into the hillside. The peeling sign over what remained of the gates suddenly took on new meaning for her. 'Stone Break House,' she muttered under her breath. 'I see…'

'There's been a quarry here since—'

'Spare me the detail. I'm thinking…' How long had Aunt Maud been in the nursing home? It was hard to be sure since she hadn't even known she'd had an Aunt Maud until the solicitor had tracked her down.

'What are you thinking?' Galem prompted.

'I'm trying to evaluate the potential of my inheritance, actually.' And that was the least of it!

Instead of sympathy or concern a very attractive crease appeared in the side of Galem's beard-roughened cheek as he stared up at the house and his gaze had a faraway look as if he were already picturing the pitfalls she would face if she were foolish enough to attempt a restoration project.

'Someone had a sense of humour leaving you this,' he said, though his own mouth had set into a grim line as if the humour in the situation had bypassed him.

Caz had to admit that Aunt Maud's intentions were a mystery to her. The solicitor had told her that her late mother hadn't spoken to her aunt for years, to the extent that Maud hadn't even known Caz had grown up in an orphanage. Having managed to track her down, Maud had changed her will accordingly. On hearing the news and with no emotion to cloud the picture Cassandra had immediately pictured herself in gaiters and deerstalker hat entertaining her London friends. But as Caz looked at the house now she just felt sad. She could feel the house pulling her in, as if laughter had rung there at one time, and a family had lived and thrived.

She discounted the feeling. Ghosts calling to her? She was still suffering from shock after the accident. But her feelings towards the house made Caz wonder if Cassandra had drifted further away than she thought. Did the country have this effect on everyone?

Not Galem, she gathered, risking a glance at his

glowering face. She wouldn't share her feelings with him. He would only laugh and tell her she wasn't up to the task.

She thanked him for the lift and mentioned the car again; she didn't want to be trapped here.

'When it's recovered I'll let you know,' he said in that weary way men had when a request was repeated.

Leaning across the cab, he opened the passenger door for her. Automatically she pressed back in the seat. She didn't want to get any closer to him than she had to, and she certainly didn't want to become an object of fascination to those piercing sea-green eyes. Galem saw far too much as it was.

He was having a very strange effect on her. Caz could only describe it as the 'bird in her chest' syndrome, and it was growing worse by the minute, and as if that weren't bad enough she couldn't get the bulge in his jeans out of her mind. How did women go on with a thing like that? Surely you'd have to lead up to it? Would she need to be prepared? She had no idea.

It hardly mattered as she wouldn't be finding out, Caz told herself sensibly.

'I guess seeing this must have put you off for life...'

As Galem shouldered the driver's door open Caz almost tumbled out of the cab in her hurry to get away from him. Only when he jumped down after

her did she rationalise her thoughts and realise that
he had been staring out at Stone Break House when
he'd made the comment.

'Not at all,' she shouted back at him, staggering
on the uneven ground.

'Why didn't you wait for me?' he said gruffly, appearing at her side. 'I would have helped you down.'

And have him feel her naked butt again? Caz
smiled Cassandra's most insincere smile and said
nothing. 'Do you have my bag?' she said, remembering it. It was important to her. It was crammed
full with every type of beauty product you could
think of, plus a bottle of Krug, which her London
friends had kindly had delivered to the Leeds office
to celebrate moving into her country home.

'Your bag?'

Galem raked his fingers through his hair as if he
was having trouble remembering what he'd done
with it, but then he brightened up.

'I threw it in the back with the paving slabs,' he
said, his voice laced with amusement.

Caz didn't dare to speak. Her brain formed the
words, but there was no possible way she could
allow her mouth to speak them, not if she wanted to
keep Galem on side.

'For safety,' he explained, plonking it down at her
feet like a well-trained gun dog.

She didn't want to risk grinding her porcelain
veneers and so she decided to forgive him this once
and do a little prying. 'So, you're a paver?'

'Something wrong with that?' His mouth turned grim as he held her stare.

'No, of course not,' she lied hastily.

He was standing very close, and it was impossible to miss the fact that his thumbs were lodged in his belt loops pointing the way to his bulging button fly. She quickly looked away, but not before Galem caught her looking. 'I thought you were a farmer,' she said, to excuse her red cheeks.

'Toiling on the land?' he said with irony.

The expression in his eyes shot heat to every part of her. 'That's right.' She formed her lips into a tight line of disapproval. It didn't do to get too familiar. Plus she had a sigh to hold in.

As she refused to meet his gaze she allowed hers to slip, taking in the wide spread of Galem's shoulders and the hint of black chest hair beneath the open buttons on his shirt. The thought of that scratching her—

'Are you all right?'

'Perfectly.'

'You still seem a little shaky to me,' he observed, working his jaw as he thought about it.

'Shaky? Not a bit.' She pulled herself round quickly. 'Thank you once again for tonight…' She turned to go. 'Don't forget to let me know about the car…'

'Nagging woman' appeared in neon lights above his eyes; at the same time he said, 'Sure.'

'Tomorrow?' she said, refusing to be daunted. 'Before lunch.'

'You're not going to be sleeping here tonight.'

His remark sounded dangerously like an order.
'Of course I am.'

Thick black brows drew together over eyes that
had suddenly turned a darker shade of green. 'You're
kidding me, right?'

'No. I'm perfectly serious.' Swinging her bag
onto her shoulder, she reached out to open the gate.
'Thank you again, Galem. See you tomorrow as
arranged.' She pushed against it but the gate refused
to budge. She kept her cool and tried again, throwing
her weight against it this time.

'Too proud to ask for help, Cassandra?'

Caz's jaw set. She tried again. And again. Until
Galem took matters into his own hands and leaned
across to open it for her. He smelled so good—good
enough to eat.

Douse that thought, Caz told herself firmly,
flashing him a grateful glance. Galem was a working
man, and one who could prove useful if she played
her cards right.

Caz walked through the gates towards what she
could now see was around six thousand square feet
of crumbling ruin. No way was she turning back, but
there was no getting away from the fact that Stone
Break House was definitely not the manor to which
Cassandra had hoped to become accustomed.

'If you intend camping out here I think you'd
better take my number,' Galem said.

He was standing somewhere behind her. She

guessed by the gate. She was at the foot of the steps now and had no intention of turning round to see his smug expression.

'I can take you back to the village, if you like?'

He sounded hopeful. Too hopeful. 'I don't like. I'll be fine.'

'This is enough to put anyone off…'

But not me, Caz thought stubbornly. Galem was blatantly trying to persuade her to turn tail and run. Why? 'I'm not put off,' she said, turning to show him her determined face. 'And I'm not hesitating either, I'm simply evaluating the situation.'

'Well, don't take too long about it,' Galem advised with a distinct smile in his voice.

The more certain he sounded that she would take fright, the more Caz became convinced that this was where she belonged, and that Stone Break House needed her. 'There's really no need for you to stay,' she said pointedly.

'Okay,' Galem agreed. 'But before I go I'd better give you my number—'

'Why?' So he could rescue the little woman, no doubt. And if he was local she didn't need his number, she could find it in the phone book. 'If you give me your name I can look you up if I need you.' If there was a patronising note in her voice he deserved it.

He gave it to her anyway, writing it on a scrap of paper with a pen he extracted from his pocket. He came right up to the door and then leaned against the wall to write, giving her ample opportunity to admire his tight buttocks clad in work-distressed jeans.

'Enjoy,' he said, with a last glance at the house before pressing the paper into her hand

'Don't worry, I will,' she assured him. Swinging her bag off the ground, she attempted to appear non-chalant as she secured the strap on her shoulder and her knees threatened to buckle beneath the weight.

'Are you sure I can't help you with that before I go?'

He was still draped casually against the wall. She wished he would go so that she didn't have to do any of this in front of him. 'No, thank you, I can manage.'

He was in two minds, but in the end he let her struggle. If she wanted to wave the feminist banner in his face, so be it. He'd allow her a honeymoon period; he could afford to. What did he have to lose?

Easing away from the damp stone, Galem added, pointing to his list of things to do. He turned to stare back at the house as he walked down the path and tried to feel nothing. He couldn't. How could he when the new owner was just about to step inside? He looked at her. Up. Down. And back again to the determined chin and the firm lips. She would be a hard nut to crack. He looked forward to it.

He was swamped with feelings, some of which he wasn't proud of. Trouble was, the old place meant more to him than bricks and mortar. It was a symbol of his father's struggle. Stone Break House encapsulated something his father had said to him when he'd been starting out. If you didn't care you didn't win. It was a simple philosophy he had taken to the nth degree. It had always served him well, though, perversely, caring as he did had given him the reputation of being hard. And maybe that was true. He didn't want people who didn't care around him.

It was the same with Stone Break House. He cared, and he knew for certain that the new owner couldn't care half as much. He'd planned his tactics well before tonight. His strategy was simple. He would humour the new owner, and then buy her off. But then Cassandra Bailey Brown had landed in a ditch in her silly little suit and high-heeled shoes, and everything had changed when he'd yanked her from the car.

How long would she last? He glanced at her again. He knew what was waiting for her in the house; he'd had a preview. Knowing that meant he couldn't just leave her; he had to be sure she was safe.

He reached the shadows of the outbuildings and chose a spot where he could see everything that was happening at the front door. She was battling with the padlocks. It hurt him to see the place chained. The solicitor had insisted the place was locked up tight, but that hadn't stopped him climbing in through a window. Brushing a hand across his eyes,

Galem grimaced. Feelings as strong as these were inconvenient—they clouded the brain.

The chains fell to the ground. She pushed them to one side and opened the door. The house had fallen so quickly into disrepair he could hardly believe it, and it carved a wedge out of his heart just to see it neglected like this. He was impatient to get started, to buy it from her and restore it. He wouldn't rest until it burst with life again.

She turned around before stepping inside, almost as if she sensed his presence. Or maybe she was having second thoughts. He might have brightened if he hadn't been so concerned. He didn't want her to hurt herself. He should go to her, go round with her and help her, but that would make it too easy for her, and she might decide to keep the house. He couldn't risk it. He just had to stand here and wait for her to break. Wait for the scream…

'Double two, nine five seven triple zero…' Every part of her was tense, but at least she hadn't resorted to a wussy scream. Yet.

Caz listened, and then groaned when she heard the familiar voice of the local butcher. She'd already got him to the phone once already. She made her apologies and tried again. 'Double nine two five seven triple zero…' No, that was someone else's fax machine…

Galem, Galem, Galem. Cursing softly, Caz redialled. She resented Galem climbing inside her head, but he was the only person she knew to call. And she couldn't find the scrap of paper he'd given her. She'd glanced at it, and then stuffed it in her pocket, but now she couldn't find it. Still, her brain should work, shouldn't it?

Dithering about wasn't like her and neither was forgetfulness, or spiders the size of dinner plates and nests of mice in the bath. 'Bath!' Caz exclaimed to the empty room, running a distracted hand through her designer do.

Pacing the floor, she glared at the phone in her hand. If there'd been any hot water at Stone Break House, any water at all, or even one room with a door or ceiling intact… The list of disasters went on and on. She guessed tiles must have come off the roof and the rain had got in, and after that it was a short journey to disaster—rafters collapsing, systems failing. And now it was pitch black outside and she had no light other than the screen on her phone, and that would soon run out of battery. Added to which, she had no heat, no food, no sanitation, and nowhere to sleep—short of curling up in the bath with the mice, of course.

But she did have that fortune of beauty preparations, which she had brought with her in anticipation of some serious self-indulgence, Caz remembered, taking a well-aimed kick at her designer bag.

Brushing up against the suspiciously furry walls, she shuddered. Stone Break House stank of damp and decay. It was a prize-one example of a dump, and she knew a lot about dumps. But even the children's home had been a palace in comparison to this. So why did she feel so determined to restore the place? How was it she could picture Stone Break House becoming a place where people would feel warm and welcome?

She laughed into the silence. Impossible tasks were her speciality, weren't they? Or, at least, they were Cassandra's. There wasn't a problem at work Cassandra couldn't get around. But this... Caz shuddered and tried to feel brave.

Double two five nine seven triple zero... 'Yes!' It was ringing, but, so far, no reply. How many more chances would she have before her battery went flat and she was alone in the dark? If only she could remember Galem's number. She started chomping on what was left of her nails. Cassandra wouldn't have lost the number. Caz Ryan, however, had been too busy drooling over the gorgeous man as her body had prepared for some high octane fantasy adventures.

CHAPTER THREE

SHIFTING the phone to her other shoulder, Caz occasionally shuddered as she brushed imaginary spiders off her jacket. The trouble was, even if she got through to him she just had to hope Galem knew the number of a local guest house…

'Galem?' She brightened, hearing his voice. 'Galem, is that you? Galem!' Caz shrieked, clutching her chest. Galem was standing right behind her! 'How did you get in?' she shouted, angry that he'd surprised her.

'The door was open…' He flashed a torch in her face.

'Turn that off. All right, turn it on again.' Better to be blinded than blind-sided; she wanted to keep track of him. She was in the middle of nowhere at night in a ruined house with no means of summoning help if things turned awkward with a man she didn't know.

She refused to listen to the inner voice assuring

her that Galem wasn't the pouncing type. She had been dragged up in the school of hard knocks and knew you could never take anything for granted. 'How did you know I would need you?' she said suspiciously.

'Now let me see,' he said dryly, looking around.

She had inadvertently massaged his male ego. Big mistake. 'There's nothing here I can't handle— Okay,' she admitted when his lips tugged up with amusement, 'I'm glad you're here.'

His gaze moved to her mouth and settled there.

'Yes, I'm glad to see you,' she said, pressing her lips together to hide how plump they felt, 'because things aren't quite as I expected them.' The truth was she had never needed Galem's solid presence more. He was a dragon slayer—a mouse would be nothing to him. The temptation to throw herself into his arms and seek shelter from all the as-yet-unidentified monsters in the house was overwhelming, but fortunately with the effect he was having on her she had more sense.

'Does the house scare you?'

He wanted her to be scared. He wanted her to admit she was wrong and ask him to take her to the nearest station.

She wanted to be brave, more than anything she wanted to prove her courage, but here amongst the creatures who had taken up residence in her house she was an unrepentant coward. 'I'm not scared,' she said, pulling a face. 'What on earth made you think that?'

'Let's call it intuition, shall we?' he drawled in a way that made her shiver.

Let's not! She didn't want him reading her mind. 'You haven't told me yet why you came back.'

'I thought I'd better check up on you.' His brow wrinkled as he stared up at her through a dark fringe of lashes. 'You sounded pretty strung out when I walked in. What's up?'

What's up? Couldn't he see? 'Could you lower that torch, please?'

As he did so he then tapped it against his thigh, drawing her gaze to the very place she knew she mustn't look. She dragged her gaze away, relieved when Galem straightened up and walked away a few paces to lean his weight against a supporting beam.

'I've always loved ancient structures,' he murmured, caressing it.

As she heard her ragged sigh creep out Caz had to wonder if she was jealous of a beam now. She had to tell him the truth. The longer she waited to do so, the harder it would get. 'Galem, I'm going to need your help.' Was that a little smile of satisfaction? Caz wondered. If it was it couldn't be helped. She did need him. There was no point in allowing her pride to stand in the way of a sensible decision.

'I can see that,' he said with an annoying degree of assurance.

Humility clearly wasn't his style, Caz conjectured. She pressed on. 'We can both see the house is a wreck, and I need to see a way forward—'

'Why? Why don't you just sell it—let someone else do the worrying?'

Because she wanted to. And why was he so quick off the mark with that suggestion? Did Galem want the house for himself? She pushed that thought away; it was too ridiculous. What would he do with a house of this size?

'I'd just sell it, if I were you.'

Oh, would you? she thought grimly. But then she welled with emotion, which she hadn't expected. The house touched something deep inside her. She couldn't even fully explain why to herself, so the chances of explaining why to Galem were nil.

He touched her arm lightly as if he sensed the way she felt, but she knew he didn't want her here. She could feel it. She could also feel her heart turning somersaults just because he'd touched her, which was very inconvenient.

What he couldn't know was that that consoling pat was one of the most intimate touches she had ever received. That was the trouble with emotional starvation—you never knew where boundaries lay. Sometimes as a child she used to think she would even exchange the rag doll she'd made in sewing class for a hug.

And there was something about Galem's touch, even that impersonal touch. His fingers had slid down her arm from shoulder to elbow so lightly she'd barely felt them, but it was something to put in her emotional bank and draw on when she needed. Of course Cassandra had shown her lots of ways to feel good about herself, but you couldn't cuddle up to money on a cold night.

'Not so good—'

She jerked to full attention as Galem spoke. He was swinging the torch as he examined the crumbling ceiling, some of which was open to the rafters, she noticed now. 'But all repairable,' she insisted doggedly. If this old house was what it took to make her feel she had a home, she would do anything to restore it. This wasn't a project for her any longer, this was a mission.

To her surprise Galem agreed with her, saying that everything in the house could be made right at a price. That was good news and bad news; she didn't have a bottomless pot of money. 'It's a pity the solicitor didn't warn me so I could have organised a proper loan with the bank.'

'They probably didn't want to frighten you off with a long list of "things to do".'

It was the most reasonable thing he'd said to her—factual and without edge. It made her wish for ridiculous things, like that they could be friends, maybe.

They were standing on opposite sides of a huge divide. She wanted the house as much as he did. There was no resolution to that problem. What he should do was walk away. But he didn't want to.

Instead he wanted something he couldn't have—the house and her. She was feisty and determined, and she touched something inside him.

'You were right, it is a dump,' she said, forcing him to refocus. 'And as for basic amenities?' She was smiling. 'Let's not even go there.'

He laughed. 'Not to mention the décor—'

When Galem laughed it was a rich, warm, engaging sound.

'The Barney Rubble School of interior design,' she suggested.

'You could be right.' He trailed the beam of the torch across the ceiling.

'I've noticed Barney Rubble lives next door,' she said.

'You have?'

As Galem rasped a firm thumb pad across his stubble she was fascinated.

'The cartoon character Barney Rubble,' he prompted.

Humour was tugging at his lips, and a lock of his inky black hair had caught on his lashes. Imagining him stretched out on a sofa watching cartoons made her smile broaden.

Get a hold of yourself, Caz Ryan! Cassandra warned.

'I was given to understand no one else lived on this road,' Caz said on a serious note. 'But there's definitely an old man living in the shack next door.'

'You mean old Thomas?' Resting his weight on

one hip, Galem held her gaze in a way that made her heart pump faster.

'Yes…' Clearing her throat, Caz tried to order her thoughts. 'That must be him.'

From the tone of Galem's voice she gathered 'Old Thomas' was no threat to her. He was surely less of a threat to her than Galem! 'I don't know his name,' she admitted. 'All I know is that I saw an elderly man chasing chickens by torchlight next door…'

'Keeping them at home can't be healthy, can it?'

'Maybe they keep him warm at night…'

The way Galem was looking at her made it impossible not to think what it would be like cuddled up with him in a big, cosy bed. He had a way of staring into her eyes as if he could see everything she was thinking. She quickly looked away again.

'This house is a listed building,' he said, easing the tension by walking away.

'Really?' She was relieved just to breathe again.

'It's going to take a special type of dedication to bring it back to life.'

That sounded very much like a challenge. 'I've got all the dedication it takes.'

Galem's jaw firmed, but he didn't rise to the bait, he just kept on with the *son et lumière* effect he was creating on the ceiling. 'This central area dates back to the sixteenth century…'

'And most of the original dust is still intact,' Caz felt driven to observe. This idea of his that she was

incapable of handling the project was getting
under her skin.

'Someone loved it once,' Galem murmured.

'And someone will again.'

He turned to stare at her. For a moment she
thought he believed her, but then his expression
changed.

'I recommend you hoover the walls,' he said,
running the flat of one hand across them.

She'd had enough. 'Are you determined to put me
off?'

'Not at all…'

But a shudder was already speeding down her
spine. What sort of creatures did he suggest lurked
between the stones? Caz wondered, screwing up her
eyes to stare more closely at them. Unconsciously
she gravitated towards Galem, just in case.

They were standing very close now, and as she
looked up he looked down. She felt compelled to say
something…anything. 'Is the ceiling safe?' How
beautiful his mouth looked when he frowned.

'You'll be light enough to walk up there in safety,
I expect…'

He expects? What if he proves to be wrong and the
floor gives way? Ground floor only, Caz concluded,
not that she had the slightest intention of revisiting
the upper rooms after her earlier encounter with the
mice. With a shrug Galem smiled into her eyes, and
she guessed that remark about her weight was
probably the closest to a compliment he ever came.

'There'll be woodworm, too, I expect,' he said, shining his torch on the banister leading to the first floor.

'So there's wet rot, dry rot, woodworm, mice and spiders as big as dinner plates—'

'You'd better use earplugs.'

'Earplugs?' Was the house on a flight path? Or in the middle of the army training ground, perhaps?

'To stop anything crawling in while you're asleep…the same with your mouth.'

'And nose?'

'You choose…but I wouldn't recommend both.'

She held her breath as he raised his arm; she was so sure he was going to brush her hair out of her eyes, and her face was already tingling. But then he clutched the back of his neck instead, and looked at the door. She didn't want him to go yet. As if he read her mind he pressed her back against the wall. She was instantly melting, eyes closed, heart—

'Look out!'

Heart stopping! Caz's eyes flashed open at Galem's warning, and then she screamed. Far from being the prelude to a romantic moment pushing her back against the wall had been to move her out of the way of a troupe of marauding mice. She hated mice. They moved even faster than spiders!

Without thinking what she was doing Caz launched herself at Galem. Locking her hands around his neck, she cried into his chest. 'I thought I could handle this…'

Her voice was muffled, which made her seem more vulnerable than ever, and her breath was warm against him. He couldn't remember the last time he'd felt like this—the last time anyone had clung to him like this. 'There's no shame in admitting you were wrong,' he told her.

'I'm not wrong,' she retorted stubbornly. 'I just need time to get used to things here.'

His face was buried in her hair. He inhaled deeply. She smelled so good, like wildflowers in a summer meadow. 'That's quite a colony of mice you've got there.'

'I'll get used to them, too,' she lied, clutching her chest.

'Get real... You can't stay here overnight. I won't let you.'

'You can't stop me—'

He put up his hand before she could get into the feminist issues again. 'I wouldn't stay here. Is that good enough for you? Plus, you've had one bad shock tonight, you don't need more.'

She gazed around and he could tell she was coming round.

'I can look after myself, you know.'

'I never doubted it, but not here, not tonight. While I'm here why not take advantage of me?'

He saw the flicker in her eyes. So, she'd like to. But she was still as wary as a doe that hadn't been covered by a buck. Then he saw the answer to the

problem hovering in a corner. 'Hey, look at this…'
One of the little fellers had got left behind.

'What are you going to do with it?' She clutched
her throat.

Walking across the room, he picked up a spade
that had been discarded on top of an old sack, and
advanced on the mouse.

'Don't kill it! *Don't kill it!*' She ran to him and
clutched his arm. The mouse looked helpless
suddenly, frozen in the beam of his torch. Twitching
up the sack, he tossed it over the mouse and sho-
velled it up. 'I'm not going to kill him, don't worry,
I'll take it outside and dispose of it—'

'Don't leave me! *Don't leave me!*' Panic-stricken,
she hobbled after him.

'Okay,' he said in a soothing tone, 'I'll let you
supervise his release.'

Was he mad? He was mad. Caz was shuddering
so badly she had to do a little dance to get over it.
'Wait!' she commanded as Galem ducked his head
to go through the door.

'What?' He stood frozen, arm outstretched, with the
mouse balanced neatly on the shovel beneath the sack.

She almost cannoned into him and had to take a
moment to restore her equilibrium while Galem
lounged back against the door frame, waiting for her.
Even through the grainy miasma of shock he looked
amazing. He was all shoulders and chest, clad in
something darkly Aran, and down from that, skim-
ming some important bits, were those long, lean,

denim-encased legs, tipped with kick-the-door-down boots.

Caz refused to compute what she'd seen on the skim. Galem had very big feet, she concluded. 'I'm ready to help you with the mouse,' she said, in case he was in doubt at all.

Lowering the spade, Galem rested it gently on the ground. 'Just take the sack away, Caz, and then he'll run…'

Something leapt inside her as he called her Caz. It moved through her body until it grabbed something in her stomach and twisted it.

CHAPTER FOUR

MUSTERING all her courage, Caz approached the sack. Plucking up one edge with her fingertips, she sprang back with a sound of revulsion.

The mouse was surprisingly slow on the uptake and surprisingly tiny. It looked straight at her with its bright beady eyes, and then, once it was satisfied that she had no intention of moving, it stared to the left and then the right as if it had reached some mousely crossing before shooting away.

She stood motionless at Galem's side, feeling they'd done the right thing. 'I need somewhere to stay tonight, don't I?' she said frankly.

'Yes, you do,' he agreed, lips tugging up at one corner in a way that made her heart rate quicken.

She narrowed her eyes just to let him know this wasn't a total climb down. 'I'll be back in the morning, of course.'

'Of course.' Galem's mouth settled in a way that

put a crease in his cheek. 'So what did you have in mind for tonight?'

'Somewhere with a ceiling,' Caz suggested. 'And doors would be a bonus.'

'You don't ask for much.'

'There's more,' she told him promptly. 'I want water. Lots and lots of water. And I mean hot, clean, running water, not a stream or a stagnant puddle—'

'And you expect to find all this in Hawkshead?'

The way he dipped his head to tease her ran heat into parts of her that had remained inactive for years, but he was the best hope she had of finding a warm bed for the night. 'All I want is a respectable guest house with hot and cold running water.'

'I'm afraid there aren't any guest houses in Hawskhead. So what do you plan to do now, Cassandra?'

'No guest houses? You're kidding me?'

'I'm perfectly serious,' Galem assured her.

Where had she landed up—Desolation Alley? Her fantasies were slipping down the drain one by one. The big house, living in the lap of luxury, lady of the manor, all that stuff, everything lay in tatters at her feet. Plus the car was a wreck and she was stuck here for the foreseeable future. Great.

Right on cue Caz's stomach rumbled, reminding her how long it had been since she had last seen a plate of food.

Galem raised a brow. He could afford to. He was

warm, clean and confident, while she was starving, freezing and filthy. How had that happened?

She was the executive here, Caz reminded herself, and Cassandra was always immaculate—if not well fed. Cassandra's calorie-conscious diet could scarcely be called satisfying. The thought of rich northern delicacies cascaded into Caz's mind, egged on by the fact that all she'd eaten that day was one low-fat yoghurt and a handbag-size bottle of water purchased from the petrol station. 'There has to be a pub in the village.' She spoke with determination.

'Not one that you can walk to.'

The way Galem was looking at her suggested he was waiting for her to break down and howl. 'Well, can we drive there?' she persisted.

'Possibly.'

'Possibly? What does that mean?' She frowned at him ferociously, brushing aside all the beauty tips she'd ever read about facial expressions encouraging lines.

'There's a possibility I might drive there,' he elaborated.

Well, don't do me any favours! She didn't like the way Galem's lips were tugging up in a predatory way as if he was enjoying every minute of this. 'Does the pub have rooms?' Right now she would have sold her grandmother—if she'd had one—for a lift to the pub, even in Galem's tractor.

'I suggest we go to my place so you can clean up first.'

His place? Not a chance. Was he mad? He was mad, and she already knew that, or why was he here staking his claim to a house they both knew was a wreck? 'I wouldn't dream of putting you out,' she said, trying to keep the sarcasm from her voice.

'You wouldn't be,' he said matter-of-factly.

She broke eye contact to give herself chance to think. She couldn't risk going to his house. 'I'd rather eat first. I'm starving.'

'Fine. I'll take you for dinner.'

Dinner? Could he afford it? She had given him the once-over before she could stop herself. And he'd seen her. 'Don't worry, I'll go Dutch.'

'It won't break the bank…this once.'

The Cassandra in her reacted positively to the suggestion of dinner. The glossies were full of fabulous restaurants tucked away in unsuspected places. 'Well, if you're sure about this…that's very kind of you.'

'You look like you need something inside you.'

Her heart started pumping like a steam train going downhill. She didn't dare contemplate what he meant.

'I know just the place,' Galem said, leading the way to the door. 'The lightest pastry you'll ever eat,' he said, 'and the gravy…' He smacked his lips, drawing her gaze back to them.

It was hard to concentrate and remember that however fragrant and tasty, fat-filled food did not appear on Cassandra's diet sheet. 'Is it a good res-

taurant?' Caz asked in the faint hope of a Michelin
star to ease her conscience.

'The best,' Galem said with a winning smile.

She couldn't hold back a tiny, contented sigh.
The thought of food, warmth and Galem was a hint
that things were going to turn out better than she
had expected. She had already located the nearest
salad bar to her office in Leeds, but quite suddenly
the idea of counting calories didn't appeal.
Cassandra had grown used to the best things in life,
and Galem had declared his intention to introduce
her to the best of Hawkshead—what more could
she possibly ask of him?

Her suit was ruined, and the mouse incident had
persuaded Caz to change into an outfit that didn't
leave her legs bare. She didn't have much choice in
her bag, as she had packed for Cassandra's anticipated five-star stay.

Rummaging around she found a cashmere track
suit, which the assistant in Harvey Nichols had
assured her would be perfect for the country. She
could change into it in a small pool of light cast by
Galem's torch, which he had kindly balanced on top
of a crumbling wall for her before politely turning
his back. She didn't want to risk any member of the
animal kingdom community running up her legs,
and nor did she want to linger a moment longer than
she had to at Stone Break House in its present condition.

She had no option but to trust Galem, Caz thought as she pulled off her clothes, and she didn't want to let him go, not yet. She wanted him, the house needed him; right now she needed him to show her the ropes in the village. But at the same time she felt naked and vulnerable with so much man standing by. She could hear him breathing in the stillness. She could sense his presence like some mighty power source. Being close to him felt good, especially in the dark in the country, and especially under these circumstances…under any circumstances.

'Are you ready yet?'

Was she ready? Galem's promise of crisp golden pastry and rich, succulent gravy made Caz race into action. Plucking out the first pair of briefs she came to in her ruined designer bag, she wriggled her nakedness into them. They were skimpy see-through red lace. All her underwear reflected a life full of sin and sex. She might be virginal, but that was no excuse for white cotton, and her lingerie was anything but.

'Hurry up!'

She drew in a fast breath as Galem shifted position, but a discreet check proved he hadn't turned around. She hurried to make herself decent, and pulled on the final part of her ensemble, a fabulous two-ply cashmere hoodie.

'Only we don't want to give old Thomas a heart attack, do we?'

She whirled around in time to see 'Old Thomas' raise his bony hand in greeting.

'Not good for his blood pressure…'

'You knew he was there?' She threw a furious stare at Galem.

'You knew he lived next door. It was you who told me about him.'

'There is no next door!'

With a huff of frustration Caz touched a hand to her forehead, trying to block out the reality that had so quickly overtaken her fantasy. 'Okay, there is someone living next door,' she conceded. 'Old Thomas lives next door, and I will remember to be more careful in future…' This was an instruction for herself, and not for Galem.

'I'm hungry, too,' he complained, drawing her attention to his super-flat belly with a pat, 'and if you want to arrive before the food runs out I suggest you get a move on…'

A restaurant where the food ran out? It had to be exclusive. Stuffing the rest of her things in the bag, she hurried down the path after him.

'Are you sure you don't want to go back to my place first?' he said when they reached the gate.

'I'm quite sure.' She was in no hurry to see *his place*. She knew better than to risk her safety with a man she didn't know, and, had she been feeling reckless, a scruffy bachelor pad—there was no ring on his finger, she'd checked—was hardly a draw. Plus, she had a plan. When they arrived at the upmarket restaurant she would ask around. Surely someone would know if anyone in the village took in paying guests. She was prepared to pay double whatever anyone asked for the simple luxury of a clean bed and a hot shower.

'The village hall…' It wasn't a question, more a resigned statement of fact.

Michelin star? The Cassandra in her raged inwardly. Are you crazy? Restaurant? Cassandra sneered rather unpleasantly this time. Forget it!

It was hardly the smart wine bar she was used to, Caz had to admit. Plus, from the sound of it there was a well-attended hoe-down underway. Brace yourself, Caz's inner voice under the instruction of Cassandra commanded. She'd just keep thinking about the golden pastry and rich succulent gravy, Caz decided, adopting a brave expression. Or was that one of Galem's tall stories too?

'I take it you like line dancing?' he said, mistaking her smile.

'Line dancing?' Caz's jaw dropped in horror. But then Galem turned his face to the porch light. It was the first time she'd got a proper look at him. She'd been freezing in the brisk north wind moments earlier, but now she was blazing with feelings so intense she would have welcomed a snow shower to cool her down. Galem wasn't just good-looking, he was phenomenally good-looking. He was the rough, tough alpha women obsessed over. And she had sexual needs she had never acknowledged before. Luckily she was standing in the shadows where she could self-combust unseen.

'Line dancing?' Galem prompted, offering her his arm.

It took her brain a moment to click into gear. And then she had to remind herself that Hawskhead was in the countryside where people had different interests from people who lived in the city. They were lucky, Caz told herself sternly, and if she only opened her eyes she might find a world waiting for her in Hawskead. The first of those opportunities was standing right in front of her.

'You can stand outside in the cold,' Galem said, lounging against the door jamb, 'or you can come inside with me.'

Caz didn't need much persuading, and was deeply conscious of the difference in their sizes as Galem nudged the door open with the toe of his boot. When he offered her his arm a second time she took it. They were only role-playing; there was no harm in it. She was safe.

His arm felt warm and strong and she barely reached his shoulder. Through the open door, she could smell the warm gravy and it made her mouth water, though the scent of warm, clean man was just as appetising. Closing her eyes, she inhaled deeply. The better to appreciate it.

'Hot hash?'

Galem was speaking very close to her ear and his warm breath made her neck tingle. 'Can I eat it?'

Opening her eyes wide, she looked up at him. She
was flirting with him, Caz realised. And this time
Galem didn't take the opportunity to tease her, he
just looked straight back into her eyes and held her
gaze so she could see his eyes darken. Her heart
juddered and missed a beat when his glance moved
on to her lips. She hadn't thought him interested, not
even remotely. She was melting from the inside out,
and heat was coiling round her hips. 'Can I?' she
whispered, having forgotten the question.

'If you like,' Galem murmured very close to her
lips.

His cheek had creased again. 'It might lead to
something more,' he warned.

'Really?'

Her eagerness made him smile. 'Yeh, like a
chassé and a lock step shuffle…'

He was talking about dancing. She wasn't sure
whether to be disappointed or relieved.

'Well?' he prompted. 'Are we going to stay here
on the doorstep all night, or are you going to take a
chance in the hall?'

Caz looked past him to where she could see
people milling around. Taking her hesitation as
assent, Galem held the door open for her. As she
walked through it his tanned fist was only just inches
from her face. It made her belly hot to think of that
strong hand unfurling to trace the lines of her body.

She welcomed the distraction of a packed hall.
There was barely room to move, and she was shoved

---

up against Galem, which felt good, excellent to have him at her side like a rock defending her. The dancing had begun and everyone seemed to know the steps. She felt a ripple of alarm. She hoped she wouldn't be put to the test. She was a hopeless dancer. 'When do we eat?'

'You have to dance first.'

'What do you mean?' Caz looked at him in alarm.

'I mean you have to dance first to earn your supper.' He shrugged, apparently unaware of her sudden attack of nerves.

'You can't be serious?'

'Why not?'

'You are.'

'I am.' His lips tugged up, proving yet again how much he enjoyed her discomfort. Well, if he was trying to scare her off he'd failed again.

'It's too late to change your mind now.' His green eyes were dancing with laughter. 'Courage,' he said. 'I'll be with you every step of the way.'

CHAPTER FIVE

THE temperature inside the village hall was approaching tropical, and Caz was in the wrong outfit again. No one else seemed to care that their cheeks were rosy red and heat radiated off the walls—they were all far too busy strutting their stuff. It surprised Caz to see how much trouble people had gone to with their outfits, so many of them were wearing stetsons, cuffs and boots, and when Galem tugged off his Aran sweater she saw he was wearing a dark shirt, which, with his snug-fitting jeans and rugged boots, made him look the part.

'No stetson, sorry,' he said dryly when she looked at him, but from the expression in his eyes Caz deduced Galem didn't have a sorry bone in his body. But at least he fitted in. Fitted in? Galem looked great. He would have fitted in anywhere from Rodeo Drive to the village hall. And when he rolled back the sleeves of his shirt and she saw the size of his arms she nearly fainted.

She was still frozen to the spot when he caught hold of her hand and tugged her with him through the crowd. It was then she saw another sight that made her gasp. Resplendent in a yellow jump suit and with his wild grey hair tamed and swept back beneath a Brylcreme sheen, Old Thomas was mounting the steps at the side of the stage with a guitar slung over his shoulder.

Galem was ready to dance from the moment he hit the floor, and had none of her inhibitions. Soon everyone was dancing; except for her. She had spent too long as Cassandra Bailey Brown to let go now. The mould had set around her and she didn't know how to break free. Being jostled, feeling awkward and getting hotter by the minute, Caz was dreading the moment when Galem made her dance. She couldn't dance. She didn't know how. She had never learned. She'd never had the opportunity to learn.

'Come on,' Galem insisted. 'Let's see what you're made of.'

She rose to the challenge, tipping her chin and this time ignoring the helping hand he stretched out. But she was tempted. Holding Galem's hand wasn't something you easily forgot, and the truth was she wanted her hand back in his. His hand had felt warm and sure, and she liked the roughness of it against her soft skin. He was a working man; who wouldn't be turned on by that?

He led her past a raised platform where a team of nubile lovelies clad in little more than white fringed bandages and high-heeled boots were demonstrating the finer points of each dance. They paused as Galem passed by and all of them fluffed a step. He stared back, Caz noticed, openly winking! Brazenly smiling! She stalked ahead. He belonged to her. Or, at least, she was on the point of taking him on as her official handyman and caretaker at Stone Break House. In her mind his services were already booked for the foreseeable future. And when he worked for her she would not permit any distractions. 'When do we eat?' she said, feeling grumpy. 'I've had enough of this—'

'Already?' Galem's lips tugged down in mock concern and there was laughter in his eyes. 'If you've had enough already I'm afraid you won't eat tonight. And I thought you had more guts, Cassandra…' His voice had hardened.

'More than you know.'

'The rules are strict here,' he told her with too much satisfaction. 'They go something like this: no dancing; no eating.'

'Fine.' She glared at him, wondering whose rules he was talking about. 'Let's dance.'

He dragged her close and suddenly her bravado deserted her. The trouble was he felt so good she couldn't think, and when she couldn't think her feet went everywhere. 'I can't do it,' she said impatiently. 'I just can't.'

'Everyone can dance. You just have to let yourself go.'

Could she just *let go?*

'Come on, follow me. I'll help you.'

Galem was still holding onto her, and she was still wanting him to hold onto her—anywhere but on a dance floor.

'I can't—'

'Yes, you can.' And to prove it he held her closer still so she had no option but to move with him.

'No, I can't, and I don't want to.'

'Is that why your foot's tapping in time to the music? I did wonder. Who cares if you make a fool of yourself?'

Caz had rather hoped Galem might.

'Are you afraid to break the mould for one night?'

His question was too close to the truth to answer.

They stood without moving for a moment on the centre of the dance floor. Galem's warmth was flooding through her; she could feel it in every fibre of her being. Could she let go this once? Could she let go enough to dance with Galem? She glanced up, only to see his face crease in the familiar grin again. She looked away quickly, conscious that her face was already burning. Old Thomas was singing his heart out. What was wrong with her? Wasn't Hawkshead supposed to be an escape from Cassandra? Or was she inviting her to take over every part of her life?

'I'm not standing here all night,' Galem said.

'Sorry, I just needed a moment.'

'A moment? You've had half an hour.'

He made her smile. She needed more than a moment to get over the way Galem made her feel.

'You can't resist this music,' he said as the infectious rhythm gathered pace.

'Well, it's hard to ignore it when it's playing at twenty decibels.' The best she could hope for was to jig about in her clumsy way and try not to tread on him. But then reprieve came in the shape of a trolley loaded with plastic cups and orange juice.

'Better grab a drink while we can,' Galem advised. 'Orange squash?'

He had to ask twice because she was looking at his lips...his beautiful, *beautiful* lips. And then she had to do a quick reality check: Cassandra/London wine bar/Chardonnay. Caz Ryan/Hawkshead village hall/orange squash. 'Thank you, I'd like that.'

Lifting a giant-sized jug, Galem poured her a glass. She was so thirsty, and the orange squash was refreshing and delicious. Cramming a handful of the crisps he offered into her mouth, Caz studied the lines of dancers. They were jigging away without partners like cowboys of old who had felt the need to dance, but not with each other.

And in a mirror there was Caz Ryan hovering; no confidence at all. It reminded Caz of her need for Cassandra and of the fact that she had only ever been successful as Cassandra. Caz Ryan never tried new things, because she knew before she did so that she would fail. Caz Ryan didn't expect anything from life, or from anyone, except Cassandra; Cassandra had never let her down.

But Cassandra wouldn't be standing here on the edge of the dance floor in Hawkshead village hall trying to decide whether or not to join the party, Caz reminded herself impatiently. Cassandra had been left outside the door.

'Are you ready to walk the line, Caz?' Galem said, taking the plastic cup from her hand.

Concentrating fiercely, she nodded her head.

To begin with it was a disaster. Each time she thought she knew what she was doing and took a firm step everyone shot off in the opposite direction. Galem had no such difficulty, he had obviously been born to dance. He had a natural rhythm and, far from making a fool of himself, was attracting a lot of attention. An admiring circle had soon formed around him. Caz longed to retreat to the sidelines, but Galem wouldn't let her. Each time she tried to sidle towards the edge of the dance floor he brought her back. She stumbled left and stumbled right, and nearly fell into him at one point. She could run or she could get a grip of this... Tearing off her hoodie she saw Galem watching her out of the corner of her eye. He was waiting to see what she would do. Well, he'd find out. She was going to be the best dancer there if it killed her.

Or not!

Caz jumped a mile as Galem's hand landed on her shoulder.

'What are you doing?' He had to bring his face close to ask the question above the noise and she could see the humour in his eyes.

'I'm dancing.' But what was he doing, was more to the point. His hand was sliding slowly down her arm, drawing her towards him and provoking stampedes of sensation as it went. 'What do you think I'm doing?' she managed faintly. 'You can let me go now…'

'I'm afraid that's not possible.'

'Not possible?' she said, putting up some token resistance. 'Why not?'

'Because this is a couples' dance. Are you normally so confused? I do hope not, Cassandra…'

So did she, Caz thought. She had to relax, and she might as well start now. If she was going to relax anywhere, Hawkshead was the place to do it.

But. Having adjusted his grip, Galem was pressed up hard against her. She could feel every inch of him. She'd never been held like this before by anyone, never been held like this before ever…

'I like it when you look bewildered,' he murmured against her face. 'It's almost as cute as when you dance.'

Cute? No one had ever called her cute before.

'Come with me,' he said.

She hesitated, resisting the tug on her hand. 'Go where?' she said. She had been comfortably nuzzled against his chest and there was nowhere she would rather be…except perhaps alone with him. But then the music changed, spoiling everything. It was too fast, too loud, and the whole place erupted into shouts, stamps and whistles. The one good thing about it was that Galem was forced to sweep her out of the way of the super-efficient chorus line that threatened to mow her down.

'You'll never get the hang of the dancing if you don't pay attention.' He laughed.

At that moment Caz couldn't have cared less about the dancing. She hid her smile. They were almost flirting. She wished she had the nerve to tell him she wanted to get the hang of it. She had never held a man before, and it was something she was keen to investigate further. As he took her hand she went with him willingly, anticipation of what was coming next making her tighten her grip.

But he stopped at the steps where some of the better dancers were performing on a platform. 'Where are you taking me?'

'Up there.'

'Oh, no…'

Galem just grinned, and, putting an arm round her waist, hoisted her up onto the platform.

'I can't do this,' Caz exclaimed when Galem sprang up beside her. 'And you know that.' She turned on her heels, fury propelling her.

He caught hold of her and brought her back. The last thought in his mind was to humiliate her. Maybe it had been in his plans at one time. At first he'd considered all sorts of plans to drive her away. But in the past hour he'd realised how unhappy she was. Beneath her Cassandra Bailey Brown brittle shell there was a tender, quirky woman, striving to break out; the type of woman who would be an asset to any business. If Caz could only lose her big city pretensions and realise that money wasn't everything, she might even make a good job of Stone Break House. The house had never been intended to impress, it had been built as a home. He wanted her to understand that, to see things as they were. 'I'm not trying to humiliate you,' he assured her, holding her in front of him.

'You'd better not,' she warned him, holding his stare.

He kept his promise as the music overtook them. Holding her round the waist, he made sure she was travelling in the right direction. As soon as he was certain he changed his grip to her wrist to give her more freedom, but then he noticed how slender it was; fragile. He changed again to draping an arm across her shoulders. He decided to lead her to a part of the platform where she would be less exposed. Dancing with her felt good, even when their fingertips were barely touching; she felt good. He was more relieved than he could express. If she had retired into the shadows or had refused him and bolted it would have been a giant step back.

'Galem, I—'

'No…' He wouldn't allow any hesitation now. Dipping his head so he could stare her in the eyes, he placed a finger over her lips, stifling her complaint. No, he mouthed with a smile of encouragement.

'I'll break your toes...'

'I'm prepared to risk it.'

He proved it, swinging her into the air and carrying her as they danced so that her feet didn't touch the ground once. She glared into his eyes, pretending to be angry, but he could see she was enjoying herself. It made him smile. He didn't like pushovers in any area of his life; they were no use to him. He liked the idea of being a wall for Caz to kick against, especially when it made her lose her inhibitions and relax.

CHAPTER SIX

'IS THIS your idea of dancing, Galem?' Caz said as he whirled her round.

'It's the safest option,' he said with honesty.

She looked at him, undecided for a moment, and then her face broke into laughter. He laughed too. He felt as if he'd just cut the greatest deal of his life. After that she melted a little and then a little bit more. She was starting to trust him and feel safe, which made him feel good. They were having a good time; a great time. She could hold his gaze with confidence and laugh into his eyes. It was as if she'd crossed some huge divide and found it was fun on the other side.

When he set her down he steadied her with the greatest care, one hand on either arm. He was in no hurry to let her go, no hurry at all. He'd never felt like this before. They stood in silence for a moment staring at each other and then, and only because he felt it was too soon to move things on, he said, 'I promised you'd enjoy this, didn't I?'

As the musicians had sensed a change in mood was called for the music slowed to a seductive rhythm, and a plangent melody rang out. The urge to draw her close overwhelmed him. He gave in to it.

This time it was easy, she melted in his arms, and it was he who had to adjust his position. He didn't want to frighten her, she felt so good, but the vulnerability he had sensed made him check the desire to pull her as close as he wanted to. What he wanted was to feather kisses all over her face, and run his tongue down her neck to her cleavage and hear her moan. He wanted to suck her ear lobe and rub his stubble against the sensitive hollow above her collar bone. He wanted to make love to her.

'Come here, come closer, townie...' He noticed how she quivered when his warm breath brushed her neck. He inhaled deeply, or maybe that was a sigh of contentment; he made them so rarely, he hardly knew.

This was like nothing she'd ever experienced before, Caz thought as Galem's arms closed around her. A lifetime of no hugs and then these hugs from this man. What was a girl supposed to do?

Galem was the first man, the first person to take her in his arms and hold her close. She was deeply affected by it, and perhaps in danger of reading too much into it. She was glad to have the steady rhythm of the music soothing her. If nothing else she had this to bank, along with all the other things she'd felt since meeting Galem.

He coaxed her to move gently with him until she

relaxed. First her shoulders and then her arms, and now one of her hands had crept up to rest alongside her face against his chest. Her other hand was enclosed in his, though that was different. She was frightened to move it, even a little bit in case of the wrong messages.

The wrong messages? She wasn't sure how much more she could afford to relax brushing intimate parts against him. She guessed a man like Galem would be used to more sophisticated lovers and would think nothing of it. He would expect her to be like all the rest, but she wasn't...

His hands tightened around her as if he sensed her anxiety. She had to stop thinking these thoughts. He could read her too easily.

Caz tried to persuade herself that she was over-reacting. She told herself firmly that this wasn't an earth-shattering moment, or even an occasion for examining all the stuff in her head—it was just a dance.

Just a dance?

Nothing so far had been that simple with Galem.

She straightened up and eased back, smiling up at him to show she was enjoying herself in the most platonic way. He brought her close again, nuzzling against her briefly in a gesture she was sure was meant to give her confidence. She consciously relaxed. She didn't want to make a scene, or have Galem thinking he was wasting his time trying to entertain a sulky woman who didn't know how to enjoy herself. This was just a bit of fun, and there was nothing wrong with that.

Caz was surprised to discover how well they fitted together even though he was so much bigger than she was. She couldn't help wondering if he found her attractive, and then told herself not to be so silly. Why would he? There were lots of pretty girls around, girls without issues, girls who loved the countryside as much as he did, and would slot into his life right away.

'Are you enjoying yourself yet?' He dipped his head to ask the question, staring into her eyes so she couldn't look away.

He had no idea how much. 'Yes,' she said, with a smile that was both genuine and guarded. She didn't want him to think she was making a play for him. She didn't want him second-guessing her thoughts either.

And then instead of looking away as she had expected he kept on staring at her. His eyes were warm and kind, and she had to stop staring at his lips. Kind. He was kind. Galem was just being kind to her.

She was like a feather in his arms, and the thought of matching his strength against her softness, of placing that strength at her disposal, was dangerously appealing. He knew more than anyone that just occasionally you had to give in to temptation. He made a signal towards the stage she couldn't see to keep the tempo of the music slow.

This time when he brought her close she came to him as if she belonged there. She was growing brave enough to tease him, testing herself against him before pulling away. He found that a real turn-on.

The rhythm of the music throbbed suggestively all around them; it reached up through the soles of their feet, making every part of him vibrate. He wondered if she felt as aroused as he did. He wondered about her inexperience. Did she have any experience of men at all?

He fixed his stare on the rapid pulse beating in her neck. She'd had fun and relaxed and had opened up to him. She had revealed herself to him in more ways than she knew. And he couldn't deny he was puzzled by what he'd learned. She was a woman in two parts, which only made the urge to know her better all the more tantalising and pressing.

As the song ended she tensed as if she was unsure what to do next. He held her lightly in a way that allowed her to break away should she want to do so, but she didn't move.

Caz hesitated as the lights dimmed still further, heralding the end of the evening. As the silence between songs lengthened she thought it the longest moment she had ever endured. She wasn't ready to stop dancing with Galem, but she was poised to pull away, to smile brightly and thank him—for the most erotic experience of her life, though, of course, she wouldn't tell him that.

As the music started up again Galem's hands

made her quiver as they moved slowly and confidently to draw her back; she sank against him, stifling the urge to whimper with pleasure as he traced the length of her spine with one firm hand. He continued on again, moving up with his fingers splayed until he reached her hair, and then, cupping the back of her head, he began massaging her with his thumb at a very sensitive place just below the base of her skull. His other hand had found the sway in the small of her back above her buttocks. She arched towards him, she couldn't stop herself. Her breath caught in her throat as she realised what she was doing. It was a blatant invitation for him to explore further.

A small shift of his fingers told her he'd got the message. Her chest felt as if a band had been tightened around it, and very intimate parts of her were growing so heavy. The sensation was new to her, and it seemed to take her over. She had never done this with anyone; she had barely acknowledged her sexuality. Needs were for other people, not for her.

Was Galem aroused? Caz wondered. His gaze was darkened. Was that a sign? When it transferred to her lips she stared openly at his mouth. Then, closing her eyes, she tried to imagine what it would feel like to be kissed by him. The music must be to blame, she realised, dragging herself back.

He watched all this, anticipating it and understanding it. He was in no hurry. He wanted Caz to feel her need, to feel it growing, and he wanted the pleasure of seeing it roll out until she couldn't hold onto it any longer. Every part of him was intensely aware of her, and of the hunger that was breeding inside them both. Lacing his big fingers through her tiny ones, he brought her hand to his lips and kissed it. She made a tiny moan deep in her throat and pressed against him. It was enough for now.

Their hearts were beating in unison and their limbs were as close as limbs could be. Each tiny space between them had disappeared one by one. With a sigh she angled herself, bringing his thigh between her legs. He could feel her warmth brushing against him, and his imagination filled in the sweet swollen spaces. Holding back like this was agony. He wanted to sweep her into his arms and carry her away and make love to her all night, all day, for as long as it took to feel sated.

He couldn't think of anything else, and she was making it impossible, resting her head against his shoulder, leaning into him, applying subtle pressure to his thigh, which she must think he was oblivious to. He helped her, just a little, just enough. He didn't want to frighten her or have her suspect what he was doing. Tiny thrusting movements answered him. She was desperate for firmer contact, but so was he. He loved to hear her sigh. He loved to dip his head and see the focus disappear from her eyes. He loved watching her, and he wanted to see more. He wanted to watch her in the throes of real pleasure, and he wanted to be the one bringing her that pleasure. And above all that Galem thought, easing away, he wanted to see wonder take the place of the wariness in Caz's eyes.

'Bravo,' he whispered, when the music died away. 'You're relaxed...'

Relaxed? This was full and total meltdown. 'I'm a little hot,' Caz admitted. Hot? She was on fire, inside, not out. She was suddenly aware of how far things had gone.

Whispering in her ear, Galem suggested it was a good time to take a break. The next moment her heart was thundering with panic. She was suddenly shy and bitterly aware of her own inexperience. She had led him on, and now no doubt he expected...

They were halfway to the door when Galem tipped his chin towards some hay bales where all the other wallflowers were sitting out. It was a gesture to suggest she join them.

Realisation swept over her in a hot cloud of humiliation. She should have guessed, he'd had enough of her. There were still some dancers on the floor, pretty girls...he probably wanted to partner them. 'I'll be fine,' she said brightly as he excused himself and walked away.

It was time for another reality check, Caz realised as the minutes passed with no sign of Galem. There were two possibilities, neither of which reassured her. Either she had failed the test and he had dumped her in favour of a go-faster model, or she had passed with flying colours and he was visiting the men's

82   DIRTY WEEKEND

room to equip himself for whatever came next. And
she still didn't have a bed for the night. She would
wait here for a few more minutes, and then she'd
start asking around. Someone had to know where
she could stay, and if all else failed she still had a
nice big bath to share with the mice.

But it wasn't in Caz's nature to sit around waiting
for things to happen. There was nothing to be gained
by dwelling on the fact that she was sure she had just
made a complete and utter fool of herself with
Galem. Her glance strayed to the door leading
outside.

Once outside she was able to gain a little perspective, to remember who she was and why she was
there. She was Caz Ryan, and she'd always survived
whatever life threw at her. After a while standing
outside in the night air proved a lot colder than she
had imagined, and, hugging herself tight, she
returned inside the hall.

'You have to join the line for food, love,' a helpful
voice suggested.

The line snaked right round the hall, Caz noticed
now, and she had seen enough of lines tonight to last
her a lifetime.

'Too late—'

It wasn't just her heart this time but her whole
body that gave a little leap at the sound of Galem's
voice. For one crazy tilted second she felt like a
teenager on her first date.

Cassandra would have been ashamed of her, Caz

thought. 'Too late for what? Another dance?' She
kept it casual.

'Too late to join the line for food. It's all gone.'

'What?' Her face crumpled. Galem had no idea
how hungry she was.

His cheek creased in his trademark smile,
warming every part of her except her empty
stomach. 'I'm afraid so. You'll have to be quicker
off the mark next time, Cassandra.'

'Caz,' she reminded him. 'You can't mean it's all
gone?' The scent of food was still heavy on the air.
She refused to believe it until she saw the people in
the kitchen pulling the shutters down. 'But that's not
fair.' She turned to Galem as if he could do anything
about it. 'We danced our hearts out. Haven't we paid
our dues ten times over?' She was certain Galem had
never worked so hard for a meal in his life.

'Lucky for you I had two put aside, isn't it?'

'You did?' Her face lit up and before she knew it
she had thrown her arms around his neck. He felt so
good it frightened her. She drew her arms back the
moment she realised he'd made no attempt to recip-
rocate, quickly adapting her smile into something
more prudent.

'That's where I've been,' Galem said, eyes
burning with amusement as he tipped his chin
towards the kitchen. 'I wanted to make sure you got
something to eat—'

'And somewhere to stay,' she reminded him.

'That too,' Galem reassured her.

As he smiled at her she had to tell her arms to stay where they were and behave.

'Come on, townie. I'll sort you out.'

There was a distinct possibility she might let him, Caz realized, heart pounding as she followed Galem across the floor.

CHAPTER SEVEN

IT WAS agony standing waiting for their food to be dished up and Caz was practically dribbling by the time Galem had coaxed an extra portion of chips out of the plump lady in charge.

He found them a window sill outside in the hall where they could perch and balance their paper plates on their knees.

'So you found me somewhere to stay?' Caz prompted him as soon as the first few delicious mouthfuls had slipped down her throat.

'Somewhere I think you'll like,' Galem promised, forking up some food. 'Here, open your mouth.'

She stared at him blankly.

'Open,' he repeated.

She had plenty on her plate, but Galem wanted to feed her, and he was picking out the best bits for her.

'I guessed you'd like that,' he said when she'd finished.

She had. But it was the teasing tone of his voice that carried warmth all the way to her toes. 'This is all very—'

'What?' he interrupted.

His arm was brushing hers: warm, strong, hard.

'Casual? Nice? Or not posh enough for you, Cassandra?'

Caz drew back a little. Galem had a way of looking in her eyes as if he could read every secret she had. There was no point in bending the truth with him, anything less than a straight answer and he'd know immediately. 'It's nice,' she said. 'Very nice.'

Crazy but true. She was eating off a paper plate with a plastic fork in a village hall painted municipal magnolia, seated on a window ledge overlooking the dustbins, and it was wonderful. Normally she was allergic to anything that came within a mile of a deep-fat fryer, but tonight? Well, tonight was different in a lot of ways…for the first time in years she felt relaxed.

She looked up at Galem and couldn't believe the impact he had on her. Was it really only hours since her car had slipped into a ditch?

Galem's lips were really beautiful…

As Caz's mind continued to ask questions that her brain resolutely refused to answer Galem pointed to the pile of mushy peas on her plate.

'Don't you like them?' he said, forking some up and eating them.

'Not so much.' They held too many memories,

though she wouldn't tell him that. As a child growing up in a series of dreary institutions she'd often begged them from the fish and chip shop together with the chunks of batter that fell off fried fish. The small amount of money she had received as her allowance had invariably been directed towards, if not to the improvement of her diet, then at least to its diversity.

'Mint sauce,' Galem said, breaking into her thoughts, 'that's why they taste so good.' He murmured with pleasure as she accepted a mouthful from his fork. 'Didn't I promise you'd like them?' As he spoke he reached and brushed the hair from her face.

He took his hand away too soon, she wanted to feel his touch again, wanted it to linger this time, wanted to be alone with him, far away from here, from everyone, but...

Caz gazed down at her hands. She wasn't ready for this. She wasn't ready for Galem. Everything was moving too fast, and a man like him was for advanced students only, not novices like her.

He found more tasty morsels for her to eat, and finally she joined in, feeding him chips. It became a race to the finish, which ended in a very messy finale.

'Greedy townie, I ought to punish you for that.' Catching hold of her hand, he held her firmly so she couldn't feed him any more. The look he gave her sent her pulse rate soaring. If she was trying to be sensible she was going the wrong way about it. She was relieved when he had to turn away to take a call.

She tried not to listen, but it was hard not to when he was sitting next to her. He seemed to be talking about some big project and vast sums of money; that surprised her. 'Business on a Friday night?' she said curiously when he slipped the phone back in his pocket.

'Business twenty-four seven, I'm afraid.'

'Your employers must be very demanding.'

He missed a beat. 'Yes, they are.'

She guessed that talk like this must graze his ego, and so she dropped the subject, but it worried her to think she might have to pay a lot more for Galem's services than she had originally thought.

'Let me take that for you,' he said, piling her plate on his. 'Did you enjoy it?'

He had no idea how much. 'Delicious,' she said carefully. She watched him cross the room and dispose of their paper plates in the dustbin bag provided. It was strange to think of this powerhouse of a man being at the beck and call of anyone, let alone people who intruded on his Friday night. But if he loved Hawkshead and had a yen to own Stone Break House one day she could see how it might hold him back.

'We'd better go,' he said when he returned, glancing at the door. 'You still want a bed for the night, don't you?'

'You haven't told me where yet.' Her heart rate doubled.

'Come and see,' he said, holding out his hand. 'I think you're going to like it.'

She wanted to trust him, wanted to go with him, but whatever little common sense she had remaining kept on nagging at her—she didn't know him. On the other side of the argument she'd had a great night. For once she'd let go and become the person she really wanted to be. Plus just about everyone in the hall seemed to know Galem, seemed to like him too…

Okay, she had to make a decision. Like most big men Galem was growing restless; inactivity killed him. She needed somewhere to stay and by going with him it might help her achieve her original thought to employ him as a handyman for Stone Break House. If she went with him now it would give her the chance to find the best way to steal some of his time away from his present employers. Lots of people held down more than one job and were glad to do so, why should Galem be any different?

'You'll feel better after a nice hot shower…'

Caz realised she was frowning at him. But the thought of a nice hot shower certainly got through, especially when she remembered the bathroom at Stone Break House. What Galem was dangling in front of her was the prospect of heaven. 'A hot shower with a door?' A bathroom door had always been an obvious fixture until she'd seen the state of Stone Break House.

'The last time I looked there was a door.'

'With a lock?'

'Naturally.'

'And a window with a curtain I can draw?' Remembering Old Thomas, Caz thought it better to be sure.

'Two, but they have blinds, both working.'

Galem was waiting, but her mind was already made up. Her new home, Stone Break House, wasn't fit to live in yet, and she needed somewhere to rest her head for the night. 'Where is this place? And don't tell me it's a surprise.'

'My place...'

'Your—' Caz's voice stuck in her throat.

'Best I could do at short notice.'

His lips pressed down. Was that with regret or reluctance?

'Ready?' he said, glancing at the door.

As she nodded Caz took it as confirmation that she had finally gone mad. She was going to accept the invitation of a man she didn't know to take a shower at his place and spend the night there.

Her heart drummed a tattoo as she thought about it. Men like Galem were great to admire stripped to the waist on a building site, or in some cheeky advertisement, but she had never come this close to the real deal. Could she handle it? Galem was so big and so confident, while underneath her Bailey Brown shell she was still Caz Ryan from the children's home, still uncertain of herself and her place in the world.

People brushed by as she hesitated. Uncertainty crept in...

Snap out of it! Caz told herself impatiently. She'd made a good life for herself in London, and she could do it again in the north of England. She wasn't a weakling, she was a survivor, and she'd survive this night just like all the rest. 'I'm ready if you are,' she said.

'We're here,' Galem had stopped outside a smart-looking cottage, which formed part of a neatly kept terrace.

Caz's heart leapt as she viewed the newly painted front door and the clean step, but she had learned in life not to take anything for granted. 'Is this your place?'

'It's your bed for the night.'

It was perfect! She turned her face up to thank him, and got the same shock she always got when she looked at Galem. He affected her more deeply each time. His thick dark hair refused to be tamed and as he raked it back she longed to run her fingers through it. Caz stood transfixed as Galem put the key in the lock.

'Well, are you going to stand there all night?'

'This is fabulous,' she said, taking everything in as she walked inside. Fabulous? It was incredible. The cottage was nothing short of a miracle in Hawkshead. It was London chic in a charming Yorkshire shell, all stripped pine floors and cool cream interior, with terracotta throws and hand-knotted rugs. There was even a touch of black tinted glass and steel in the tiny kitchen to make her feel at home. 'I love it,' she said honestly, turning full circle. 'And your employers loan you this?'

'No.'

'So who owns the cottage?' She didn't mean to be rude but her thoughts just blurted out.

'I do,' Galem said as if it were no big deal.

'You?'

'Now, Cassandra,' he drawled disapprovingly, 'surely you of all people could never be accused of judging a book by its cover, could you?'

His voice rose at the end of the question as if he expected an answer. Had Cassandra's fame spread to Hawkshead? Something in Galem's eyes made a chill run through her. She was overreacting again. She was just telling herself to relax when she remembered her overnight bag.

'What's up?' Galem looked at her.

'I've got nothing with me. My bag—'

'Is already here. I put it upstairs in the bedroom.'

Bedroom singular? Was there only one? 'Look, Galem, I can't take your room.'

'Why not?'

'I don't know you.'

'I don't know you either,' he pointed out. His lips were starting to curve. 'Would I be safe?'

She met his gaze, raised a brow and chose not to answer.

'Shower?' he reminded her, shrugging off his jacket.

As Galem hung his jacket on a peg by the door Caz tried not to notice how powerful his shoulders were. Instead she made some fast calculations. There were two comfortable-looking sofas, and she could sleep on either one of them. A wood burner was chuckling happily away, so she would be warm, and the throws looked cosy. 'I'll take the sitting room you take the bedroom—how about that?'

'Shower first?' he suggested, sidestepping the question.

That made sense.

Galem opened the door on a small, neat bathroom that smelled as clean as if it had just been installed. Pointing to a cupboard, he said, 'And you'll find lots of clean towels in there.'

Bliss! She guessed this must be a guest bathroom as there were no personal items on show. The master bedroom had been created out of two smaller rooms, he had told her, and that had an *en suite*.

A smart terrace with two bathrooms? She was going to have to revise her budget if she wanted to entice Galem to work for her. Whatever type of building work he was involved in, it was certainly profitable. The cottage was like a luxury apartment, only far more spacious.

She would have to find the money to employ him from somewhere. Everywhere she looked in the cottage the workmanship was of the very best, and that was what she wanted for Stone Break House.

The proceeds from the sale of her London home had gone on the penthouse in Leeds—she hadn't been able to resist the views—and so she didn't have a lot of spare cash to play with, but the thought of abandoning the old house to its fate was out of the question. The setting in the quarry might look grim at first sight, but she had seen restoration projects where even ugly mining scars had been planted and softened. In the visual sense Stone Break House was a romantic ruin, but she was sensible enough to know that in practical terms there was a lot to do. And do it she would. Each time she thought about the old house she felt a tug. The project was on, and so was Galem. Somehow she had to find a way to afford both of them.

Caz waited until she could hear Galem banging about in the kitchen before stripping off her clothes. It excited her to be naked in his house while he was just a few feet away. Her nipples tightened as she turned on the shower; just the thought of employing him was addictive. By the time she switched off the shower Caz was doubly determined to sign him up. Bathrooms like this were exactly what she wanted at Stone Break House. She could have stood under the power shower all night...

She might have to, Caz discovered when she looked in vain for the towels Galem had promised she would find in the cupboard. She searched every inch of space before considering her options: she could jump up and down and shake herself dry, or she could stand dripping, naked, and yell for help.

When he heard her Galem chuckled. Knocking on the bathroom door, towel in hand, he added, 'My apologies…'

She had opened the door a crack to reach through it, and to his credit Galem kept his gaze fixed firmly on her face. It was inevitable that their hands would brush, and maybe because she was warm from the shower and naked fire shot to her elbows and all points beyond. Galem's hands felt wonderful: warm, dry and smooth.

Leaning against the door jamb, he glanced inside. 'Do you have everything you need?'

Caz glanced at the bundle of fluffy white towels Galem had just placed in her arms and then at him. 'No' rang in her head. 'Yes, thank you.'

'There's a robe hanging on the back of the door you can use.'

The thought of snuggling into a soft towelling robe seemed like bliss. She'd rinsed her underwear in the shower and was intending to risk commando again. A Galem-sized robe was as good as a tent. Perfect. No risk of exposure this time.

And she might as well douse that disappointment. She wasn't a wanton sex kitten, she was an inexperienced virgin with a problem on her hands. Galem earned a lot more than she'd thought, judging by the quality of everything at the cottage, so she

was facing some serious competition on the remu-
neration front. She would have a serious rethink
about his package.

Or not.

CHAPTER EIGHT

As SHE emerged from the bathroom Caz could hear Galem pottering about in the kitchen. As far as he was concerned her desirability factor score was zero. She should be grateful. If Galem had decided to turn up the heat she would have turned tail and run, and where would she sleep then? 'Without milk for me, please...' He was brewing fresh coffee in the kitchen.

The kitchen was small, but surprisingly well equipped. It was also extremely clean. Someone liked cooking, Caz gathered, gazing around. Galem continued to challenge every opinion the Cassandra in her had formed of him.

There was one problem with a small kitchen: space was at a premium with six feet four of solid muscle taking up most of it, which meant that she had to press back against the wall to let Galem pass. She tensed as his body brushed her lightly and hoped he hadn't noticed.

He carried the coffee through to the living room for them on a tray. She was still staring into space daydreaming about what it would be like to have a man like Galem want her. Having put the tray down he came back, squeezing past before she had chance to move.

'Sorry,' he said, reaching over her. 'I need the sugar. I'm guessing yours is without, right?'

Caz held her breath as Galem paused halfway across her. She felt as if she were wobbling on a tightrope with all sorts of forbidden pleasures lurking underneath. When the green eyes looked into hers she blurted the first thing that came into her head. 'Don't you know sugar's bad for you.?'

'They say that all the best things in life are bad for you.'

Caz closed her eyes briefly to absorb this, and when she opened them again it was to find Galem's lazy smile only inches from her mouth.

'But I can tell you with absolute certainty,' he said, murmuring the words so close to her lips they started tingling, 'that *they* are wrong. But maybe not about sugar,' he conceded with a shrug. 'So, I'll let you put it back in the cupboard for me, shall I?'

She was staring at his lips, Caz realised, quickly reorganising her eyeline.

'Sugar. Cupboard,' Galem prompted her. 'You've saved me from myself, Caz. Does that please you?'

If he moved maybe she could breathe again and answer him.

'I'll do it, shall I?' he said, moving past her.

As Galem put the sugar jar in the cupboard Caz's stomach turned over. She couldn't pretend she wasn't disappointed. If he had wanted to kiss her he'd had plenty of opportunity, so she could put that out of her head once and for all.

She hovered by the kitchen door as he settled down on the sofa. Having drained his mug, he put it down on the table, and, reaching forward, he started to unlace his boots. Kicking them off, he wriggled his toes and then, turning to her patted the seat next to him. 'So come here and tell me about yourself, Caz.'

She froze. 'Nothing to tell.' That was far too much man and far too little sofa.

'Nothing?' Galem's brows drew together as he stared at her. 'There must be something. You inherit Stone Break House from an aunt you've never met; you hold down an important post in the city. Fill in a few of the blanks for me, Caz. That's not asking too much, is it?'

It was a great deal too much to ask. She never discussed her private life with anyone—how could she when Cassandra lived one life and she lived another? How could she explain that to Galem? A man like him would never understand. He had probably lived in Hawkshead all his life and wouldn't understand the pressures. He wouldn't understand the need for Cassandra. 'I'm very boring,' she said. 'How about you?'

'Not boring at all,' Galem assured her. 'And I wouldn't describe you that way either...Cassandra.'

She didn't like the way he said the name, it made her nervous. 'Let's just say I'm a very private person,' she said, hoping he'd take the hint.

'That I can live with,' he said. 'Now, are you going to sit down, or are you going to stand there all night?'

If she wanted Galem to work for her she had to re-establish her credentials and fast. And lurking by the door as if he terrified her was not the way to do it. Caz clicked into business mode. 'Before I leave Hawkshead we must make an appointment to conduct a proper inspection of Stone Break House.'

Did she imagine it, or did he flinch at her use of the word 'must'? If his current employers were into coaxing perhaps she had better try it. 'I'd really appreciate your opinion,' she modified, 'and I promise not to take up too much of your time.'

'Tomorrow's Saturday,' he responded flatly.

She should have been on the point of nailing the deal, but instead she was floundering on the back foot like a novice. Patience, Caz instructed herself firmly. Had Cassandra ever failed to win a suitable candidate over rival companies? Leaving her mug in the kitchen, she went to perch next to him on the sofa. 'I realise it's Saturday tomorrow,' she said in a concerned voice, 'but I return to work on Monday—'

'And?' He frowned.

And she couldn't expect him to understand the demands of a high-powered job, Caz reminded herself. 'And so tomorrow is the only chance I have to sort out what we're going to do about Stone Break House—'

'We?'

'I thought you wanted to be involved?'

'You're jumping the gun, aren't you? I haven't agreed to anything, yet.'

Moistening her bottom lip, Caz looked up at Galem through her lashes. 'But you will…' She had everything crossed.

Lust roared up inside him, obliterating every rational thought he'd had about her since they'd met. She was sitting very close, and the look she'd just given him had made him hard. As she leaned towards him he could see the swell of her breasts beneath the neck of the robe. Pressing back against the sofa, he kept his distance, but that couldn't help him when her hand came to rest on his thigh. 'Caz—'

'Galem, I need you…'

His intention had been to remove her hand from his leg, and warn her that the sort of tactics she was employing could get her into a whole lot of trouble, but as his fist closed around her tiny hand she sighed. That was it. Instead of pushing her hand away he twined his fingers through hers. The ache in his groin had grown into a raging agony and inch by inch he drew her slowly towards him. 'Tell me to stop any time you want,' he begged her hoarsely.

'Don't stop,' she said breathlessly.

Her lips were rosy pink, the bottom lip full and slightly damp. Her top lip was beautifully etched in a perfect cupid's bow. Her eyes were slumberous, and her breathing was already rapid. The rise and fall of her chest drew his attention to the swell of her breasts beneath the robe. He wanted to part it and touch them, taste them, knead them, suck them, lave them with his tongue. It would only take the smallest move to close the distance between them and do that. Holding himself back was growing harder every minute and it was a glorious torment for a jaded palate.

Eyes closed, head back, she was offering herself to him. He feathered kisses on her throat to hear her whimper, and when she locked her fingers round his neck he kissed her lightly on the lips, brushing them, teasing them mercilessly. She was hot and sweet and eager, everything he had imagined she would be and more. She pressed into him hungrily, and the knowledge that she was naked beneath the towelling robe tormented him. Finally his hands found their way to her breasts. He could feel her nipples hard and extended even beneath the soft towelling fabric. He stroked them firmly with his thumbs on top of the robe while she clung to him, her eyes black with desire and her lips parted to drag in air. It pleased him to watch her pleasure unfold, just as he had always known it would. 'Do you like that?' he asked her roughly. 'Do you want more?'

Her answer was to lace her fingers through his and drag him close. The tender skin beneath her bottom lip had been abraded by his stubble and her lips were swollen from his kisses. He wanted her naked; he wanted to pleasure her in all the ways he knew how. He wanted to kiss her, nip her, taste her…

She dragged his shirt from the waistband of his jeans and placed her cool palms flat against his hard, warm, naked chest. It felt so good he gasped. Tugging off his shirt, he tossed it aside. She looked at him and he could read her mind. She wanted to feel his chest hair rasping her nipples against it. She wanted to feel his weight pressing down on her. She wanted him to part her thighs and ease the unbearable ache between her legs.

His hands moved swiftly to remove the belt on her robe. He tossed it aside impatiently. Opening the robe was like opening a very special gift. He kissed her again, pressing his hand against her belly and feeling her quiver. She couldn't keep still; her need was furious. She was beautiful, soft, round and rosy pink. As he dipped his head to tease her nipples with his tongue she strained against him, begging him not to stop, never to stop… He told her to be patient and she railed at him. His answer was to kiss her again, plundering the dark recesses of her mouth while she ground her body against him, on fire for him.

'I need you, Galem… I want you…'

He cupped her heavy breasts in his big hands, loving the weight of them and loving the engorged nipples that tempted him on. He suckled one and then the other while she encouraged him, calling out his name and making wordless sounds of need. She was showing him in every way she knew how much she wanted this. Her impatience drove her fingers cruelly into his naked shoulders, but whatever he did to her it wasn't enough—she wanted more.

'Do you want to make love?' he whispered against her mouth. 'Is that what you want, Caz?'

The need to feel her naked against him was over-whelming. He kissed her again, deeply, passion-ately, his hand tracking up her thigh, thrusting the towelling robe impatiently out of the way. She helped him in every way she could, writhing and thrusting against him as he kissed her neck and then her breasts. She was raking his back, exploring the hard muscles, and then she started fighting with the buckle on his belt. It came free in her hands and then the button fly yielded. She looked down, and, real-ising what she'd done, drew her hands away, leaving his jeans gaping. His erection was pressing hard against them; he was in agony. She made it worse, clinging to him, moaning, but some part of him still held back.

'Touch me,' she begged. 'Touch me there…'

He laughed softly against her mouth while his hands continued their exploration. 'You feel good,' he said, parting her lips gently.

'Do I?' she breathed.

'Oh, yes…warm, wet and very, very good…'

She was swollen and ready for him and as she exhaled raggedly he started stroking her more firmly. 'Is that what you want, baby?' he murmured, touching her rhythmically with just the tip of his finger.

She was keening softly, her hand pressed lightly over his. 'Yes, yes, do that, please…more…'

Little of what she said made sense, but it gave him a rush to see her in the throes of so much pleasure. She was ready for more and as he stroked her with his thumb he moved to go deeper, but as he did so she flinched and drew back. He knew right away.

'Why didn't you tell me?'

She sat up and hugged her knees to cover her nakedness, staring at him wordlessly with her big blue eyes.

'I'm not surprised you can't think of anything to say.' Reaching for his shirt, he put it on. He buttoned it up and tucked it into his jeans. Fastening those too, he secured his belt. Swooping down to pick up the discarded robe, he tossed it at her. 'Put that on.'

She looked at him sheepishly as she belted it. 'Galem, I'm—'

'Forget it, Caz. I'll sleep down here tonight. You take the bedroom.'

'I couldn't—'

He ignored her. 'There are clean sheets on the bed. And, Caz—'

'Yes?'

'Don't try that again with anyone. Ever. Understand?'

She paused without turning at the foot of the stairs. At least she had the good grace to blush.

'Good night, Galem…'

She could only see him in profile, and his jaw was set in an unforgiving line. He didn't answer; she didn't linger. Picking up the hem of the robe, she ran as fast as she could up the stairs and didn't stop until the bedroom door was firmly closed behind her.

Too humiliated to think, Caz dropped the robe, climbed into bed, and turned her face to the wall.

It was two o'clock in the morning. With a heavy sigh Galem put his wrist-watch back on the side table next to the sofa. His mind was in turmoil. He'd drifted off only to reach a half-world somewhere between sleep and waking, where Stone Break House had become more important to him than ever, and Caz was a virgin he could never touch. Would never touch again. The end result was a waking nightmare during which he tossed and turned, locked in an impossible quest to find a solution.

There were three burning questions going round and round in his head. Could he live with this level of frustration? Could he seduce a virgin? And what was going to happen when she found out who he was?

104   DIRTY WEEKEND

CHAPTER NINE

CAZ's cheeks were still burning when she woke the next morning. She couldn't believe what had happened with Galem. Couldn't believe she had let things go so far.

Cassandra Bailey Brown and Galem going forward into the future was never going to happen and she needed her career. If Cassandra ever found a man it would be some rich city type. But without Galem to keep the project on stream there would be no Stone Break House. The only thing she could do was to put her embarrassment to one side and pretend last night had never happened. She had to convince Galem that they could still work together.

Caz lay and listened to the silence, wondering if Galem was awake. If only things had been different, if only she had stayed away from him. There were good things in Hawkshead, though it made her smile to think of Cassandra accepting a future that included a crumbling ruin, a peeping Old Thomas, and a paver who liked throwing his weight around. But she had to think past Cassandra to a future when she could be herself. If she could be Caz Ryan in Hawkshead it would all have been worthwhile.

Having decided the best thing to do was take Galem a cup of tea and act naturally, Caz crept downstairs trying not to wake him. She made the tea and then took it into the living room where she could just make out his dark shape on the sofa beneath the throw. There was just enough light outside for her to draw the curtain a crack without putting the light on and disturbing him.

'Tea,' she whispered.

Throwing the covers back, Galem swung his legs over the side of the sofa, rubbed a hand across his eyes and stood up. He was completely naked. Retreating to the door, Caz hovered. 'Sorry, I didn't mean to. I mean, I—'

'You didn't mean to what?' Throwing himself down again, Galem held her gaze as he dragged the cover across his legs.

She mumbled something about tea and started backing out of the room.

'Caz, wait…'

'Shall I put it down here?' she said, skirting the sofa to put the mug of tea down on a side table. She was just straightening up when Galem caught hold of her wrist. She froze, but she didn't look at him.

'Caz, you can't brush this under the carpet.'

'Brush what…?' She kept on staring at the wooden floor, noticing how attractive the knots of wood were in the antique finish.

'What happened last night mustn't happen again.'

Galem released her wrist, but it took her a moment to react.

'I don't want to think of you putting yourself in danger like that,' he said. 'Not with anyone else. You mustn't risk it.'

There was a stinging sensation in her nose that always heralded tears. She straightened up and turned away. He was talking to her like a big brother.

'Promise me,' Galem said.

Silently, she nodded her head.

'Thank you for the tea.'

His voice was easy and relaxed—the old Galem. He was trying to make this easy for her, which perversely made it worse. She heard him put the mug down and reach for his wrist-watch.

'It's barely six o'clock in the morning, Caz.'

She turned round to see Galem raking his hair into some semblance of order.

'To what do I owe this honour?'

'I just thought we should make an early start.' She could see him curbing a smile.

'Well, you certainly did that.'

He flashed her a glance and scratched the stubble on his jaw, a stark reminder that parts of her were still burning from the rasp of it.

'I don't want to ruin your weekend, so I thought

we could start early on the tour round Stone Break House.'

'Good idea.' Sipping his tea, he sighed with approval, and then he gave her another of his penetrating glances, searching for anything more she might have on her mind.

'Would you work for me on a formal basis, Galem?'

'I already have a job.'

'I know that.' Buckling on her confidence, she went for broke. 'I also know you must be very good at it. You're obviously hugely appreciated by your employers, and I can see you wouldn't want to lose your position, but what I'm offering you is something you could do in your spare time.'

'I'm not sure I could work for a woman.'

She wasn't sure if he was joking or not.

'You see, I'm a traditionalist—'

'I would respect you absolutely. I wouldn't dream of throwing my weight around. I'd ask your advice every step of the way.'

When Galem winked she knew she'd been had, but would he take the job? Cassandra was always confident of the outcome of an interview, but she had messed up royally since coming to Hawkshead.

At least teasing her was an effective damper for his libido. He was relieved. After what had happened the previous night he was as keen as she was to get things back on an even keel. Even so, it was impossible to forget how she'd felt in his arms, hard to forget his sheer incredulity at discovering that anyone so sexually naïve could have survived intact for this long in the twenty-first century.

'I would pay you the fair rate, of course,' she went on thankfully, unaware of the track his mind was taking. 'And I'd be here every weekend, of course, pulling my weight…'

Pulling her weight? He had to hide his smile. She weighed around the same as a sack of feathers. But having concluded she must have swallowed a fistful of pride just to get to this point, he nodded sagely and let her go on.

'I'd like you to oversee the project and advise me. Team work, Galem,' she said, offering him the idea like the winning ticket in the lottery. 'Perhaps you could do some of the manual work for me too. We'll have a better idea when we go down there and take a proper look.'

She took it for granted that they would. Putting down his mug, he straightened up to face her. She didn't flinch; she squared her shoulders. He got a mental image of her in the boardroom: she'd be effective; she'd be good. 'I'm listening,' he said, reminding his eyes to curb the smile.

'My problem is time,' she explained. 'I've just taken on a new job, just moved up from London to Leeds, and I can't risk short-changing the work I do.'

'It means so much to you?'

'Yes, it does,' she said, honesty shining from her eyes. From her very beautiful eyes.

'So why Stone Break House?' he said, broaching the subject closest to his heart if not uppermost in his mind with Caz in the room. She was wearing faded pyjamas with teddy bears all over them. They trailed over her naked feet; her tiny naked feet. Clearly these were not one of Cassandra's designer purchases but something cosy she travelled with to feel safe in at night. She hadn't answered him he realised. They were staring at each other in a trance. He quickly snapped out of his. 'Why not choose an easier project than Stone Break House?'

'I never expect anything to be easy. And the amount of work ahead at Stone Break House doesn't frighten me.'

'There are plenty of beautiful conversions in the valley. You could sell Stone Break House and buy something smaller, but truly spectacular, with better views...' He had to try.

'No,' she said, firming her jaw. 'My mind's made up.'

He could see that.

'To be honest with you, Galem,' she went on without prompting, 'I can't even tell you why I want the house so badly. I just know I do. I don't think I ever met my aunt. There's no connection between us, or between me and Stone Break House, nothing that could explain how I feel about it—'

Her cheeks turned scarlet. She mashed her lips together, drawing his gaze.

'If you keep the house you'll need me to help you.'

'Yes, I will.' Hope sprang in her eyes as she looked at him. 'So will you help me, Galem?'

Better that than risk someone else interfering. 'You'd better go and get dressed,' he said, stirring. He saw her flinch and glance down to be sure the throw was still in place, covering him. Satisfied, she relaxed.

'Can't you see it, Galem?' she said as she was on the point of leaving the room. 'Can't you see Stone Break House when it's finished?'

He'd always been able to see it, but what interested him now was the way Caz's face changed as her imagination coloured in the spaces. Her expression was euphoric, and she looked truly beautiful. For a moment he bought into her dream, but then he reminded himself that Stone Break House was his home, always had been, and always would be.

'Well?' she said, prompting him. 'Will you help me?'

'What's in it for me?' Galem the paver had returned.

'Tell me if you can do it first,' she countered, showing him a glimpse of the businesswoman she would be during the week. 'Project management would look good on your CV,' she coaxed, her eyes burning into him.

'On my CV?' He tried not to laugh; this really wasn't the moment. He could practically see the cogs in her mind whirring, telling her that she'd made a blunder, and that men like him didn't have CVs.

'It would be good experience for you,' she modified quickly.

She could think on her feet and her professionalism wasn't in question. 'And do you think I need more experience?' he said, wrinkling his brow as if her opinion really mattered to him.

But she saw through that and her cheeks flamed red again. She blushed so easily it was wrong of him to tease her, but irresistible all the same. He could feel her willing him to break eye contact now, and so he held it a little longer. 'I tell you what I'll do,' he said at last.

'Yes?' She sat forward.

'I'll come to look over the house with you now, and we'll make a plan.'

'You will?' She wanted to go to him and throw her arms around him, tell him how much this meant to her, but, of course, there was no way she could do that now. Just to clear the air completely she said, 'This is strictly a business proposition, Galem.'

'I'm always open to propositions…'

Cocking his head to one side, he looked at her quite seriously, but then slowly the look in his eyes changed and he smiled his long, lazy smile that fired up every part of her. But she could sense the microscopic changes in his eyes that told of something hardening inside him; resolve, she guessed. He wanted the house as much as she did; she must

never forget that. She knew that Galem resented the
fact that she had inherited it, that anyone had inherited it. He thought Stone Break House should
belong to him. As he looked at her now she was
struck, both by the beauty of his eyes, and by the
calculation in them. It suited him to indulge her for
now, but eventually he would find a way to take the
house from her.

The thought of an enemy as attractive and potentially dangerous as Galem clutched her innards and
made them play circus games that involved lots of
spinning and clenching. It couldn't be helped. For
now he was the best chance she had. 'I'd like you to
think about co-ordinating the project for me.'

'You don't know anything about me, or my abilities.'

True. Cassandra wouldn't have taken such a
chance. Rasping a thumb pad across his jaw, Galem
gave another of his cool, assessing glances.

Who was assessing whom here? She had never
come up against anyone like this before. Lucky for
her Galem was a one-off.

Caz's hand crept unconsciously to the tender spot
below her lips where Galem's beard had abraded
her. She felt a tingle of delicious dread at the thought
of working with him on a regular basis, but never
coming close to him again. 'We can soon put that
right. You can tell me all about yourself as we go
round the house.'

'You don't give up, do you?'

'Never.' She held his gaze. Galem's was pure irony. Had he never been through an interview process before? She guessed not. In his line of business recommendations would take him from job to job. 'It would just be a casual chat,' she reassured him.

He remained impassive.

'I'm more interested in you telling me what you think about the house.' She was trying to shift the emphasis so he'd feel he was on familiar ground.

His silence was unnerving.

'So there's no way you'd sell the house,' he said at last.

'Put that out of your mind, Galem. It's not going to happen. I'm going to restore Stone Break House with or without your help. If you agree to help I should warn you I'm short of funds right now, but I'd be able to take you for more hours quite soon.'

He held up his hand to stop her. 'Don't worry about money now, I'll think of a way you can repay me.'

Her body responded immediately, but her head intervened. Galem was always teasing her, or lecturing her; he didn't mean anything by it. The glint in his eyes still ran a quiver of awareness down her spine. She had to remind herself that Galem was simply telling her that she could keep the house just so long as that suited him, and not a moment longer.

But it didn't matter what his terms were, Caz realised, because the die was cast and she couldn't turn back now.

CHAPTER TEN

CAZ elected to walk to Stone Break House with Galem. She wasn't in the mood to be cooped up with him in a rusty Land Rover, or beat-up tractor. There was no pressure to talk to each other while they were walking in spaces that were vast, beneath a sky that was huge.

The early morning air was bracing, not cold, and even the hills didn't seem quite so daunting. Galem had been okay so far, quiet but relaxed, but as they approached the rusty gates his mood changed again.

His jaw set as his hand closed on the rusty gate latch. 'That lawyer really did spin you a yarn.'

'Perhaps.' She said it in a way that didn't encourage any more conversation on the subject. She could be just as stubborn, and use just as much imagery. She ran her fingertips possessively along the sunken railings, telling Galem without words to get over it and get it through his head that the house was hers and was going to stay that way.

As he pushed the gate open he said, 'It's a disaster,' as if that was an end of it, the end of the tour too, even before they set foot inside.

'I prefer to think of it as a blessing in disguise for both me and Stone Break House.' She strode ahead of him down the path.

He caught up with her at the foot of the steps, stopping her there. 'Meaning?'

'The house has been neglected and needs some love, and I need to get out of the office—'

'Job too much for you, Cassandra?'

Galem's question, plus the speed of it, startled her. 'Of course not,' she said, quickly refocusing. 'I like a challenge.' He started off round the back, and now she had to run to keep up with him. 'My legs are shorter than yours, in case you hadn't noticed.'

Noticed? He had conducted a full inventory, not once, but several times, and last night he'd almost completed his inspection. Sexually she was corked like a bottle of champagne waiting for the stopper to be removed, which puzzled him. She was a beautiful woman—not in the conventional sense, she was too quirky for that, but he liked quirky. So why was she so inexperienced?

He slowed to match her pace as they walked round. They had to find a way to get along. It was better he had a hand in the renovations from the start.

As they crested the hill and she saw the lights of the village down below them she turned to smile at him. 'It looks welcoming, doesn't it?'

It gave him a jolt to realise she was settling in, at least in her mind. But something inside him glowed. She was such a mix of stubbornness, assertiveness and eagerness. Just the sort of person you would want working for you…

'Do your employers live close by?' she said, distracting him.

That was one question he was never going to answer. 'Roundabouts…'

Why could she never get a straight answer from Galem? She was the one with a past to hide. What was wrong with him?

Country manners, Caz concluded. People were more reserved in Hawkshead. They liked to look at you and weigh you up before committing themselves to a conversation, and Galem was no different. But she had to find out something about him. Her plan could fail before she launched it if his employers felt they were entitled to Galem's services every waking moment. 'Do they give you plenty of time off?'

'Enough.'

Perhaps he worked in isolation and monosyllables went with the territory. She would just have to rein back her impatience for now. He would surely have a few hours to spare for her each week.

The dilapidation they found was worse than she had expected; it looked a lot worse in daylight. Caz's heart sank as they walked round together. It was a sad old house, not even close to being habitable. It would take more than money, it would take a miracle to make it right.

'Structurally, it's sound enough, though it needs a proper inspection by a building surveyor,' Galem told her as they continued their rounds.

'What about the roof?' She bumped into him, then hastily drew back, staring up to avoid looking at him. Any form of physical contact, even accidental, had to be avoided at all costs if she was going to pull this off. Employing Galem, not making love to him, was the future.

'I'd need to get up there to be sure.'

He brushed up beside her to take a closer look and she wasn't sure whether she'd give more away by moving or staying still. She opted for a return to the interview. 'Have you handled anything of this magnitude before, Galem?' She stood back to give him space.

'Similar things,' he said vaguely. 'If you'd like to check the quality of my work I could give you some addresses.'

'That would be great. Thank you. It's not that I don't believe you…' She forgot what she was going to say as Galem turned to look down at her. Prolonged eye contact like this was almost as bad as touching him. 'Bank managers always want proof,' she blurted, ripping off a chunk of plaster and with it half a wall.

'Hey, steady on,' Galem exclaimed, grabbing

hold of her arm. 'Damp has made this wall unstable. You don't want to start doing that.'

I really don't, Caz agreed with him silently, his warm hands coming into contact with her body as he started brushing the debris from her clothes.

'Let's go through to the kitchen,' he suggested. 'I'm thinking we could take this wall away without impacting on any of the original features.'

'You seem to know your way around pretty well?'

'I climbed in through a window. Your aunt's lawyer kept things locked up pretty tight.'

He didn't just want it for himself, he'd been making plans to restore it for some time, Caz thought as she watched Galem moving around. And he was right about taking the wall down. The large open-plan space that would create would make a fabulous family kitchen.

'Be careful! Don't tread there… Too late,' Galem murmured, catching her in his arms as a floorboard gave way and she lurched towards him.

She froze in his arms, not daring to move a muscle. Her heart was pounding so loud, surely he must hear it? His arms were so strong and he smelled so good; all of it, all of him reminding her… Reminding Her To Turn Her Face Away. But she couldn't. She just couldn't. She closed her eyes, melting…

'You follow me in future,' Galem said, setting her back on her feet again. 'You follow exactly in my footsteps, and you will not wander off. If you don't do as I say you'll have to wait for me outside. Do you understand?'

Her jaw worked. Her eyes filled. Who did he think he was talking to? But he was right, Caz conceded. Some parts of the house were more unsafe than others, and Galem had already been round. She firmed her mouth and nodded briefly. 'Bottom line, can it be saved?'

'Definitely,' Galem said with the air of a man who had already come to that decision.

She should be glad he shared her belief. They both felt Stone Break House was worth saving; didn't that endorse her decision to keep it? Their individual reasons for doing so were irrelevant. 'So, we have a deal?'

'I don't know, Cassandra… Do we?'

The tip of her tongue crept out, testing the redness beneath her lips. Could she work with him, or was she kidding herself? What if he had a girlfriend? What if he brought her here? How would she feel then?

Caz knew how she felt. Galem's fabulous eyes and wicked smile hadn't been wasted on a man who wasn't interested in women, and she doubted she could stand by each week and watch him walk away with someone else after they'd been working on the house together.

Unconsciously her gaze slipped to his lean hips, skirting past the well-worn fabric on his bulging

button fly. She couldn't have him, but if she even suspected anyone else of taking an interest in her project
manager she'd be hard pressed not to scratch their
eyes out.

'Something on your mind, Caz?'

'No. Why?' She had to calm down, and ease
back. Acting defensive was not the way forward.

Galem let it go. Easing his shoulders in a shrug,
he suggested, 'Shall we continue our inspection?'

They carried on, the tension sizzling between
them, until finally he said, 'That's enough for today.
I've got another appointment.'

What he said gave her a jolt, but after the way her
thoughts had been turning she should have known.
'Okay,' she said lightly. 'Where are you going?'
None of her business, but it slipped out before she
could stop herself.

'The dogs.'

'The dogs?'

'Greyhound racing. You can come with me if
you like.'

She was relieved by what he'd told her and by the
way his face creased in the familiar grin. Maybe they
could get on. Maybe this was a test. Galem was
offering her a real taste of northern life. Rough and
ready, casual fun, something Cassandra would have
loathed.

'Just remember,' he said, planting his legs and
folding his arms, 'I don't do waiting.'

'And I don't do tag along.' She had to be sure. Her

head was still full of the high-kicking glamour girls at the village hall who'd been drooling over him.

'I'm on my own, Caz.'

'Do you want me to say ah-h-h?' It was her turn to grin. She felt like saying a lot more than ah, she felt like cheering. Couldn't be helped that he saw how pleased she was to hear that.

'Well, are you coming with me, or not?'

She had to keep him on board, but after last night it was dangerous to show too much enthusiasm. 'Thank you for inviting me. I'd like that,' she said primly.

Galem scratched the side of his face and looked her up and down. 'Don't you have anything else to wear?'

So he'd noticed the cashmere suit was ruined? Right now it was all she had. 'I'm stuck with this,' she said, brushing her hands down the matted wool. 'It's seen one too many puddles, I guess, but I don't think my business suit would be appropriate.'

Galem's look told her she was right.

'No problem,' he said, moving towards the door. 'We'll go back to the cottage, pick up the Land Rover, and then I'll take you shopping.'

Her mouth fell open. 'You'll…' She was speechless.

'Do you have a problem with that?'

'No… No problem at all. Are you sure you don't mind?' Her heart was already lifting at the thought of shopping.

'It would be my pleasure.'

There was a glint in Galem's eyes that should have made her suspicious, but any man who took a girl shopping had to be a paragon of all the virtues. Didn't he? Caz thought as Galem quietly shut the door.

'Wash-and-wear trousers in Sherwood Green and a nice bright yellow shirt...'

Caz could only stand and wait for the shop assistant to ring her purchases through the till. Galem was standing guard at her back, preventing her from fleeing the shop. This was the best ladies *fashion* shop in Cleckhampton, he had assured her. And now she had to try not to notice how much he was enjoying this.

'A royal blue zip-up jacket...comfort-fit brogues *and* cushion-heeled socks. My, you'll be comfortable in that lot,' the sales assistant assured Caz, her rosy cheeks glowing pink with approval as she handed the bundle over the counter.

'I'll pay for them,' Galem said, pushing Caz's hand with its precious piece of well-worn plastic aside.

'No,' Caz protested hotly, but then he pointed to a sign: 'cash only'. 'I see,' she said, cheeks reddening. She hardly ever carried cash. 'Thank you,' she said meekly, vowing never to be caught out again.

'The changing room's over there,' the assistant said, pointing. 'And when you've finished I'll put your emergency outfit in a nice paper bag for you to take home…'

Home… The mere mention of it brought Cassandra back full force, forcing Caz to take a back seat. The contrasts were too stark to sustain her through an ordeal like this. Home was London or Leeds, both of which were blessed with one of the finest fashion stores in the world. Home was black, tan, beige and winter white, with the occasional shot of pewter grey. Home was not green and yellow and royal blue, with extra-wide comfort brogues and stay-high, cushion-heeled socks. Home was trophy carrier bags, design statements in themselves; home was not a paper bag.

'Happy now?' Galem said brightly as they climbed back into his beat-up Land Rover.

Ecstatic! Though she had the good grace to thank him for stopping off at the shop. Worst of all he looked great. He always did. Galem would have fitted just as well on Sloane Street as in Clackhandle, or wherever the heck they were.

She almost lost it when his warm hand briefly covered hers.

'Stop wringing your hands, Caz. You're sorted now.'

Sorted? She almost laughed out loud. She was about as far from sorted, as… She stared at her hand. Emotion washed over her. She could feel the imprint of each of Galem's fingers burning into her. Something to hold onto, she guessed.

He stopped in front of an unpromising pebble-dashed entrance. The building was single-storey and rambling and streams of people were already making their way inside. It was impossible to see anything beyond the high walls marking the perimeter.

'Security,' Galem explained. 'The race track is on the other side of that fence. You don't want anyone climbing over.'

'Where to now?'

'I'm meeting Old Thomas in the paddock. He's got my dogs.'

'Your dogs? You race greyhounds?'

'It's a team effort with Thomas.' He switched off the engine. 'He used to race with my father and now I've taken his place.'

It was the most he'd ever told her, Caz realised.

'Are you ready?' Galem said, leaning across to open the door for her.

The brush of his arm, the faint tang of his shampoo and his warmth enveloped her, forcing her to drag in a huge draught of fresh air as he opened the door.

'I bet you're glad you've got a jacket now,' Galem said as they got out.

It was nippy, but she'd have preferred the shelter of his arms to a serviceable jacket, Caz thought, zipping it up.

'Come on,' he said, finding her hand as if she were his kid sister. 'I'm going to take you to meet my babies.'

He drew her along behind him while she told herself not to get excited, and that the only reason he was holding her hand was because the place was packed and he didn't want to lose her. The way he talked about his dogs, his *babies,* that threw her a bit. Reining in feelings wasn't so easy when Galem could be so nice.

Caz's heart turned over while she watched Galem hunker down with his animals. The greyhounds clearly adored him, and were doing their best to lick the stubble off his face.

'They're gorgeous. Can I stroke them?'

'Of course you can.' He turned his face up to look at her. 'Do you like dogs?'

'I love all animals.' She didn't care if he thought she was trying to win him round. She had always wanted a dog, but her life had never allowed for one. As he rumpled their ears she said, 'I can see they mean a lot to you.'

'I love them,' he said simply. 'Thomas and I both do. They've got a home for life with us.'

Weren't dogs supposed to be good judges of character? Caz thought wryly as she watched the two greyhounds continuing to make a fuss of Galem. 'What are they called?'

'This is Hawkshead Sally,' Galem said as he stroked the smooth head of an intelligent brindle, 'and this black beauty is our champion, Stone Break Sid.'

Named after the house! 'Named after the house?'

Galem was so busy with his dogs he didn't appear to hear her. 'I'll just put their muzzles on before we take them in. You'd like to see them race, wouldn't you?'

Both dogs wagged their tails appreciatively as she patted them. 'Of course I would.' Who could resist those keen, bright eyes? And that was just the brown ones.

Galem handed the dogs over to their handlers for the meet, and then took Caz trackside to a prime spot alongside the winning post. It was an important race, he explained, in which Sid was up against some stiff competition. Galem stood behind her as the stadium filled up, keeping one arm either side of her body to protect her, trapping her between him and the rail. Having him so close was distracting and it wasn't until she saw the parade of dogs approaching Caz could think of much besides the warmth of Galem's breath brushing the back of her neck. It had raised each tiny hair and made every part of her tingle.

'I don't see Sally?' she said, turning to him with concern.

'Sally's an expectant mother, so she's not running today.'

'She's having puppies?' Caz's face relaxed into a smile. 'So why did you bring her?'

'Because Sid won't race without her. Look,' Galem said, leaning forward.

Caz snatched a breath as the sleeve of his shirt brushed her face. She could feel his warmth, and his

legs were pressed into the back of hers. Her heart
was racing so fast she could barely concentrate on
what Galem was pointing out to her.

'The first dog in the line,' he prompted.

'Sid,' she said excitedly, transferring her attention.

'You can tell Sid's looking for Sally.'

It was true, Caz thought, looking at Galem. She
knew how Sid felt. Leading the parade, Sid was
definitely straining his leash looking for his mate.
Galem's cheek was so close to hers she could feel the
heat coming off him. And he was so pleased to see
his dogs it was only natural he should drape an arm
over her shoulder to point her in the right direction.
Gradually she relaxed and started sharing his
pleasure.

'Sid will run this race for Sally, and he'll win,'
Galem predicted.

The idea of one dog depending on another
made Caz smile. The fact that Galem believed it
made her all warm inside, or maybe that was
because Galem had been forced against her again
by the weight of the crowd.

'Excited?' he whispered in her ear as the dogs
were loaded into their racing traps.

'Extremely,' she said honestly, glad he couldn't
see her face. The place was so packed they didn't
have any option other than to be cuddled up close
together. It was a relief when he started telling her
about the race and what to expect.

It would be over in seconds, Galem explained. He

pointed out Sid's most likely challengers, and moments after that the electronic hare was released. It whipped in front of them at incredible speed, and then the trap doors sprang open. With a dip of their sleek heads the greyhounds broke for freedom in a pack. Caz had to rely on Galem giving her a commentary because to her inexperienced eye the racing dogs were a blur. Hearing Sid was in the lead, she jumped up and down, screaming with excitement, and when the dogs streaked past a second time she saw one black muzzle nudging ahead of the rest. 'Sid won!' Ecstatic, she threw her arms around Galem's neck.

'Yes, he did.'

Galem was staring down at her without making the slightest attempt to draw her close, Caz realised; if anything he had stiffened.

She slowly unlatched her fingers and stood back. 'Can we go and see them?' She was all hot and cold inside and feeling awkward again.

'I have to go and collect the prize,' Galem reminded her. 'You'll be coming with me, won't you?'

He never made it easy.

CHAPTER ELEVEN

IN THE winner's enclosure Stone Break Sid was looking as pleased as Caz guessed a dog could look, and at his side his sweetheart, the pregnant greyhound Sally, looked on adoringly. The dogs' history seemed to be tied in to Galem's, and that was perhaps the only clue she was going to get about him.

One clue was better than nothing, and she was determined to make the most of it. 'Did Sally ever race?'

Galem had just collected Sid's trophy and a cheque. He gave them to her while he took the leads to lead the two dogs away. 'Sally loved racing, but she always came last.'

'Was that a problem for you?'

'Never. Sid can't live without her, and, even if he could, Sally enjoys running. I wouldn't dream of stopping her while that's the case. When she isn't expecting she takes part in some racing I organised to give older and slower dogs a chance of glory.'

The more she learned about him, the harder it became to keep Galem in the pigeon-hole marked impersonal. She was touched by this new caring side of him, but she had also learned that he sponsored racing, which cost money. A lot of money. Before she could probe any further he said, 'Come on. Let's get out of here.'

Crowds were streaming past them in readiness for the next race, and they were being jostled. To protect her Galem held the leashes in one hand and steered a safe path for her with the other. Old Thomas was waiting for them in the car park, and he insisted on taking the dogs back with him. He made the comment that Galem should relax while he could.

He must work every hour under the sun, Caz concluded. He must do to be able to afford such a lovely house as well as keep racing dogs.

'Hungry?' he said, distracting her.

'Starving,' Caz admitted. Since arriving in Hawkshead her appetite had quadrupled.

They ate in the Land Rover outside a fish and chip shop, using plastic forks, and glugging everything down with a can of cola.

Something Cassandra would never do, Caz reflected as Galem disposed of their rubbish, but Cassandra wouldn't be here in the first place.

Swinging back into the driver's seat, Galem threw her a glance. 'Better now?'

'Much.' She held his gaze momentarily. It was the

best time she'd had for ages. She'd really enjoyed his company, and she had no doubt that if they'd been a real couple the date wouldn't have been close to reaching its end.

Forget that thought, Caz told herself firmly as a sheet of lightning lit up the cab. She wasn't Galem's type and this wasn't going anywhere, and now it was time for her to get on with her life.

But getting on with her life had to wait because when they returned to the cottage they found the storm had brought a tree down across the door. Several neighbours were out on the street, sheltering under umbrellas. As soon as they saw Galem they clustered round him as he got out of the car.

It had only just happened, apparently, and the general suggestion was to call the fire brigade.

'No need, I'll get the tractor,' he said, taking charge. 'You stay here,' he instructed Caz. 'I need to make sure the cottage is safe before you go in there.'

'Be careful…' He was gone before she could stop him, and she could only watch anxiously as he climbed over the branches and disappeared inside the house.

A tense five minutes passed when an ear-splitting crack made Caz cry out with alarm. The giant trunk had shifted and become more firmly lodged. Like many houses in the village the cottage backed onto another, which meant the front door through which Galem had entered was the only way out. The windows were old-fashioned and tiny—another example, no doubt of Galem's thoughts on keeping the essence of a house intact, but this time it would work against him. He would never be able to fit his shoulders through them.

Right on cue Galem's head poked out of the window as he tried to assess the situation.

'What can I do to help?' she yelled, coming as close as she could.

'Not much.' Galem scratched his chin and sighed.

'Call the fire brigade, mate,' someone yelled.

Galem squashed that one right away. 'They'll have enough to do tonight. This isn't an emergency.'

'Why don't I get the tractor?' Caz suggested. 'You can tell me what to do,' she insisted, determined to ignore the expression on Galem's face.

'Don't be ridiculous—'

'Why can't I drive the tractor?'

'Because you can't even drive a car!' he pointed out with a certain amount of logic. 'Plus you'd have to attach a rope—'

'Would I have to tie a knot too?' she said, growing angry.

She knew this was the worst kind of torture for him. Galem was used to being in charge, instead of which he was imprisoned. 'Just tell me what to do— where I can find ropes, how to start.'

'Absolutely not.' His voice was adamant.

'So what do you suggest?' Caz demanded, squaring up to him. 'Shall I start whittling?'

'Maybe we should call the fire brigade…'

She could see him reaching for his mobile phone, and called out, exasperated, 'This is hardly a life-threatening situation. It's something I can deal with, if you'll let me.'

Snapping his phone shut, he tried again to force his shoulders through the open window.

Caz pressed her advantage. 'I've had my accident for this weekend. Now are you going to trust me, or are you going to sit there and wait for men with better things to do to come and rescue you?'

That got a reaction. She could feel his indignation lashing her harder than the rain.

'Driving a tractor isn't like driving a car,' he said after a tense silence. 'And the tractor I've been using here in Hawkshead is ancient—'

'Is that the one that tipped me into a ditch? The one parked round the back of Stone Break House?'

'I was moving some rubble. And I didn't tip you into a ditch. You managed that very well all by yourself.'

So, her driving was hopeless—it could only get better. 'I don't care what you were doing,' she said, overlooking the fact that the renovations on Stone Break House had already started as far as Galem was concerned—and probably before she'd even arrived in Hawkshead. 'I'm well acquainted with your tractor,' she told him pointedly, 'so I know how old it is. I presume it dates from the time when men were men and women did as they were told?'

She had to admit it was a relief to hear him laugh.

'Can you use a gear shift?' he said, turning serious again.

'Of course,' she lied. How hard could it be? 'Where are the keys?'

'Here,' he said reluctantly, dragging them out of his pocket.

'Thank you,' she said as he tossed them down to her. 'And the keys to the Land Rover?'

Caz listened carefully as Galem gave her instructions on what to do when she drove the tractor and where to find the ropes she would need. 'I'll be back as soon as I can,' she promised, ignoring his sceptical hum.

'Half an hour and then I'm calling the emergency services.'

'You do that,' she told him, stalking away.

Caz's over-confidence was short-lived. Galem was right about the tractor. It was ponderous and unpredictable, with a wobbly gear lever as long as a walking stick. Just getting it started up was an achievement. The mud-caked pedals were each the size of a small paving slab and about as heavy to press down. Adjusting the seat wasted more precious time and even then she had to half stand to stamp the clutch into submission. Several false starts later she had managed to lurch forward an inch. Gritting her teeth in fierce concentration, she gripped the wheel firmly and stamped her foot down on the accelerator pedal.

'Slow down, slow down,' Caz cautioned herself grimly, arms spread wide on the huge metal steering wheel. Galem had warned her about the dangers of turning tractors over and she was rigid with fear. But she had done everything he had told her to do. The ropes they would need to lift the tree trunk away from the door were coiled at her side. But even with all Galem's instructions the thing that helped her most was the fact that she was as stubborn as she was scared. No way was she going to admit defeat.

There were ditches beckoning on either side and with the heavy rain and faltering headlights there was a real risk she might land up back where she had started on Friday night, and this time there would be no Galem to rescue her. So she would just have to travel at the speed of a slug, Caz concluded.

Galem was watching out for her when she arrived, straining his head out of the narrow window space. 'I didn't think you'd make it,' he admitted, grinning at her. 'And when you did, I wasn't sure you were going to stop.'

'Behave, or you can stay there,' she warned him, leaning out of the cab.

With Galem yelling instructions and an avid audience at every window in the street Caz managed to secure the rope. Climbing back on board, she revved the powerful engine and inch by inch dragged the tree trunk away. She pulled it to some waste land where it could be dealt with later, and then, switching off the engine, slumped back in her seat.

'You did good, Caz...' Wind and rain blew into the cab with Galem. Throwing the door back, he lifted her out. Or rather she tumbled into his arms, trembling all over.

'You did really good,' he soothed her as he carried her back to the cottage in his arms. 'You deserve a reward...'

A really big one, she hoped, gazing up at him.

'Brandy and milk?' Caz stared at the mug Galem had just pressed into her hands. He had sat her down on the sofa on top of a towel in the living room while he went to make the drink.

'With sugar,' he said apologetically. 'I know it's bad for you, but even bad can be good for you sometimes.'

She took a long look at him.

'Shock, for example,' he said, glancing away, 'needs sugar. So you have to make an exception this one time.' Wrapping her fingers around the mug, he insisted, 'Drink. You're wet through.'

'So are you,' Caz observed, slanting him a glance.

'But you've had one hell of an ordeal.' Galem couldn't help but be proud of her. Caz Ryan was beginning to get under his skin and he wasn't sure how much longer he would be able to resist her.

'Only one?' She smiled over the rim of the mug.

'You'd better get out of those wet clothes now,' he said. 'Strip. You can't sit there, dripping all over my nice clean floor.'

As soon as she got up and started peeling off her clothes he knew he'd made a mistake. He couldn't handle this much torment. Her figure was stunning, mouth-watering. Gym-toned and clad in what he could imagine was this season's lingerie—pale green with pink rosebud trim. He swallowed and turned away, trying to avoid her gaze.

Thrusting some towels in her hand, he pointed up the stairs to the bathroom. 'Strip off the rest of your clothes there. I'll stick them in the washer with mine.'

But it was too late—he'd caught the look in her eyes. He ran his gaze up and down her gorgeous body once again.

He had to get her out of his sight or he wouldn't be responsible for his actions. 'The hot water won't last for ever.'

Just as she'd thought, Galem wasn't interested. She'd proved herself with the tractor; she still felt the exhilaration. She wanted him to share that with her.

Brushing past him as seductively as she knew how, she walked up to the bathroom and shut the door. Turning the shower on full blast, she stood motionless for a second, catching her breath and trying to blank her mind to what she so desperately wanted, needed. If only he wanted her.

Once she was calm enough she stepped beneath the steaming spray. Turning her face up, she luxuriated in heat and daydreams in which she had turned

into Superwoman. It had been a lot better than being
Cassandra, because she had got to save the hero,
whereas Cassandra was always more interested in
squashing them. And where heroes were concerned,
Galem came top of the list. Fully clothed, he looked
amazing. She could only imagine how good he
would look naked. Caz wondered idly as she soaped
herself down. Toned and tanned, his abs and pecs
were made out of steel; his muscles bulged like a
proper man. When had she ever seen one of those
before? Whatever prejudices Cassandra Bailey
Brown had brought with her to Hawkshead, Caz
Ryan had just ditched them. No one matched up to
Galem, whatever his profession—no one even came
close.

'Are you finished in there, or am I coming in?'

She laughed and ignored him; Galem would
just have to wait. Her thoughts were abruptly trun-
cated when the door lock flipped open and Galem
stepped inside.

'How did you do that?' She caught her breath.

'I warned you about the water.' Parting the shower
doors, he didn't hesitate. The way she'd brushed
against him earlier had told him all he needed to
know.

Her arms flew across her chest to cover it, and she
was having difficulty balancing with her legs
crossed.

'Something wrong, Caz?'

She lost, caught up by the very sight of him. He

looked better than she'd imagine. Quickly she tried to compose herself. 'Turn your back this instant.'

The last thing she had expected was for Galem's arm to sweep round her waist, or for his other hand to cup her head and drag her close. She should put up some resistance. She really should. She did. She placed both her hands flat against his powerful chest and gave him the feeblest push in her repertoire. It didn't work. By which time her fingers had closed on the crisp black hair on his chest and, instead of pushing him away, she was pulling him towards her… *And kissing him.*

They were bathed in steam as Galem's tongue lightly brushed her lips. It was better than the first time…this was the first time, or it felt like it. She felt as if she were melting from the inside out, every part of her on fire. She closed her eyes as Galem's strong white teeth closed lightly on her swollen bottom lip. His confidence, his strength, his power, she felt that he was placing all of it at her disposal.

He teased her as he always did, but not for so long. His breathing was just as hectic as hers, his need just as pressing. The sensation when his firm, warm hand started stroking the curve of her naked bottom was indescribable. He used long, even strokes that made her arch her back for him, asking for more. She was searching for more intimate touches, and tried desperately to press against him, but every time she got close Galem pulled away again. She rubbed her breasts against him, loving how tender her nipples had become. She loved to feel his rough chest hair scratching them. 'I want you,' she sighed, and reaching up, she wove her fingers through his thick, wet black hair. 'Kiss me, Galem,' she begged him. 'Kiss me properly.'

His answer was to hold her in front of him and as he stared down she said again, 'Kiss me…'

His wet mouth closed on her lips, sucking the last rational thought from her head. His face beard was rough against her face as she strained against him, and now she wanted to feel it over every part of her. She would never get enough of kissing him, tasting him, feeling him.

Pulling back when she could least bear it, he ran one firm thumb pad across the tender reddened skin beneath her mouth. 'Did I hurt you?'

She denied it fiercely, and brought him down to her again.

'I'll have to soothe it,' Galem breathed against her mouth.

'Only when you've kissed me all over,' Caz insisted, pressing against him.

'First I'm going soap you down,' he said, reaching for the sponge. 'Where would you like me to begin?'

'Anywhere you like… Just don't keep me waiting too long.'

Galem's smile was long and lazy as he charged the sponge. 'Vanilla and rosemary…'

He held it up for her to approve. She rested against him as he began.

'I think you like that,' he murmured.

She answered by parting her legs a little more, and then gasped for air as he made lazy circles round her breasts, teasing her nipples with the edge of the sponge until she was purring her satisfaction like a pampered pussy-cat.

'And how about this?' he said softly, running the sponge down the length of her back. She could only moan her pleasure when he reached her buttocks. Arching her back to its fullest extent, she felt the sponge slip down to where she so badly needed Galem to touch her. As she moved against him she could feel his erection pressing into her belly. He was enormous and her instinctive response was to draw back.

'Do I frighten you?'

'A little,' she admitted, burying her face in his chest.

Tipping her chin up, he cupped her face and kissed her again, very gently to reassure her, and then he deepened the kiss slowly until her fears had been left far behind. But he hadn't finished washing her and he started with her feet, moving on to her ankles, her calves, and then her thighs.

'More?' he murmured, as if asking her permission to continue.

'Just don't stop…'

He brushed her with the sponge intimately in a way that made her gasp. No one but Galem had ever touched her there before, but even as she was

banking the sensation in her mind he pulled away
and the spell was broken.

Rinsing out the sponge, he squeezed it dry, and,
putting it back in the wire basket, he switched off
the shower and reached outside for some towels.
Dipping his head, he planted a tender kiss on the side
of her neck. 'We need to get out of here before the
water runs cold.'

That was no explanation. She watched him snatch
up a robe and belt, and stood unresisting as he enveloped her in towels and lifted her into his arms. But as
he carried her into the bedroom and lay her down
gently on the bed her heart lifted and began beating so
fast she could hardly think, hardly breathe. But instead
of joining her he pulled up the blanket to cover her.

'Rest now...' His hand pressed her lightly as he
turned to go.

'Galem, what did I do wrong?'

He hesitated a moment when she called him back,
then, returning to the side of the bed, he sat down
and took her hand, enclosing it in his. 'You're a
virgin, Caz,' he said softly, shaking his head, angry
with himself that he'd let things go this far.

To some men that might have represented an opportunity, Caz realised, but to Galem it was a barrier
he wouldn't cross.

'Do you want to tell me about it?' he said, lifting
his gaze from her hand to her face.

'Nothing to tell...' Her eyes widened. She was
deeply embarrassed.

He had to keep reminding himself that her private life was no concern of his. But still he sensed that more than hard work and single-mindedness had kept her intact. It was as if she couldn't risk losing any part of her to another, as if she didn't quite believe in herself enough to do that. 'Caz, why are you here? And I don't just mean why are you here with me at the cottage right this minute. I mean what brought you to Hawkshead?' What drove you here? was what he meant, but he couldn't say that to her. She was too tender, too vulnerable.

'You know why I came,' she said, turning her face away. 'I inherited a house…'

She didn't want to talk to him about her past. She didn't want to talk about sex. She didn't want to open up to him, or anyone. She didn't know how, he realised. 'Why don't you sell Stone Break House and go back to the city—'

'Forget it,' she cut him off.

Were they both crazy fighting over a rambling ruin in the shadow of a quarry? Or were they fighting because it kept them together? There were no certainties any more.

The only thing he could be sure about was that she would continue to fight him, even if she couldn't explain why. Or maybe she could to herself. Maybe she had always wanted somewhere to call home, and Stone Break House just felt right to her.

'I'm keeping the house, and nothing you can say will change my mind.'

His internal temper flared at her defiance. He couldn't believe he had let things get this far, with Caz or with the house.

'My aunt must have had some reason for leaving the house to me,' she mused out loud, 'or why didn't she put it in the hands of her solicitor to sell with the rest of her effects?'

He softened as she looked at him, taking in the straight, no-nonsense nose, and the chin that looked as delicate as a china cup, until she jutted it out at him. She had the type of passion he always looked for in his executives, but how would she feel when she learned the truth about him? He had allowed things to go a lot further than he should have done.

'I don't know why Aunt Maud left Stone Break House to me,' she said, breaking into his thoughts, 'but whatever the reason I'm going to honour it.' He could see the determination in her eyes, but it masked a deeper sadness.

Honour? Galem ground his jaw as he took in what Caz had said. Where did honour lie in his father's mistress leaving her house to a niece she'd had no contact with? The solicitor had told him that much when he'd called to ask about the new owner.

Stone Break House was his. It had been his boyhood home, and it was wrapped up in the heritage he had come back to find, and finally understand. He had intended to make the new owner an offer they couldn't refuse. But now he couldn't just put the house out of his head—it meant too much to him. It was a symbol of his father's struggle to succeed, a struggle his late mother had shown no patience for.

Caz would have been different. The thought swept over him as he took in the firm set of her chin and the determination in her steady gaze. They'd have made a great team; it was just a pity they were pitted against each other.

She looked so small and pale in his big bed, so vulnerable. Her humiliation hovered over them like a dark cloud and for that he blamed himself. Self-control was his watchword, or had been until Caz had arrived in Hawkshead. Misleading her was a first for him; plus he'd hugely underestimated her determination. And he had almost given in to the temptation to sleep with her. He had no excuses for himself. He had picked up her sexual curiosity and naivety where men were concerned. He had picked up all the clues, but had simply chosen to ignore them.

CHAPTER TWELVE

DRAWING the blanket close, Caz looked up at Galem. 'I'm sorry, Galem.'

'What for?'

'I didn't mean to—' She could feel the sting of tears; it had all become too much.

'Didn't mean to what?' He took the blanket out of her fingers and pulled it up for her, as if she were a child who didn't know what was best for her.

'I didn't mean to make such a mess of things.'

'You didn't,' he told her frankly. He was the one to blame for that.

'Just tell me one thing, Galem.'

As she leaned forward he had to fight the temptation to take her in his arms. 'Tell you what?'

'We're still on for Stone Break House, aren't we?'

He bridled, then reminded himself that he wasn't the only one with feelings, but when she shot a bolt she hit the target every time. 'If I say I'll do something,' he told her firmly, 'I will. But I can't sleep with you, Caz, just so you can return to the office on Monday morning with a post-coital glow on your cheeks. And I won't sleep with you because you think your virginity is an embarrassment.'

'It isn't like that.' Her cheeks turned scarlet.

'I hope not.' He waited a few moments for her to compose herself. 'So why?'

'Why what?'

'How did you get to be this way, Caz—so defensive, so driven? Tell me about yourself. Did something bad happen?'

'No. Nothing like that.' Her eyes were wary as she made a gesture with her hand to dismiss his concern for her. Her body language told him more. It was a small movement, almost indiscernible, but she moved back as she protested, as if he'd hit a nerve. 'Tell me.'

'There's nothing to tell.'

'Okay.' He eased off. He'd go about it another way. 'I just thought we should get to know each other a little better if we're going to be working together, that's all. How about you give me three things that matter to you, three things you care about.'

Caz froze and then tried to moisten her lips with a tongue that had turned as dry as dust. Galem was employing the same interview technique Cassandra used. It was one that helped people to focus their thoughts and open up. Once they were relaxed the truth poured out. Or, as Cassandra would have put it, you lulled the candidate into a false sense of security with your apparent vagueness, and then went straight for the jugular. She didn't like being in the firing line—how could she when her life was built on a lie? At the office Cassandra talked warmly about her supportive family, and of course she had attended an exclusive girls' school. Then there was the family membership at the tennis club and the golf club, the annual ski trip, and the villa in Portugal. Caz Ryan was a fast learner and she had soon found out what it took to fit in with the high-flying set at the top of the tree. Fortunately, no one had ever called her bluff. Why should they, when she spoke as they did, wore the appropriate uniform, and dropped the right names? They accepted her as one of them. Cassandra Bailey Brown was 'in'.

And it all counted for nothing, Caz reflected as Galem waited for her answer. The only thing she wanted now was to tell the truth to this man. But if she did he wouldn't understand. She knew for a fact that Galem would hate pretension, and would think her a fool for ever courting it.

'Can't you think of three things?' he pressed.

'Of course I can.' She ticked them off on her fingers, staring him straight in the eyes, knowing he would root out any deception right away. 'Family...' The family she longed for. 'Loyalty...' To that family. 'And...' She was about to say 'love', and then quickly changed it to 'Stone Break House', adding, 'The moment I saw the house it was love at first sight.'

The look in Galem's eyes had made her say it. Whatever he said she knew he wanted Stone Break House for himself. And why was she the only one under the spotlight here? 'And now it's your turn to come up with three things.'

Briefly she thought he might refuse, but then the humour came back into his eyes. 'Okay,' he said, falling in with her. 'I care about my work, the people I work with, and everything else that falls within my sphere of influence.'

Galem's sphere of influence? Caz felt vaguely disappointed. She had expected more passion from him; more insights into who he was. 'Game over?' she said, wanting to move things on, to get out of his bed and put some clothes on while she still had a shred of pride intact.

'Game over,' he agreed, refusing to break eye contact so it was far from over.

She took the cue for Stone Break House and ran with it. 'If we could have a look round the house tomorrow, say around lunchtime, we could draw up a schedule of work so when I go back to Leeds I can put a proposal in front of my bank manager.'

'Okay by me.'

He was still staring at her, and the air was still charged. She still craved his warmth. Too bad. She went to get out of bed. They both moved at the same time and the space around them shrank to nothing. Their faces were millimetres apart, their lips almost touching.

'Caz, no…'

Galem drew his head back and lifted his hands away from her, holding them out as if signalling his promise not to touch her. She didn't move. 'Why not?' The words were barely spoken but they hovered in the air between them like an unspoken pledge.

He held her eye contact, and it felt to Caz as if he could see right into her soul. She had lied to him about who she was but she couldn't lie about how she felt. Drawing her hand up to his face, she made the first move. Grazing her fingers down his roughened jaw, she was nervous, but she didn't want this to end. As if he sensed this, Galem leant forward and brushed the hair from her brow, and then he drew her slowly and very tenderly into his arms. His kisses made her relax. He feathered them over her eyelids and her cheeks, and on down her neck, then, pulling her up the bed, he cupped her face in his hands and brushed her lips with his mouth. 'Are you sure?' he whispered, sending a trail of fire down her arms with his fingertips.

Lacing their fingers together, he kissed her again. His restraint was arousing her beyond anything she had ever known. She nodded and started to say something, but Galem put a finger over her lips, and then he replaced that finger with his mouth, kissing the fear out of her.

Tenderness was something she had never experienced and had never anticipated. It brought tears to her eyes, and made a nonsense of all the brash talk at the office about Saturday night clinches and fast, fierce couplings. This was different, very different, this was something that grabbed at her heart and squeezed it tight.

'Touch me…' She strained against him, lacing her fingers through his hair, flying high on the point of giving away something so precious and integral, but feeling it was so right. It was a huge step to take, but at that moment it felt like the easiest decision she'd ever made. It was a step she knew now that Cassandra could never take, because Cassandra had nothing to give. And Caz wanted to give everything she had, everything she was, to Galem. He made her feel so safe, cherished, precious, all she wanted was to be enveloped in his warmth, his power, his gentle strength.

'Listen to your body,' he murmured as she cried out with pleasure. 'There's no rush…'

Easy for him to say, but her body was clamouring with sensation and she wanted more, but Galem was pacing her and so she had to be content with his chaste kisses until she grew quiet again.

'Good girl,' he murmured, stroking her.

How much longer could she bear the frustration? She gave a gasp of relief when his hands started a more interesting track over her belly, and eased her thighs apart to draw his attention. 'Stop teasing me…'

'I want this to be special for you, and if you don't lie still—'

'You'll what?' she challenged softly.

Seizing her wrists for answer, he fastened them in his fist above her head, resting them on the soft bank of pillows. 'You asked for this…'

'You wouldn't dare tease me…'

Drawing one of her nipples into his mouth, he proved he would. He suckled hard, showing her no mercy, and then made sure the other one received the same attention.

'I love your breasts,' he said, pulling back to admire them. 'They're magnificent.'

She didn't want him staring, she wanted him doing, and bucked towards him to give him a hint.

His eyes were laughing as he stared down at her. 'So magnificent I think just looking at them might be enough for me.'

'No,' she warned succinctly.

With a soft laugh Galem returned to his duties, and by the time he'd finished with her both her nipples were hard and pink. Gleaming wet, they stood extended and provocative. 'I want you,' she said, reaching for him. 'Don't make me wait.'

'In the workplace you may be used to people obeying you, but in my bed you do as you're told.'

He made a pass across her nipples with the rough stubble on his chin, reducing her in that one move to a whimpering, writhing ferment of sensation.

'Tell me what you want,' he insisted. 'You have to tell me, Caz.'

'You know what I want…'

'Tell me…'

His voice had a harder edge that turned her on.

'I want you, Galem. I want you now…'

'And what do you want with me?' His lips tugged up.

'You know what I want…'

'Do I?'

'Please stop teasing me.'

'And do what?'

'Make love to me…'

'Like this?' he suggested, slipping lower in the bed.

'Oh, yes…yes.' She cried out with pleasure and relief as his tongue found her. 'Please don't stop…' She couldn't bear it; she wasn't sure it was possible to withstand so much pleasure, but she was prepared to try.

Lacing her fingers through Galem's thick black hair, she kept him tightly in place. His tongue was warm and firm and rough, everything she wanted, and this time he didn't deny her anything.

She cried out, convulsing on the bed in the throes of pleasure so intense, so enduring, she wondered if she would survive. He let her down gently and then held her for a while until she was still.

'Good…'

'Mmm,' she managed, utterly contented and ready to fall asleep in his arms. But then he started kissing her again in a way that very soon made her strain against him.

She felt bereft when he sat up, and then went very still, hearing a foil rip. He came back to her immediately, stroking her face. 'Do you trust me?'

She gazed steadily into his eyes. 'You know I do.'

He kissed her again, tenderly, gently, and while he was kissing her his hand found her. She went to say something and couldn't. Her need was so great, the hunger had returned, and Galem was stroking her delicately and deliberately, drawing more exquisite sensation out of her than she had known was possible. The pleasure spread out in rippling waves until she relaxed completely into it, wondering at the destination, and only fearing that if it was in any way better than this she might pass out before she got there.

When Galem moved on top of her he was kissing her at the same time, kissing her, stroking her, soothing. Looking deep into her eyes, he cupped her buttocks and she felt a wonderful pressure that coaxed every part of her into readiness to receive him.

She drew her legs back, wanting nothing to stand in their way, and her breathing quickened in preparation for what was to come.

Testing her readiness, he pulled back at first, making her cry out with disappointment, but then he set up a gentle rocking motion stroking her, and it allowed her to take as much or as little of him as she wanted to. When he was sure she was ready he moved deeper still, and so he took her without pain.

Caz's lips parted in surprise as Galem stretched her for the first time. The sensation was incredible. He was so careful, so gentle and considerate. He kissed her over and over, his words caressed her, and her body responded to him as he set up a steady rhythm. There was more tenderness in his eyes than she had ever seen before, and it was that look that made her lose control. Calling out his name repeatedly, she shuddered and bucked in the intense throes of pleasure, only to collapse exhausted and replete in his arms.

They slept for a while wound around each other, and she woke to find Galem caressing her again. 'I can't,' she insisted sleepily, rolling onto her stomach.

'Is that a fact?'

She barely had strength to move her head on the pillow, but she turned it to the side and opened her eyes to stare at him. 'All right, maybe I can,' she mumbled, closing her eyes again, feigning sleep. But Galem had started stroking her bottom again, and somehow her legs parted without her having anything to do with it. 'How did you do that?' she asked him groggily, barely opening her eyes or her mouth. 'And don't you dare say years of training…'

'Let's just call it a natural talent, shall we?' Galem suggested, drawing her beneath him.

He sank inside her, pressing deep. 'Is that too much for you?'

He'd asked because she was clinging to him, gasping for breath. 'I just need a second. I can't think, can't breathe…'

'Breathe, don't think,' he advised, starting to move again.

She groaned with pleasure as Galem filled her, massaging her inside and out with each thrust. But then he did something that made her cry out in complaint. 'You love teasing me, don't you?' she accused him as he withdrew completely and made her wait before re-entering her again so very slowly.

'I love to bring you pleasure; I love to watch that pleasure unfold on your face.'

Pressing her knees back, Galem knelt between her legs, proving just how much pleasure she could take. Her cries halted him.

'Have I hurt you?'

'Don't stop!' she warned him furiously, in a real panic that he might. She was developing quite an appetite.

But as he kissed her this time Caz felt that everything had changed. And not just her virginal state. She knew Galem was wrong for her, totally wrong for her, they were wrong for each other, but she was in very real danger of falling in love with him.

'Caz…'

He was moving steadily now, firmly, drawing her attention to his eyes. Drawing her once again to the height of passion.

'How do you do that?' she asked him later when they were quiet.

'How do I do what?' Galem murmured lazily.

'All you have to do is prompt me, and I—'

'Obey?' he suggested, receiving a nudge of disapproval for his trouble.

'You know what I mean,' Caz insisted, finding it an effort to move her mouth and keep her eyes open at the same time.

'Don't you like my suggestions?'

'Love them…' She smiled into his eyes.

'That's what I thought. So here's another one…'

She was instantly awake as Galem eased onto his back. She trusted him absolutely, but she was still in beginner's class. 'Can I…can I do this?'

'Do you want to try?'

She straddled him. 'So are you just going to lie there?' She had forgotten how big he was, and, having sampled the tip, she drew back.

Taking her in his arms, Galem swung her beneath him. 'Shall I show you again?'

'I think you better had. I'm a slow learner…'

'Don't worry, you've got all night to get it right.'

'I was hoping you might say that.'

'Hold me, Caz…'

She needed both her hands to encompass his girth, but it was worth it to explore the silky hardness ridged with veins. From base to tip it was quite a journey. 'May I?' she asked politely.

'Be my guest…' Galem's lips pressed down in a contented smile as she began. Drawing him in, she closed her muscles around him. 'You're my prisoner now.'

'I yield,' he assured her. 'Is that good?'

'Perfect.'

'A little deeper, perhaps?'

'How deep?'

'Are you ready to find out?'

'I wouldn't miss it for the world.' Caz felt joy soar inside her.

'I might lose control,' he warned.

'You're not allowed until I say you can.'

'And when will that be?'

'Never.'

'How much do you want of me, Caz?'

'All of you... I want it all.'

Oh, God, she meant it. She meant it. She really meant it. She hoped Galem couldn't read her mind. She had never exposed her vulnerable inner self to another human being before in her life, and yet just now in the throes of making love with Galem she had made the most honest declaration of her life.

CHAPTER THIRTEEN

THEY woke to sunshine streaming into the bedroom early on Sunday morning.

'I should be getting back,' Caz said reluctantly.

'Who says so?'

Galem was right. There was no rigid timetable in Hawkshead for her to follow.

'The freedom here is what I appreciate most,' he said, as if he'd picked up on her thoughts. Sitting up in bed, he was gazing out across the moors.

Was that why he was content to stay here? Caz wondered, dropping kisses on his shoulder.

'We have to go to the house yet,' he reminded her, easing her down on the bed. 'So you might as well plan on staying in Hawkshead for a bit longer.'

How was she supposed to think about leaving when Galem was kissing her neck? 'I couldn't possibly impose on you,' she teased him.

'But I want you to.' His mouth tugged up into the

familiar wicked smile. 'You may have to stay the night too…'

'Really?' Sucking in a deep breath, she tried to keep her thoughts confined to the conversation, but that was impossible now Galem was moving down the bed. She capitulated gracefully. 'Oh, all right, then,' she agreed.

'First one into the shower,' Caz suggested round about noon.

But Galem had played the game before with her, and as she launched herself off the bed he came after her.

'Room for two?' he said, holding the shower door as she tried to close it in his face.

That wasn't a question, Caz realised as Galem joined her. She backed into a corner, inviting him to come closer.

'You don't mind sharing the shower, do you?' he said, turning it on.

Caz screamed and launched herself at him as freezing cold water cascaded down on them.

'I'd better warm you up,' Galem offered.

'You better had,' Caz threatened, scrambling up him.

He took her there in the shower, holding her off the ground, two strong hands clamped to her buttocks while she braced her feet against the wall. Freezing outside and hot inside was quite a combination. It was incredible. He was incredible, and addictive, Caz mused when Galem let her down gently and started kissing her.

'Why, Cassandra,' Galem drawled, holding Caz in front of him while a substantial natural divide was still holding them apart, 'I do believe you're blushing.'

For once he was wrong; Cassandra would have fainted. 'I'm not blushing. The shower's turned hot.'

'So, you'll stay?' he guessed.

Was there any doubt? Raising her arms to slick her hair back in a gesture Caz realised was deliberately provocative, she licked her lips to ramp up the pressure. 'If you can take the pace?'

'I'll hold up.'

She was sure of it.

Galem pushed the doors open. 'Now, get out of here, or we'll never go see that house.'

After breakfast Caz suggested a picnic to tie in with their visit to the house.'

'A walk, at least,' Galem agreed, brushing her swollen bottom lip with his thumb pad.

They could hardly keep their hands off each other and a rosy glow had descended on them by the time they left the cottage arm in arm.

'Why are you stopping?' He turned to stare at her when they were halfway up a hill overlooking the quarry.

'I'm admiring the view.'

'Again?'

'Is there a limit?' She couldn't disguise her gulping breaths any longer. She needed a break.

'I thought you were fit.' Galem's laugh was deep and sexy, and it resonated through her.

'For pavements.' She smiled ruefully. These hills were steeper than the treadmill at the city gym. But as Galem drew her close Caz knew she wouldn't have missed this for the world.

'Can you see the house?' he said, turning her. 'It's why I brought you here.'

Caz found herself watching Galem's face instead of looking down on Stone Break House. She loved him; it was that simple and that complicated. There was an edge of darkness hovering at the edges of her happiness because when it came to Stone Break House Galem's sense of ownership equalled her own.

She just had to put it out of her mind and get on with things, Caz told herself, looking for a place to sit as she waited for Galem.

'Not there!'

His shout was too late to prevent her sitting in a mud bath that might have been tailor-made for her bottom.

Grabbing her underneath the arms, Galem went to yank her up. 'Can't leave you alone for a second, can I, Cassandra?'

She stared into his eyes, thinking. Cassandra had been accident-proof; she'd had to be. But Caz…she was different.

'Well?' Galem said. 'Do you want to get up or not?'

His thick black hair was ruffled by the wind and his profile was a sharply carved silhouette against a white sky. There was such strength in his jaw, such kindness and humour in his eyes, and for once she didn't want to do what was right or sensible. 'Do you fancy getting really muddy?'

His eyes turned slumberous in an expression she recognised, but then he threw back his head and laughed, understanding.

The ground was soft and warm and as they wrestled Caz knew it was the most fun she'd ever had. 'Now I know why mud treatments are so popular,' she said, gasping for breath when Galem allowed her to hold him down. 'Do you think our clothes will ever recover?'

'I'm guessing you hope not,' he said, drawing her to him for a kiss.

And then he held her and she lay safe in his arms swimming in a warm, safe tide of love. Being hugged by Galem, being kissed by him, seeing the affection in his eyes when he looked at her, meant more to Caz than anything. It meant more to her than Stone Break House, more than losing her virginity even. Affection; respect; trust. However short a time they'd known each other it was all there, and she valued it above everything.

'Come on,' he said, getting up and drawing her to her feet.

'I've never had a muddy kiss before,' Caz said as Galem cupped her face in his big, muddy hands.

'Then let me be the first,' he whispered against her lips.

'This is the best day of my life,' Caz said when Galem released her at last.

'All that could change in a moment,' he warned, turning her to point out the black cloud heading their way.

'But the forecast promised—' Caz stopped. Since when had she believed in weather predictions?

'If we hurry we might get back before the downpour.'

'And if we don't?'

'We'll get wet.' The crease was back in Galem's cheek again.

They set off down the hill at a brisk pace, but there were a lot of damp leaves underfoot, and damp leaves under Caz's trainers were a recipe for disaster.

'You really can't be trusted for a moment, can you?' Galem said, scooping her off the ground a second time.

Caz brushed herself down, glad of the opportunity to hide her face. She didn't want Galem thinking she was the type of girl who took a tumble and burst into tears, though right now that was exactly the type of girl she was. What had happened to Cassandra when she needed her? Caz seemed to be losing her poise and pride by the minute.

'Take it slowly,' Galem advised, keeping a protective arm around her shoulders. 'Get your wind back.'

'But the rain—' Breaking free, she set off again.

'Caz, watch out! Don't go that way!'

'Why not?' The way she had chosen was prettier than the track Galem was taking. There were wild-flowers and…thistles!

'Or that way!'

Nettles!

'Ouch!' Galem said it for her. 'Now will you stay with me?'

For ever, Caz thought as she gazed up into his face, but, of course, she didn't say that.

'We have a stream to cross now,' Galem informed her when they reached the bottom of the hill, 'and I don't want you trying any heroics. You're to take my hand so I can get you safely to the other side.'

The stones were slippery, but Galem's arm was like a steel rod, his hand like a grappling iron welded to a winch of limitless strength. She wasn't sur-prised he brought her safely over to the other side. She only wished the stream had been wider; the Atlantic Ocean, perhaps.

The sight of Stone Break House from the top of the hill had only increased his passion for it; seeing it with Caz had only aggravated his dilemma. She was never going to sell, and he was never going to give up his rights to it either. It was an impossible situa-tion made worse by her stubbornness. Made worse by the way she made him feel, Galem admitted to himself. Who in their right mind would want to make their home in an old ruin that was overshadowed by the gaping wound of a former quarry? Only the man who had lived there as a boy, perhaps...

Until Caz had come along, that was. She felt so good in his arms. Better than that, she felt right there. But she knew that if he told her how he felt she would think it a ploy to claim Stone Break House through the back door. Things got complicated when your father's mistress turned out to have a niece as beautiful and complicated as Cassandra Bailey Brown, a woman whom he would always think of as Caz...

'Breather?' she begged him.

'When it rains here it really rains,' he warned her.

'Oh, not like anywhere else, then,' she said, laughing into his eyes.

She tempted him, and he dropped a kiss on her lips, loving the easy familiarity that had sprung up between them. He'd never felt like this before. Sex, lust, accommodations between a man and a woman, those he understood, but this...this was something very different.

He waited until she recovered, feeling like a jerk. He was in a mess. He was pushing her too hard. What had started out as an undercover interview once he'd realised who she was on Friday night had become something more, something that made him push her to see what she was really made of. She was such an enigma, but he preferred what he had now to what had landed in his ditch on Friday night.

'Is it much further, Galem?'

Her jaw was jutting out in a way that made him smile. 'Just one tiny field,' he said, using a little poetic licence. 'Get your breath back first, and then we'll set off again.'

He helped her over a stile when they reached the field. Her clothes were sodden from the mud, but he could feel her warmth beneath them. It reminded him how good she felt when she was naked. He was just making some discreet adjustments when she froze.

'Galem, what are those?'

They had only gone a few yards into the field. He followed her gaze to see a herd of bullocks lifting their heads from the grass to take an interest in them. 'Don't worry,' he said with all the confidence of a man who used to sneak a ride as a boy. 'They won't hurt you.'

'Are you mad?' she said, looking at him horror struck.

Before he had chance to say another word she took off, legs working like pistons as she ran in the opposite direction to the way they should be going.

'Cows can kill…'

Cupping his hands around his mouth, he yelled back at her, 'Only if you're careless. And those aren't cows, they're—'

'Chasing me.'

'No, they're not,' he said, loping after her. He threw a glance over his shoulder to be sure, only to see a small stampede forming up. 'Okay, they are! Make for the trees!'

But she couldn't run fast enough. He guessed her legs had turned to rubber and he could hear the drum of hooves coming up behind them fast. Sweeping her up beneath one arm, he carried her like a rugby ball to touchdown.

'Idiot!' she screamed when he landed on top of her.

He had to admit it wasn't quite the show of gratitude he had anticipated.

'How could you bring me to a field that had rampaging bulls in it?'

'Bullocks—'

'Dangerous animals!'

Capturing her flailing arms, he forced them into a puddle above her head. 'Cassandra, calm down...'

'Get off me, you great oaf!' she said, wriggling furiously.

She had never been rugby-tackled before; never been thrown to the ground by a grown man, never wrestled twice in one day in soft warm mud before. And wrestling with Galem meant extremely impressionable parts of her were rubbing into him again and again. 'Galem, I'm warning you—' *If you stop holding me down and pressing yourself against me, I'll kill you!*

They stopped fighting and she grew quiet. They

were looking into each other's eyes, really looking. Galem's green eyes were deep and mesmerising, and that mouth… They'd have gorgeous children. Swallowing hard, Caz forced the thought from her mind, but the shared dangerous incident had brought them even closer. 'The last thing I want to do is mud wrestle with you again,' she assured him in a way that brought the familiar crease to his cheek.

'Now, why don't I believe you?'

She melted into his arms when Galem bent his head and kissed her. 'You feel so good,' she murmured, sighing as she rubbed herself against him. 'I want to feel you all over me.'

'I love it when we think the same,' Galem murmured against her mouth.

He was making her ready as he spoke, undoing the fastening on her polyester trousers, and freeing the zip. She opened the buttons on his shirt and pulled up her top so she could feel him hard and warm against her.

Even on a bed of mud their love-making was sensual and tender. They knew each other's bodies, knew each other now. This was falling in love, Caz thought as Galem sank deep inside her, holding her gaze. This was what it felt like to be loved, and to love, heart soaring, body thrilling, mind flying. Oblivious to the sullen sky, she dug her fingertips into the bulging muscles beneath Galem's shirt, loving him for ever with all her heart.

As she relaxed back in his arms, panting and

glowing, he couldn't believe they'd known each other such a short time. She was different from every woman he had ever met; she fulfilled all his fantasies, ticked each box on his wish list. She was gutsy, sexy and stubborn, and stirred his competitive juices like no one he'd ever met. That wasn't just a change—for him it was unique. He was a little bit in love with her, and maybe a lot more than that. And that wasn't just his libido talking. When she'd first arrived his mind had been full of Stone Break House and he had bitterly resented her for owning it, but now he could have it all.

'Is it really only Sunday afternoon?' he murmured against her sweet flushed face. 'So we've known each other—'

She was brushing damp strands of hair out of her eyes, and, catching hold of her wrist, he brought her palm to his lips and planted a kiss on it. 'I don't care how long. It's long enough for me.'

Caz tensed, wondering what Galem meant by that. Even now insecurity was waiting in the wings ready to raise its ugly head. 'Long enough for what?' She held her breath, dreading his answer. She had travelled a long way since arriving in Hawkshead and she was miles past worrying about being in too deep.

'Long enough to know I don't want to let you go,' he said, drawing her close. 'Long enough to know I want to know you a whole lot better than I do…'

When they were dressed again he brought her

onto his knees, holding her on his lap in his big strong arms like a baby beneath the spreading branches of an ancient oak. 'It doesn't get any better than this, does it?' she said, turning her face up to him.

Galem's answer was to kiss her, and they kissed like lovers who had known each other a lot longer than a few hours. There was a new certainty between them and a sense of trust, a growing knowledge that every moment they spent together brought them closer.

A new horizon full of possibilities had opened up for her, and Caz found it hard to believe she had ever thought them mismatched. Galem was the builder and she was the dreamer; he was the man who would build her dreams. And her dreams encompassed a lot more now than an old house. She was about to tell him how much she loved him when Galem stared at her and grinned. 'Ready, Cassandra? Shall we start back?'

Calling her Cassandra brought her back to earth with a bump. This was all a sham. Galem had made love to her and spent time with her, because he wanted Stone Break House. He wanted Cassandra. He wanted a girl who didn't exist. How could she have forgotten that?

Because she wanted to, Caz realised. She wanted all the things she'd never had. In fairness to him Galem had never mentioned love once. Perhaps she expected too much of him, Caz thought as they started back, expected too much of life…

She tried not to think too hard about it as she matched her stride to his, but everything inside her had grown cold and tight. When she was in his arms Galem made her feel as if she were the only woman in the world, but Galem lived a simple life, and sex for him was just part of the natural rhythm of that life. She mustn't read too much into what had happened between them that weekend. It might have been earth-shattering for her, but for him it was probably different.

'Why don't we go and look at Stone Break House now, if you have to get back to Leeds?' he said.

The way he spoke underlined her fears. The weekend was drawing to a close and with it his commitment to her. He was already prepared in his mind for her leaving, while she couldn't bear to think about it. 'You're right,' she said, hiding behind Cassandra's no-nonsense tone. But this time the switch grated on her. She didn't want to go back to being the person she had been on Friday night at the start of this journey.

When they reached the gates of the house Galem touched her shoulder as if he sensed her anxiety without understanding the cause of it. It was the type of touch a man might give to a colleague to reassure her—brief and impersonal. Before she could stop herself she caught hold of his hand and kissed the fingertips that had brought her so much pleasure. She loved him however he felt about her, and there were still a few hours remaining. Whatever the future held she would put it out of her mind for now.

CHAPTER FOURTEEN

THE list of 'things to do' at Stone Break House was growing longer by the minute, though Galem insisted that none of the tasks was impossible. She needed his enthusiasm and energy to buoy her up, Caz realised, especially on those occasions in the future when her money ran low, or when, temporarily, she lost faith.

'The way forward is to restore rather than rip out and start again,' he commented, leading her round the back of the house. 'That way we can preserve the unique character of the building.'

The unique character of the building. Even the way he talked about the house showed his love for it. She had to wonder at the depth of Galem's attachment to a pile of old stones and rotting timbers. She had to wonder at the depth of her love for him too. Could this really have happened in a weekend? It had, she realised, taking his hand.

Galem laced their fingers together in an intimate

gesture that made her long to ask him if he felt the same way she did. It cut her up inside to think there was always part of her she would have to keep hidden from him.

'I wouldn't be surprised if we could reclaim the tennis court,' he said, reclaiming her attention.

'The tennis court?' Her brow wrinkled. He was directing her attention to what looked to her like a wilderness of broken fences and weeds. She hadn't allowed for anything like a tennis court in her budget. 'That will have to wait...'

'Perhaps we can sort something out,' he said.

What did he mean by that? She flashed a glance at him. Then as the breeze lifted her hair from her face she turned to gaze out at the miles of rolling fields, a patchwork of green and gold.

'Happy?' Galem said, drawing her close.

Happier than you know, Caz thought, snuggling into him. Nothing could spoil this moment, she wouldn't let it. She set her mind free to picture the ponies and sheep that would graze in the fields. 'We even have enough land to run a sanctuary,' she said, speaking her thoughts out loud.

'A sanctuary? What kind of sanctuary?'

'For animals,' she said, turning to him, warming to her theme.

'Go on,' Galem prompted.

Maybe he would think it sounded silly. She firmed her jaw. 'A home for racing greyhounds when they retire... Or donkeys. I love donkeys.'

Galem's expression changed and softened as he stared at the waiting land. 'My father started his business on the proceeds of the winnings from Stone Break Sid's ancestor, so yes...' His voice died away.

'The building business?' she probed, seizing the single strand from his life and clinging to it.

'That's right.'

'So you think my idea might work?'

'It has possibilities.'

'I wish I didn't have to go back to Leeds...'

'And work?'

She sounded like a spoiled child, Caz realised, but she was itching to make a start here.

'You'll make new friends in the north.'

She only wanted him. Her eyes filled. She turned her face away so he couldn't see. All she wanted was to be the real Caz Ryan with Galem. And self-pity was no use to anyone. 'I already have made friends,' she said to jolt herself out of it.

It made her smile to think about her new colleagues at the Leeds office. Fun and uninhibited, none of the girls cared what accent you had. They liked labels as much as the next, but weren't afraid to augment their shopping with supermarket bargains to get the latest look. They were real people and she had envied them from the moment she'd walked into the office.

'Caz?' Galem prompted her gently.

She looked up at him, shrewd green eyes that saw so much, and wanted to tell him everything, but if she did that she had to admit to being a fake. It was a vicious circle from which there was no escape. And Galem was as elusive as she was. How much had she learned about him since they'd met?

They both turned and frowned at the unwelcome intrusion of a car horn.

'Oh, no,' Caz sighed.

'Are you expecting visitors?' Galem asked her as a flashy red sports car zoomed up to them.

'Surprise!' a woman screeched as it skidded to a halt throwing a spray of gravel in the air. Leaning out of the passenger window, she waved a bottle of champagne in Caz's face.

'Cordelia Wentworth-Smythe,' she shrilled, holding out one beautifully manicured hand to Galem.

There was a moment when Caz thought Galem was going to salute her, but somehow he held back. They must look a sight, she realised, after rolling in the mud, whereas Cordelia and Hugo, both colleagues from the London office, were as immaculately dressed as ever. They climbed out of the car, looked around and then at each other.

'Fresh supplies!' Cordelia announced, putting on a brave face. Turning her back on Galem, she handed the bottle of champagne to Caz.

Cordelia had already dismissed Galem on the flimsy evidence of his rough appearance and muddy clothes. The spell they had woven between them during the weekend was shattered; the past had

caught up with them. As Cordelia swept a posses-
sive arm around her waist and led her away Caz
wondered if she would survive this visit, or if
Cassandra would seize this opportunity to take her
over completely.

'You didn't think we'd forget you, did you,
darling?' Cordelia flashed a glance at Galem over
her shoulder. 'Just tell me if we're in the way.'

Cordelia would have been too much at any time.

'You must have known we wouldn't abandon you
in the country?' she went on, this time staring pointedly at Galem.

Caz felt instantly protective towards him.

'Cassandra, your clothes—'

'They're practical.' The edge to her voice made
Cordelia's eyebrows shoot up.

'That's exactly what I mean.'

As Cordelia's eyes closed briefly in disapproval
Caz thought the expression in Galem's eyes spoke
volumes about his opinion of her London chums. And
it was as if she was seeing them clearly for the first
time. Hugo had just stepped out of the car and was regarding Galem as if he had only recently climbed out
of the swamp. In some ways he was right, Caz thought,
smothering her smile. But Hugo and Cordelia's pretensions grated on her, and she was mortified to think
that only a short while before she had felt the same.
But they were here, and she had to remember her
manners. 'Welcome, Hugo,' she said, fixing a smile
to her face. 'You've driven a long way to see me.'

'We were curious,' Hugo admitted frankly. The look he gave Stone Break House made Caz's hackles rise. She could feel Galem seething beside her too, and to avoid direct conflict between the two men she decided introductions were in order. 'Hugo, I'd like to introduce—'

'You can introduce us to the staff later,' Hugo cut across her.

His accent might have been cultivated in richly furnished drawing rooms rather than muddy fields, but as far as she was concerned Hugo's manners stank, but her scowl of disapproval seemed to bounce off him, making no effect whatsoever.

'I'll leave you with your friends...'

'No, Galem.'

He ignored her outstretched hand. She was proud of him. Galem had remained cool and dignified throughout. He had made a point of acknowledging Hugo and Cordelia, whether they cared to be acknowledged or not, and as he walked away she wanted to shout, 'Wait for me! These people aren't my friends. I don't know what I was thinking about.' But she had extended an open invitation to Hugo and Cordelia to visit her any time. She couldn't turn her back on them now.

Be honest for once, Caz thought as she watched Galem's retreating back. The truth was she didn't have the guts to stand up to Hugo and Cordelia and destroy her precious image.

Her image? Caz gazed down at her ruined

clothes, and then glanced at Hugo and Cordelia. Galem was long gone, his easy loping stride eating up the distance between her and his destination, which was almost certainly the cottage.

She had just made the most monumental mistake of her life, Caz realised. Galem was the one genuine thing in that life, the rock she could build on, and she had thrown all that away for the sake of her pride.

But not if she acted quickly enough. Caz firmed her jaw. She would just have to tell Hugo and Cordelia this was a bad time and she had to leave. The only thing that mattered now was straightening things out with Galem before she left for Leeds.

It wasn't hard to apologise and recommend a smart hotel in the centre of Leeds—in fact she couldn't believe what a relief it had been. Now she only had to find Galem, put her arms around him and assure him that nothing had changed.

So why did she still have the nagging feeling that the bottom had just dropped out of her world?

Caz walked all the way back to the cottage, and was devastated to find it empty. The silence was intense, just as she remembered it when she had first arrived. She had been so concerned with her own timetable, she hadn't given a thought to Galem's, she realised. In her mind he was a fixture, a paver who lived in a gorgeous little cottage. But what did she really know about him?

And she was supposed to be an expert when it came to reading people? Caz was angry with herself as she stuffed her scant possessions into the ruined bag. Cassandra, you're a washout, and you'd better pull yourself together before work tomorrow morning. Dashing the tears from her eyes, she took one last look around the room where her life had changed for good, then, swinging her bag off the floor, she went downstairs to call a taxi.

'Station, love?'

She was on the point of saying yes, but what came out of her mouth was, 'No... Could you take me to Stone Break House, please?' Maybe Galem was there; she didn't know where else to look.

'Stone Break House?' the taxi driver said in surprise. 'That old ruin?'

'It won't be for much longer,' Caz assured him, narrowing her gaze. 'And that's where I'd like you to take me now, please.'

When they arrived she paid off the taxi driver and, using her keys, walked inside. She called out for him, but she already knew he wasn't there; she would have felt his presence, had he been.

She made a tour of the house, being careful to avoid all the places Galem had warned her about. It wasn't so bad if she was careful. A fanciful side of her imagined she could hear laughter and voices; happy voices; a family... Leaning back against the door jamb, Caz pictured the large open-plan kitchen area as it would be when she had finished with it.

There would be an Aga at one end, and a wood-burning stove at the other with two sofas pulled up either side. In the winter she'd have rugs and candles and throws…

It would be lovely, Caz thought, biting her lips against the tears that threatened when she thought how much lovelier it could have been with Galem to share it with. Thinking about him now made her throat tighten and her heart ache. Another lesson learned; he hadn't even bothered to say goodbye.

And so she was alone again. But maybe that was enough. Staying here in the house where she felt she belonged was a consolation of sorts. Having accepted that, the rest was easy. She was going to stay the night, and not just Sunday night, but every weekend from now on. She didn't feel frightened by the old house any more. The wildlife was probably a lot more frightened of her than she was of it.

An old sofa faced the black iron grate, and that was where she would make her bed for the night. When she went back to Leeds she would arrange to have it recovered, and have another one made to match it. Galem was right about saving everything that could be saved. She wanted as much as he did to keep the spirit of the house intact.

CHAPTER FIFTEEN

'THERE was no more to your trip than a country hike, I bet,' her PA commented, on Monday morning when Caz walked into Brent Construction. 'Something's put that glow on your cheeks...' She smiled, sharing a knowing look with the other girls.

Like a perfectly schooled chorus line they all craned forward to hear what she had to say.

Caz managed a smile. 'If there was, I'm not telling.'

'You don't have to,' the chorus assured her.

Closing her office door with relief, Caz hit the intercom button. 'No calls, please, Julie...' She needed a minute before buckling on her business armour, a minute to mourn. The girls were right— she was glowing, but that glow was fading fast. She'd hardly slept for thinking about Galem, and what a fool she'd made of herself. She'd bought into the fable of love at first sight, which she now knew was a lie.

'When you're ready,' Caz said, hitting the intercom button again, 'a coffee would be great, Julie. And I'm taking calls now.'

'Don't forget your ten o'clock—'

'My ten o'clock?' Her mind turned blank for a moment, but then she remembered, wondering at the same time how she could possibly have forgotten. 'Young Mr Brent?'

'That's right,' Julie confirmed.

A visit from Mr Brent had been on the cards for some time. He'd been out of the country for years, growing the business into a world class concern, but now he was back. 'Better hold those calls a few more minutes, Julie.' She needed to be on top form for this meeting.

Ten minutes later Caz slammed her file shut. How was she supposed to concentrate? With an angry sound she thrust her chair back from the desk and started pacing. Galem's face, Galem's eyes, Galem's lips, Galem's body… Galem the bit of rough she had fallen madly in love with; Galem the bad boy who had turned his back on her without a second thought; Galem the unrepentant alpha, the lusted-after sex toy with his long, lean legs, powerful arms and incredible iron buttocks; Galem, the man composed entirely of muscle and appetite, with no finer feelings at all. How was she supposed to forget about someone like that and concentrate on work?

'Julie? Coffee; it's an emergency. And those

reports I prepared. Can you bind enough copies for
the meeting? If you're stuck I'll come and help you.'
Caz touched a hand to her forehead, aware that she
sounded desperate. It only made her feel worse
when her PA was at pains to reassure her. Julie
would have guessed that all the executives at Brent
would be tense this morning. But she was more
wound up than most, and coffee wasn't the answer.
And now she must forget everything but work.

'Oh, that's easy,' Caz informed the empty room.
Her body was screaming with sexual frustration,
while she was in the throes of some deeper, inner
grief. Her concentration levels were at zero.

It was just after nine when Julie came back on the
intercom. 'I know you said no calls, but I thought
this is one you should respond to...'

Reluctant to lift her head from her work, Caz
hummed agreement.

'Mr Brent wants to see you in his office now.'

'Now?' Caz's throat dried. Business was an arena
in which she excelled, but today it was as if the
essence of success were being fed through the air-
conditioning system making even Cassandra doubt
her abilities. Brent the Younger came with a formidable reputation, which had put everyone on
edge. Everyone except Cassandra Bailey Brown,
Caz reassured herself, patting her hair and then
standing to smooth her slim black pencil skirt.

'Don't worry,' Julie chirruped, 'you'll knock him
dead.'

* * *

Counting to ten wasn't enough, so she counted to ten again and then knocked on the mahogany door, which already bore the legend: Chairman.

Brent the Younger had chosen a smaller office than the one previously occupied by his father, his reason being that as he would move between the various plants he didn't need to monopolise such a large space. As long as he had a window and a view he was content, apparently. And his view stretched way down the newly restored canal. It was one of the few open aspects in the building and everyone envied him. They had also notched up the fact that, as well as modest, he was shrewd.

And so was she, Caz reassured herself. She just had to convince herself that she was firing on all cylinders, ready for anything...

'Hello, Caz.'

'Galem...' Caz stood transfixed in the doorway, and then it was as if a veil had been lifted and she couldn't believe she had been so dense. Drawing herself up, she walked forward with her head held high, her future, her life, her sheer existence hanging like a delicate silken thread between them. 'I'm sorry, I mean Mr Brent...' As Galem rose from his seat behind the desk Caz extended her hand ready for the traditional greeting.

He ignored her outstretched hand and sat down again, indicating a chair. 'Everyone calls me Galem and that includes you, Caz.'

Caz remained standing. There was no warmth in

Galem's voice, and his eyes were cold. She felt sick inside, but at the same time a catalogue of charges against him were forming in her mind. He had betrayed her trust, deceiving her in the most unforgivable way. He had misled her from the start, taken her virginity, slept with her, not once, but many times, knowing he was her boss. He had lied to her.

But she was blameless?

Caz lashed herself a few times with the word hypocrite before taking her seat, and as she did so she thought about the weekend and her anger changed to a deep-rooted sadness. Both were feelings she had no option but to stifle. Above all she wanted to hold onto her job with Brent. She had a deep emotional attachment to the company that had given her the first leg up in life, and on a practical level there would be no Stone Break House, no penthouse in Leeds, no food on the table, no car, no clothes, no Caz Ryan. And right now Galem Brent held all that in the palm of his hand.

As well as holding her life in his hands Galem was holding her personnel file, Caz noticed, flicking through it with his long, tanned fingers. She cleared her throat in an attempt to bury the thought of other places those fingers had explored, but those places were already tingling. His mouth...his lips... Caz eased her neck, trying to forget, but then Galem lifted his head from the file, catapulting her back to the present with a look that held none of the warmth she remembered from those previous encounters.

He put the file down on the desk in front of him,

lining it up next to a file she didn't recognise. She knew that everything she had worked for was about to slip away and there was nothing she could do about it but sit and wait. The thought of what was at stake launched her on an agonising journey that took her from a children's home to a ditch in Hawkshead, and on again through each preconception and glaring error of judgement she had formed about Galem Brent. The fact that she had been made a director of his company specifically because of her talent for reading people didn't escape her reckoning.

Picking up one of the files, Galem studied it. Dressed in ripped jeans and a frayed Aran sweater he had been stunning, but here in the office with his thick black hair neatly groomed and wearing a dark business suit, garnished with a silk tie and crisp white shirt, he made her heart thunder. Or maybe that was apprehension stalking her...

'I'm going to call for coffee,' he said. Leaning over the desk, he buzzed his PA and placed his order.

They were going to be there for some time, Caz deduced, sitting tensely on the edge of the chair.

'So. Caz,' Galem said, sitting back. 'Or should I say Cassandra?'

His expression told her he knew everything, and her heart clenched at the thought of what that meant. Her head was reeling and she was having trouble finding business mode, but she forced herself to examine the facts. She wouldn't be sitting here if she had fallen short in her job, but had she hung herself with the rope Galem had given her during the weekend? There'd been enough of it, after all. She was sure the answer lay somewhere inside the folders he had in front of him.

'Do you know what these are?'

'My personnel folder, and... I'm afraid I don't recognise the other one.'

He picked it up, and then there was a brief pause as his PA came in with a tray of coffee.

His eyes were tourmaline, Caz thought as her mind felt free to wander briefly, and were the same colour as the silk thread in his tie. His suit had undoubtedly been tailor-made for him, by some famous designer, she guessed, judging by the vivid lining. How could she have made such a peerlessly bad judgement call?

Galem glanced her way as his PA poured coffee for them both. His face appeared impassive, but she sensed beneath it was the confidence of a predator, who knowing all the strengths and weaknesses of his prey, could afford to toy with it for a bit.

When the woman left the room and shut the door he said, 'Your appointment as a director of my company is a significant achievement, Caz.'

'Thank you.'

'You hold down a position of great trust here at Brent.'

Warning bells rang inside her and everything started to tighten.

'You're privy to a lot of confidential financial information, for example.'

She could only nod agreement. She had discovered that directors at Brent, highly trusted individuals all of them, were given the access codes to just about everything on the system.

'Therefore,' Galem went on, straightening up again, 'it won't surprise you to learn that there are companies who specialise in carrying out security checks for me.'

Now there was only a body in a chair, and that body was Caz Ryan. Cassandra Bailey Brown was floating somewhere overhead waving goodbye to Caz and her precious career.

'Naturally, the company I employ carried out a full check on you.'

Some people could get angry in order to intimidate, while others could be equally threatening with just the use of a low voice and a direct stare. Galem was one of them. When she had compiled her CV invention had seemed her only option. She still didn't know what she could have done differently to get a job, to get a break, and wasn't going to sit mute now and not defend herself. 'I'd do it again,' she said. 'Perhaps you had the luxury of a home, a family, and a direction in life. I had none of those things. I had to live on my wits. And before you accuse me of feeling sorry for myself, let me put you right. I have never felt sorry for myself. In fact I think I've been lucky because I've always been free to take whatever path I chose in life—'

'And you chose Brent. Why?'

Galem shot the question at her while she was still recovering from his opening salvo. He was as merciless as Cassandra, but why did she expect anything less of him? Caz firmed her jaw. 'I didn't choose Brent, Brent chose me. Your father took a chance on me, spent money on my training; gave me day release to attend university—'

'So your loyalty is unquestioned?'

'Absolutely.' She held his stare.

'Your track record with Brent shows you're a highly motivated individual, as well as being a loyal member of the team.'

A loyal member of the team? Brent had given her purpose, and had become both her home and her family. She had already lost Galem; was she going to lose that too?

'This is the report I received,' he said, pushing a folder across the desk. 'You might want to look it over.'

She didn't need to look at it; she knew what it would say.

'You got a good degree,' he said, launching straight in, 'but there's no mention of a secondary school in your file…'

'Yes, there is,' she said confidently, before she could stop herself. She was so used to living in the past she had invented she couldn't stop even though this was the man who could end her career with the stroke of his pen.

'Ah, yes,' Galem said, tilting the file round as if he hadn't memorised every word, 'Princess Amelia's school for girls in Switzerland, wasn't it?' His brows rose as he looked at her. 'Swanky. You just made one elementary mistake.' He paused to ramp up her discomfort. 'Princess Amelia's school isn't a secondary school, it's what they call a finishing school. Young ladies attend post A levels in order to learn how to win a wealthy husband.' He looked at her. 'That doesn't sound like you, Caz. There was no finishing school for Caz Ryan, was there? You grew up in a children's home.'

She held his gaze, refusing to flinch, refusing to show any emotion at all under Galem's remorseless stare. What was the point in denying it, when everything he said was true?

CHAPTER SIXTEEN

'LET'S forget Cassandra and concentrate on Caz Ryan,' Galem said, settling back in his chair.

'Back-street girl from the children's home?'

'Caz Ryan from the children's home,' Galem said, ignoring the interruption. 'The same Caz Ryan who was helped, financially, through university and then managed to achieve a reasonable degree while holding down three jobs. None of which, by the way, had the slightest relevance to my business.'

She wanted to leap across the desk and shake him. Only remembering what was at stake held her back. She had constructed the type of CV she had known would get her the job with Brent. She'd been young, desperate and equally determined, and she'd had too many disappointments in the past to risk telling the truth.

'You lied to me—'

Galem was judging her? 'And you lied to me.'

But his deception had been a very personal one,

and raising what had happened between them in Hawkshead in these sterile business surroundings expanded her accusation into something stark and shocking. She went for broke. 'From the moment you found out who I was the only thing on your mind was Stone Break House, and you were prepared to stop at nothing to get it. You used me, Galem.'

Caz's words reverberated in the silence.

'Are you saying that I forced you to do anything you didn't want to do?'

'Of course not.' Blood rushed to her cheeks. They might have been discussing business for all the emotion in Galem's voice, while her head was full of Galem kissing her, Galem holding her, Galem re-assuring her… Didn't he feel anything, anything at all?

Caz's stomach roiled and her heart was beating so fast she could hardly breathe. It was all she could do to maintain the mask of composure she'd stuck on her face at the outset of the meeting. 'My point, Galem, is that I didn't know who you were, and you didn't see any reason to tell me, but you knew who I was all along.'

'And wasn't it more convenient for you to lose the virginity that had become such an embarrassment to you to a rough paver from Hawkshead than anyone else? Wasn't anonymity your safeguard? Hasn't it always been the shield you hide behind, Caz?'

She could make no excuses, but hurt was piling

high on top of her humiliation, and she wasn't going
down without a fight. 'You have a reputation for
being ruthless in business and you brought those
same tactics into our lives regardless of how that
would make me feel when I discovered the truth.
You're every bit as much a fraud as I am, Galem.'

'I never pretended to be anything other than the
person I am. It was you who assumed and drew conclusions. And whatever I did or didn't do over the
weekend, it doesn't affect the business.'

Cassandra would have known that. Cassandra
would have been as incisive as Galem; she wouldn't
have allowed herself to be distracted by personal
considerations as Caz had.

'Did you really think Cassandra would change
your life?'

She refocused as Galem barked the question at
her.

'You must have done; to the extent that you
changed your name by deed poll.' His lips tugged
down with distaste. 'I can't think of anyone who
would willingly sign up to a lifetime membership of
the blinkered, prejudiced, self-serving minority like
you did, and I have to ask myself, is this the type of
person I want on my board?'

'A name doesn't change me, Galem.'

He let the silence hang. 'Is there anything else
you'd like to say to me?' he said at last.

'No, I don't think so.' What could she say?

It seemed impossible that there would be a way

back from this. Silence was buzzing between them like an angry insect, and Caz found herself retreating inwardly from all the angry voices in her head. She took refuge in a void of sadness. She knew there was another man beneath Galem's driven shell, and that man was warm and humorous and kind, so Galem Brent wasn't so different from Caz Ryan, after all.

'I can offer you my resignation if you want it,' she said, 'but there's a meeting soon, and I have an obligation to the team. And I won't make apologies for who I am and what I did. I'm proud of what I've achieved, Galem, and neither you nor anyone else can take that away from me.' She was twisting her hands in her lap, Caz realised, stilling them. She had no intention of breaking down in front of Galem. But emotion was building up in her and something had to give. She got up clumsily, almost knocking the chair over in her haste to leave the room.

Galem came after her, moving in front of her as she reached the lift. 'Have you eaten anything?'

His hand was up by her face, resting on the doors of the lift. She stared at him blankly, her mind in uproar. Her thoughts were a crazy mix of the sight and scent of Galem, together with grief at what they'd lost, and all of it packaged in the determination not to let her colleagues down before she left the building.

'Have you had breakfast?' he said again.

Food was the last thing on her mind. After staying

the night at Stone Break House she'd called the taxi service to bring her into Leeds. She'd been too anxious for food at the apartment, knowing this was a big day for her, the day when she finally got to meet the chairman of Brent Construction. She'd changed her mind about which suit to wear at least three times and then had polished Cassandra's leather briefcase before scuffing it again in case it looked unused, and all that before closing the door on her apartment. And then arriving at the office, instead of concentrating on work as she had intended her head had been full of Galem; her heart too. Breakfast? No. She hadn't eaten a thing since the previous day.

'I thought not,' Galem said, standing aside so she could go past him when the lift doors opened. 'I'll have something sent down to your office.'

'Thank you,' Caz said formally, stepping inside the lift, but when their eyes met her stomach jounced, and her eyes threatened to fill with tears again. She was in love with him. Whatever the future held, she loved him, this man who held her career in the palm of his hand. She had felt comfortable and relaxed with her sexy paver, and for the first time in her life she'd had the courage to be herself. But this wasn't her affable, sexy paver this was Galem Brent, the chairman of Brent Construction, a man who had taken his father's business and turned it into a world-class corporation. And he hadn't done that by being soft.

'Or on second thoughts… Perhaps I should come with you and make sure you don't fall into anything, or over anything, or stamp on anyone's feet.'

The air left her lungs in a rush as Galem stepped into the lift just as the doors were closing, but his face remained impassive, so she had no way of knowing what was going through his mind.

She'd already keyed in her floor but he hit the button for the basement car park. 'The view's spectacular, isn't it?' he said, refusing to explain this as the panoramic lift swooped down the side of the building.

She was still stunned, still wondering why he was in the lift with her, added to which she hated lifts, hated heights, hated being in this impossible position. 'The view? How can you act as though we've never met?' Caz was instantly furious with herself. She'd been so determined to say nothing, to keep her cool and preserve what tiny shreds of her pride remained, and now, not only had she thrown all that away she had done it with the crassest of theatrical flourishes.

Galem's expression didn't change, but he touched something on the control panel and the lift stopped mid-floor. 'I'm sorry,' he said coolly. 'Did you expect me to send round a company e-mail announcing the fact that we'd spent the weekend in bed?'

'I'll give you my resignation' Fumbling furiously in her briefcase, she dragged out a pen and some paper. 'Here,' she said. 'I can write it for you now.'

'I don't want it,' Galem said, brushing her hand away. 'You're too good for Brent for me to lose you.'

But not good enough for you. Caz shook her head. 'I won't stay. How can I? How do you expect me to work alongside you now?'

'That's up to you, Caz,' Galem said, touching the control panel again.

So that was it, Caz thought, squeezing her eyes shut. She was back to square one. She only cared about work, and that was the coin by which she was valued. Cassandra won, after all.

But as the lift started down the woman inside her told Cassandra to beat it. 'You left Hawkshead without even saying goodbye to me, Galem—'

'So did you.'

'I tried to see you before I left.'

'Was that before you put the keys to the cottage through the letterbox, got in a taxi and drove away?'

She stared at him. 'I spent the night at Stone Break House.'

'And I left you to say goodbye to your friends and then I went to check the dogs and say goodbye to Thomas. When I got back to the cottage, you'd packed up and gone.'

And the last place you would have looked for me at night was Stone Break House, Caz thought as Galem stood to one side to let her pass when the lift doors slid open.

'What are you doing? Where are you taking me?' He was steering her towards the car park.

'On a journey.'

'No, I can't. I've got work to do—'

'And I'm giving you the rest of the day off.' To close off her only escape route, he placed a call, postponing the meeting to the next day.

'Get in the car, Caz.' Galem opened the passenger door of a black Range Rover Vogue. 'This is something we both need to do.'

'Why?' She hesitated. 'I can't see the point. I can't see where this is going—'

'Get in.'

It took Cassandra to remind her that her job hung in the balance.

They drove in silence through the city and took the link road onto the motorway. Galem was a good driver, smooth and controlled, and the vehicle he drove was the epitome of luxury. Caz knew he was taking her back to Hawkshead, but she was curious to know why. When they approached Stone Break House she asked him. 'I got the impression you didn't want me here in Hawkshead. What's changed, Galem?'

'I don't seem to have made a very good job of getting rid of you, do I?' The glance he shot her made her heart race.

'So what is it about Stone Break House?' she asked as he drew up outside.

If he told her she would think it another ploy to soften her up and buy the house through the back door, but he hadn't made the journey to say nothing.

'Stone Break House was my childhood home where I grew up. I came back here to retrace my roots, to understand what made my father tick, and, of course, to buy it back from the new owner.'

'So the weekend with me was all part of your plan?'

'I didn't plan for you to drive your car into a ditch.'

'But once you realised who I was you realised you had a golden opportunity.' Caz was warming to her theory when Galem stopped her.

'Nothing half so complicated,' he said, leaning forward to stare her in the eyes. 'I wanted to take you to bed.'

His frankness shocked her; made her angry too. 'How long have you known you were my boss?'

'From the moment you told me your name. I felt sure there couldn't be two Cassandra Bailey Browns in the world.'

'So, where do I stand?' Caz said as he switched off the engine.'

'This isn't about work, Caz. There are more things in life, in case you hadn't noticed?'

She had. 'So why are we here?' She stared out of the window at the house.

'Because I think Aunt Maud intended this all along,' Galem said, removing the keys in readiness to get out. 'Maybe she blamed herself for not being close to your mother—for not being in a position to rescue you from that children's home. I can't be sure of anything; I only know she grew fond of me when I used to visit.'

'That's a pretty wild supposition.'

'Can you come up with a better idea?'

'Coincidence.'

'That's just as unreliable.'

'I can see why Aunt Maud might leave the house to me, but why would she want to bring us together?'

'My connection with your aunt goes back to the days when my mother had an affair with a rival contractor. She left Stone Break House one Christmas Eve, wrapping a scarf around my neck and hustling me down the road in the dark. My father never recovered from that, though eventually he was consoled by his secretary.'

'Aunt Maud?' Caz said quietly. 'And knowing all this you slept with me?'

'I made love to you.'

She looked at him, wanting so desperately to believe that was true.

'I fell in love with you,' Galem said, with a self-deprecating shrug. 'No one was more surprised than me. Love at first sight; that's what they call it, isn't it?'

'Or love in a ditch, maybe...' She smiled a little, wanting to believe him so badly.

'I suspected you felt the same—'

'I did.'

'I have my own insecurities. I had to be sure you were falling in love with me, and not with Galem

Brent, the chairman of Brent Construction. Cassandra might have seen that as a career move. But as I got to know you better I wanted more than that, I wanted to challenge *all* your perceptions.'

'And you wanted Stone Break House?'

'Yes, but I'm greedy; I want it all.'

'You really mean that, don't you?'

'Let's do this together, Caz…you and me.'

'What are you saying, Galem?'

Leaning across, he placed a finger beneath her chin and tipped her face up so he could stare into her eyes. 'Let's bury Cassandra in the foundations of the tennis court where we can jump on her every day. Let's get married and share the back-breaking work that lies ahead of us if we're going to stop this old house falling down. And…' reaching inside her briefcase, he plucked out her scribbled letter of resignation '…let's never talk again about unsettling the delicate balance I have established on the board of Brent Construction.'

'Dinosaur,' Caz accused him softly as Galem ripped her letter to shreds in front of her eyes. 'Do you think you're going to get everything your own way, from now on?' Her heart was leaping around insanely as he stared into her eyes.

'I think we've both got a very challenging future in front of us, and I for one wouldn't have it any other way. Will you marry me, Caz Ryan?'

Her mouth moved but no sound came out. Caz glanced at the house and then at Galem.

'I love you a lot more than bricks and mortar.'

'And what if I won't marry you?'

'We'll just have to live in sin.' His lips tugged up, sending heat flooding through her. 'But one thing's for sure, that house won't come to life until we're both living there under the same roof.'

'The same leaky roof.'

'Is that a yes, Caz? Only I'm an impatient man.'

'How impatient? It's just that maybe I need a little more persuading,' she teased.

Galem reached across and pulled her onto his lap. 'That's fine with me.' It was a tight fit in the Range Rover, and hugely difficult wearing constricting business clothes, but somehow they made it with Caz telling herself that it had to be a lot more comfortable than the beat-up tractor. The luxurious leather seats were comfortable and firm, and the broad span of windscreen was a great place to rest her feet. The windows were soon steamed up, and it was quite a while before they were ready to start their tour of the house.

They were just walking through the gates arm in arm when Galem's phone went off. From the set of his shoulders Caz knew immediately that something was wrong. 'Is it bad news?'

'Sally's gone missing…'

Their world was like a see-saw that went up and down. Sheer happiness was instantly replaced with sheer horror at the thought that the adoring grey-hound with her big mournful eyes could have been hurt or worse. All Caz could think was how lucky it

was that they had arrived in Hawkshead just at the
right time. She turned straight back to the Range
Rover, but not before she noticed Galem's glance
sweep over her smart black business suit. 'Forget it,'
she told him. 'We have to go right now and look for
her. Is it possible she ran away?'

'That's one possibility, but with Sid as their father
her pups will be valuable.'

'You don't think she's been stolen, do you? Oh,
Galem, come on...' She grabbed his arm. 'There's
no time to lose.'

He smiled as she did her tottering little run in her
too-tight skirt and five-inch heels; there were some
parts of Caz Ryan he hoped would never change.

They eventually found Sally in the grounds of Stone
Break House. The contented mother was curled up
in a ball beneath some bushes, and for a moment as
Galem cradled the greyhound's head in his arms
Caz thought she might be hurt. Her mouth dried as
she asked the question. 'Is she all right?'

'All right?'

Caz's heart lurched as Galem turned to smile at
her. 'Come and see for yourself.'

There were six tiny, blind, pink hairless puppies
scrabbling for position around their mother's milk-
swollen belly. Caz knelt in the mud at Galem's side,
exclaiming with pleasure. 'They're so beautiful...
Do you think there's a champion in the litter?' she
said, turning her face up to Galem.

'Maybe, but they're all beautiful to me. Will you help me get them in the car?'

They made a bed of leaves in the boot and Galem very gently laid the greyhound Sally down on top of it. Caz followed him with the puppies in her arms, carrying them three at a time until mother and babies were reunited and made comfortable.

They took the new family back to Old Thomas, who had remained at the kennels to be there in case Sally wandered home. The rest of the village was out searching for her and Thomas promised to ring round and make sure everyone heard the good news. Sid was ecstatic and couldn't stop licking his beloved mate's face. Caz was sure the handsome greyhound stood a little taller once he had surveyed his litter of new pups.

'Thank you for coming to search for Sally,' Galem said as they strolled back to the car.

'I'm just so relieved I can't tell you...'

Galem could stare into her eyes like no one else on earth, and at one time she would have been frightened by how much he could see, but now she couldn't hide how much she loved him. He could still make her blush with that look. 'I must look a mess,' she said, staring down at her ripped tights and ruined skirt.

'I think you look very sexy.'

'You do?'

He nodded but then laughed. 'Okay, I promise to buy you some rugged outdoor clothing,' he said, draping an arm over her shoulder, 'if only to hide those parts of you I find so distracting.'

Air shot from her lungs as Galem nuzzled her neck. 'That would be a shame.'

Then they both looked at each other and laughed as Sid and Sally started barking.

'They're encouraging us,' Galem insisted.

'Will they be all right now?'

'Of course they will.'

'Why do you think Sally ran away?'

'Even dogs need space sometimes.'

'Is that a hint?' Caz slanted a stare at Galem, daring him to agree.

'No, that wasn't a hint.' Stopping, he turned to face her, and, taking her face between his hands, he drew her close. 'We work well as a team, Caz.'

'Do we?'

'You know it. I'm on board for Stone Break House, aren't I?'

'But am I on your board?' Her anxiety was showing, Caz realised.

'You're part of everything I do,' Galem said, turning suddenly serious. Then grinning his bad-boy smile again, he brushed her mouth with his lips, teasing her and nipping her in a way that could only lead to one thing.

'Do you have nothing better to do than make love all day?' She pretended to complain, but this time it was Galem's turn to think of practicalities.

'I'd better feed you first, hadn't I? Don't want to wear you out before the wedding. And I know just the place...'

'Steak and chips?' Galem said, picking up the menu at the pub. 'Or would you prefer something lighter?'

'Like pie and peas?'

They shared a look, which made Caz feel all warm and fuzzy inside. In just three days they were sharing a history. She liked that, it felt good. But she couldn't help thinking that there was too big a gulf between Galem Brent, boss of Brent Construction, and Caz Ryan from the children's home.

'Penny for them,' Galem said, leading her to a table with a little bit of privacy. 'All right for you here?' He held her chair.

'Fine.' She sat down.

'So, what's on your mind, Caz?'

'Nothing...'

'You can't lie to me, not any more.' Leaning across the small round wooden table, Galem caught hold of her fidgety hands and enclosed them in his giant fist.

'I never could lie to you...'

He smiled at her. 'So, what is it? What's worrying you?'

'We come from different worlds—'

'Not that old chestnut.' Galem threw himself back in his seat, lips pressing down in mock disapproval. 'You were Caz, and then you were Cassandra and now you're Caz again. But here's the thing—both Cassandra and Caz live in the same world I do. And that's an end of it, as far as I'm concerned.' Leaning across the table, he held her gaze. 'Cassandra Ryan, will you marry me?'

'You know I will.'

'Well, there's your answer. Now, what do you want to eat? For goodness' sake, hurry up and make your mind up. I'm starving.'

'Pie, peas *and* chips?'

'Your wish is my command, lovely lady,' Galem said, dipping to plant a tender kiss on Caz's neck as he left the table to place their order.

EPILOGUE

THERE was always a handkerchief of blue sky over Hawkshead. That was what Galem had told her, and he was right, except that it had rained all night and the ground over which she had hoped to sweep her Vera Wang wedding dress was thick with mud.

That was no problem for Caz, except that the vintage Rolls Cassandra had pictured herself arriving in at the small village chapel got stuck in the approach to Stone Break House.

Caz quickly found a solution: wellington boots and a lift on Galem's ancient tractor. Now, admittedly the tractor was garlanded with white roses picked from the garden and the buckles on her Hunter boots were threaded through with white ribbons, but she cut quite a picture all the same. In flowing tulle, with a sweep train tucked into her boots, and a beautiful lace overlay on a low-cut sweetheart bodice topped off with a sensible waterproof jacket, just in case. She had to laugh at her image of country chic.

Well, this was Yorkshire, not Mauritius where Galem was taking her to spend their honeymoon in a wooden hut suspended over the ocean in a sumptuous five-star resort.

Caz didn't know what to expect when Old Thomas drew the tractor to a halt outside the chapel doors. Would she find Galem, her sexy paver, waiting, or Galem, the chairman of Brent Construction?

The one—or, rather, two things she could be sure about was that Stone Break Sid and Hawkshead Sally were waiting for her at their door, their leashes in the safe keeping of the plump lady from the village hall. Each greyhound had a tasteful silk ribbon in shades of peach, ivory and aqua round their necks, as, naturally, the tasteful colour scheme for the wedding had been chosen by Cassandra.

The low throb of country music greeted her as she walked through the door on the arm of Old Thomas who had cleaned up really well for the occasion, and was wearing his best Elvis suit, complete with diamante studs. Hugo and Cordelia sat down quietly at the back after politely showing everyone to their places. Galem had decreed that their business acumen far outweighed their snobbishness, and with the mettle of true survivors both of them had adapted quickly to his ways.

This was a fairy story, Caz thought as she walked up the aisle towards her prince. And there just weren't enough of them these days—not for grown-ups, anyway.

I love you, Galem mouthed as she approached, and she was thrilled to see the tears brightening his ocean-green eyes.

'I'm so proud of you,' he murmured.

'Me, too,' Caz replied as Sally the greyhound panted her approval. Each dog had been given special dispensation to enter the church and Sally had been given the special honour of bearing the rings.

Galem's was a simple platinum band—suitable either for a paver or for the chairman of an international corporation—while Caz's was a little more exotic. Cassandra and Caz had come to an accommodation in the months following Galem's proposal. Cassandra was pleased to accept Galem's solitaire diamond ring from Tiffany's, and, if Caz almost fainted with shock when she saw the size of it, Cassandra had helped her to maintain her cool and poise so that in the end she didn't disgrace herself. Her wedding band was a similar fabulosity. A band of diamonds flashed like fire on the ruby velvet cushion suspended on a golden chain beneath Sally the greyhound's head.

'If you've got it, why not flaunt it?' had been Galem's flimsy excuse for the extravagance. And who was Caz to argue when she had Cassandra prompting her from the wings?

'Oh, okay, then,' she had managed graciously, trying not to pass out from pleasure as Galem had tried it on her for size.

And now old Thomas was placing her hand in Galem's. She looked up at him. Galem was the same man, with the same rugged face and the same thick black hair that she had first fallen in love with. His ocean-green eyes were the same, his sensual lips just as kissable, and the broad spread of his shoulders beneath the formal tail suit still rang her bell.

'I hope I haven't disgraced you?' he said.

'How could you?' Caz murmured, thinking him the most handsome man she had ever seen—not to mention the most well dressed.

Until Galem discreetly glanced towards the ground and she saw his feet.

Cassandra gasped. Caz laughed. Those kick-the-door-down boots looked just great to her.

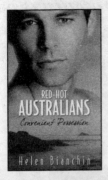

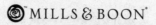

millsandboon.co.uk Community

Join Us!

The Community is the perfect place to meet and chat to kindred spirits who love books and reading as much as you do, but it's also the place to:

- ■ Get the inside scoop from authors about their latest books
- ■ Learn how to write a romance book with advice from our editors
- ■ Help us to continue publishing the best in women's fiction
- ■ Share your thoughts on the books we publish
- ■ Befriend other users

Forums: Interact with each other as well as authors, editors and a whole host of other users worldwide.

Blogs: Every registered community member has their own blog to tell the world what they're up to and what's on their mind.

Book Challenge: We're aiming to read 5,000 books and have joined forces with The Reading Agency in our inaugural Book Challenge.

Profile Page: Showcase yourself and keep a record of your recent community activity.

Social Networking: We've added buttons at the end of every post to share via digg, Facebook, Google, Yahoo, technorati and de.licio.us.

www.millsandboon.co.uk

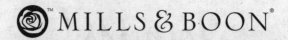